han return

Barbara Brown

Published by bodytao imprint
www.bodytao.co.uk

First published 2013

© Barbara Brown 2013

ISBN 978-0-9926512-0-6

Printed and bound in Great Britain

PREVIOUS PUBLICATIONS

Qi Gong: The Chinese Art of Working with Energy
(co-author Gunter Knoferl)
Published by Harpercollins 2001

Looking for Doris
Published by The Tenth Bull 2008

ACKNOWLEDGEMENTS

Thank you to Rina Minervini from Jo'burg for superb, astute and delightful accompaniment as editor

Thank you for love and encouragement from friends and fellow pilgrims along the Way:

Warren Kenton, Paul Taylor and Peter Chatalos from the Kabbalah Schools

Hameed Ali, the founder, Sandra Maitri and the tutors, and my friends from the Ridhwan School UK

My teachers from schools of T'ai Chi and Qi Gong: Chung Liang Al Huang, Master Chu, John Solagbade, Master Chen Xiao Wang, Zhixing Wang, Dr Li and Ken Cohen; fellow practitioners and my Qi Gong students

Belinda Budge for her loving and generous accompaniment

Patrick Budge for cover design

Kate Codrington for patient technical support

Graeme Chaves for his unstinting and generous clear mind

Robert Downes for supporting a whim

Anne Geraghty for her courage and appreciation

Marilyn Kernoff for being a treasure

Roger Lichy for his consistent and loving belief in the whole project

Stacy Mackishi and Vick Ryder for creative accompaniment

Katherine Tetlow for her wisdom and perception

Caroline Ward for her intuition and good faith

To my dear family, thank you for love and encouragement

... and to Han-Shan for his inspiration

Dedicated to Roger
Sasha & Ethan

… and to the blessed presence of the Eternal Elders

Poem No 269 from Cold Mountain by Han-Shan

Ever since I 'left home,'
Bit by bit I've acquired an interest in nourishing life.

I've stretched and drawn back, making my four limbs whole;
With diligence listened, making my six senses complete.

My coarse woollen robe is with me winter and spring;
Unpolished rice sustains me morning and night.

Today, earnest and eager, I practice,
Hoping to run into the Buddha.

Reprinted by permission from The Poetry of Han-shan: A Complete, Annotated
Translation of Cold Mountain by Robert G. Henricks, the State University of New York
Press ©1990, State University of New York. All rights reserved.

1

My last incarnation upon Earth happened in what you would call the Ninth Century, when I made my home in the T'ien-T'ai Mountains of China. The final glimpse of me was when I disappeared through a crack in the rock, avoiding the official Lu-Ch'iu Yin who was sending food, incense and clothes to my two companions, Big Stick and Pick-Up. I left behind poetry, written on bamboo, rocks and the walls of people's houses. I left behind memories of my wild hair, birch bark hat, patchwork robe, big wooden clogs and gnarled staff.

Don't imagine that because I haven't been on Earth for all this time, that I have not been utilised. Everything is made use of, believe me. Whatever realm you inhabit, whether you are incarnate or discarnate, you are part of the warp and weave, you are a thread in the whole Design.

I dwell in the Heavenly House of Discourse and Apprenticeship. We are overseen in this House by a Being of Abiding Wisdom, a feminine Being whose beauty and intelligence lightly enfolds us as we come from and go to schools and ashrams across the diverse and multiplied firmament. The tales we bring upon return from the Earth School are particularly poignant to us. You may not know it, Dearest Brothers and Sisters, but we are in constant, compassionate accompaniment to you. Some of you gaze up into the bejewelled night sky with wonder and longing, looking for signals from us. Please understand, Dear Ones, we do not inhabit material reality. If you were to stand up and extend your arm, you might even be cutting through the dimension, unseen by you, untouched by you, in which we now have our habitation.

We have no Time in this dimension, referring rather to Long Whiles and Short Whiles and Intermittent Whiles. These cannot be indicated by your measurements, horizontal measurement, overseen by the Lord Chronos. We live more in the vertical time experience whose Lord is the Mighty Chairos, Lord of the Endless Moment of the Immediate Present.

As I say, I have been in the Heavenly House of Discourse and Apprenticeship for the Longer Whiles. You could say this has been the Home Place for me, from which I have come and gone to Further Constellations, each time, upon return, reflecting upon knowledge and experience – in solitude or through dialogue with others.

Ah, what a wondrous Learning! Through all this I sojourned with beings of wit, empathy and creativity, and particularly with those deep in spiritual apprenticeship, coming and going from the Earth School. These companions of course were no longer physically embodied, but the force of incarnation and its physical and emotional imprint could sometimes still reflect as a fading pattern within the distilled remnant of soul-being. Thus it was that I could witness and enjoy the robust form of Master Yang long after he'd left it behind on the dusty roads of the Earth. Master Yang's consciousness, in communion with mine, could remind me of what it felt like to perform the movements of t'ai chi – the sinking of the mind, for instance, into the tan t'ien – a point below the navel and deep into the body – accompanied by the fluid turning of the waist. I could feel the memories of visceral expression. I could remember the sensation of flesh resting upon bone, and blood moving through flesh, even after more than a thousand of your years.

We informed our companions in the House of Discourse through a coded calligraphy of knowledge shared and implanted from one to another, its appropriateness subtly tested through delicate systems of alignment and balance. Master Yang and I, and the blessed feminine sage Madame Li, drew our Learning from the Tao in this way. I shall speak further of these Beloved Friends ....

I wish to make it quite clear: we were not sitting in God's lap just because we were in the Heavenly Realms. No one shall see the face of the Holy One and live. But, oh, put it this way – in these realms, the perfumed essence of the hem of the Holy Garment feels more prevalent, more accessible. And to the degree that we here are conscious beings existing within the laws of manifestation and holding still the privilege of free will, we are not yet absorbed and mysteriously vanished.

In human form, we all intimately know the body of Our Mother, the Earth; we abide upon her, clinging as she tilts, and yet of course we are mostly unaware of the Great ·Perennial Dance she performs, rotating and travelling around her sun at great speed. She is accompanied by her moon, offspring of a vast collision which wrenched her very innards and yet left a residue of life-promoting ingredients. She is accompanied also by great brothers and sisters, and the brother Jupiter indeed offers itself as protecting shield, receiving the onslaught of debris which otherwise might damage his smaller sister.

It was during a quiet moment of contemplation of the nature of the Earth Mother's body that I heard a call from the Being of Abiding Wisdom.

She requested me to appear at the Quiet Edge of her Field of Influence. I poured myself into the allotted space and calmed the music of my consciousness until She and I were in Accord.

'Han,' she said (and of course it was not like this, but rather like the movement of the wind through a field of newly opened grass, a small soft wind, gently touching the foreheads of the stalks just as the first light appears).

I bent my head to receive her communion.

'Han, the Scribes of the Records of Coming and Going have received communion that Your Blessed Beingness is required on Earth.' Even within the bliss of our Accord, I felt a ripple of un-peace.

'Blessed Being,' I replied, 'for what purpose am I required?'

'There is pain in this Great School. And yet at the same time, the teachings you were part of have spread from their home in the region of China and moved to the Western part of the Earth Being. They are seized upon with hunger and some are taught with impeccable care. We request that you visit Earth to quicken this particular Illumination and to be available to those beings who are able to calm themselves into Accord with you. This will enhance vibration and bring added solace.'

I remembered the experience of density and weight that is part of being on Earth. Yet I also felt joy at the possibility of tasting the Earth experience for a Short While, feeling again the ten thousand footprints, languages, experiences and phenomena evident upon her surface. And then the possibility of Service to humanity drenched my heart and made of it a Mountain of untold dimension, an Ocean of immeasurable depth.

'Will I be taking a human body?'

Her compassion radiated through me.

'We are leaving you to take a While of your choice so that you may meditate upon this request. You can refuse. One possibility to dwell upon is that you may visit the Earth within your Subtle Body, taking form according to your discernment, in order to reach anyone who might be able to receive your influence. So you will not have the sweet burden of a physical body unless you so choose, and then for as long – or as briefly - as you wish. You have reached a beautiful state of integrity, Han, and we entrust you with advanced responsibility and capacity.'

I felt a swirl of soft gold move from my field to that of the Being of Abiding Wisdom. Love vibrated between us as she silently acknowledged my gratitude and respect. I gently vacated the space I had taken, and focussed into my Core. The cold, bright perfume of plum blossom, newly opening into the frosty sky, accompanied me, leaves still tight, yet the valiant blossom unfurling itself, symbol of perseverance and bravery, the winter flower of the four seasons, the winter gentleman along with its seasonal companions, orchid for spring, lotus for summer, chrysanthemum for autumn. I do love this delicate flower-being. Lin Bu, my friend and poet from a later While upon the Chinese Earth did so love plum blossom that he considered the Plum Blossom tree of Solitary Hill to be his wife. And the cranes to be his children.

There did I abide, meditating on the request. Clouds

and mists drifted through my being, harbingers of duality and separation. which Earth dwellers commonly term reality. However, the luminosity arising to disperse this obscuration told me that my long sojourn in the Heavenly Home had created in me a sustaining chord, an orchestration of union that would now never leave me.

Beloved Brothers and Sisters: on Earth, our Incarnations, in whatever form, are ultimately vehicles of learning, moving us through the belief and desolation of separateness and – when we are ready - returning us to the One Reality. We are invited to step through the Portal of the Opening of Heart as this, indeed, is how the Great Mystery Unfolds ,and brings us home Most of us, when we receive this invitation, see it as a terrifying plunge into the Tiger's Mouth. It can be a slow journey to turn towards that which we fear.

The earth number forty-nine came into my awareness. I took this as a sign and agreed: forty-nine days and nights. The seven repeating seven of this sacred number then hinted to me that the impending journey might request an additional number to keep in my pocket, so to speak, to spend if necessary. The dynamic number three emerged, and repeated with seven to create: twenty-one. I understood then that forty-nine was the primary number, but that twenty-one could be added to create seventy days if required. I remained in anticipation for a short while, to see whether the seven, or any other number, would communicate with me further. The quality of stillness which emerged indicated that the numbers had withdrawn. The arithmetic was complete. Seven, three and ten, generating forty-nine, twenty-one and seventy would accompany me on the journey, creating a firm and yet flexible container.

In this moment a colour arose, and a sound, which is how it is when a thread of the weaving of collected souls in the Heavenly Realm is gently pulled from the Shimmering Pattern, and is required to extend itself into a different dimension. This pliant and loving cloth of being, into which for Many a While I had been woven, allowed a gap to remain where the separating thread still had its purchase, firmly connected even as I set off on my Holy Task.

I entered a space which rippled with celestial winds and tides. I slowly became accustomed to the magnetic roar that took me. Utmost sorrow did I know at first as I withdrew from my home, and then I was pervaded by necessary movement ... diving, spiralling and penetration of layer upon layer. Singing and chanting followed me, notes of seed-pearl and miniature diamond, strung together in patterns of flowers and shells upon silver and gold. Notes and cadence of unparalleled salutation met me as I rode through a Corridor of Great Ones. They were burning with humility and wisdom, and extending their love and protection to me as I began the long journey to the Emerald Planet.

2

The figure of a man crosses the car-park. In the uncertain light of dusk he appears to be of medium build, moving easily on the rough ground, a shoulder bag swinging against his left hip. He reaches a car, a Golf Cabriolet, long past its best, dark green in colour. Even in the half light it looks dusty, except for an arc of clear space on the windscreen left by movements of the wiper. The man pauses, and searches in his pocket. His mobile phone rings and he exclaims in irritation before answering.

'Yes. Miriam. Yes. Yes … I'm coming.' His voice rises. 'I've only just finished the class … And I have the car this time – I told you I was taking it for a service, remember? I won't be long'. The call is apparently abruptly ended, for the man sighs, deeply and audibly, switches the phone off and gets into his car.

Shrouded by the dim and lonely light of the car-park, he sits in the driver's seat, motionless, but for his chest, slightly rising and falling. Five years ago there would not have been this conversation. There would have been talk about meeting somewhere in town, out and about, and the lovely fleet woman he finds and claims would fly into him with joy and mischief and passion. He recalls Miriam's face, her dark beauty, and relocates that face, pale and rather exhausted, fixed upon a baby sucking at her breast. He is out of the picture. He understands this rationally. New father syndrome. He is not prepared for a persistent feeling of resentment and counters it by stepping forward and claiming the infant, changing his nappy, holding him as he yells, putting him to sleep, taking him out. Bonding with him. But what of the bond with his woman, now become his wife? He can never have that rapture, that sexy feeding that the two of them share, that narcissistic milky exclusion. He sits behind Miriam as she feeds Paul, his husband-arms loosely around her, contemplating the baby-face of his son. The infant gaze is fixed upon its mother. However he moves and twists his head, Jack does not come into his son's range of vision.

Jack tries to cajole himself into delight at the Pietà before him. These enforced responses are not long sustained. He is frustrated and ashamed at his banal reaction. He is like a sulky boy.

Recoiling from all of this, Jack makes a decision. He takes himself no longer towards, but away, into hours of practice, extra workshops for the class and for his substantial number of private students. He watches YouTube replays of t'ai chi masters, and feeds himself on these. He becomes especially watchful of his students – encouraging and supporting their development. His son is about four months old and developing fast, when Jack catches sight of Miriam looking at him in a stricken way, her face drawn and tense.

'Jack, I feel I have lost you.'

He turns and puts his arms around her.

'I haven't gone anywhere. You've been preoccupied, really.' He smiles at her, a meaningless smile, and continues rather hastily: 'Well you have to, of course.'

'Your work. Feels as if you're living in it – even when you're here and with us.'

'But I include you, love ....' He'd tried to be glad when she came to the class a few times with Paul.

'Yes, and it's not my thing. We know that.' She speaks sharply. 'I can't help it, It's dance that's more my thing and I haven't got back into it.'

He steps away, withdrawing his embrace. 'Something I just have to check from last night's class ... sorry, I know this isn't quite what you want to hear right now. Won't take long and then shall I go get a take-away?' Jack is unhappy at how abrupt he is being. It's as if it is not he who is speaking. Some unpleasant alter ego is sitting on his tongue and speaking for him. As he turns away he hears Miriam mutter: 'Bloody marvellous timing, mate.'

The last time Miriam visits the class – with Paul in her arms – she arrives by arrangement just before the end so they can go home together. Jack notices her awareness of Marie, one of his best and most diligent students. He is giving Marie precise instruction, carefully and slowly, and he suddenly feels a painful and hostile stare from Miriam. He is fed up and wishes she were not there so he could get on with his work. They are both disturbed by this episode and talk circuitously about it later at home. They agree each has become a little distant from the other, that nothing is seriously wrong, but that they need to pay attention and mend a little rupture that is setting in. Babysitters are found, they go out sometimes with his friend Maliphant and at other times her best friend Tilly, and Tilly's husband. Riotous nights are cut short, however, and they leave before midnight. 'Babysitter,' they say apologetically. Miriam is sometimes too tired anyway to go past midnight, and then those stains appear from her full breasts, on her clothes. She is a milk machine on call. Sometimes Jack wants to stay on and let her go home alone but he knows without doubt this would be a grave mistake.

Jack shakes himself out of the narrative he is recollecting, opens the glove-box abruptly and takes out a packet of mints. Absently, without really wanting it, he puts one in his mouth and sinks back into uneasy reflection.

They hook up with other parents, finding them in the Gospel Oak corner of Hampstead Heath, within the gated playground of swings and slides and the sandpit. Jack finds these chance encounters largely tedious. Miriam insists they will surely find friends who are parents and also interesting. Jack grimaces. She shoots him an angry look. Over the days, the weeks, they make attempts to heal and mend, and then sharpness seems to come out of nowhere, ripping into good intentions.

It takes him a while to insert the key and start the car.

Approximately four miles away, on the ground floor of a brick terrace house guarded by its sentinel pavement tree, a woman sits in a room dimly lit by a bedside reading lamp. A small child lies sleepless in a bed, his eyes open and fixed upon her.

'Read it again.'

'I've read it twice already ....' The child's face puckers and the woman, as if the rearrangement of the child's expression is tied into her belly, winces and says quickly, 'Okay, okay ... but the last time, now.' The child settles back. Even with eyes closed, he is watchful.

'Once upon a time there were three bears ....'

The woman wonders whether the room is dark enough to hide her tears. She blinks them back, swallows hard and forces animation into her voice. She feels sad, and puzzled. As she reads, she glances at her watch. He should be back in half an hour.

As Jack opens the door he adjusts his posture, shaking his shoulders to let go of some degree of tension.

'Miriam,' he calls softly. She emerges from the child's room. Stares at him.

'Jack.' Their eyes meet. Layers of accusation and longing

move between them. She stifles a wish to grab at his face, scratch it and then kiss it. 'Do you want something to eat?' she asks tightly.

'No, I ate before the class.'

'Who with?' The words jump from her mouth. She doesn't want them to. She doesn't want to be saying this. Something feels wrong. The only discernible place that the wrongness emerges from, it seems to her in this painful and querulous state, is the place called Jack, the nearest one to her, the one to whom she is tethered.

'No one ... In the caff. Those samosas they have, you know ....'

'Look.' Bitterly. 'I'm not interested in what you ate.' She crosses to the kitchen door, glances through the window at the street. 'And I thought you had the car serviced.'

'Yes, I did, I told you.'

'Didn't they clean it as usual?'

'Buggers. Didn't do it this time.' An unpleasant silence hangs between them. Jack clears his throat. 'So,' he says, 'What is it you are interested in? Punishing me? Accusing me of things I don't do? What's going on, Miriam? Things never used to be like this.'

'We are going to wake Paul – let's go in the kitchen.'

Unpleasantness accelerates. Miriam wants to say help me – I have lost my way. My life has become narrow – you come and go and have a life outside. Does this mean having the child isn't enough? I love my child ....

Miriam won't reveal that this is what she wants to say. She throws out sulky ropes, hoping he will pull at one and make his way hand over hand until he is up close and then he will say I know you don't mean this. Faintly, she knows that she is alienating him so that he cannot make his way to her, rather has to protect himself. And the compulsion for her remains to poke and stir, and then feel alone and rejected. This is an old story.

From his bedroom, the child, fighting sleep, strains to listen to his parents. He thinks about calling but, against his will, sleep comes thick and dark through his veins and the initially demanding noise he attempts turns into an inaudible murmur.

In the kitchen, Miriam and Jack sit at opposite ends of the table. Jack remembers a night – how long ago? – when they eat together, chairs as close as possible, each feeding with one hand as the other roams beneath the table, beneath clothes, seeking mutual excitement, teasing, smiling. His face darkens.

Still life: the kitchen. Jugs of parsley and basil. Unusual, colourful bowls on the window sill. A carved Buddha on the shelf next to smaller, unmatched bowls. A striking black and white photograph of a man in Chinese loose trousers and jacket, body in a t'ai chi pose. Jack. A few years younger. The expression on his face is tranquil. A photograph of Miriam and Paul, he maybe six weeks old, in her arms and staring at the camera with an imperious look. Miriam's hair is longer, a hint of shyness in her eyes. The photographs are at an angle to each other. There are a few unwashed dishes in the sink and a pot on the stove.

'Whatever's going on, I want to sort it. But I always feel wrong in your eyes ... no, not always. Sometimes.' Jack looks at his wife. He's choosing words carefully because he knows what he actually wants to say is I don't want to be here. Well, not day after day when it's like this and I feel you tugging at me to make you feel all right.

'How did your class go?'

'Well enough. It's slow, teaching the form. People are impatient.'

'Was she there?'

'Who?'

'Oh come on, Jack!'

'For God's sake, Miriam – she – I am not interested. You know that.' What he wants to say, if only the truth could safely be told, is, yes she was there and I am not going to pursue her, I am not romantically interested in her, I don't want her to replace you. But I am aware of her and she does interest me because there is something of a mystery about her and she loves learning ... she is a good student. What he wants to say is: Miriam, don't show me this naked pain. And this desperate accusing questioning. It makes me want to walk away from you. And I don't want to walk away from you.

Miriam, panicking at the prospect of losing control, draws herself straight and tries to bring dignity into the situation. She begs the desperate child staring towards him from her eyes to drop its gaze a little and give her a chance. 'Jack. I'm tired.' Jack – unwilling, but knowing that this act is absolutely necessary, and remembering that he loves her, gets up and prepares to put his arms around his wife.

They meet, but not quite. And the gap yawns into the kitchen until every object arranged on shelves and on the worktop seems to hold its breath.

Miriam, before she gets into the bath, winds her long hair and fastens it on top of her head. She lights a candle and drops rose essence into the water. Maybe tonight they might talk together in a real way, not this mouthing through broken glass stuff that's been going on. She wishes she was as absorbed in something. Paul – yes. But it's not the same. Anyway, Paul is growing up. Not a baby any more. Something will change. She loves Jack. If only he would come in the bathroom now and look at her, he would see it. But she won't call him. He must come in of his own wish. The water starts to get cold. This is a strange passage they are walking through, damp and grey. The rest of the world madly dancing past – tossing skirts, colours and sound. She drops the soap and fishes under the cooling water for it, hating the feeling of the slippery wax under her fingers.

3

In another part of London, further east, a woman in her thirties, slight, of lithe body and symmetrical of face, a pleasing face, inward-looking and quiet, is slowly folding the black cotton trousers and long-sleeved black cotton jacket she wears for her t'ai chi class. Her room is sparsely furnished and each object is of quality. A futon bed, an old wooden chest of drawers, a rail with several garments hanging on it, an ornamental box on which stands a feminine figure, the Chinese Kuan Yin, goddess of mercy and compassion; next to this delicate form, a candle and a fern, its fronds wavering just below the edge of the box, teasing at embellished carvings. Two drawings on the wall demonstrate postures from the martial arts. The figures could be male or female.

The woman stares into the long mirror to the left of the drawings. She neither adjusts her appearance, changing an expression to meet the reflection in the glass, nor pulls at her hair to alter the frame around her face.

She watches as tears begin to gather and fall, noticing her numb expression. Closing her eyes, she drops into the pain in her heart, a queasy dissonance of longing and confusion.

He's your teacher. Love him as that.

I want him; we should be together; we're meant to be together.

Two unknown stories – nothing to do with present thoughts – play within her like thin lines of smoke from hidden fire. She is oblivious to them.

Silence more or less gathers in the room. The twenty-four-hour roar of traffic from a nearby main road in this borough of

Hackney creates a sullen rumble, a cold ocean dashing itself endlessly at a coastline of dark shingle. The woman, Marie, lives on the fourth floor of a mansion block, originally a council building, now most of the flats within it bought by the tenants who originally rented. She gets to her feet slowly, lights the candle on the ornamental box and from the same match lights a thin stick of incense. A savoury spiral ascends, carrying an aroma of sandalwood. She selects a CD. A compilation of songs by Purcell. The deep notes emerge, and also circle slowly upwards, suggesting a conversation of yearning and loss, a dialogue that Marie finds particularly familiar. A companion, speaking to her through the centuries. Dido's song. Remember me. Remember me.

Marie moves gracefully, accompanied and partially comforted, as she goes to the adjoining kitchen and puts on the kettle. She feels it to be an act of generosity and compassion, the way in which the instruments hold and support the human voice. The cradling extends into the room, it holds her too, lets the forlorn tale safely be heard. Nothing to do. No help. No resolution. Only listen.

She has work to do before the next day. She is ghost writer to Hannah Bloom, beautiful, antique, demanding, irascible, and the consequence of this collaboration is to be the memoirs of her life as a dancer. Marie is beginning to resent the odour of Hannah's house, the smell of her narcissistic flamboyance and the sharp rattle of her tongue as she dictates words which are often just as quickly erased and then re-stated. At the same time, she loves the world Hannah pulls her into. The precision of exercise to imprint ballet on the human form is very different from that required by t'ai chi, but the expression of love for movement, clearly within the essence of Hannah, touches Marie and keeps her committed to finishing the task. Marie promises to remain in employment with Madame Bloom for the next year, or at least until the work is complete. As she begins reading, seated at her computer and bringing jottings from pen and paper to the screen, the tumult in her heart subsides, a tide pulling slowly out as she wrestles with terminology, paragraphs and fractured grammar.

At precisely ten past ten, unexpectedly, a memory of Jack rises to the surface; she remembers a moment in the class when he demonstrates to her how to settle her energy substantially into her belly, hips and legs; working on postural alignment and the presence, simultaneously, of the qualities of both rising and falling. She feels as if he is in the room.

At ten past ten, in his home in Kentish Town, several stops west of the overground station nearest to flat 97, 136 Granville Buildings, Hackney, Jack feels disturbance as he lies quietly behind the sleeping form of his wife. He sees with vivid clarity the face of his student, Marie, as she watches his movement and listens to his instruction. He puts his hand over Miriam's hip; she doesn't stir and yet he has the sense that she is awake. He holds tenderness for her. Somehow in the dark nest of their bed, he knows that she knows. That which is going on is known in some unspoken way. And yet he is not setting out to cheat on her. He loves her, he loves their life together as man, wife and child. He hasn't looked for, nor asked for the feelings running through him in this instant, that there is something intensely necessary in the young woman Marie, for him. He experiences urgency when he sees her. He is not going to act on it. And yet Miriam is responding as if he were about to betray her, or had already done so.

Has he betrayed her? In some way, yes. And in a way which

carries inevitability, in the way that all humans fall out of the Garden of Eden, through uninvited thoughts, feelings and actions. If only ... those two terrible, damning words ... if only Miriam took it more lightly, wasn't so seared by it. And – again – there's nothing he has actually done. Except that glances, sensations, thoughts, non-spoken interactions seemed to be doing themselves. If only Miriam could be a little more intact and mysterious about all this, and about herself. He knows her so well; she is naked and this nakedness is no longer erotic.

What an irony. He used to long to see her naked. Now he longs to see her clothed, clothed in a way that suggests she is not so available to him. That would give him air to breathe, a chance to go into solitude within himself, prevail with the currents that come and go. Jack sighs. He knows it will be a long while before he sleeps.

Miriam hears him. She is lying in unpleasant stillness, rigid, feeling the desired and dread weight of his hand upon her hip. She feels deficient in herself. She's lost her sense of separate confidence. A flash of anger passes through her, both for the heavy hand upon her hip, and for the loss of a separate, creative self. And then there's the irritation of that slow quiet woman.

How can she slough his hand off her body without his knowing she's awake? Her doleful mind chews on this dilemma until sleep pulls her away and she turns over without thought so that their two bodies separate. Jack wraps his abandoned arm around his own body and turns his mind to a calming practice: breathing down into the soles of his feet. Imagining the breath to be cool and tranquil. His mind quiets, but sleep is still a long time coming. It is windy and cold outside and he thinks of the rowan tree outside their kitchen window. He and Miriam follow its veiling and unveiling through the seasons.

Night parcels day into semi-darkness, darkness shot through with artificial light. A thousand imaginings stir the sleeping populace and fuel those still up and about, going about business and pleasure, legitimate and covert.

Still awake, Marie continues to listen to Purcell. Who was he, she wonders. Died young. An organist at Westminster Abbey, a choirboy previous to that. How would it be – imagine if it could be – that one day she could travel back in time, and seat herself, invisible, in the chamber of this court musician and observe him as he composes. Would he look anguished, straining for harmony – or would his face be impassive, empty, calm? All this froth, she thinks. The passing of history. The creative drive that pinches him between its teeth, not killing but holding – is not of linear time, and space – it is always present, prevailing – and we find it if we are lucky. Or blessed. Or diligent enough. Or of such impassioned yearning that we would give up everything to know of this dangerous, brilliant, tender grip.

Marie returns to the chapter currently overloaded with exclamation marks and contradictions, and re-directs her attention, the cup of tea next to her forgotten.

4

Without digression, forethought or map, obedient only to Agreement did I tumble through inter-penetrating dimensions of cluster and galaxy, before entering the Earth's canopy. Through a dark sea of energy, pierced with flickering forms of light, silent and beautiful, like lost jewel-fish in a forgotten corner (though of course nothing is lost or forgotten) did I continue the trajectory.

I simply fell, and landed, and quite particularly did I land for I realised myself to be in the corner of a sleeping room, and a man and wife in the bed and I saw sorrowful colours around them. There was neither equivocation nor sense of query: where am I? Am I meant to be in this place? I was drawn thus towards a small, ancient, green country, the other side of the planet from my long-ago habitation and then followed a magnetic pull to this house. I came in through the Emerald Vortex and emerged on this unfamiliar side of the planet, away from the ground of my previous earthly origin, away from the language of the Tao, that which expresses the longing of the heart to be full and yet unknowing. Trustfully I arrived, allowing the requirement of my task to deliver me.

I was curious, as is every traveller. I arrived in the time of day revolving into night, so the impact of the panoply and effusion of Things became mercifully softened. Finally, the night-mantle covered all. Even so, I saw and sensed not only the foreignness of physiognomy and landmass, but also the foreignness of a Much Later While.

Beloved Friends, in your measurement, you would understand that I had been located away from Mother

Earth and in the Heavenly Realms for one thousand and two hundred years. In what raiment did I perceive the Mother to be dressed after my period of absence? Her beautiful covering of earth, water, mineral, plant and animal was still in evidence, though much manipulated and – yes – hurt by the minds and hands of Humankind. Human not always Kind. Human also Unkind. My listening and feeling picked up groans and cries from the Mother, telling of piercing and plundering. Also did I hear songs from her, songs in answer to love, devotion and respect uttered by some dwellers on her surface. I could tell, from listening to the constantly unfolding, malleable and diverse web surrounding her, that the human creature had developed the faculty of mind and thinking to an extraordinary degree but that this capacity did not generate an equal development of heart and belly intelligence. Indeed, I expected to witness a change in the human body – imagining I would see a very large head and smaller, weaker hands and legs. This was not so, but what did turn out to be true was that the electrically charged aura around human heads was dense and dominant. Particularly in the corner of the Mother's body where I landed, and manifesting with equal intensity in larger landmasses near this ancient island. I tuned swiftly into echoes from distant habitations and these told that small groups of people, living very simply and close to the ground, were being contemptuously treated, that their understanding of forest and creature was not appreciated, that their number was slowly and sadly diminishing, with very little sorrow or mourning from the humans whose lives were more elaborated.

Thus did I absorb, rapidly and in many-dimensional

detail, the history of the Mother. While I received this intelligence of a cosmic nature, I was drawn into a singular and precise place: to behold a man and woman in a sleeping room. At the same time, I was given access, furthermore, into the room of another sleeping person, in a dwelling place some distance east within this great city, and received sight of a young woman with long dark hair which spilled over a white pillow. There was a palpable cloud of sorrow around these three human beings. A connection travelled from the solitary woman to this house, and back to her. I saw this connection distinctly. And of course this was one line amongst countless myriad colours and patterns and shapes in flux within space and time.

I saw cast-off forms that had history with the incarnated forms presently sleeping. A weight of story and consequence began to seep into both rooms. An extraordinary profusion of narrative and consequence surrounded this entire city which stretched for many a length this way and that, bisected by a river and with stretches of green relief mercifully breaking up the solidity of houses, large and small.

During the last part of my descent I journeyed through a density of multiple, layered exhalations of energy carrying words and thoughts and intention. It was quite difficult, before the cessation of my movement, to discriminate astral bodies from disembodied currents of conversation which flew between the small buzzing objects people held in their hands and to their ears. The movements humans made were much more nervous and rapid than those I recalled from my previous time upon Earth, the forms were larger and of course they had

Occidental patterning rather than the Oriental patterning
I was used to before. The disappearance of nature under
heavy building materials was hurtful to me. Do not forget
I lived in the mountains before, the wild mountains, quite
without neatly signposted paths and cleared forestation.
The smell here too was quite different. Poisonous and
metallic is the best description I can give. I observed an
extraordinary number of complex objects I had never
seen before, including moving carriages that brought
humans from one point to another. Some of these
carriages moved through the sky, and I saw in them rows
of people, as I was directed onto Earth. What Things!

I was finding it easy to keep my inner balance through
all of this. The Laws and Principles of course prevailed,
unchanged. The Great Yin and Yang and the Way of the
Tao govern all – and the Ten Thousand Things simply
assume different shape. I suppose if anything shocked
this unshockable old rascal, it was the pervasive affect of
nervous excitation, and the unhappiness and desperation
emanating from many of the tangled energy fields. At the
same time, I also witnessed beings of extraordinary
beauty and refinement, moving with clarity and quality
through the heaving waves of interpenetrating influence.
And the children! There seemed to be a rush of souls
visiting at present who carried the Indigo Ray of
Enhanced Sensitivity. Ancient Beings winked at me
through the eyes of babes in arms as I tumbled in!

May I bring your attention to a key principle I have
learned over the time spent in the Heavenly House of
Discourse and Apprenticeship, Dear Friends? Deeply
embedded in True Practice is that courtesy is a primary

element in all transactions, even transactions with the Dark Forces. Not that they should be let through to plunder and disrupt, there always has to be strength, protection and discrimination. Let me say that the Opposition cannot be excluded from courtesy. We bow, without discrimination, before each event that comes before us in our life.

I narrate this as preparatory understanding for you, Beloved Friends.

In the room of the married man and woman, I sensed a Darkness. Not of a worrying order, not of the nature of profound dishonour or evil, but of the nature of unbalanced whispering, promoting judgement through the heart's disquiet. I saw also elements of revenge and unfinished business. These aspects emerged from remnants, shadowy figures in the darkness; ancestral discarnates, who had not yet fully left the Earth plane's influence. One of the figures was rather uncomfortably aware of my presence. I could see the transparent husk of a physical body still clinging to its astral pattern: a stocky, strongly masculine figure he had been, with an over-developed will and an under-developed sense of receptivity.

When I say 'saw' I am of course not talking of physical sight, but of a refined capacity to know, a capacity to decipher the subtlety of the Akashic Records, that complete reference to All that has Been. I knew that there were superior instruments manifested upon the Earth which brought forth information at the touch of a finger. This process minimally and crudely emulated the profound and instant knowing which comes when a being has passed through Cleansing and Initiation of a very high order.

Returning to the issue of courtesy: I received an opening Portal which indicated that I had been given permission to engage.

The masculine figure became aware of my presence.

'What do you want to tell me?' I was not hearing his voice. We were communicating through the medium of thought. His thought-transmission carried hostility. I responded:

'You are possibly carrying unfinished business.'

I received a hard, aggressive jolt of energy as response. His field moved nearer to mine and I sensed him sniffing around me. I protected myself, but nonetheless remained available. Curiosity took the better of him and he indicated that I should show him what I knew, but that he would cease the exchange if anything displeased him. I respectfully requested evidence from the Thread of this man's journey. Instantly, a frail but tensile vibrating line emerged for our vision. It was almost like a necklace of smudged pearls, heavy pearls, small and dense and sitting upon the Thread in differing shapes. Oh, how I struggle with these images and metaphors, they offer such a poor imitation of what I am trying to reveal. It was not at all a necklace of pearls, more a momentum of incident, profound, accumulated incident, each one in relationship to the one emerging after it. Cause and effect.

He and I saw – and received the seeing each from our own perspective – we saw an encoded transmission spinning between him and the embodied man on the bed.

'So what?' he communicated gruffly. 'I never liked my son, why should I like this grandson? People have to earn your respect. They have to follow the family rule.'

A signal of Intention came from the shadowy horde of discarnates gathered around and the pale relic of another man emerged.

'I am your son.' The Thread sagged with pain and spun out a distilled rendition of aggression and passivity, the mode between this father and son. The sleeping figure turned and spoke unintelligible words. I could see that the incarnate man had suffered from the shame of his father being made deficient by the grandfather's bullying; of his father perpetually suffering from humiliation, and secretly hating the old man, seeing him as the cause of his unhappiness. From grandfather to father to son passed a line of cause and effect: punishment, resentment and displacement. The sleeping child I sensed in the next room was as yet free of effect, but as always with young ones, his field was porous and vulnerable.

Now I must tell you forthwith that I was not there to mend, change or make good. I was there to occupy a Place, and around this Place, events would occur, but they would not be of my making. I would embed myself into this situation as an anchor, a still point, an Offering and a Radiance. That's all I can say.

The grandfather suddenly withdrew attention; the father faded back to his place in the shadows, and the

Thread re-wound itself into the Records. I spent time in deep silence, without reference or consequence; I spent time in the place where there is no time.

Let me deliver to you a small fragment at this point, Dear Ones. If I had been in this or a similar situation as an incarnate being within a finite physical vehicle, I would be heavily engaged in the process of thinking and feeling within the limits of time and space. That is, my thoughts would be dwelling upon the situation and engaging forces of logic and consequence and obligation – to see what I should do or where I should go, and to try to guess what it was that was required of me. I would be puzzling about the discarnate ancestors and studying the moments that had passed between us. I would have been having opinions about what had happened. I might also then have engaged feelings, and be experiencing unease and anxiety. I might have felt dislike for the grandfather, pity for the father, curiosity about the young man on the bed. And before you perhaps feel irritation with me, and want to justify the attributes of incarnation, let us agree that of course this is How It Is. Divine engineering fashioned a time-limited phenomenon with its marvel of mind and body as a vehicle for experience, and its nature moves it along the horizontal procedure of causality.

The Awakening that is the Essential Quickening of human life upon this planet comes from the blessed vertical shaft of light that pierces this horizontal, and appears and disappears according to its own law – the unknowable law of Grace.

Permission to withdraw from you, Beloved Friends, at

this point so that the entry of the vertical into the narrative may be felt by you unencumbered by further words. A prolonged moment, if it so pleases you, of silent absorption.

5

'I had a lousy night. Dreaming,' says Jack, reaching for his wife as morning light fumbles through plain, thick cotton curtains. She opens her arms to receive him and their bodies take purchase and find familiar resting place. Jack stirs with desire and she answers with a movement of the hips. Happiness of a sort touches them, they kiss and search each other's bodies with eager hands. The bedroom door opens and Paul, dragging a soft toy, regards his parents with steady severity.

'What you doing?'

'Kissing mummy.'

'I want to ....' The entire rumpled bed, the geometry of their embraced bodies, the light moving into the room, all seem to sigh as the adults, reluctantly but willingly, welcome their child into their bed where he triumphantly lies between them.

'Did you have a bad dream?' she asks, running one hand along Paul's arm, at the same time touching the outer line of Jack's shoulder.

'I had a dream!' says Paul loudly. 'I was an elephant ....'

'A big elephant?' asks his mother.

'A normal size,' he replies, correcting her, working hard to retain the success of his interruption, between their bodies and between their words.

'Let daddy tell us his dream ....'

'I want to tell mine!'

'You told us yours – daddy's turn.' Jack turns to Miriam and yawns.

'I could do with another hour – is it you to get his breakfast or me?'

'I think it's you but I'll do it ... I want to hear about your dream.' Something urgent speaks through her body, rakes at him through her otherwise soft gaze. She is clutching at the dream; it might have information which could help her with that which threatens to rupture something safe between them. Jack recoils from the sudden demand, but dishes up something to placate her. He is disturbed by the unpleasantness he is producing in himself at the moment. He doesn't like the way he is treating Miriam. Baffled, he watches himself, wanting to come out of a kind of obstinacy and yet not willing to make that shift.

'I don't know if it was a dream … it was more as if something was trying to speak to me ….'

'Like what? Or who?' Miriam frowns at Paul who is now tugging at her arm and asking for breakfast.

'Darling, can't say any more – let's sort out the little fellow and maybe if something comes back I can tell you later ….'

'You mean I sort out the little fellow ….'

'Miriam! You offered!'

'Oh all right ….' Bundling up her pleasing curves into a dressing gown Jack particularly dislikes (it reminds him of grumpiness and sour milk) she picks up her son and trails from the room. Jack rubs his nose into the warm place beside him. Shadowy voices and figures tease at him; he tries to recall and then sinks back into fragmented sleep.

Miriam wants to scream. She feels the warm snake of desire still pressing in her belly and wants Paul to understand and to go into his room and play for an hour and then she will go back to bed and rip the dream out of Jack and comb it for meaning and clues and then she will lay the length of her body upon her husband and draw him into her.

'Porridge? With raisins?'

'Yes, yes, yes, with raisins and can I have two spoons one for porridge and one for raisins … no I want a fork for raisins so I can poke them ….' Laughing and near to tears, Miriam gives

Paul a cushion for his chair, a spoon for his porridge and a fork for the wrinkled, black, juicy raisins.

Jack turns and comes up from sleep, remembers his father and feels sad; remembers his grandfather and feels angry. Feels the conviction within himself – resurrected and reiterated almost daily, sometimes even without his knowing – that he will never, Never be like either of those men, not like the old bully, and not like his son, who soaked it all up, even his body, round-shouldered and pigeon-chested, soaked it up. Jack stretches his own body, enjoying the lengthening of muscle. A momentary feeling of guilt catches him. Poor dad. What else could he do. He was fucked, basically. What else could he do. What can you do when you're a kid and your dad beats you. Okay, some kids get gritty and fight back. But if you're not made that way? Jack thinks of his mother, small, round and tough. She was gritty. Bullied his dad. Yes, she did. But that was more affectionate, wasn't it? An uneasy knowing enters his body. His mother bullied his father. Where's the affection in that? Growling at him, teasing him, making fun of him and then putting her arms around him and saying don't mean it, sorry, sorry – just a joke. But too late. The soaking had already happened, the shoulders full of sorrow. He would slope off, in his sloping shoulders, yes, slink away with a half smile, a shit-eating smile. And Jack would collude with his mother's betraying arms and hands, knowing that she wanted to slap the old man straight, have him stand up for them, do manly things for them, and that her frustration and disappointment came out as teasing and then her arms would embrace him in the Judas embrace and they would watch and not smile at him as he left the room. Never, never, the mantra begins in Jack's mind and in his body at that time. Never, never. And he goes to the boxing ring and then – because actually he hates boxing – very quickly changes to karate and then to aikido and finally – with relief and a sense of joy – to t'ai chi.

Why does his mother marry such a man? Jack remembers their wedding photographs. Pa is handsome, has a gentleness and gallantry about him that Ma probably goes for. She comes from a rough-house too, but it is a warmer rough-house. Cuffs and slaps but also big loaves of bread baking, and lavish butter and cheese for sandwiches and all of them around the kitchen table, joking and slapping and teasing and their mouths full of warm bites of bread, mingled with strong cheddar.

Jack listens to the sounds of his wife and son from the kitchen. In his half-awake, half-asleep state, he is aware of something he can't grasp. This ungraspable quality doesn't feel like a dream, more like a knowing on the edge of his consciousness. Opening his eyes, he stares into the eyes of a small oriental man in the corner of his room. The man, wearing a colourful patchwork cloak, is clearly not of present time. His hair is long and matted. Ancient patina burns from his outlined form in fierce luminosity. The gaze Jack receives contains an incandescent quality of love and detached interest. Jack blinks, and the figure disappears.

Jack's eyes fill with tears and a deep sob wrenches itself through his body. Shocked, he sits abruptly upright and then begins to haul himself out of bed. Groping for loose trousers and shirt, Jack frowns as he pictures again the figure of the small man. Is this a picture he has seen somewhere? The sensation of being observed, and the illuminated quality of the observing gaze, however, remain present and unmistakeable. Jack wonders whether to tell Miriam but then recalls the discomfort of her sharp response to his dream. Not his dream, his night experience. What the hell is going on? Jack feels the aftermath of the sob that arose in his body. He wants it back. The gaze from the little man, like a key of precision and exactness, opens a door deep in him. Behind the door: a wave of unknown water, of a hue peculiarly light green. A wave shot through with shrieking seabirds and prehistoric salt quantities. He cannot cry now. Anyway what is he crying for?

Full of thoughts, and yet privy to an indescribable experience distinctly new, host to breath and blood now prickled with unearthly capacity, Jack goes to the far corner of the living room, near the bay window, and looks out onto the apple tree as he begins, as is his regular habit, settling into his feet, his belly, loosening his shoulders, releasing the tension in his upper body, breathing down into his centre. He opens up his stance shoulder-width apart and begins the slow process of energetic alignment.

6

Hannah Bloom waits for Marie. She is arranging her features into a casual and reflective portrait, hoping that, precisely now, Marie will walk through the door and be impressed by the elegant, philosophical woman sitting on the burgundy red sofa. (Rich material; thick brushed cotton, several scattered cushions placed on the left side, each one carrying a version of the burgundy … a stripe here, a flower there. Hannah, today, is wearing a variation of burgundy … a touch more red in the purple.) Hannah moves slightly and rearranges to the full, the calf-length, deeply gathered skirt she has chosen. In the large, gilt-edged mirror at the far end of the room, she sees herself. Straight of back and neck as a ballerina should be. The room is shadowed, even though it is morning. Heavy, thickly lined curtains partly conceal the long windows of the living room, keeping out the raw yellow of a late summer sun – ruination to a dancer's pale skin. On the desk, neatly laid out, photographs, programmes and letters.

The serene features of the living portrait begin to crease slightly into annoyance. It is ten o'clock and the girl should be here. Ten o'clock is the agreed start time. Hannah knows she is a reasonable employer. This is a job any girl would covet, helping the exquisite and adored ballerina of the London scene write her memoirs. She won't quibble over a few minutes. She knows public transport is unreliable. Nonetheless, knowing this, the girl should leave earlier. Hearing the key in the lock just at this moment is a signal for Hannah to retrieve the artfulness of her original expression. She is gazing casually and reflectively towards the shaded window as Marie walks in. A small smile just touches Hannah's carefully sculpted lips, tinted with the exact red of her skirt.

The obedient employee flinches slightly as she sees the

Great Lady. Tense again. Might be a difficult session. 'Morning, Miss Bloom,' she says. 'How are you?'

'Ready to begin,' says Hannah. Marie brings out notebook and pen. She is quick enough to be able to type interview notes and initially brings her laptop but Hannah cannot bear the sound. 'The noise of the fingers on the keys, darling, goes right through me. I simply can't take it.' Time and time again, for Marie, working with Hannah Bloom brings a combination of fascination and distaste. Her life is interesting, her commitment to dance unflinching. Her instinct for the truth? Marie frequently feels that the truth is being embroidered. However, it is not her job to scan for biographical accuracy. Her job is faithfully to record what is being said and then, later on, to review the contents and structure with Hannah, and to edit.

'Darling, today ... the golden years,' says Hannah. 'Please bring that pile of programmes.'

Hannah is the only child of Barney and Sadie Bloom, who find themselves within a displaced shoal – a desperate and frightened community from Lithuania – dispossessed and washed from their homes by a violent and evil tide. By no directive or inclination of their own (they faintly think New York might be the best destination for such as themselves) they end up in Bethnal Green, soon finding enough of a familiar community within this unfamiliar place to rebuild some sort of a life. Barney is a dogged and reliable tailor. Nothing fancy, but what you get is good quality, plain and simple. Sadie helps him at the machine and, later, in the shop. They have one child – Hannah. To their astonishment, they produce an exquisite, precocious daughter. 'I think it must come from auntie Greta,' Sadie frequently says, looking at her daughter's thin, pale, delicate face, the long shining black hair, and innate grace of movement. Auntie Greta has disappeared – with so many others – herded into a queue, eyed up and fingered, moved along, taken away … no one knows where. But no one can forget her beauty. There are story-fragments of the haughty toss of her head from the last known days. Even in old and dirty clothes, emaciated, she stands out, her face sculpted and proud. Hannah begs for photographs of this auntie. But there are none. In an archive in her mind, Hannah stores many images of Greta. Images she fashions from longing and the desperate need to have someone special other than Barney and Sadie, her solid, decent, boring parents who let her rule the roost and who sacrifice a great deal so that she can go to dancing school.

In a manoeuvre almost psychopathic in its rational intention, Hannah mislays her parents when she can, forgetting them somewhere, dropping them on the road, left in a cupboard, in a handbag given away. Eventually, Barney and Sadie come to believe, building up a rationale of their own, that Hannah lives a life so demanding, in a world so different, that the world itself – not her, not their Hannerle – has to take this swan away from their rude duck nest. That this is within the natural order of things. Truth be told, if there is any truth, if one could scour to the bottom of their souls, beneath conditioning, strategy and defensiveness, one might find relief … this child is sometimes a difficult creature to have in the house. They might prefer a simple, plump child who fits into the tribe around them, who is amused by their jokes, delighted by their food and willing to care for them when they get older. Who gets married to the boy next door and has children. There are times (many times) when Sadie feels a heartache close to anger. Sometimes she wants to slap this child, and then feels ashamed at the thought, slaps herself instead, laughing bitterly. 'Oi, what kind of a mother am I?'

'You know what?' Barney says one day, unexpectedly. He is

not generally an expressive man. 'At least she kept the name. You'd think she would have changed it to Pavlovitskaya or something like that ....' 'Hannah Pavlovitskaya,' says Sadie, in a deep, exotic voice. 'Hmmph. No – it would be Anna Pavlovitskaya.' A moment of pure, unacknowledged hatred of their changeling passes intimately between parents, and then drops far out of sight beneath the carpet which covers all possible unmentionable things.

Hannah's version of her childhood (a short chapter) presents her parents as two artistic, slender and tubercular creatures, melancholic and poetic, singing together as mother played the piano, their heartbroken, deeply sensitive daughter dancing in the corner as they sang, oblivious to everything but their exclusive and undying love for each other. When Hannah dictates this chapter to Marie, there are tears in her eyes. Marie sees them, and feels oddly unmoved.

'So,' says Hannah. 'Now we are in the time when I start to become known. Well, just a little known,' she smiles modestly. 'I was asked to dance the lead role in *Coppélia*.' Her next sentence follows rapidly: 'Well, you see, I was stand-in and the original principal took ill. I was particularly suited to this role as it was playful.' She shows a photograph to Marie and there is a beautiful girl, body drawn upwards on one pointed toe, the other leg sharply bent at the knee, the glistening ballet slipper anchored softly onto the side of the vertical leg. Dark eyes shining, black hair drawn into a classical bun, this is lovely Hannah, in the splendour of her youth. Marie's heart turns. How could one not love this girl, simply for the poetry and beauty of her expression, the buoyancy and joy of her body?

'Ha! I know what you are thinking?' Hannah's tone is warm, almost girlish, Marie notices. 'Yes, they adored me, the men I mean. They were always there backstage, bearing bouquets.'

'Anyone special?' asks Marie.

'Now you're asking,' Hannah's tone changes. 'And that would be telling.'

'But I thought ...' begins Marie, and changes her mind. She is going to say: I thought that's what you wanted to do. Tell.

'They were all special, darling,' says Hannah sharply. 'I attracted a superior kind of man, you can be sure.'

Hannah and Marie move into a known routine of Hannah reporting and Marie writing – and occasionally asking Hannah to stop and repeat or stop and explain. Marie is skilled at noticing gaps, or inconsistencies. Hannah appreciates this quality in her but at the moment is working on autopilot. She remembers, she produces facts and opinion. She is not present in the procedure. She is caught fully by memory and pain. Special. Of course he was special. But this is not for telling. This is buried, gone, dead. A time I was crazy, she thinks, hoping that Marie won't notice the turbulence suddenly arisen. Of course she won't notice, she consoles herself. I am a trouper. On with the performance. No matter what is happening underneath.

'Let's have tea, darling,' she says abruptly. Marie is surprised. Tea is usually precisely at eleven thirty. It is not quite eleven fifteen. Marie rises.

'Lovely idea – I could do with a cup.'

Hannah leans back into the sofa. There is no thought now of facial expression, or presentation. She is oblivious to the smear of pain across her features, forcing itself through now that Marie is out of the room. Jeremy. Oh God.

She notices him – a tall, unsmiling man with intense eyes – when she performs in *Coppélia*. Her concentration slips for a moment, she glances into the audience and there he is. For the next few performances she looks deliberately, not expecting anything. And a week later, on Wednesday, there he is. Sitting in the front row. Sending shivers down her spine from the first day of noticing him is that his eyes seem to be on her alone. This intense man, unsmiling, disregards the other whirling and expressive dancers, even the gorgeous Beatrice as Swanhilde, and she, Hannah, after two experiences of this focus, starts to dance just for him. She opens her arms, twirls – just so – and comes back into the dark hollow of his eyes, landing there, just where she wants to. Will she ever meet him? Not knowing is painful, but delicious. She feels like a doll in his gaze. It is up to him. Nothing she can do but dance. After three weeks, by the time she is performing the lead herself, she receives a bunch of three dozen red roses in her dressing room. Without a note. She receives them on Wednesday. Taking a chance, this time she allows herself to smile at him. A brief smile. Who else would notice? He does not smile back, but she knows his expression changes. A look of satisfaction. A look of confidence. The following week, three dozen red roses. No message. She smiles again. His face seems to deepen in the shadows where he sits. Always in the same seat. The same seat occupied and flowers every Wednesday, no matter that *Coppélia* is over and she is back in the corps for the next production, until – on the sixth Wednesday – he isn't there. Her heart drops and her dance carries a quality of fire, of bravery in the face of loss. After the performance, in the dressing room, she is told there is someone to see her. He walks in, carrying one rose. He gives it to her and says (his voice captivating, deep and slow and musical), 'You are the most beautiful woman I have ever seen.' He extends his hand to her, his left hand, and she sees the plain glimmer of a band of gold. 'Yes,' he says, 'I am married. This is how it is. And you are the most beautiful woman I have ever seen and I have to get to know you.' He smiles slightly. 'I am obliged to worship you in whatever little way I can.'

Leading up to her breakthrough star performance in *Scheherazade*, he is present in the front row every week. And as well as flowers, sends her gifts. A necklace, a pair of soft leather gloves. He comes to her backstage after the performance. A pair of turquoise harem pants hang loosely over a chair, and he runs his finger almost carelessly over the silken material.

'Tonight I will escort you home.'

'What about your wife, won't she worry about you?' questions Hannah lamely.

'I request you not to think about these things.' The man is courteous, and firm. The exquisite little creature obliges him.

She takes him home, she takes him to bed. Not her first lover but her most wonderful. He ravishes her with adoration, asking her to turn around for him, slowly, in her clothes and then without them. She obeys his request. She banishes thoughts about his wife, his life. Thoughts seem to drop away like spun sugar melting. He makes love to her meticulously, seeming to anticipate just the quality of touch she is wanting. She has never known herself so abandoned, voluptuous, capable of ecstasy. Every now and then, even in moments of passion, he stops, moves away – and asks her to arrange her body, her features, into a dramatic or romantic or sometimes savage position. And he looks, and moves her to a mirror so she too can see what he is seeing. As if he is taking photographs. (Later, he does take photographs. She doesn't want to think about this.) As if in a trance he murmurs – almost not to her but to himself – 'It cannot be that I have her now ....'

Sometimes he is in tears. And then he is away from her, in his own grief – never talked about, but expressed, and witnessed by her silent gaze. Then he turns back to her body with ferocity, gentleness and strangeness, for she knows very little about him but that he has a wife and son and that he works in the city. He says to her early on: 'I probably love my wife. And she is in the world with me. You are not in the world, you are a being from another world, the ordinary should not tarnish you. She doesn't know about this but she knows I need to be away regularly. Let us not dwell on outer realities. They do not belong here.' Swooning, cherished, she takes into herself his words. She becomes, in her own mind, a being of unearthly excellence – and she tells herself she doesn't want anything else. Not for her the mundane arrangements of people like her parents. Even if he were free and … she tosses this idea away. It does not become them, the purity of their liaison. And then, late at night, after he's gone, she chews, like an unhappy dog with not enough meat on its bone, she chews on the word 'probably'. He's not said, 'I love my wife'; he's said, 'I probably love my wife ….' What does that mean? And she cannot, will not contaminate the atmosphere by asking him.

He informs her: 'And sometimes I won't be here. Don't be concerned. I will be back as often as I can to my queen … and I will feast on you, and you on me. What we have, my darling, is so special, it does not run by normal rules.'

He puts no strictures upon her – but doesn't need to, as she finds she is too obsessed by him to see other men and can't bear their presence if they approach her. None will ever be as he is. Her king, her worshipping king. She has her dance, her body, her secret lover who loves her more than anyone could ever be loved, bringing her treats and sweets and feeding her little pieces one by one, licking her lips to taste what she has tasted, who bathes her and dries her and dresses her and undresses her. They don't talk much, but he likes to ask her to look in the mirror and tell him, in as much detail as possible, what it feels like to look at that image and know that it is her.

At last, her dream come true. Someone who really appreciates and sees her beauty, reflecting it back to her so that she can fall in love with herself. 'Look in the mirror,' he says, 'and see the most beautiful face and body in the world. Love yourself ... you are Helen of Troy, Cleopatra ... they are dust next to you ....' And she looks and then looks away and sees, behind her, a handsome, intense, broad-shouldered and lean-hipped man – ignoring the sometimes disquieting expression in his eyes, around his mouth – frightening, if she were truthful at those moments – and she tells him he is a god come to find her, a god from the heavens, from the godplace. And he chides her and says he is a mere mortal and she was to hush her mouth and he kisses her and watches her dissolving against him, watches in the mirror this woman who is giving him a secret life beyond his fantasy, beyond his imagining – a bird in a cage, surrendered and willing to sing and flaunt her feathers. He is now the keeper of the captive one. Hannah decorates her studio flat with flair and artifice and he brings velvet hangings and satin covers and soft lamps and, over time, new mirrors, so the luscious textures can be amplified.

Marie comes back with tea and as she pours, notices Hannah's face, looking somehow younger, very beautiful, sad .... She is touched and looks up as if to say something to her employer. But at that moment, Hannah draws herself together and her face ages and sharpens and she says the tea isn't quite right and can Marie pour it out into the sink and make another pot – perhaps the teabags are stale, try the new box.

7

He watches the woman with the turned-out feet. That's how he comes to know her within his own frame of reference. He is fascinated by the way she sits. She sits down in one movement, not looking first at the seat or going down in pieces, or collapsing, as some people do. She swoops down, that's what she does. Then she arranges her skirt in a wide arc around her, and then, the feet turn out. They make a V, with the heels together. He is mesmerised by that V – it is so certain and yet so unnecessary. What the hell difference would it make if she let her feet just do what they wanted to do – tuck under, or one foot jiggling at the end of a crossed leg? What is she trying to tell him – or anybody – with this performance? But he really likes it. It's as if it's for him. His reaction is not sexual – she's not his sort of woman. She'd make a fuss about everything. And he wouldn't want that bloody V around the house all day, he'd have to hit her if she kept doing it. It's just that here, within the wide, bench-littered grasslands of this common, she doesn't know the way that he is watching. And that he is looking out for something particular which has now become a totem for him.

And what's with the head scarf and the glasses? He knows they're not for real. Is she disguising herself somehow? Her dresses are pseudo-gypsy. Big colours and big skirts and a scarf wrapped around her obviously dyed blonde hair. Or a wig? Compared to all the fucking tarts in beehives and mini-skirts littering the grass she is old fashioned. A librarian maybe, who acts different off-duty? And the newspaper? She's not really reading it – just looking at the headlines. 'Kennedy shot!' What the hell does he care. Never trusted the guy. Big insincere smile, rich family, that stupid wife with those eyes on the side of her head. Serve them right. Or she brings books – they keep her eyes lowered as a change from that strident gaze she has – at a diagonal, looking aslant at the house across the road. And stiffening when someone emerges from it. The woman with the child. It's always them. Out of curiosity he goes there in the early morning one day and sees the gent – smart-looking, tall and dark – leaving at about eight. And the woman – the woman of the house, his wife probably – comes out at odd times. The bench woman – the one with the turned-out feet – is not there everyday. He should know. He knows everyone who settles here. This is what he is doing at the moment. Nothing else to do. He watches, and speculates. He's got plenty of time right now; he parks his motorbike, wanders around and then sits.

He sees himself as a helper. Not in the way you would automatically think, oh no. He helps people when they're on the edge – and not quite going over. It's the final nudge they can't give themselves. Too much fear. Or conscience. One bored afternoon he picks up a book someone has left at the barber's: *The Screwtape Letters*, by C.S. Lewis. He starts reading, and this astonishing piece of writing burns itself into his thinking. It is his book, written for him. Takes him out of a feeling of endless inner accident, where nothing works, where there is always collision. He is irritated by the inept learner-devil who has no idea of how to help people off the edge. He has sympathy for the uncle, who is trying to train this simpleton into the skilled task of devilry. He himself doesn't need any training. He knows exactly what is required.

To start is to know the smell of it. It is a distinct kind of smell, it's on someone when they are on an edge. It is a hunted smell, the V-feet woman has it. And after you follow the trail and find the leaking human being you place yourself and watch until you understand the situation and then you move at just the right moment. This asks for extraordinary capacity. He has it; he knows he has it. That's why he calls himself The Helper. Some things just need to happen. If they don't, there's a scratchy, angry, impatient thing going on under the skin. His skin, their skin, what the hell, it doesn't matter. And it can get really serious. Nothing stops it – except Helping. It's like sex. You just have to get it in and do it until the anger and the impatience have gone. But sex is a nuisance. Girls are a nuisance. They don't understand about how to do it like that. So much extra stuff has to go on. And even those who pretend they can just do it and get rid of their own impatience, they either want money or sooner or later there's something ... where were you, why don't you ... and then. Time to get out.

The light in the park shifts and writhes in front of him, this darkly thin young man, tense and muscular, a surface tension evident even in the way his worn black leather jacket twitches on his form. Some women find him attractive. They take the interrogative line of his dark, graphic eyebrows and make it into sexual questioning and curiosity, they look at the cynical turn of his lips and imagine they might be the one to make him gasp – and soften. Hannah notices him, but is so charged with her own febrile activity that she discounts him as another loser, lost in his own sorrows and disappointments. He never encroaches on her; he sits at a distance. She knows that he watches her and assumes without question that it is because he finds her extraordinarily beautiful and is dreaming about possibly one day finding a woman like this who might even look at him.

Hannah spends a long time planning her outfit. The blonde wig, carefully rolled longish hair, is so unlike her, no one would ever know. The scarf allows the fringe and side pieces to be evident. She wears make up she normally would not touch: green or blue eye shadow, and pink lipstick. The hot feeling of these colours feels like a disguise in itself. He could walk right past her and never know. Her usual sleek and svelte blacks and browns are discarded for a riot of colour and excessive shape. The first time she saunters onto the wide spread of grass, having located precisely the bench that overlooks obliquely – not obviously – placed at an angle, this bench – nothing to do with anyone wanting to look directly at their house, she feels boldly, completely, not Hannah Bloom. As she does not need to speak, no one will notice the planes of beauty which are her inner unique state: the artistry and sensitivity. And the external frame of reference? If she were to walk past known colleagues, who would possibly guess? Her posture and walk – well, could this be a give-away? Not many have the grace and turn-out she does. And she couldn't – even if she tried – walk without her back straight and feet poised. She will always look like some kind of dancer. But for this purpose not the soloist at a great company. She has taken away all those trappings. Her archetypal persona has disappeared. She could be a music-hall dancer perhaps. Something more ordinary. And what would Hannah Bloom be doing on a park bench with a newspaper?

Nobody knows of the overwhelming compulsion to see the house where this undeserving woman lives with a god among men, a man who should be with a woman of exceptional quality. Not just occasionally – but as partner. As wife. He as husband. She has to see this woman. What is it that keeps him to her? Yes, of course, without saying very much he has hinted at the sense of honour and duty that binds him to a woman who has had a child for him. Ah! What a noble man this is. Who suffers for principle. But underneath this thought – and pushing at it with intensity of pressure – is a river of hatred and jealousy and disappointment; a river of dark shapes, hideous crawling fish with gaping mouths, a blackness of environment where silt and bitterness feed these creatures as they prowl and push the muddy depths with their scavenging jaws.

She can't quite believe she has managed to make this happen. For months, she pulls and presses and half-murders the thought that, somehow, if she were able to see that woman, something would become easier. If she doesn't ease this burning misery and hatred, her face might crack. Up till now, Jeremy does not notice anything but charm and love and a smile of melting beauty. Occasionally, after he leaves, she tugs at her cheeks, desperately massaging the aching muscles. The glorious smile is half a thread's breadth from becoming a gargoyle's grimace. And that would never do. It would be completely unworthy of their divine love. But lately – is it real or her imagination? Is it possible that her King is slightly – ever so slightly – less attentive than earlier? Of course not, he looks at her and his eyes glitter and their love-making is a hymn to perfection ... as he says ... so what does she catch with the corner of her awareness? Oh, foolish woman. She comforts herself with replays of ecstatic moments, and now and then – angrily, with a rage that catches her by surprise – plots a takeover bid by another – an unfettered Adonis who will grasp her and take her away and then he will suffer for having kept her now for months – how many months – near to a year ... she doesn't want to count, this is too ordinary .... So yes, it is quite obvious, she has to get hold of the situation and it is a strong and purposeful action to go to the scene of the crime, as it were, and see for herself. Maybe he hasn't told her that the woman is disabled – or disfigured – and this in a way would help. But no point imagining. She has to go and see.

She is aided and abetted to make manifest this thought: rapidly patting his coat pockets while he briefly dozes one night, she finds an envelope. His name. And an address in Ealing. She vaguely knows that part of London. Large houses, set back in their well-tended gardens, and across the road from areas of public grassland. A long ride by underground. Well, has to be done. The weeks of planning bring a vigorous and meticulous quality to her practice at the barre. A look of radiant intention gives her performances extra hue, and reviews are pleasing. The first day she finds herself disguised and on her bench, she is almost happy.

8

Miriam gazes at three pots on the window sill. The outer two pots, wider at the rim than at the base, hold, each of them, a profuse red geranium. Some of the flower-heads are drying and shrinking, others display themselves in their full, orange-red vigour. Small orange-red petals fold one against the other into a circular shape, each full bloom settling itself onto a long, green stalk. Further down the stem, green leaves fan their veins subtly from core to curly periphery. A faint frill-line of a different colour, reddish-brown, lies in a circle some distance from the edge. Each leaf sits proud upon a vertical stem, smaller leaves near the top, larger at the bottom.

The wind blows, small drops of rain fall, the leaves and flowers bend and dance in submissive unison.

The pot in the middle is decorated with a band of zig-zag squares. There are only two geranium flowers settled amongst this greenery; small pinkish-red clusters of petal, not quite round, not quite full. These flowers emerge from variegated leaves – pale yellow, green background – upon which are impressed – each leaf different – a darker green and a blood splash of dark red. As with the neighbouring leaves, the veins fan out to the stalk. Each leaf holds its gentle form up to the light. Miriam moves her eye from one to the next.

The rain quickens. The window gathers drops of water to its surface. Some are larger than others. The window is alive with congregating movement, and momentary stillness. New drops fall, and disturb the old from their temporary position on the glass. 'Neither dread nor hope attend a dying animal.' An unidentified line from a poem disturbs her. Who is the poet? Yeats? Auden? A fat drop arrives and gathers smaller drops to itself as it slides to oblivion at the bottom of the frame. They look like glassy tadpoles, but without tails. Some slide very quickly. Miriam stares at the changing patterns.

Wife and mother, daughter and sister. In the morning, in the change-room at the swimming pool, she observes a woman, probably in her sixties, as she steps out of her costume and reveals long flat empty breasts, the slightly bulbous nipple-end nudging nearly at the waist. Not big breasts, must have been normal-sized breasts. Once. Miriam turns her head quickly, does not want the woman to see her looking, to guess at her thoughts. Bit like hers. Normal-sized, and still okay after months of feeding Paul. Miriam thinks of her mother and the manageable breasts kept firmly to herself. Firmly? Well, yes, bolstered into small alert shapes no matter what. Her sisters? She feels always separate from them, not included in their bonded sorority and closeness to mother, she is a stranger in the family cluster, dark and alien. As if a cactus had suddenly sprouted in the geranium pot and mistakenly thought itself welcome and compatible. One sister is now in Los Angeles, married to an American banker; the other is in Brighton, married to a businessman who buys houses, does them up and sells them. Money and houses. Oh well.

Miriam sighs. An uncomfortable sensation hovers in her heart. The sensation wants to fall, but it's as if a gate won't open. Miriam breathes out slowly. She looks at the table, then again at the geraniums. She notices the way one particularly curved leaf is holding, like a bowl, drops of rain water. She looks beyond, at the houses on the other side of the road, noticing a particular distinction of colour and form.

Miriam is ten years old and is going with her friend Lucy and Lucy's mother to see Lucy's grandfather. From being a brisk and sometimes insensitive, handsome, demanding man, he is now, in his nineties, bedridden and refusing to wear his false teeth. He is propped up on large cushions, a small fridge hums in the room, medicine sits in a jumbled pile on the bedside cabinet, through the windows the view is of trees and a distant road. The room is large, as is the house, stately and decrepit, like the old man himself. Past grandeur, on the edge of Highgate. Miriam sits, appalled and fascinated, next to Lucy. Her mother, downstairs in the kitchen, calls out to Lucy to come and help. Miriam hastily rises too but the grandfather asks her to stay, he hasn't seen her for a while, he remembers her as a unique little girl.

He waves a ruined hand at the window. 'I am losing my sight,' he says, lisping a little without his teeth, and soft-voiced. Miriam remembers how in awe of him she was when he was up and about, white-haired but still vigorous. This has been a rapid collapse. She searches desperately for a reply and finds none. She looks warily at him and finds that he is looking at her kindly. 'I am storing memories,' he says, 'of the trees, of your face, of colours, and then when I can't see the external world, I can still see inward; I can still see without eyes.' Miriam is captivated, anxiety forgotten. She thinks the old man is a hero to talk with such bravery about something so terrible. 'And do you know what?' he continues, waving his hand again at the window. 'I can still hear all right and when I hear the traffic it sounds like the ocean, waves coming in and out. And when there is an accident – it is like the waves crashing on a rock!' He grins as if he has said something naughty and then a sweet look comes over his face. 'You dance, don't you? Will you dance a little – just over there in that space ....' Miriam rises, uncertainly, stands in the empty square of carpet, and does a solemn movement, rising a little on her toes and circling her arms. The old man claps, his eyes shine softly. Lucy comes into the room, and Miriam, suddenly abashed, sits down again.

Later, downstairs, Miriam is eating omelettes with Lucy and her mother and a neighbour who calls by each day. The adults are talking intently.

'Well, he has that morphine pad – and it's dripping into him all the time and then he takes extra stuff. Addicted now, but what the hell, he is in the clouds. Off with the fairies.'

Miriam, suddenly hungry, gets up to open the fridge, and thinks about the pasta left from the night before. Re-heated with black pepper and olive oil? The house is quiet around her. The middle floor – and its mostly absent inhabitants – seals her from any sounds that might emerge from Madeleine's odd existence on the top floor. The lone rowan tree on the pavement shares its life with her through all seasons, producing leaves, red berries, white flowers. It perseveres with foliage as long as it can, coming to an inevitable stripping in the late winter. Footsteps rattle past on the square, functional pavement stones. A woman in high heels. A car is being manoeuvred into the space opposite, in and out, second attempt, third attempt. The driver – a woman hampered by a bulky coat - finally makes it, just enough space between the car in front and the van behind. She remains in the car, head down, maybe on the phone, perhaps reading.

Miriam's mother can never park successfully. She is too nervous and impatient. 'Aim for the centre and straighten out,' her husband counsels her. This remark causes shrill castigation, the car often stranded in a diagonal as the discussion continues, he increasingly mild, she the opposite. If young Miriam is in the back seat at a time like this, she writhes in embarrassment, hoping desperately that no one they know will come by, hoping that no one will come by, known or not. A time of helplessness. She cannot get out of the car, she cannot block out the sight or the sound of her parents' interaction. She cannot soften her mother's sharp corners, or find a way to win the smiles and glances of approval that seem to come the way of her elder blonde siblings. The most frightening and helpless moment of all is to experience jealousy and hatred, a mean, dark rush of something putrid and oily. Desperate. Eyes lowered, chin trembling, not wanting anyone to know the awfulness she is harbouring. When her father fails to rescue her, she finds an anchor: a small black notebook, carried on her at all times, and under her mattress during times of sleep. And into this – poetry of exactly how it is. The worst feelings, the darkest words.

The odd thing about the geraniums, Miriam thinks, not for the first time, is that they rest on the outer window sill and no one has ever taken them. Jack is sceptical when she first brings her spoils back from the nursery in Camden Town. 'They'll be gone in a week, my innocent darling,' he says and kisses her. They are bought, the pots filled with soil and the geraniums planted before Paul's birth. When it is very cold, Miriam covers them with protective material bought from the nursery. She does think it would be more sensible to put them in the tiny backyard which belongs to their flat, but she loves sitting in the kitchen and seeing the geraniums on the kitchen window sill. She wills them to survive, and to fend off thieving fingers. Do they bring her hope? This is a crude query. It's not to do with hope. It's to do with consequence. She puts them there. They stay and thrive – or they don't. No way of knowing what will happen. It is a risk. In the summer, Miriam picks off a stem here and there and places them in rooting compost and water. Some survive and some don't. She has an ongoing story with three pots and three geranium plants.

They both think it odd that the kitchen faces onto the

street and the living room to the back of the flat. The previous owners make the alteration. Miriam in time comes to love it, being in the kitchen and including the passers-by, the geraniums, the rowan tree before her as she prepares food, cooks, sits at the table. A cup of tea at the kitchen table means including the geraniums and the rowan tree. Mad Madeleine is walking out of the gate. She mustn't call her that. Perhaps Madeleine calls her Mad Miriam. She picks up a postcard from her parents, ten years resident in Spain, in a sea-facing apartment block in Alicante. Their postcards have an odd quality. Jack points this out to her. It's as if they have just arrived and are having a fortnight's holiday. The last visit paid to Alicante by Miriam and Jack is not the greatest success. The flat is without charm, and rooms seem to have not enough privacy from each other. However, the balcony affords wonderful views of the sea, and of the sunrise, and Jack, if he is up early enough, finds it perfect for practice. One morning, repeating the movement Wave Hands Like Clouds, he looks up and sees his mother-in-law watching him from behind the glass door leading from the balcony to the living room. She catches his eye, remains in position, looking neither towards him nor away, says nothing. Her face is impassive, her hair shining and immaculate. He waits with mild curiosity during the day to see if she makes any reference to this incident. She does not.

Miriam looks steadily at the picture on the postcard. Palm trees, a seafront, blue sky, blue sea. She is doing this partially to avoid meeting Madeleine's eye. Unlike Miriam's mother, Madeleine is quite happy to behave as if there is no barrier to conversation. She talks through the window, as she moves through the gate and as she plots her course down the road, inconsequent words tossed behind her like derelict streamers. Does she hope that someone (anyone?) will pick them up and come running to her? Here are your words, I found them. Ever hopeful that someone will find them and pick them up and run to bring them back to her.

9

I emerged from silence as my first Earth day ended and light had again shaded into night. I found myself gazing once more at the same young woman whose dark hair I had seen spread over the pillow. She clearly had some attachment to the young man suffering disturbed sleep. She had not the bond of marriage and child with him, as did the woman in his home and his bed, but their link had significance, and its vibration was unsettling. She became conscious of my presence while asleep, and I was able to connect with her through the medium of dreaming.

She had entered into dreaming which led her to wishes and to fear. A silky, treacherous path she walked and then stepped upon a slippery rock which changed quality and began to crack. She feared for her safety. Water poured from the rock and boiled and swirled beneath her. I took presence in the dream, after obtaining permission for this from her Guardian Spirit, a being of gentle nature. This permission was communicated to me through the instant recognition and respect that passes between those who have the well-being of others and the Unfolding of the Holy Way as their sole purpose. In the role of watchful Guardian, this spirit had no permission to enter the dream or the life, but could only abide in the invisible realm alongside the young woman, available when called by her to give discreet signs of companionship and subtle hints upon the Way. Having had discourse with many a Guardian Spirit in the Heavenly Realms, I know of the sorrow these beings experience when they are unable to give succour to their earthbound charges. They cannot move if not called upon. Some have guarded humans for life after life without being called upon. I salute their patience and love. As we know, sometimes it is at the moment of death that a being first calls, the threat of physical extinction prompting a desperate cry for help.

In the dream I extended my arm to the woman. She looked at me and I looked at her. She rested her hand on my wrist and I knew the sensation as something familiar for all of my life. We withdrew gaze from each other and I walked her down the treacherous path and back onto dry grass. There was a moment when words could have been exchanged but I knew this was extra to my task and I willed myself to fade out of the scene. This was difficult. And I didn't know why. A strange sigh rose from my being, and I took a while to settle.

When quietness returned to me, I requested sight of the Records and an unfolding showed itself. This took place in the great capital city of the country I inhabited in my time as poet. I saw the Emperor's Palace and the Emperor walking along the grandly constructed raised pathway which was built for him. Down below, a guard, one of many, stood to attention, clad in the bright colours of the Emperor's protective regiment. Nearby, a woman servant from the palace loitered anxiously, keeping her face down, but obviously intensely aware of the man. I could read their thoughts and understood that the woman was newly pregnant, and soon to be married to the man, and that he was soon to be sent on a long journey, travelling with the Emperor's entourage as it visited a feudal lord further south. The scene dissolved and re-formed and I saw the young man laid upon by bandits from the south, and I saw his body ripped and robbed of heart and breath. I saw the young woman running to the hills near the great city, and living a desperate life. The child, a boy, was born. She died young, of a disease of the lungs, and the boy scavenged a life for himself from the dust heaps outside of the city. He joined a group of desperate and marauding youngsters in the same plight as he was; and became adept at sword and knife combat. This young man, ruthless and intelligent, had also a side to his character that wanted to live a less bloody life, and he one day took a wife and raised a living from the making of weapons, having apprenticed himself to a master craftsman. The young man, Liu, settled into the quieter life of choice, becoming a craftsman of note himself. He fathered three sons and died in old age. Liu, just at the time of his passing, came to think of his parents. This side of his life had for all the decades of his active life been shut down and closed off. The shedding of defensive walls as his soul prepared for departure had brought the memory of a desperate mother and her worn-out stories of a brave and handsome father. Tears rolled down Liu's face as his wife and sons sat by him. Before he died, he told them in a whisper that he had never known tears before, and that he wanted to see his mother and father and show them the moist sorrow in his eyes as a form of respect and gratitude for his life. His wife, unthinking, had taken a cloth to wipe the tears from his face but the oldest son beckoned her to leave the watery trail as it settled on his cheeks.

'Let him take these pearls with him for his ancestors,' he said softly.

I felt my heart touched by the words of his oldest son. The Records closed and I knew that the young woman whose dream I entered had experienced the life as the young abandoned mother; and that the young man who was her teacher in present time had been the slaughtered guard.

I withdrew focus, folded myself into a misty cocoon and called up remembering from the time I was Han Shan, poet: boiled rice, sweet green vegetables, steaming water for dumplings, a dark plum sauce; the smell of early morning filtered through the foliage of great trees and ferns, how cold and damp it was when I lived on the Mountain; the taste of hatred towards me, and from me when my life was threatened. As it was on many occasions. In youthful, hot-headed days I was adept, Beloved Friends, with the knife I stole from the kitchen of a wealthy house. I used it for chopping food. And once or twice had to use it to defend myself. Life was short and cheap. When it was the choice of him or me, I chose me. How vulnerable is the physical body to illness and death. And to pleasure. Ah yes, the pleasure of caressing a woman's body!

And I remembered also the joy of running, swift and heedless through forest paths. My toughened feet collected burrs and thorns, but nonetheless, the perpetual motion flung me forward and deeper into wild places. And then, exhaustion threw me onto thick swatches of grass and flower, to rest and quieten the panting heart.

10

Jack as child is not far from Jack as man. His mouth has always been distinctive. It never hovers in a loose smile, or so it seems. He often feels irritated if he is with someone whose mouth forms uncertain shapes, whose lips tremble and hover, who allows – shamefully – to settle on their face a queasy I am trying to please you smile .... The impression Jack leaves with most people is one of authority, of economy of movement and expression. As a child, he is allowed to be the leader. In early photographs, Jack is not openly smiling. His shapely mouth is distinct, closed, purposeful, the corners slightly drawn up so that he looks ironic and as if he is dwelling inwardly upon some secret amusement. When the cajoling adult with camera poises himself before the assembled family and particularly focuses on Jack, when the call comes to smile, he remains impassive. He is just there, that is enough. He is not going to have his face pulled upon by any camera-wielding joker. It is his face, his expression. The world has no right to ask him to be anything other than he is.

Mostly, however, it could be said, he doesn't want his face to turn into his father's. He cannot bear the tentative, beseeching smile that creeps onto his father's face, especially when his wife is in a mood and crashes about the house with tight lips and a tendency to put kitchen equipment away noisily and aggressively. There! Saucepan hurled into the cupboard; frying pan smashed into the lower shelf. Instead of getting out of the way at these times, his father anxiously shadows the angry woman. You fool! Jack wants to scream at him. Can't you see? ... It's you. Stand up! Close your mouth, put your chest up. This woman can't stand it that you are so placating.

Jack can't remember a time when he doesn't wish his

father were different. And yes, of course, this is a very kind man who loves his family and wants everyone to be happy but where the hell is he? Who is living inside that anxious body? Kindness isn't enough, Jack says to himself, and once finds himself whispering to his father, hard hissing words under his breath, kindness isn't enough. And what does the old man do? Smiles at him, of course. And Jack wheels away from him and goes into the yard to practise his kick-boxing, or karate, or any one of the sequence of martial arts he has found that takes his body into hard shapes and brings his breath out harshly.

'That's it son, kick the hell out of him!' his grandfather yells, dragging a chair out of the kitchen and settling it into a corner – watching his grandson with a proprietary look, a plastic toothpick hanging out of his mouth and his belly sitting loosely over his belt. Jack hates the old man watching him. And the old man never seems to notice that Jack concludes practice very shortly after his grandfather has settled his bulk into the kitchen chair, training his eyes upon his grandson.

In his early twenties Jack begins to sense that he is looking for a quality beyond the fighting skills he learns, some kind of configuration that the martial arts so far have not yet offered him. Strength, yes; authority, yes. Agility. And something else … what is it? He doesn't know what it is; he knows he hasn't found it.

A girlfriend drags him to a performance at Sadler's Wells. A combination of dance and martial arts by a company from Taiwan. He is cynical, expresses doubt about this adultery before it starts. Folds his arms and settles into a particularly firm creasing of his lips as the curtains rise. A solo musician, on a dais in the orchestra pit, begins playing from a selection of Bach's cello sonatas. An unexpected, small knot of fire begins to creep up Jack's spine. He hears a thrilled intake of breath from Marcia, his friend. Two dancers emerge from the wings. A man and a woman. The man's upper body is bare; he wears soft white flowing trousers. She wears similar trousers, white and loose, with a simple flesh-coloured top. They circle into and around each other with strength, balance and liquidity, two skeins of silk, plaiting, wrapping and then separating and emerging. She is smaller, and flows into the male dancer with a quality of release and dissolving; he flows into her with a quality of intensity and precision: fire meeting water. Their legs are bent into pliant, willowy shapes, one foot rising and empty, the other planted and full. The movements are slow, repetitive, co-ordinated. The interacting qualities of dissolving and precision seem to spiral into a new power as a group of twelve dancers, six men and six women, dressed in the same minimal fabric, emerge from the rear left-hand corner, moving as one breath, close together in an oblong shape, arms soft and melting, strong and controlled. Tears spring to Jack's eyes. He has never seen anything as beautiful, powerful, mysterious, evocative. It is like watching breath take form. The two original dancers melt into the oblong shape and two more emerge who then weave and move around each other. Man and woman again. Rising and falling, bending and stretching, reaching into each other, sexual and not-sexual, an expression rather of infinite possibilities of power and tenderness. The cello follows the dancers, the dancers follow the cello. Jack is both man and woman, feeling mutuality and difference.

In the second half, the stage is swept with a sheen of water. Large mirrors cover the two sides and the back. The images multiply in ephemeral fashion, a watery world fills the eye. At the end, each flawless dancer leaves the stage, one

64

after the other. Taking time, unhurriedly, until a solitary woman remains. She moves as if in deeply personal reverie, as if unwatched, private and committed to each movement, and then, pausing between seconds, allows her left foot to disappear behind the curtains on the left hand side of the stage; then her leg, slowly her body, only right ankle and foot visible, and an aching period of almost cessation of movement as this too is softly removed ... and is gone. The empty, wetly glimmering stage is left, the curtains still and white. Jack cannot move, cannot speak. He and Marcia are almost the last to leave their seats.

Jack can feel Marcia's longing for him as they move out of the theatre and into the streets. She brushes against him, her fingers linger near his. He does not clasp them. How difficult he finds this. She introduces him to this experience, she is a sensitive and sweet companion throughout the evening, and he wants only to detach himself from her side and stride off, uncluttered, into the night. How is he going to do it? He makes an effort and thanks her, takes her to the station and sees her on her way to the Northern line. As she disappears through the ticket gate, she turns a wan and disappointed face towards him and he feels that he is an unpleasant and ungrateful man. An argument arises within him as he walks further than he needs, picking up his train two stations along the line, giving himself air and movement and aloneness. It is better to be truthful than to try to be nice. It would be awful to go back to her flat, maybe have sex. And not really want to. If he goes to the most honest place in himself, he wants this experience for himself – the dance, the water, the last sight of the last dancer upon the stage. He can't share this at the moment. Why even say at the moment. He doesn't want to share it. Full stop. Well, not with Marcia. Maybe one day there will be someone he feels generous with. But now the bliss of his own step, his own hand swinging, no little hand begging to be taken. He pushes troubling thoughts from his mind, guilty feelings, irritation, sorrow, shrugging his shoulders, lengthening his stride.

11

I insinuated myself into a corner in the hall where the one named Jack teaches his class, and stilled my field into quietness and watchfulness. This was a difficult word for me to savour. Something odd needed to happen in the mouth for this sound to emerge. When I felt the vocal impression, something in the middle sound would not open. Perhaps if I actually spoke it would sound like 'Dzukh'. This, with respect, is how I shall refer to the young man who has – whether he knows it or not – invited me into his life.

I settled into the corner. I was not physically visible, of course, but certainly one or two students approached and then backed away puzzled, as though they could not stand there or put their coats on this area of floor.

I closely observed Dzukh, to check whether my presence in any way disturbed him. If this had been so, I would have left. However, to my joy, I could tell that he was once more drawing breath and power from my direction, and that this breath was nourishing him and making thick the air around him so that his energetic presence became substantial – an effect from which I knew the students would profit.

The students, filling the room, formed four rows with five or six in each. The structure happened in an informal way and I noticed that there were mostly men in the class, of differing ages. Some were new souls, and the one or two who had approached my corner were of maturity. This had me winking and bracing myself, knowing that I could dive through the colourful stuff of experience around them, and come to the point of implicit recognition. This would not have been appropriate, so I veiled my presence adequately. Simplicity and discretion were necessary for the Inquiry in its initial unfolding.

I saw the woman-soul whose dream I had briefly entered. A quivering stream of energy moved from me to her and back again. And back again, creating staves and octaves of an unknown music. A different melodic strand moved between her and Dzukh. Notation which was craving completion. Neither of them knew of the nature of this music, but each was stirred by it, felt disturbed by it. I could sense the linear, geometric patterns of their minds trying to name and organise the unknown melody, to control it, make a neat packet of it and put it out of the way. This effort increased disturbance.

Until we Know, thus do we deal with the unknown music of our stories, a music we dance to and hear in blind obedience until it begins to tell its tale. And for that moment, I held Knowledge of the event from their past, the tragic severing of their union, as if I were holding the most precious liquid in a jar finely wrought; without any sense of having to pour it and thus present evidence. This is true Guardianship, Dear Friends. Sacred containment until the time is ready.

Jack adjusts his posture in front of the class, loosening his shoulders, softening his knees, presenting a demeanour of vigorous calm. He notices a flock of random thoughts, some of which appear earlier as he travels to work. Thoughts of Miriam. What is the disconnect that comes between them these days? He notices Marie. She impinges on him, but not in a way that wants relationship other than that as teacher–student. He sees her, head lightly held, concentrating within.

There is pleasure in observing her but no more that. She tugs at him. No more than that. Deeply. And no more than that.

Jack still finds it slightly incongruent that he should call this activity work. But of course it is. He does it at agreed times in a designated place, earns money from it and has made it an area of study and practice. Yes, of course it is work. And these are his working clothes. And why not? Soft trousers and a loose top. Most suitable. Why not? Jack knows himself as willingly diligent. As long as he is doing something he likes. So what's bothering me, he asks himself as he directs the class into an initial exercise, aware of a nudge of dissatisfaction curling softly through his innards. It's not the group, he thinks. They're committed – most of them come regularly. There are a good number of private students and invitations to give weekend seminars. It's not Miriam, even though things are tricky at the moment. And sometimes he feels he could cry. And does. And he knows couples go through this kind of thing. It's normal. It was sexy the other night. With the lights off. Dark and strange.

'Gently swing the arms,' he says, 'no effort – turn the waist and let the arms simply follow.' He enjoys the sensation of weight in his belly, the centre below the navel moving powerfully from left to right, the tan ti'en leading all movements, the initiating impulse from the depth of the body.

Yes, he loves this work, the discipline and artistry of it. Pragmatic and poetic, he thinks. And there's more. What of the experience in the morning, the figure near his bed? The encounter leaves him in both ecstasy and grief. He knows this encounter was not of imagination. He was visited…. Don't go! Who are you? Stay with me! Is the Ancient One announcing some kind of test? He has to jump, does he? Is there something around the corner … A skill? A technique? Another form? Double sword? Something quite unknown and extraordinary? In the midst of the thoughts pulling his mind lightly hither and thither, Jack notices a student making more effort than necessary. He goes to the man, and indicates carefully how he could minimise the struggle. The man smiles, his solid body agreeing to the suggestion – releasing a certain stress around the shoulders. Jack returns to the front.

The Natural Language that I have imbibed, is a language of seeming contradictions. The beguiling phrase 'effortless effort' comes to mind; the phrase 'doing by not-doing' comes to mind. To a minor degree in Dzukh, to a greater degree in his students I saw the interference upon natural beauty and divine harmony through too much striving. Of course in the tumble and thrust of life we do not remain passive; of course we make effort. I am discriminating unnecessary effort from Natural Effort – that is, the capacity to align with what is already In Place and Unfolding.

Dzukh – I bow to him – encouraged the student to minimise the struggle. He understood that each movement carried an Essence of Divine Implicate Order. To understand t'ai chi, to be In Accord with it, is to dive into Natural Effort. Breath is a beautiful example of this. We are being breathed – we don't have to think of each breath and make sure it happens. We can alter the pace of breathing, encourage slower, deeper breaths – but THAT we breathe, is not up to us. The last breath of our allotted store is not up to us. Equally, if we grasp the great principles of the shifting of weight and the turning of the waist, the co-ordination of limbs and trunk with the tan ti'en, the compatible and necessary qualities of Rising and Falling, Expanding and Contracting, Release and Storage of Energy, we can enter the activation of these principles as lightly as a leaf in space drifting from branch to ground.

I watched the members of the class. I saw in them the longing for easy relaxation and grace, and then I noticed rigid pathways through the muscles and tissue as a consequence of uneasy thought-forms and timid or aggressive reaction to life experience. Terror and dissatisfaction make stagnant and moribund the flowing plasma of the soul. We often do not know that we are thinking the uneasy and fearful thoughts that move like white noise in the hinterland of our mind. We fear loss of control without the often restraining injunctions of these thoughts, imagining that the soul will flood and roar and carry us to unlimited regions where we will drown and die.

And yes, of course, there needs to be order, limitation, boundary and naming. And thoughts can be beautiful tools of precision. And we don't have to strive for this precision! The Implicate Order contains both the nature and practices of the Great Yin, the Abiding Mother, and her discrimination, naming and containment, and the pouring of creativity and energy from the Great Yang, the Abiding Father.

Think not about this, my Friends. I am earnestly requesting you to restrain thought and here do I be, in this very discussion, cultivating further thought!

Gaze upon the symbol of the Great Yin and Yang, two fish forever swimming together, equal but different, mutually necessary.

Disturb yourselves not through trying to understand. Breathe the Image into your Being and feel that the

swimming and the overlapping and the mutuality Is You.
And when your arms slowly rise you are That; and when
they slowly fall, you are That.

Jack works the group through initial exercises and then
guides them into the form. Some have learned the whole
sequence, and they slowly move together, taking almost
thirty minutes to complete it. Others are in various stages of
learning and Jack skilfully moves from group to group,
imparting whatever is necessary. He is delighted to feel a
quality of attention in the room. At one point, he is about to
explain the shift of weight from left leg to right leg to a group
of near beginners, when his gaze is suddenly pulled into the
far corner of the room. Sitting there, as plain as could be, the
same Chinese Ancient, yes – with the face of kind and neutral
intimacy, and clothes of an eccentric stuff and orientation
from the past; the same Beloved, bearing qualities of Vastness
and Aliveness once more, to feast upon and absorb, body and
soul.

'Who are you?' The Ancient One sends him a word: Han.
Jack smiles. Mouths the name back – Han. A pandemonium of
hot delight fills his blood, his blood roars to and from his
heart and his heart chamber fills with the name Han and the
scarlet profusion swirls towards the corner, and, Han, smiling,
lifts himself into it, and rides off like a mischievous Emperor
on a sedan-chair made of red silken stuff.

Has anyone else seen him? Jack scans the room. Everyone
is absorbed. Only Marie is distracted. She is not looking into
the corner, but her face is pale, shadowed with thought. She
catches his glance, holds it for a moment and then looks
down, and resumes her practice. Jack picks up the thread of
where he was and demonstrates the transfer of weight, not

explaining as he thought he was going to, but imparting the experience through his own clear movement. He feels an unhurried, unruffled powerful quality within his body, and this calms his thoughts. He ceases to puzzle about the reappearance of Han and carries the image and the sensation as a taste of something clear and foreign, an unusual taste, like the flesh of a lychee fruit, silky and perfumed. Not robust like an apple or of zest like an orange. A sweet, provocative taste has entered his being. The taste of lychee fruit, the aroma of plum blossom. Jack moves to the next group, the senior students. He smiles at Marie. 'Any questions?' he asks. 'Any movement you particularly want to work on today?' Marie smiles at Jack. Her face takes on more colour. 'Well,' she says, 'the joining section between part one and part two ... I get confused.' 'Let's go through it,' says Jack. The seniors group together and take a position, right leg about to step forward, hands to the side, right hand pressing forward; left hand palm up.

Well now. This young man and I were touching each other. He was clear enough to begin to abide with me. He was about to enter a new phase of knowledge and authority. Something in him was maturing as a teacher. This was because of his diligence and his natural aptitude. He was also a soul of integrity, although he was somewhat troubled. Troubled by things of the past and the continued influence of this congealing into the present. Unresolved complexity was creating knots in his field of relationship and influence. I imagined that to dwell with him was a useful expenditure of my time. And how beautiful for me to be within the field of the practice of the Tao. (I sent a smile to Master Yang and Madame Li.) Making good with one stays not still but has passage through a much wider field. Each One influences the All.

Jack encourages the smooth integration of the movements, illustrating the spiral effect of a rounded hand moving slowly and softly through space – and moving also with intent, so the softness – and strength – is focussed and connected to the movement of the tan ti'en, the belly centre ... but if he could he would lie on the floor and laugh; his whole body wants to shake and tremble with laughter. At the end of the class, he invites everyone to shake. As he begins, loosening his wrists, his neck, his knees, laughter bubbles through his lips. The sound is contagious. Soon everyone is laughing. After the class he goes to a pub nearby for a beer. He stares at everyone he can see, candidly and openly. He wants to drink it all in. The beer is wonderful, German wheat-beer, dark. He doesn't get drunk; he is already drunk.

12

It is cold when Jack gets in. A sudden bite to the air, the earlier benign quality of September lost to a sharp flurry of wind, brown leaves starting to appear in flight and on the ground.

'Glad I took my coat,' he says. He hangs it up, taking from the inner pocket a satisfying fold of cash and cheques. His private clients pay well, particularly those in the corporate sphere. He goes to kiss Miriam. She is slowly moving around the kitchen in a way he recognises. Anyone not knowing her would imagine her aimless and distracted. Jack knows that she is clear about what she is doing, the supper has been planned, the ingredients are ready. The movement is a singular choreography she has; no straight lines, she innately prefers to meander. She is not distracted. It's as if her body likes to keep itself in motion, weaving and touching and making an embroidery around any possibility of intention which might lead to one straight line and then a corner, and then ... stopped. In the early years of watching her in this meander, Jack feels that the habit originates in her hips and then has to follow the contours of those hips. And the movements between them happen in this way; she takes the straight line, the intention of his body, and makes a movement around it. And so his early watching of her has a sexual excitement for him whenever she starts her stately dance – but now, though loving and wildly touched still from the delight of the class and the wonder of the presence of Han, it is cold and he is hungry and she is peeling potatoes and he wonders what else is on the menu.

'What we got?'

'Well, potatoes,' she smiles at him. Her mouth curves but he sees agitation in her eyes.

'What's up?' he asks, though he doesn't really want to

know. But he wants the agitation to stop so that she can become absorbed in one of her tasty sauces. 'Carry on cooking,' he says sweetly, 'and tell me meantime.'

'Paul's asleep,' she says.

'Do you want me to look in on him?' He is wondering whether the agitation is from that quarter and perhaps soon settled if he wanders in to his son's room.

'No, he's fine.' She starts chopping the parsley and mushrooms spread before her on the wooden board and then stops. Jack invisibly grits his teeth.

'Shall I do these?'

'No darling, I will.'

Well for fucksake get on with it, he growls, silently, inwardly, his face rather stiffly pleasant.

'Don't worry,' she says quite sharply. 'You'll get your supper.'

He decides to come clean. 'I am hungry, love. I'm silently cursing you. I ate a sandwich at twelve.'

She looks at him with something tender in her eyes. He smiles.

'Tell you what,' he says. 'Let's make a deal. I help you and when it's done, you tell me. Okay?'

They work together in peaceable silence. The food is soon cooked, and tasty, the potatoes made interesting with a sauce of mushrooms, parsley and sharp cheese. Miriam also makes a salad. Jack looks at her with inquiry. 'Do you want to tell me now?'

Miriam raises a fork to her mouth, then puts it down. 'I was with Paul today – in the park. It was lovely before it got cold. We saw friends, we had fun. And then something came over me so dense and frightening – from nowhere, Jack. No reason.' Her face grows tight. 'It's mad – I just had this thought ... we've made God up – we can't bear the hugeness, the not-knowing, the death we all face, illness, accident, cruelty. We've made it up, Jack. There's no consolation. It's unbearable.'

The half-filled fork remains on her plate. Miriam sits like a stone and cries. Jack has not seen her cry in this way before. There is no meander, no movement to this. She is still, and the tears run along her cheeks and continue down her neck. Jack watches them form and slowly descend. He has an odd sensation – as if she is unavailable to him – he can't touch her.

'It's crazy. I know nothing's wrong, Paul is fine, here we are, we are safe and all is well and there is nothing ... not like for some people, war and ongoing terror and earthquakes and hurricanes and lack of food ... we are protected here on this damp island.' She looks at him, her eyes flat with a curious mixture of pain and anger. 'I haven't really got words for it.' She gestures to her body. 'It's in here. In this sack that's going to die and I don't know how ... how am I going to perish?' There is an avalanche of tears now. Jack pushes away his plate and moves his chair close to her. 'And the improvisation dance class I loved has closed and I don't like the new one with prescribed steps and I don't meditate any more, each time I sit down my mind just fills with thoughts ....'

'Miriam ... Miriam. Let me hold you. Let me hold you, baby.' With a curious, jerky movement – like a marionette and her strings suddenly cut – she drops herself into Jack's hands. The hard tears continue. Jack has a sense that whatever he might say would not be right for her. His hunger is forgotten. He wants to say ... it is all so brilliant ... he can't understand her fear. The eruption of everything, the tease of never knowing what's going to happen ... out of the blue ... the unexpected ... Han in his class, the perfection of the martial art, galaxies, black holes, the infinite mathematics of the cosmos – the unfolding of time and space, an unending formation of stuff bending and looping into itself, the Earth tilting at an angle and moving around the sun at 100,000 km an hour, the large rocky intruder smashing into her side and then out of the rupture, debris emerging, spinning out, caught into the gravity field, and the moon forming, and the recipe just correct, precisely, for life to begin. Water delivered in vast ice-packs from asteroids. Why should we want to know everything, be safe? There'd be nothing to explore, to quest for. If the Earth had no tilt, there'd be no seasons. Jack stays quiet and then wonders – appetite returning, slightly abashed – whether he might finish what's on Miriam's plate if she doesn't want it. Carefully, lovingly, he brings her to her feet and steers her to bed. He washes her face, undresses her and tucks her under the duvet. Miriam stares at him like a wretched child, relieved and unknowing.

'I'll go and do the dishes.' As water fills the sink, he spoons the last of Miriam's potato into his mouth. It tastes delicious. He finds a bar of chocolate in the cupboard and brings it to her. 'Do you want a little piece, darling?' She shakes her head, and holds onto his hand. She holds it very closely as if the only possibility of safety and a reasonable life were located there, in his grasp, in the warm, hairy certainty of this broad hand.

Later, they make love, in darkness again, as if the dark is closing in with no light available to relieve it. Jack feels excited and powerful. Miriam feels as if she is being pummelled to death but there is some relief brought by Jack's weighty and ruthless, intentional body. She is the one to fall asleep first. Jack remains awake for a while, looking through one small gap in the curtains at a piece of black sky beyond. In his class he sometimes ends with a meditation, suggesting that his students forget about everything they have learned, and fall momentarily into deep, velvety blackness, a blackness of unknowing. With his hand on

Miriam's back, Jack leaves the confines of bed and wife, shoots through the gap into the sky, punching and yelling, ripping through the dark, his mouth wide with joy and rough love.

13

The house they live in is a solid Victorian structure. It has been skilfully remodelled so that they – on the ground floor – have their own entrance. The occupants of the first- and second-floor flats have an entrance on the side, share a small lobby that takes them straight up the stairs to the first floor and then, through a narrowing of the staircase, to the second. The middle flat is owned by a man and wife who moved out of London. They are conscientious as landlords, brisk and rapid whenever required to do something practical. They are fortunate in their tenants. So far, quiet and reliable people have come to occupy the space. Jack and Miriam always make sure they identify themselves to new tenants and occasionally favours are asked, both ways. A tacit mind your own business but help when necessary urban co-existence. As opposed to the top floor, where it is a different story.

This is home to Madeleine, a woman in her sixties, struggling half-heartedly to curb an unhealthy appetite for alcohol; she is dramatic and prone to misadventure. Madeleine seems to have a private income, the flat is hers, left to her by her husband, she has no children though a niece visits sporadically. Madeleine locks herself out, she falls over the last step into the lobby, she loses her wallet and her travel card. Madeleine is occasionally to be found in Miriam's kitchen but after Jack says to Miriam that he is not interested in seeing her there too frequently and Miriam finds that she agrees, Miriam starts a new kind of meander, a rapid sideways lurch away from Madeleine, waving too brightly and chattering about have to do and see you later. Miriam decides that she will help Madeleine when the situation is urgent, but is stepping back from enforced altruism. The sideways movement and the bright waving are indicators of the new regime. Madeleine is puzzled and angry, then tosses her head and decides the hell with them, smarmy bastards.

Madeleine navigates through the small front gate and finds her way through the dark towards her front door. The bottom flat is dark. They must have gone to bed. Or away again. All very well for them, wait until they are old and one is dead and life is precarious. Day after day precarious. All very well having fancy notions but this is what it comes to. No one to walk home with you or to switch on the light so that you can see. Her ankles are hurting, the right one particularly. Must be arthritis. Do you get arthritis in an ankle? My she had lovely ankles as a young one. So thin. Still would like to know what kind of job that young one has. Jack. Probably doesn't earn that much, their furniture isn't posh. Not a decent matching set of crockery anywhere. Guiltily, Madeleine runs her tongue around her teeth. Can still taste the beer. Just one pint. That was nice. Can't hurt. And quite a nice old gentleman talking to her until he started that nonsense and the rude language after his second beer. And the ugliness of his false teeth. Can't abide that. Not supposed to drink any more. Made that promise. Well, one beer. As long as it's no more than that. A moving shadow disturbs her. Could it be a rat? That's one thing she doesn't like. Rats. Heard there's more vermin in London than people. You're never far from a rat. Planning to open her door very quickly and just minimally ajar so she can slip in unaccompanied, Madeleine holds her key out like a spear, slips in through the narrowest angle, and marches, falsely ferocious, up the stairs. After her awkward ascent of the narrow climb, a light shows on the top floor. Another little London life arrives into its nest.

14

Paul is asleep in his bed, his cheek roundly pushed into the white cushion, decorated with occasional miniature embroidered sailing boats. Miriam sings him into temporary oblivion, pauses and gazes upon her son, at the shape of his left arm, pushed into an energetic angle. Tonight he makes an instantaneous shift from activity to sleep. Miriam walks quietly from the room. She enters the hall and notices – as if for the first time – the division of the wall into rectangular shapes, doorways inviting entrance into different chambers. In herself, a shift – slight, but evident – a movement away from melancholy and unease into a wish for excitement. An excitement not yet present, but hinted at; a door glimpsed but not yet opened.

Two days previous she talks to her best friend Tilly, robust Tilly with the capacity to counter any possibility of uncertainty with a crisp and simplified menu of certainty. At least, this is how Tilly supports her friends during their periods of doubt. The recipe she offers so generously to those she loves does not very often work for her. Her well-known phrase 'Beyond a shadow of doubt, my love!', seems, ironically, to have created a mischievous doppelganger, one which snaps at her very heels, even as she speaks good cheer, tripping her up in her own life, landing her into confusion concerning her own affairs. Somehow, this contradiction, known to her friends, does not reduce the value of the commentary and advice she offers to those who request help. At times, when the discrepancy is challenged, Tilly laughs ruefully and says, 'Well, you know what they say about therapists – they're all in need of therapy.'

Tilly is not a therapist. After a short acting career, where she meets Miriam, she creates a fusion of her two interests, drama and community work, and develops a reputation as a gallant worker in the field, entering poorly funded centres for the aged and for children, creating diversion and amusement from seemingly endless resources of time and energy.

She is separated from Luke, her husband. They live in the same house, in different wings. Tilly declares that they get on better since separation; if they'd stayed together, one would have ended with an axe in their back. Miriam and Tilly – centre of a cheeky posse of women in their younger years before their marriages. Friendship continues after marriage and Jack and Luke get on with each other, especially after a pint of beer. Then Tilly and Luke separate, and Jack and Miriam have Paul and meetings are less frequent, and different in quality. The other women of the posse marry and go to other cities, one of the group dies after a car accident. A warm, intimate, sometimes bitchy continuum disbands, dissolves. It is easy to look back and sense something heedless and powerful and free. Tilly, without children, still seems to have some sort of freedom. Or so it seems to Miriam. No husband; no child. Lonely sometimes? Yes. But free. Not a young woman's freedom any more, decked in a ragbag of brilliant clothes, but young enough, surely, to feel sometimes sassy and sure-footed in the city.

'No worries, honey,' she says to Miriam. They are in a café in Islington. A wooden chair hangs on the wall, a headless wooden torso in clown costume decorates the far corner, the coffee is good. Miriam hasn't confessed the deeper sorrows she's been feeling about Jack – she says nothing about the quiet and diligent woman in his class, and the dark corners she falls into, thinking about this woman. She takes the unholy threads of paranoia and jealousy and weaves them into a story of temporary loss of confidence. 'No worries, honey,' Tilly repeats, stirring her cup vigorously until the last flecks of cream and sweet dusty points of chocolate disappear into the dark coffee liquid. 'You need to get out more – the kid's adorable but you can't be cloistered with him all the time. Does Jack look after him?'

'Yes.'

'Well then – '

'Well then what?' Miriam feels belligerent. This isn't a problem to be solved, so why is she setting it up as such and inviting solution?

'There you go,' says Tilly with alacrity and firmness.

'Where do I go?' Miriam wants to laugh. And cry. 'Tilly, this isn't what I want to be talking about. It's not a simple thing.'

'I know,' Tilly touches Miriam's hand. 'What we need is distraction.'

'You too?' Miriam rubs her hand where Tilly has touched it.

'Me too always. I always need distraction. You know me. You look peaky, my friend. What are we going to do?'

'Not talk about Jack's duties as a father.'

'Shall I adore you? Shall I order you a gorgeous cake? Trouble is with adoring you it can't last for long today – as a practical demonstration of everlasting love of course – have to be off soon – this is a quick pit-stop.'

Miriam gazes into Tilly's eager face. Tilly's straight red hair falls in brisk swatches around the bright triangle enclosing her features. Broad forehead; pointed chin. Miriam knows she is slipping around a surface. Her words are sliding about, they mean nothing. Tilly, in her kindness, is trying to step alongside her but she can't. Several rocky layers further down, a different dialogue is trying to hack its way into awareness. She feels confused, uncomfortable and clumsy. Come on Tilly, look at me with your diamond eyes and tell me about clarity.

Tilly's long and shapely mouth is moving inside its coat of vivid red lipstick, the same colour as her hair. Miriam has no idea what she is saying. She is suddenly aware of a tall man standing next to Tilly and smiling at her.

'Sorry,' says Miriam.

'Oh Simon, wouldn't you know – friend of mine – fancy seeing you here – this is Miriam. Simon.' Tilly's friend has the face of an artistic man; quirky, rather sardonic mouth, thick dark brown hair skilfully cut, tailored jacket which looks as though it is part of a suit. Dark grey with a slight stripe. Faded jeans. Simon sits down. He and Miriam exchange a glance which – in a brief second – in a neutral, cool, inevitable way – agrees an inventory of acceptability.

'I think we met a long time back,' says Simon. Pleasant voice. A further rating on the score-board. 'Maybe at Tricorn Theatre – were you there?'

'Oh, very briefly. I did some organisation for them.'

'Still doing that?'

'No. Well, I ....' She is interrupted as Tilly stands up. She looks at Simon and Miriam.

'Honey, I have to go – we must talk again. Simon, you haven't changed a bit.' Tilly gives Miriam a kiss and a meaningful look. Miriam cannot decode the meaning. Having sat still during the parallel arrival of Simon and the departure of Tilly, Miriam is more caught up with knowing that the arrival – Simon – has performed the miracle Tilly has been unable to do. Under the persistent gaze of a nice-looking man in a well-cut jacket, she suddenly, successfully forgets that her world is confusing and fearful, that her husband stares regularly at a woman of quietness and discipline. Graciously accepting another cup of coffee, Miriam feels appreciatively looked at. She likes the attention. She has another half an hour to spare, and she is now an organiser of a theatre company, not a woman at home. She will see if she can remember elements of that persona, and bring them through.

No effort is required. Connection with that whole world returns. Simon is familiar with current events in ballet and the arts. He is some kind of director, Miriam doesn't ask too many questions. All she has to do is listen, speak and smile, and let his eyes roam over her face, and let her eyes linger – just a little – on his.

Standing in the hallway, her sleeping child in the smallest room, Miriam, in excitement and nervousness and guilt, thinks again about the arrangement to meet Simon for coffee in three days' time. The inner voice whose job it is to harass her with stories of Jack's betrayal and her own deficiency and loss - now articulates a different conversation. A defiant one. Well, there's nothing wrong with this. He could be a colleague. He might know some interesting courses she could go on. A lower voice, savage, the beast, barely audible, barely known, expresses triumph and hatred. You're not the only one. I could have some power too.

Miriam is elated and horrified by the fresh piece of meat thrown at her to chew – or choke – on. The beast knows all about comparison. If someone has something, it is no longer possible for you to have it. If you are feeling less than, or done to, the beast provides the face of someone who has surely caused this injury. It occupies a sour underworld of positioning and poking at those who are top dog or under dog. Jack is not yet home. Will he see the hatefulness in her face, will he come home to a wife shrouded in fur and teeth, glittering and skilful, a small knife concealed in her gloved hand? What a menagerie, what a pantomime she is creating. And all because of a woman with a quiet face and a man in an attractive jacket. Louche – it makes him look louche, is that the word? No, it's not all about them. It's about her and some kind of loss. Some part of her missing, lying exhausted in a cave as the desert winds howl past her closed eyes and the prickling sands assail her nostrils.

15

It is organised. Paul stays at the playgroup for the afternoon as well as the morning. Carefully covering all her tracks, Miriam tells Jack the night before that she is meeting a friend of Tilly's who might have part-time work for her. 'He's theatre-based,' she says, 'connection to dance.'

'Hmm,' says Jack absently, 'that's nice, darling. Lovely if you can pick up some of that again.' Miriam looks at Jack with love, observing his firm mouth and wiry frame. He is thoughtful, making notes from his class the night before, papers spread before him on the kitchen table, a cooling cup of tea nearby.

There really is a difference. Miriam keeps Jack within the frame of her gaze as she clears the draining board of dishes and cups. If he'd drop a remark like that to her, she'd oh-so-casually ask about the 'friend', ending with the most casual question of all – is she pretty? And then mortified at the give-away she would want to erase the whole line of questioning. Is it men and women, she wonders? Or me and Jack? Abruptly swerving, she wonders what to wear. And no, she is not going to go to any great trouble with this. Take me or leave me. Take me where? What am I thinking – what do I want? Just a diversion, she suggests to herself defensively. No harm meant. Just a cup of coffee and a conversation. And yes he is in the business so that isn't a lie. She resolves also to tell Tilly. A Tilly version. Also not altogether honest – but something similar. Nice guy – interesting. Might be a lead there in terms of her getting back into theatre. Then if anyone sees her with him, it's all legit.

They are meeting near Leicester Square, at a little patisserie he swears is the best in London. She likes this phrase – best in London. Something special. And she likes the assured and immediate way he chooses the place. Not would you like to or what do you think but we will. Jack wouldn't do that. He's more democratic. Says what he wants and then waits to find out her preference. Simon's style is very masculine. Not that Jack isn't, she tells herself hastily. And she loves Jack's masculinity. Miriam leans forwards and strokes Jack's hair. He looks up, smiles at her and covers her hand with his.

She leaves the kitchen, thinking to herself that it's a good thing she is doing, this excursion outside of her boundaries – this innocent excursion. It is already having an effect. Like yeast in bread, vanilla flavouring in a cake. She gazes at her wardrobe, selecting and discarding with her eyes a not very important outfit for tomorrow.

She chooses a slim black dress in cotton jersey. She wears low-heeled black shoes and a small red jacket. Not her best, probably not warm enough, but something she loves for its nipped-in waist and gathered shoulders. Chooses a warm scarf in case. She wears her favourite silver earrings and her hair is bundled up and loosely held by a dark clasp. She sees herself mirrored in the patisserie window before she goes in (carefully 10 minutes late) and likes the look and feels her heart beating rapidly. Tell him, she says to herself, tell him very fast about Jack. Make it clear you are attached. She smiles, imagining herself walking in and saying hello Simon, I live with Jack.

He is there, and gets up to grasp her hand, looking at her with appreciation and then pulling her near – in a friendly way – and kissing her cheeks – in a friendly way. She sits down, takes out her mobile to switch it off and then says, 'Actually, do you mind if I leave it on – my little one is at the nursery; and my husband is teaching ... so ... just in case.' He looks at her with a mocking glance (or does he? is this her imagination?).

'Of course, sweetie. Well then – various exquisite cakes, your choice of tea or coffee and then let's get to know each other.' Now the friendly approach is altering – a steamroller made of velvet is simply obliterating the domestic information she gives him. And she feels so distinct delivering it. Now she feels a little gauche. What the hell. The cakes look good. She chooses a strawberry tart, and coffee. 'Good choice, good choice,' he says and calls the waitress over in a familiar way. 'Hello, honey. How are you? We'll have a strawberry tart – and I'll have your gorgeous Portuguese custard tart. Two coffees. No milk?' She nods. 'Yes or no?' he asks pleasantly. She shakes her head. 'No to the yes or no to the no?' he asks. The waitress stands by holding her pencil and small pad. She is blonde, sexy and big boned, her black top slipping a little off her shoulder, revealing milk-white sculpture.

Oh for heaven's sake, Miriam hisses at herself. Climb out of this. He is playing with you. It's not nice. Miriam addresses the waitress, smiling: 'I'll have black coffee.' The waitress leaves. Under the black apron, she is wearing pink shorts and lacy white tights. Miriam gives Simon ten out of ten for not following the luscious woman with his eye, and instead maintaining a friendly gaze – yes, and appreciative – towards her, her black dress and red jacket.

The steamroller parks itself in a lay-by but Miriam is sure it will make another appearance.

Simon is wearing jeans which sit firmly on his masculine hips, and a black t-shirt. The same jacket hangs over the back of his chair. After the coffee and cakes arrive, they fall into easy conversation, and Miriam discovers an attractive quality in Simon. He has a vivid, eclectic mind, and moves easily from one area to another. He makes ideas sound and feel exciting and he rides into absurdity with glee.

'On the one hand; on the other, five fingers ....'

'You're not Jewish?' asks Miriam.

'No, but I could be. It's also a matter of choice and inclination – not only the way the racial or cultural or genetic dice rolls. You are, my lovely, aren't you?'

'Half.'

'I know which half. The half with the eyes ... yes?'

'Well, my father was Jewish; my mother not.'

'Hmm. So you're not.' His arm is lightly touching hers. It feels warm. Miriam is enjoying herself.

Simon is administrator for a community arts project. 'Yes – I am the cynical, hard-headed businessman of the outfit. Artistic? Me? Forget it.' However, when he lets his sophisticated mask slip, Simon has an appreciation for culture and creativity, especially for anything innovative, and before long she is talking with surprising frankness to him about an idea she'd had once, an idea she'd shelved as impossible. 'Gravity? A visual essay on gravity?' His tone is warm, interested.

'Yes, I don't know what category it might fall into. I would like movement, music, words. Film, ultimately.'

'Say more.'

'You need to know the basic theme. We are held captive here on earth by gravity. We can jump, we can get onto a plane – but we always come back. And of course if we didn't stick, we'd be floating – untethered. It fascinates me ... just that correct amount of gravitational hold. They've done experiments on the possible effect of being on another planet with a greater field of gravity. Our faces would suck inwards and downwards.'

'Charming. Thought that was called age.' He covers her hand and moves nearer to her. 'You're a bright sweetie.' She feels as if her usually distant father has given her praise. Her sense of herself expands, She feels pleased beyond requirement.

'God in this context is called The Captor. But turns out he is captive too. Or is he? Is he the captor or the ravisher? Because of course it is so ravishing to be formed into a shape by gravity, and then to experience the whole of life ....'

'Have you written any kind of script or plan for this?'

'No. A couple of pages written when we were on holiday at the coast. One of those lazy holidays where the mind empties and then an idea comes up seemingly from nowhere.' She is astonished at the way she is speaking. And then something tells her this is enough. This is only the first date after all. Date? This isn't a date, she isn't on a date. She is a grown woman meeting with a mature man. Just that. And the exchange has been fun. Detach, Miriam, she tells herself. Slow down.

'Write it,' he says with the masculine air she has noticed. 'You must write it. Ideas are for exploring.' He looks at her speculatively and then changes gear. 'And your partner? Does he write? Is he artistic?'

'No, I mean yes.' Oh, there she goes again. Coffee black or with milk madam? 'He is a t'ai chi teacher. And yes, I would say he is artistic.' Simon makes sweeping movements with his hands.

'I know. They're in the park, greeting the dawn and the trees.' There is nothing offensive in what Simon says but for a moment the absent Jack feels like the odd one out. Not a sophisticated, creative man talking about metaphysics in a patisserie where the waitress wears pink shorts and white patterned tights. No, he waves at trees at dawn. Miriam feels upset and guilty and wants to defend Jack.

'It's a beautiful, complex system,' she says. Something lame in her tone and delivery.

'I am sure,' says Simon in a comforting way, and puts his hand on the back-rest of her chair. 'Now where do we go from here?'

'Oh,' says Miriam hastily and looks at her watch. 'Oh my – I need to get back.' She turns in her chair.

'No, sweetie,' says Simon, 'I mean shall we meet again?'

'Yes, no, well, that would be nice. Not for a few weeks. I am quite busy,' says Miriam, rapidly in contrast to his measured pace.

'Don't worry, honey. No pressure. Nothing you have to do or provide for uncle Simon. I have greatly enjoyed your company – not the least how nice it is to sit for a while with a beautiful woman who has good taste in clothes. Love your outfit.'

'Well,' says Miriam, 'I have enjoyed talking to you. Nice to bring out that idea, you know, the gravity.'

'Why don't you send me what you have written so far?'

'Why?' asks Miriam, suddenly suspicious.

'Oh, not if you don't want to – you are good with language. I'd like to read it.'

'Let me think about it,' says Miriam, pleased with herself for not leaping forward. She wants to leap forward. She wants to put it in the post tomorrow.

'Okay.' He pulls out a card. 'Here's the address if you want to send it.'

Miriam and Simon embrace each other briefly. He insists on paying. They walk off in different directions. Miriam, flushed and happy and guilty goes straight to the nursery. Simon, as he walks away, wonders what the pink-shorts waitress might be like in bed. Miriam has stirred his balls, but bedding her would probably be hard work. A lot of effort without guaranteed results. Attractive girl, he thinks. Quite a cute idea. Won't work in theatre. No story. No plot. He gives a short laugh, disturbing himself. And for no reason at all, damn it, Tina comes to mind. Tina, who compelled all his attention and who didn't need him to show her she was lovely.

To Miriam's surprise, Jack is home early. He offers to put Paul to bed. She feels breathless, scratchy in the company of the two of them, staring at her with their brown eyes, playing together noisily, and says she will go for a run on the Heath. She takes her Ipod, rides the train one stop to Gospel Oak, listening repeatedly to Puff Daddy, a cover of *Missing You*. Released onto the lower curve of Parliament Hill, her feet pound the grass, and tears come. Angry tears. She is enraged, battling with a sense of something forbidden, something longed for and out of reach, teasing her. She can't get what she wants, and she doesn't know what she wants. Yes, I am missing you. Who am I missing? Other runners pass her, breath coming in unpleasant gasps, or in smooth pleasure. She keeps herself to herself; finds a steady pace and loops back to the station after about an hour.

Light is fading as she gets home, sweaty and happy and unhappy. She is firmly lodged somewhere in herself in a way which feels self-righteous. There is a gap between her and Jack. In that gap is hatred; of herself, for him. In bed, Jack reaches for her, pleasantly, without urgency. She says no, too grumpy. Without argument, seemingly equable, Jack turns over and is soon asleep. Miriam lies in irritable darkness, thinking of her mother, remote, elegant, perfumed – and under the perfume a sour odour, subtle but present just above the skin: floating, as it were, a signature of her lack of goodwill. Floats towards her husband and Miriam, the oldest daughter, so like her husband in appearance, olive skin and dark hair. The two younger girls are fair, more like her.

Miriam's father incurs family wrath by marrying out of the faith and culture. He brings home a fair Anglo-Saxon woman, blue-eyed and wasp-waisted. In the early years, romance and passion flourish. Later on comes vitriol and bitterness. You see, say the sisters-in-law, Miriam's aunts on her father's side: you see, we told you. Mild and stubborn, their brother Eric – his mother's favourite – protests that marriage always means trouble no matter who you marry. Different woman; different trouble. The sisters spend wonderful hours picking through the sorrow and pain Eric brings to the family. Miriam fiercely champions her father. Within herself, never spoken. She believes she understands him better than anyone else, including her mother. She looks for moments of his noticing how she understands him. She shows him her poems. Kindly, but absently, he puts them aside, saying how lovely and he will read them later. Now she is putting Jack aside. Isn't she? Is it the same?

Miriam twists to see the bedroom clock. Three in the morning. Shit. The hour of spectral haunting, misery and confusion. She pulls the duvet towards her, Jack turns in his sleep, murmuring. Miriam wants to get out of her body, she feels encased, trapped and punished by her continuing sense of herself. She is sick of her dissatisfaction, her shape, the way her mind works, the way her feet get cold in the winter. She wishes she had never been Eric and Anette's daughter. She wishes she was … who? Missing who? She thinks of her conversation with Simon. Why the hell did she talk about her idea so freely? That man is not sincere, he is a tease. She doesn't like him. She stares towards Jack in the dark. He has a steady, contemplative mind. No mental acrobatics. Her thoughts collide and collapse, re-assert themselves and collide and collapse again. Miriam tries breathing into her feet as Jack once told her to when she couldn't sleep. They are too bloody cold. The night slowly passes.

16

Miriam remembers: the process of Jack becoming beautiful in her eyes. Before he begins to inhabit the invincible place of the desired one, he has, she thinks, a strange way of constricting his lips and taking in a sharp breath when he is shy or unsure. She doesn't like his brown corduroy trousers. She wants him to have more hair on his chest – like Christopher the year before whose silky chest-flowering she can rest her head on, studying at close quarters the curl, the twist, the texture. But then, as she becomes more familiar with Jack and as his mouth and hands start to delight her and as his body becomes familiar with hers, she happily discovers the smooth ivory quality of skin stretched over the rib formation. She rests her head on this surface and the experience starts to delight her and the foliage and decoration upon Christopher fades into memory, seeming even, on reflection, over-elaborate.

During the first months of their courtship, she feels a movement in her heart, and then stops whatever she is doing and invites the thought of Jack into her awareness. She feeds upon the taste, detail and particularity of this man. These experiences carry an exultant sharpening of vision, a private happiness. She walks the streets, catches the bus, does her work with the knowledge that she is loved. She has abode in the world of another. He mirrors her beauty and shows her how delightful she is. He cant wait to see her and pull her to him and gaze at her, his beautiful lips (no longer constricted) in a wide smile, and his eyes looking, looking ...

And in Jack's memory: the first glimpse of Miriam's hips (he is invited, together with some of his students, to take part in a theatrical improvisation she is organising). She is wearing a black dress. The material clings to her and follows the curve of her body; the black stretch moves down, and around, cupping her in a friendly, familiar way ... oh the tease of it, this black dress hanging between use nonchalantly in her wardrobe. He imagines how it might feel to follow so closely the hip-bone connected to the thigh bone connected to the thigh ... He contrives to brush past this woman more than necessary. Her smell lingers on the air, in his nostrils. Vanilla? Does she bathe in it – or rub the stuff on her wet skin? He could do it for her, following swell and fold and intricacy. He could rub it in softly and then insistently. He experiences a singular, particular desire as he looks at this woman, enjoys saying to himself her biblical name. Some people shorten it – Mirry – he wouldn't, it doesn't suit her. Miriam – who was she in the bible? Desert air feeding her nostrils, black hair, the rough feeling of working hands. Jack pursues Miriam methodically, firmly. He fantasises about her at night and feels certainty in his heart when he sees her in the day. He loves the high bridge of her nose, the way she gives complete attention when you speak to her. He is going to have her; he knows that.

The night they make love for the first time, Jack hides tears from this soft, rough biblical woman – as he comes to define her in his thoughts, in his longing.

As hunter, he moves up the track, the elusive desert path to find her. Shadowy creatures flee from him as he walks swiftly through scanty undergrowth, seeing only by faint moonlight. He finds a small hut – opens the door and she is there.

Marie remembers: a ride in a mini-cab one cold winter night, coming away from a party in a restaurant in Shoreditch, a modern place serving minimalist food of unusual elements, figs marinated in balsamic vinegar, cashew nuts heated and then smoothed into a buttery paste. Conversation swells and subsides up and down the long table, as wine bottles are emptied and replaced. At eleven, Marie decides to go home. She has no more conversation and there is no special leaning toward anyone in the group. She calls a mini cab. Feeling indulgent, she steps into the back of a silver Audi estate and rests pleasurably into the corner of the seat. The driver steers the vehicle neatly and swiftly into the traffic, passing the wonders and delights and tragedies of London on a Saturday night. He is completely silent and Marie explores the back of his head, the line of his shoulders, his hands on the steering wheel, her exploration punctuated by glances outwards at the passing lines of buildings, the variation of light through darkness, human forms, and slight drizzle against the window, this falling of water seen more lucidly under the illumination of lamp-posts, spraying gently outwards, a shower of water and light. The driver has thick, sleek, shiny black hair tied in a low curly pony tail. He has shapely ears, coiling flat against his head. He wears a dark jacket and his shoulders are wide and substantial. Marie watches his hands on the steering wheel; they too are shapely, large and strong looking. She begins to find it erotic, watching his hands lightly and firmly moving on the steering wheel. She cannot recall exactly the face she sees briefly through the window before stepping into the car. An olive-skinned face, Latin American maybe. She falls in love with the experience of being the woman wrapped in a coat in the back of a car, and a strange man with a pony tail and competent hands driving her just exactly where she wants him to. He has control of the car, but she tells him where to go. Marie falls in love with the raven black quality of the man's hair, his silence, the way his hands dominate the wheel. They speak not a word, Marie begins to gloat over the movements of her mind, the movements of her desire. For the short duration of the trip, this is the man she desires. He fills the world, his wide shoulders, the black hair, his hands. Rain falls against the car as it follows a swift route towards her home. She hardly sees him as she leans towards the driver's seat, sorting out, beneath a dull light from the front of the car, coins and notes, including a tip, aware only of a suggestion of an aquiline profile. Just before they turn into her street, she taps his shoulder and reminds him to avoid road-works at the corner. Solidity deflates as her finger pushes through empty material, the dimension of the jacket clearly enhancing a body not quite filling the available volume.

Hannah remembers: the company is putting on *Scheherazade*, faithfully following Fokine's choreography from decades previous. She is to dance Zobeide, partnered by Mikhael as the Golden Slave, a dancer with the cheekbones of a Cossack, and the brooding eyes of Rasputin, despite his origins in the east end of London. Hannah remembers the pale turquoise harem pants, slit over the thigh so that pale flesh shows through, and banded by elastic at knee and ankle. Her midriff is completely bare beneath the sequined top that covers her tiny breasts. Mikhael wears bronze loose trousers, also tethered at the ankle, glittering tattoos on his torso, and dark eye make-up. He is tall and rippling with discreet muscle; she is pliable and sensuous, her ribs, delicate willowy twigs, pushing at taut skin. Their interlocking moments, he stroking her torso and she lifting her face, her mouth, to him, have the audience holding its breath, a perfect erotic combination. Hannah feels triumphant in partnership with Mikhael. As she melts and swoons, and places her hips against Mikhael's perfect thigh, she draws into her the man she knows is in the front row of the audience, his eyes fixed upon her, his body motionless and rapt.

That night, the night he comes home with her, in those rapid and fleeting hours he ravishes her with his words, telling her what he sees, how she dances, how graceful the curve of her head and throat, how she breaks his heart with her beauty. He propels her to the mirror and outlines with his finger her face, her shoulders, her waist, murmuring all the while that she is his enchantress, his prisoner, dancing only for him and now she will receive his kisses and caresses and he will hold in his arms the flower of English ballet, his exotic darling .... She drinks this in, loving the view in the grand mirror of the two of them, she even more delicate-framed against his masculine bulk. He keeps his coat on as he devours her reflection, taking it off finally and abruptly as they make love before he leaves. Each time after this, at each departure – she can't help it – she expresses sadness at his going and he assures her that it is with a heavy heart that he has to leave, that his duties and a complex life await him outside of their world but that he will be there the next week, nothing would keep him from his passionate love, the ballet, and his need for – his desperate need for – her, his prey, the queen, the ultimate .... Mollified, pacified, she melts, and as the door closes, returns to the mirror to find the adored one, the beautiful one, telling herself as he tells her that it is lucky, so lucky, to have even ten minutes of rapture – as opposed to a lifetime of duty. How lucky she is to have this sensitive man who absorbs everything about her and then feeds it back to her, so that each time after his visit she is renewed, re-established in her own eyes as beautiful, an object of reverence and wonder. She falls asleep with her hands clasped over her flat belly, feeling sorry for the wife who has lost her shape through the carrying of a child and who has never been loved like this.

Simon wrenches a pretty picture from its frame next to his bed and tears it up. 'Fuck you. The biggest love of my life, and you fuck off.' Simon finds girl after girl in the next few weeks, smiling and seducing. Some of them ask why he keeps an empty photograph frame next to his bed.

17

He is accustomed now to sitting next to her. Not immediately. After a little while. He knows just the moment to get up, smoothly, and to wander across in a calm unhurried manner. He sits a little distance from her, avoiding the full skirt, avoiding her eyes behind the dark glasses. He too is protected by dark glasses. The full skirts, he remarks to himself again irritably, are no longer fashionable. Mary Quant sees to that. Does she not notice the mini-skirts, beehives and black-circled eyes around her? She's not that old, she could still wear them. But what would the V-feet look like in mini-skirts? Forget it. Anyway she is hiding herself, any fool would know that. And now – she is wriggling, this little fish. She is opening her tiny mouth for the hook. He loves this feeling of small tension, a slight prickling of the skin, a skip of the breath. Nothing serious, but a knowledge that the bait has been taken.

He greets her in formal, polite fashion, and says nothing else for a while, taking in her watchfulness, the direction of her interest. The house, the zebra crossing. Her body is upright, alert. Well, more than that. She is seized by something, her body stiffens. She tries to pretend it isn't happening by laughing. Nervously. The door of the big house opens and a woman with a small boy and (this is new) a pram – move down the front path. The woman shuts the gate carefully, and places the small boy's hand onto the pram handle. It is a little high for him and his arm stretches directly upward. Come to think of it, she has been wearing fuller clothes lately, the pram woman. Broad woman, tall. Easy to hide pregnancy.

He looks at his companion on the park bench. She is flushed, a pale pink radiation rising to her cheeks. And underneath that colour, her face is an unhealthy, chalky white.

'Hmm,' he says lazily, 'look at that, will you. Mother and children. Must be a nice life for them. Rich husband, big house, park opposite.' Her mouth tightens. He continues. 'Some people don't know how lucky they are. Silver spoon, eh?' He pauses. And his tone of voice sharpens. He leans towards her a little – not too much – his voice barely audible but somehow sharper, as if he is directing a dart into her ear. His mouth is aimed towards her. A metallic, acid aroma rides from his mouth to her ear. 'Tell me, miss – don't you sometimes just want to rip that silver spoon from their mouths? Why should they ... when we ....' And then he stops and looks away into the middle distance. Breaks the line of intent. Looks away into nothing.

'Why ....' she begins. And then stops. Compresses her lips firmly together.

'Why what, ma'am? Can see you're a lady, ma'am. A beautiful lady, if I may say so. You deserve a rich man and two little'uns you do. Although ....' He turns his body and looks directly at her. ' 'Scuse me ma'am, perhaps you do ... beg your pardon. Of course you must! Lovely lady like yourself. Thought you were Jackie Kennedy – when I see her on the news I always think what an elegant lady. Like yourself, ma'am. Only the colour of the hair different.'

'What business of yours!' she says, but without heat or courage.

'Just imagine,' he says, deciding to allow himself one sharp thrust and then to leave it, 'just imagine that she disappears and you walk into her shoes ....' He is not looking at her but he knows her face is undone. 'Oh well,' he says cheerfully, and stands up, 'must be getting on. Very nice talking to you miss, always at your service.' This time, standing, he faces her directly, takes off his glasses, and gives her what he calls a hot-shot from his dark eyes. He saves these for last. Doesn't overdo them. Less is more, hmm?

She takes the blast, right in behind her presumptuous disguise. His surmise is correct. In some way this pram-pusher is her rival. Her sister maybe? That she hates. Or maybe she has the hots for the city gent husband. Silly tart. He feels triumph and then hatred. Smiles and walks away.

The next time she is there, he takes his time coming to join her. Notes a frozen quality to her posture. Stays only a short while, and says nothing but 'Good morning ma'am, I trust you are well.'

The time after, he sits for a while, and then leans towards her. 'Ma'am, excuse my liberty in talking to a lady such as you, I know my place believe me, but I have a heart, believe me, and I can just feel there is some trouble in your life. I am not asking you to tell me, perish the thought, miss, but believe me, I understand. I understand perhaps more than you know what's hurting you, what's on your mind.' Though he now averts his gaze, he knows – bulls eye! Bingo! Gotcha! She has reddened, and tears start to fall beneath the dark glasses. She dabs at them with a lace handkerchief taken hurriedly from her handbag. After a solicitous silence, he speaks. Softly. 'I feel for you, ma'am, and I know a way to ease the pain a little. I won't tell you what ... just I know ways to take the smile off her face. That one. Nothing serious. Just wipe the smile off.'

Hannah flinches. She is crazy to keep returning to the scene of the crime, as she now sees it. It is torture. And she has to come, she has to see. This man is presumptuous, and yet as he speaks, a deep savage agreement runs through her, exultant, vicious. Yes! Wipe that smile off. A wild tremor seizes her mind. Today, particularly, she is angry and panic-stricken. The pram! How does that affect the story she tells herself?

One child is already there when they meet. She knows this. It is fact. The pram happens since the initial encounter. Two children now. The story she hitherto has in her mind is not like this. In that story, and surely he encourages it, sex happens only with her. The child already in existence is an accident that has to be cared for. And she cannot say anything about this pram, this heavy black exultant object on big superior wheels, carrying the undisclosed new infant. She cannot say she has been spying – for months. The bastard, the betraying bastard. And – yes – he leaves earlier than usual these days, and doesn't come as frequently, mentioning abstractedly travel for business. What is he really doing? Cooing over the baby? And the roses don't look quite as abundant, or as newly picked. One of the current bunch is hanging dolefully from its stem. Ruined. She has to throw it away. After he leaves. She wants to throw the whole bunch away but arranges them in the cut-glass vase, smiling at him, moving gracefully in the new black skirt she has bought for him. And in the cupboard, a Jackie Kennedy box-jacket. Smiling. Smiling. Behind the smile, the grace, an enraged creature wants to plague him with questions. Mr Jeremy Faulks. That much she knows. Big deal. His name. And that only seen by chance on the letter in his pocket. Still, after – how many? – almost two years. Yes, one year, six months and three days. Always the same words. No promises, nothing represented in the outside world. Nothing real for pity's sake. They never step out of her flat. 'I am your king, your lover. This is all we need to know. The mystery darling, for us the mystery. Not for us the mundane world.' And how the hell to pronounce it? Folks – forks? Stupid bloody name, (who'd want to be Mrs Fooks) ... who are you kidding, Mr Jeremy Fucks? Why should she be banned from what everyone has? Home, a public face, children, and even if she is not sure about that – children – she wants choice. And the worst, yes. Not telling her that his wife has another baby. The first time she sees the pram vomit rises into her throat. And her mind accelerates with stories: she is baby-sitting for someone else. Yes, that's right. He would tell me. No. He just wouldn't do it. And the pram is there each time. The repetitive thought arises: this means he is still having sex with her. Not the impression he gives. He gives the impression of a separate life, a dutiful life, devoid of emotion, physicality. Wait a minute, now she thinks of it, he never says he doesn't. He cunningly implies it – but never says so specifically. In these moments, she hates him desperately. In the desperation, folded in, lying in wait for her, is always the lie of hopeful redemption. She loves him, she trusts him. He is her king. He will explain all. The wife forces him; someone else has impregnated her and now he is stuck with two children. Hating, excusing ... she circles on a demented merry-go-round of thoughts, fear and panic, creating ever more elaborate scenarios in which he, on bended knee, weeping, comes to her and says, 'At last my beloved. I have been longing for you to fill my life and now – at last – I have created the possibility. She has gone.' Instead: less passion, longer intervals between meetings, a certain distracted quality in him sometimes. No amount of strutting or coquetry can bring him back to the earlier days of magnificence and perfection. She goes to the beautician more often, her dancing takes on a frantic quality which sometimes suits the role and sometimes doesn't. The director shakes his head at her after a performance which requires tranquillity and depth. Bastard. Who did he think he was? Men. And now another bastard sitting next to her. The cheek of it. Who does he think he is? Well, anyway he is subservient and respectful. Knows his place, and for all his rough looks, he seems to be a bastard with a quality of understanding. Not that she'd ever go near someone like this.

But she has grown accustomed to his presence. The first time he sits beside her, he says 'Excuse me ma'am, I know this is a little presumptuous. I have always liked the view from this bench. I won't interrupt your peace, but do you mind if I sit here too?' As he is asking this, she thinks that perhaps his proximity provides extra cover for her, so she gives a cold nod, not looking at him. 'Oh thank you, miss,' he says, arranging his legs carefully so they came nowhere near hers, nowhere near the neat V she creates with her feet. She thinks the story about the view is false. He fancies her, that is what it is. But knows she is far above his station. As long as he behaves himself, he can stay there. It suits her, after all. But one inappropriate move and the bastard will get it. The full flash of her wrath towards all self-seeking bastards, that's what he'll get.

And now he's sitting next to her, telling her he understands what she's feeling, and saying this extraordinary thing: wipe the smile off her face. How often does she think this, seeing the woman smile at her child, smile at that baby. Yes, with an abrasive cloth, something that hurts, something that cruel nannies used in the nursery, wiping harshly ... or that the smile could literally be wiped off, leaving a gaping hole, a shriek, just a hole, no mouth, no face. How often does she want to wipe the smile off her own face and shriek, shriek out of the black hole of misery and longing. And then her damn body, obedient to his amorous love of her smile. 'Smile darling, look at my naked body and smile ... slowly darling ... look in the mirror at us ... I want your eyes on me and that luscious slow smile of yours.' And she gives it. And gives it again. From her aching jaw, from her raging heart. This is an addiction, a craving. The way he loves her ... no one can do it like that. No one else will ever do it like that.

And now – these damn tears. She must go. As she rises,

without words, she has the oddest sense that some agreement has been reached between her and the strange nobody on the bench. What nonsense. This stupid man poking at her feelings. And yet, when she goes, she feels excitement. Something is going to happen to ease her pain. Someone can see her pain, can understand how badly she is being treated and is going to help her. Who knows how. She walks to the station with her head even higher, the tied ends of her colourful scarf pulling at her chin. And there. She is not looking back this time. Just forward.

18

Marie is thoughtful as she travels to Hannah. She is impervious to sights and sounds of the journey, the creaking of the elderly tube carriages and the arrival and dispersal of varying human forms. Stopping and starting and gradual emptying and filling create barely noticed background accompaniment to the movement of her mind. She feels empty and a little sad. Jack, she supposes. It's a nuisance, this Jack situation. She doesn't want to think about it but her hungry mind lurches there. Perhaps nothing happening enough in other directions. Maybe just life in a flat patch. Can't be happy all the time. Noticeable in this rueful stoicism is a well-learned pattern. Lou is the one who creates drama and language and turmoil. Marie learns to watch, carefully to soak excess colour from a situation, to re-route it into a quiet receptacle, and then to observe the splashing and roaring caught within this designated container. That is how it is. If you can't change it, observe it and understand it, but do not go flailing into the currents and back-waters. Especially if they are coloured red and purple. Any colours of violence are to be contained and observed. This alchemic procedure, herself as dedicated alembic, gives Marie patience and depth. Her nature is not spontaneous and sometimes she misses the quality so freely evident in her sister. Lou, always the elder, persistently the initiator, is experienced by her through their childhood to be dangerous – and admirable. Enviable at times, and then the container displays a disconcerting blackness, a troubling liquid of sibling rivalry and resentment, the gap apparently unbridgeable, the dye cast. Each sister with her given set of trials and treasures from the fairy godmother.

She walks along the canal. The boats and the water seem

arrested into uneasy stillness, it is too cold for anyone to be out on deck with beer, or tea, or with a dog or a child. The pavement feels cold and hard; Marie notices the irregularity of the paving stones. Her feet, as she walks up the steps to Hannah's flat, are heavy. Detached from the rest of her somehow. She rings the bell – a leaden sound from within – and then lets herself in with her key.

Hannah is reading the newspaper, the curtains are drawn as usual, and a lamp on next to the sofa. She is wearing cream silk and her face looks small and pinched. Marie feels a softening of the heart towards Hannah. Poor old thing.

The young woman is quite unaware of waters gathering and near to uproar.

Hannah, disguised by the day's modestly elegant outfit, is a bent twig forced into movement by a sodden, racing, filthy river. She is covered in oil, detritus and dark water. In the night, unexpected and unwanted memories come to her so real that she is back in time and then is now and she is screaming into the muffled curtains of her bedroom. No one there to calm her. And he who could have been, who should have been, just gone – no word after that thing that happened. Gone, as if he too had died. And she should have died then. Mortified, crushed, bereft and not able to show it to anyone for no one was allowed to know. All very well to want someone to help her, it is not possible. She cannot speak of this thing. She will die stuffed to the eyeballs with it, it will turn into a cancer, she will die a horrible death. In the morning, she is a mess of exhaustion, woe betide anyone who walks in.

'How are you, dear?' asks Hannah. She has never before

addressed Marie in this way. Doesn't often inquire how she is, or, if she does, the question is asked without waiting to receive the answer. A question without interest. This time there is a pause. Marie looks at Hannah. This nearly-famous beautiful old woman is observing her steadily. An offering of friendliness? But at the same time the attention is unnerving. Something glittery and fractious about her today, liquid and poisonous.

  Don't trust her Marie

  'I am okay. I suppose. Shall I make tea?'
  'Plenty time for that. Why do you only suppose you're all right? You either are or you aren't. And if you aren't it's one thing only, isn't it? Boyfriend trouble?' Marie is astonished. Hannah has never before asked her if she has a boyfriend. And the word sounds odd in her mouth, as if she's speaking a foreign language.
  'Don't have a boyfriend, actually.'
  'Pretty girl like you, what nonsense!'
  'Well,' says Marie (ignoring a second warning of the inner voice, low and precise, this time urging: Go Now, and falling into a net which will shortly drag her onto a stage, exposed and humiliated), 'Well ....'
  'Must be someone,' says Hannah with frightening deliberation. 'Tell me, dear. An old bird like me might be able to help.'
  Marie puts her notebook down. 'I'll make the tea,' she says. 'Anyway. And thanks. That's sweet of you.' When Marie returns from the kitchen, Hannah is standing up.
  'Yes, well,' says Hannah coldly from her erect posture, neck elongated, 'we were looking at men, marriage, that sort of nonsense. What's that funny exercise you do? The waving

arms?'

'T'ai chi?'

'Foreign words.' Hannah sits again, crossing and uncrossing an elegant leg. Marie hears the soft sound of silk grating on silk. 'Aren't there eligible men in the class?'

'Not that I ....' Marie flushes uncomfortably.

Get Out! Get Out!

Disagreeable stuff is floating from the ceiling, a sticky canopy unfolding, catching and swaddling Marie's thoughts.

'It's always about me – well, yes, that's your job. But I know nothing about you, your hopes and fears, your longings ....' Hannah's face darkens. 'When I was your age I was just leaving my peak. Of dancing success, that is. That was the time to cast my eye around.'

'Didn't you?' asks Marie,

'No,' snaps Hannah. 'Should have. Big mistake. The married ones are the trouble, aren't they dear?' Marie is silent. 'Oh good heavens,' says Hannah, 'now I've gone and upset you. Should stick to the task, eh? Did I tread on a corn there? Are you in love with someone married?'

'I ... shouldn't we have tea ...?' Marie finds a tissue, wipes her nose. 'Must be getting a cold.' Hannah gives her an appraising look, and then, to Marie's relief, stops speaking as Marie pours from the delicate, painted teapot. The sound of cups being replaced on saucers is noisy and uncomfortable within a developing, tight silence.

'I remember where we were,' says Hannah. 'Something terrible happened. Don't write. This is not for the book. I am not telling what the terrible thing is. Just know that there was a love beyond description. And that's not going in the book.

Do you hear? And never will I say anything of such matters.

'Never.

'Because after that, there were many, but never the same. And never could I settle with any that came after. So now I am on my own.'

Hannah's voice is pinched, she looks as if she has a fever. A stale odour permeates the room, as if it has been shut for many years. The smell is unwholesome. 'Where is that t'ai chi school that you go to? And who is the teacher?'

'Jack.' Marie feels a muffling sensation settling around her. She can't think straight, is unthinkingly, childishly obedient. Hannah's eyes stare at her; two black holes. 'And his surname?'

'Goodman.'

'And is he? A good man?' Marie's face reddens, drains of colour, and reddens again. 'Women do terrible things to good men if they turn out not good,' says Hannah in a strange voice.

'Miss Bloom, I don't know what you are talking about. Do you want me to be here today? Shall we stop for now and I'll see you tomorrow?'

'You need help, dear. You are doing something bad!' Hannah's face is drawn, crumpled, ugly, her eyes glassy.

'I'll go now. Getting a cold, anyway, I think.' Marie rapidly gathers her note-book and jacket. A shrill voice follows her, shocking, a voice from the foetid room, a mad voice bent on helping. 'You are making trouble and something bad is going to happen. You can't wipe the smile off someone's face. If they are smiling, they are smiling.'

Marie runs, tears streaming, down the road and away from the house.

Something knotted in the field, the field where I had

been still and meditating day after day. Beloved Friends, when the silence deepens and grows, it is quiet and yet riotous with sparkle and plumage, none of which is visible or audible! How to explain this? But now I emerged from peace, and followed the trail of un-peace. I reached an embattled place, a shuttered room near a stretch of water, and waited. A congregation of harpies emerged, their shadow spread through the room. I waited. A gentle voice called to me through the pestilential shrouds that draped the empty forms of dark creatures and clouded the ethers. I traced the presence of a Guardian Angel. This beloved being told me that it had guardianship of a group. And that one in the group – an elder one – was suffering and that her mind had slipped and was creating distortion. As is courteous and appropriate concerning the actions and responsibilities of angelic beings, there is an abiding and never an interfering. If they are not called, they cannot move. I have mentioned before, and will mention again, the extraordinary patience of angels. Who abide and wait. Until it is asked of them. If this tormented one was able to wake up, even a little, and understand that her suffering was of her own making, she would be assigned an angel to walk with her specifically, for an awakening human being is a precious jewel and needs support. I communed with the angel and asked of it permission to attune to the suffering elder. Permission was given. I felt my way toward the knot. I found Pain, the pain of an event from this lifetime. A terrible event. Kept locked. In the absence of speaking this pain, it was being manipulated and dirtied and pushed onto someone else, and in this pushing something was beginning to erupt and emerge ... There was no access to me from this old one's soul. She had fallen into an abyss, and was lost, embattled. Madness drifted away from her like black smoke, toward a being of familiarity to me. I left the suffering old one, sadly, blessed the angel, and followed the trail. I found the young woman from the t'ai chi class. She had overlooked several warnings from her Guardian to leave the company of the old woman earlier. I brought myself into stillness, noticing again the odd, familiar effect of being in her company. Something known and not known. I attuned to her Guardian, and we both understood that her usual sensitivity had been clouded with some kind of inattention and weariness. She had fallen into the net of distortion woven by the old woman and could not hear the Inner Voice. Dear Friends, suffice it to say, this being usually had awareness of her Guardian and ability to commune with him and open her heart to his wisdom.

Her Guardian agreed we two would accompany her and attend upon her.

She travelled rapidly back to her home, took to her bed and allowed sorrow and fright to speak their experience. She stayed close to herself as she shook and trembled. She began to recognise that she had ignored the voice of her Guardian, a voice that is also her own, this still, small voice often called the intuition. She wept for the loss of awareness.

I sat within one point of what you call a Triangle and felt the pleasure of accompaniment. The Guardian Angel, the suffering human and I. What more can we do for a suffering soul than be present? Without argument, discussion or applied helpfulness. The impending pressure of consequence was also in the room. We three all knew it, each in our own way. The vulnerable human creature felt fear; at the same time, parallel, the deep presence within her soul provided equanimity. Beloved Friends, the three-pointed energy has a vitality not present in the line between two points. The line between two has direction and apparent certainty but the arising into three brings necessary mystery and a sense of Other. It is like sitting within the structure where the roof is not flat, but pulled into this Pointed Shape. Dear Friends. May I pass on to you a sweet practice called The Pointing of the Way? If ever you are in distress and the two-pointed Way has you wandering there and back and back and forth without realisation, raise your arms above your heads and with your fingertips create this Pointed Shape. Breathe your way out of the Two and into the Three. And wait without expectation or knowing for a clearer quality of air and ether within the soul to bring you refreshment and respite.

Inside the darkened flat, in the curtained room, a shard of horror, a memory, is disturbed from its burial in the past and impaling an old woman. Her mind yields up its banished content. All she can see is that young man, getting up and sauntering towards the pavement, to his motorbike. Revving it up, driving fast down the road, towards the house, the zebra crossing, just as that woman, the child and the pram open the gate and step onto the road. A car swerving to avoid the rapid and seemingly heedless bike, the collision, the still form of the child on the ground. The motorbike and its rider disappear. She never sees him again. 'Not my fault!' she screams silently. 'I didn't ask him to do it!' Frantic, her mind presents her with an action which could redeem her, which could undo the horror from fifty years ago. Over fifty years. Why should she feel bad any more? She didn't ask him. He just did it. But now she can stop another woman causing an accident and this will cancel out that other thing. There is a sorrow to the young woman just like the sorrow she felt on the bench on the common in Ealing. That is how it works, isn't it? She knows the man with the motorbike is heading towards that girl. He is everywhere, everytime. If someone is unhappy he finds her and there will be an accident again. Is that good man married? His wife better look out. Hannah must find out before the accident happens and the smile is wiped off .... She can make inquiries, someone will find out for her where he works. And she can go and warn him, and warn her. Triumphant, almost redeemed, Hannah stands up rapidly. She has a lot to do.

19

As the babysitter Claire arrives and Paul runs to meet her, Miriam receives a text message from Simon. As before, an instruction. 'See you outside Liberty's main entrance 3'. She likes the instruction, and she bridles against it. It is terse, brooks no contradiction. No question such as '... okay for you?'. She argues with herself. If you don't like it, tell him. Assert yourself. Tell him 3.30. At the side entrance. Wasted thought. She is not going to do it. She is heading for the front entrance. And she will be on time, at 3. Two weeks after their first date. Not date. What's the matter with her. Meeting. He emails her. She waits a day – no, a day and a half, before replying nonchalantly.

A copy of the pages on Gravity is folded into a side-pocket of her handbag. She might show him. It depends. Well, his enthusiasm helped. No. Hers. All hers. Walking into Regent Street she is not the Miriam who waits a day and a half before replying to Simon. She does not know what kind of a Miriam she is. She is powerful. She is subservient. She is curious and free; she is afraid and not yet free.

She remembers last night's love-making with Jack. They hold each other, reach for each other without permission or preamble. She pulls at his hair, at first stroking the dark tufts, and then pulling a little harder. He takes a fistful of her long dark hair, winds it round his hand. It hurts a little. She doesn't say anything, enjoying the wordless erotic battle between them. A dark strangeness falls between them as they fight each other for pleasure. It is disturbing, she feels – and necessary. As Jack falls asleep, Miriam follows the pulsing in her body, a swollen quality of her heart, and a sense of balancing, within her heart, mysteriously, on a small space, not knowing what lies before or behind her. And she must choose. And not know specifically what she is choosing but it is a crucial choice. It is a movement of the heart. Miriam falls asleep, folded onto her right arm.

Simon arrives a few minutes after her. Seeing him, Miriam feels a frisson of guilt, power and attraction. She can see from his eyes that she looks appealing. She's twisted her hair and clasped it low into her neck. This sets off her silver earrings. She knows that a turn of the head will reveal graceful shapes. My god, she thinks. At this moment I am indifferent to everything else in the world. All that matters is that he sees the shapes I organise for him. This knowledge brings within her, immediately, sadness. Where is Jack in all of this? This is not to do with Jack. It is something she needs and she will take it and it will not be betrayal, just a moment in time where she takes something. Simon takes her hand, kisses her on the cheek, and sweeps her into the shop and the sadness, disrupted, makes way for a sense of disorientation. She surrenders to a scene within a play by an unknown author. She has no choice but to act. And she loves the theatre, doesn't she? Could this be her way back in?

'I'm taking you to a lovely little space,' he says, moving swiftly through the milling shoppers, hand behind her back, not quite touching, through the handbag palace and the scarf emporium. In a small carpeted corner, beautifully lit and sodden with perfume, he brings her to an elaborate two-seater sofa, curved and sensual, made of wood and tapestry. The sofa is in the middle of the space, and all around are bottles and jars and pots of ointments and liquids, some of which are viscous and golden in colour. Two assistants wait elegantly at the serving desk – a smooth and empty surface – and behind the sofa and against the wall, on small, curved feet, stands an elaborate, decorative glass cupboard, bejewelled and painted like a courtesan, proud and in her prime. Simon sits her down and surveys the surroundings with a satisfied smile, as if he has – just in this moment – conjured the whole scene up for her delight. Miriam's coiled hair and her earrings take on a patina of luxury as she absorbs the presentation. Just for her.

Miriam and Simon occupy the sofa, and present themselves to each other and to the few people exploring the contents of bottles and jars, flirting with each other as if the surroundings demand that only this behaviour is permissible. They speak of travel and exotica. She contributes in a fanciful and elaborate manner which sits uncomfortably with her. What the hell is going on? The scene is being played with such exaggeration and untruth. Why is she doing it?

'Come away with me,' he says. 'Let's have a few days in bed in a foreign country.'

'You're a beast,' she says, 'and I a mother and wife.'

'Hmm, of course. Nothing beastly about you, saintly one.' She doesn't like the smile on his face. In a parallel seduction, spiders weave webs and small flies fly into them and cover their wings with sticky substance as they struggle to get free.

'Don't you have available women who could go to bed with you in foreign countries?' she asks lightly. She doesn't feel light. She is angry and anxious; without balance and teetering on an edge. No gravity. The pages rest quietly and privately in her handbag pocket.

'Yes – '

How dare he be so confident. That's what she is here for. That's all that this is about. She is to pluck confidence from his smile and his jacket and then return, renewed, to Jack. And then Jack would ... and they would ... Simon's face is near hers. She sees the dark bloom of tomorrow's beard under his skin, and feels his hand on her knee. She puts her hand onto his, to take it off her knee, remove that proprietary gesture. He puts his other hand over hers. Nearer his face now, his skin looks almost dark blue and the cabinet against the wall seems to expand and include her on its shelves among the decanters and silver-topped containers of potions and liquids.

'What do you want from me, Simon?' Stupid question. So naïve. How does it manage to fall out of her mouth? She completely displaces any advantage she might have. She knows what he wants: not only to lay his dark blue face upon her thighs, but also to conquer another man's wife. And mostly – she supposes – to alleviate boredom.

He removes his hands, looks up into the ceiling, examines the dark black wooden decorative fixture so typical of the shop.

'What do you want from me, honey?' He looks at her. The glance is not unkind. 'We want a close encounter ... isn't that right? Nothing heavy – but two people giving each other a little pleasure in an exciting way and' ... he leans back towards her, giving her a quizzical look ... 'a little affection?'

Darkness falls into the nape of Miriam's neck, smudging the graceful shape of her hair and making tarnished the silver of the earrings. The dark word affection clubs her on the back of her neck. What the hell is she doing here with this man? Whatever she tells herself to the contrary, she is betraying Jack, that's what she is doing. But then isn't he betraying her in a similar kind of not-quite-doing-it way? She teeters and rolls. Fanciful mind-embroideries drag her from the vivid place in her heart where she balanced, crucially, the night before.

'Do you like jasmine oil?' asks Simon gravely. 'I think it would suit you.' Aghast, she regards him. Touché, Simon, that is a master stroke. With a sigh, dreamily, she agrees to experience a drop on her wrist. He applies the oil from the tester bottle as a surgeon would apply anaesthetic on his favourite patient, buys her a small bottle and puts his arm around her waist as they navigate the chambers of the shop on their way to the exit.

Leaving the sensual environs of the perfumed corner, coming into the mess of Oxford Street, the pavement roped off in parts where paving stones are being replaced, a policewoman with a megaphone herding pedestrians who are trying to cross, the seduction bursts, the perfumed play drifts into polluted air, and Miriam feels irritated and inappropriate. She is not betraying Jack, she is betraying herself. The bulge of paper in her handbag nudges against her as she walks. Now what is she going to do?

He emails her 'Lovely time we had. Let's continue. Friday afternoon?' She obediently returns a message 'Yes' and, in her mind, in her fantasy, there follows another delicious discussion and after that she will dream and then write again. She does not expect a jasmine oil anaesthetic.

'Simon ....'

'Yes, sweetie.'

'I'm not up for this. I think I will cut it short and go home.'

'Up for what? Nothing's happening to be up for, is it?' Miriam feels stupid, deflated, unsophisticated. She tries to pump herself up and it doesn't work. She is a little flat tyre rolling down Oxford Street next to this pneumatic marvel, bowling along on its plentiful supply of inflation. The image brings a small private smile to Miriam and her secret document brushes in a substantial way against her. Her secret, her delight.

'Don't be so frightened, little girl,' says Simon in a teasing way. 'Let's at least have a cup of tea before we part. I know a lovely place near Marylebone High Street.' Well you would, thinks Miriam. But she agrees. She is not a little girl, a frightened little girl. If she were she would run off right now. Yes, cup of tea and she grows up. And then leaves.

'Yes. Good idea, Simon. I know the place you're thinking of.' Seated in the window of a small café, she orders an Earl Grey with just a small amount of milk, and watches him order an espresso, repeating her order at the same time as if somehow she hasn't quite ordered correctly. Or is that her imagination?

'So what are you not up for?' says Simon with an expression of kind amusement in his face but not in his eyes. 'You can speak freely.' Miriam pauses before responding. She is monitoring herself fiercely – a director with a protégée caught before a demanding script.

'I don't want to do flirtation with you. I enjoyed the conversation last time – but this time, our meeting didn't feel right.' Leave yourself alone now Miriam, the director instructs. That's fine. Don't look down. But don't look too intently at him.

'Hmm. I wasn't aware we were offending the grand estate of holy matrimony. Oh dear, Miriam, did I misunderstand you?'

'What do you think you understood about me?'

'That ...' – he pauses, staring into his small cup of coffee as though reading a message within its dark fluidity. His face looks handsome. 'That,' he continues, 'you are one of these lovely women I meet occasionally who is discovering that the holy state has reached a point of stagnation – temporary maybe, but stagnation nonetheless – and along comes Prince Charming – mois – and ....'

'Simon,' – Miriam puts her hand on his in a friendly, neutral way – 'my husband and I do get bored with each other now and then. That is true. And you are an attractive man, that is true. And I did flirt with you a little, also true. But what I really enjoyed was the good conversation last time. And what I didn't enjoy was the way I fell into a flirty thing without really meaning it.' Bright with sincerity, Miriam believes she is picking her way carefully into something truthful. Well, truthful enough. 'I am not looking for Prince Charming,' she continues, looking him squarely in the eye, righteous, honest, faintly indignant. Liar, she tells herself. You did think he was a possible lay, didn't you? Not quite as baldly as that! No! she didn't. She doesn't. She impatiently shrugs off the drama coach, accompanied now, it seems, by a Zen inquisitor, staring into her lying soul. She fires the drama coach. She is not a little girl. She is managing. And he is an arrogant bastard and soon she will leave. And there is something she is leaving for which is suggested by a rumour in her heart, and she feels the tug, the pleasure of arabesque and poesy in the night, just hers, abundantly hers. The Zen master is neither to be hired nor fired. He appears and disappears of his own volition.

'Fair enough,' he says meekly. Miriam grins spontaneously. Simon smiles too. Miriam could start to like him again but no, she decides. Out of here. Away. And pay for the tea. Simon lets her pay, joking that he should have ordered the expensive chocolate cake.

'And thanks for the gorgeous perfume,' says Miriam, kissing him lightly on the cheek. 'You are quite someone, Simon. Good luck with the bored wives' club. Do you want the perfume back?' she adds hastily.

'Yes, of course I do. Wasted investment.' She opens her bag.

'No, sweetie. I'll put it on expenses for failed projects.' They walk together for a while and then Miriam turns left for Oxford Circus and Simon heads for Bond Street.

'Fucking stupid bitch,' he thinks as he walks along, his eyes gazing into shop windows, and then ruefully smiles as he acknowledges to himself that it's quite a gas to be turned down. For a change. It's usually very easy with women. Except of course for the one he really wanted, the one whose lovely face used to inhabit the picture frame, now empty, next to his bed.

Miriam is longing to get home. She still has time and could go shopping or wander around but no, she wants to be home. She wants Paul to run towards her when she opens the door and to see Jack. She wonders if she should tell Tilly about all this. No, not necessary. What if he says anything derogatory or gossipy himself? Perhaps she could just say something casual. And then drop it. Oxford Street tube entrance yawns at her like a dirty mouth. She treads swiftly down the stairs, vanishing from the street and entering the labyrinth. Her heart is beating quite fast. She is feeling a little sick. A bit dirty herself to be honest. She feels as if she is back in adolescence, unsure of the rules. You are walking along safe ground and suddenly a hole opens. Before you know what's happening you're lost. There are no seats in the train and she is pressed against strangers. The air smells bad. Home. Please. Home. And please no Madeleine at the doorstep. She doesn't want any extra thing to deal with. She wants her baby and her Jack. A large woman with a badly applied scarlet mouth looks at Miriam. Another Madeleine. Her fleshy body pushes against Miriam's. Miriam adjusts her eyes so at least she doesn't have to look at this stranger. They're everywhere. Inappropriate women who want to interrupt her, get in her way. She reddens as she thinks of Simon. She has made a fool of herself. The scarlet-mouth woman stares at her with a sharp, amused expression. Miriam tells herself the woman knows nothing of her, she is not complicit in the Simon fiasco, laughing behind all that red. How could she possibly know, this is ridiculous, she is tired and embarrassed, that's what it is. Her mind is racing, delivering thoroughly unreliable material for her to choke on. Just hold onto the yellow pole, everything will be all right. Soon home. Her heart beats in time to the rhythm of metal upon metal. The yellow pole becomes a rooting point into the ground, racing and swerving with the movement of the carriage, but stable enough.

20

The woman of my brother in the Tao was troubled when she came back from visiting the man with an angry heart. She was looking outward to another to give her beauty and value so she was vulnerable to the fractured shining of this other who was restlessly drawing her in. Her attraction towards the presentation of another, and her mistrust of her husband, had created an instability in her, and clouded her awareness.

Discreetly did I turn away as she and Dzukh expressed through their bodies the combination of love and unease they currently felt towards each other. When sleep absorbed them I stationed myself near to her and attuned to the Records to discover whether it was appropriate for me to receive the past soul-journey of this particular being, and equally, whether it was permissible for me to attune to her in the present. Permission came in the form of an unfolding of colour and shape. I felt her to have a quality of humour and artfulness but that this essence was shadowed with doubt and memories of pain and fear. Quietly I stayed as she lay, curled onto her right side, breathing steadily. Into her dreaming mind came images of gravity and substance, and thoughts about form compressed through weight. And then an image – a memory – of desert sands. Hot and compelling. And trudging feet. In this experience, her body was in pain, heavy with pain, and there were blisters on her feet and she felt the weight of a sack of belongings, and of responsibility for a small other. As I sat with her, I found a way to say the name she has now: Mi'lan. She shook in her sleep as recollection arose within her. Steadily did I abide with her, and knew her to be remembering a form she had inhabited as a woman from the Nabatees, a Middle Eastern desert tribe. She had been born with the capacity of word-profusion and crafting called poetry (yes, Dear Friends, yes – of course I know of this state!) but although women had held quite a strong place in this culture, she had stepped too far out and forward, desperate to be part of the band of poets in male form, and for this was denounced and cast from the tribe, and with her came an idiot boy who had become her friend. Cast away himself from his family he had befriended the woman. She was the only one to show him kindness, all others derided him and imitated the agonised expression on his face as he tried to formulate the simplest sounds, and the drool that came from his mouth, and the occasional scream that emerged when he became frustrated. She took him in. The tribe threw them both out. They walked, day and night. She wanted to die. They were picked up by a group of Bedouin nomads. She closed her mind to poetry, and a part of her life ended. The rest of her life – and the boy's life – was qualified by hard drudgery. He died before she did. Her bones gradually succumbed to exhaustion. The loss of poetry was a bigger weariness. The marrow in her bones dried up, her singing soul dried up long before her physical body perished. Her karmic line followed more gently from there, each time a Thread of poetry offered, and each time picked up with a little more trust. Never again was this soul so deeply separated from its humorous, expressive tendency, but the shadow of this long-ago life cast its darkness over each incarnation.

In the earlier part of this present life, the woman Mi'lan was drawn to theatre. When she left this world of stage and story to care for their child, she watched Dzukh practising his martial art and was struck by the poetry of the movement and she felt that which we may call envy, enmeshed with anger, for the essential expression of her soul was parched with longing for her own poetry. There was no refreshment or outpouring of that kind in her life at that time. T'ai chi was neither her mode, not her method. Language and theatre spoke to her. This was why the restless man had a hold over her. He was of the nature suggested by the black and white bird xi que – magpie. He picked up bright things. He had a sharp, expressive beak! Language attracted him where it shone and sparkled. But this was not his interest in Mi'lan. His playing with her was to feed the emptiness of the loss of the one who came before. The one who didn't need him and in that became beautiful and desirable.

I felt a questing tendril of request coming towards me from her soul. In sleep, she felt my presence. I received the gentle messenger and allowed streaming to return from my knowing-being to her. Poet to poet we signalled to each other, wordless, but of a cadence and a melody which was understood. Back and forth it went, and her animation increased and language and poetry began to stir. Her body moved, she saw me with her inner eye and wept for the recognition. Han Shan am I, I told her, of Cold Mountain. I am he who wrote his poetry wherever he could, upon plants, stones and sand. She remembered writing poems in the sand with a broken stick, the drooling boy pointing and shouting. Poet to poet we communed. Then our exchange ceased. The tendril withdrew, folding itself peacefully back into her consciousness. I re-assembled myself, staying still and quietly joyous that another soul had come to recognise its particular music, for each of us has a music quite unique, to be once sung and then to be gone, never to be repeated. Some of us sing through poetry, music, painting and sculpture. And Dear Friends, in addition, there are the simple forms of the music of a life lived in harmony with itself: attention to nature, to animals, to people. We each of us have a note, Once sung and then gone.

To know this is also a form of awakening, Beloved Friends. The Awakened Life is not necessarily one of renown and magnificence. There are many whose song quietly emanates, without applause. But they know. Their Beingness has a quality manifested similarly by that object called tuning fork – or singing bowl. Yes, surely we will dwell on this thought again, for it has a charm to it, does it not? The charm of simple possibility?

One more thought: when that which is called interrogative or question mark appears in this narrative, this does not require you to give that which is referred to as answer; and especially not that which could be referred to as The Correct Answer. The question is a living device which brings freshness into a landscape of statements. It opens up other questions, and a field of possibilities. We might rest time and again at a place of steady understanding, and the question might for a moment cease. And then – when movement and change are required, the beautiful Interrogative arises again.

In the morning, Miriam asks Jack to take Paul to the nursery. She is bright, her eyes shining. She must write something, does he mind? Please Jack. Her olive skin is glowing. He wonders what has happened but doesn't want to ask. Maybe she had a dream. Leave it alone.

'Of course, darling.' Paul screams for his mother as he is taken through the door. Miriam gasps, but closes the door behind them. He will settle down quickly. She gets to her computer. Simon comes to mind but doesn't stay. He floats off in his sexy jeans and man–hips. She creates a heading: 'Gravity – and the Captor.' When three pages have been written, she puts on 'Fields of Gold', Sting at his expressive best, and dances. The music lifts her up like a puff of wind, and circulates her far above the ground. She is aware of an experience from the night, but doesn't know what it is. The more she searches her mind for the night-story, the more evasive it becomes, until all she has is an experience of retrieving something hitherto lost; and around her and within her whirling and ululation. What now? she wonders. Don't know. Just this. Just this – for now – is enough.

She knows not, but I danced with her, shadowing her beautiful movements as she dipped and soared in the small room. She kicked the dust from the long-ago desert sand and this time, instead of it entering her nose and choking her, it rose up, a cloud of language, all the words she wrote in the sand remembering …

21

Miriam feels as if she has shed a headache long endured. No, not a headache, more a tinnitus of the soul, a disturbing sound layered onto thought and experience. Language feels all at once precise and alive in her, the ceaseless drone somehow packed up and departed. All she knows is she wants live words, not dead ones. Miriam shreds the pages still folded up in her handbag as offering to Simon and writes anew, spine curved into an eager S-shape, hands spread and active over the keyboard:

Gravitas pulling, gravity pulling, so we cannot escape, float off, untether our moorings. Ambivalent commitment. Because we have to. No choice. So! Come out of ambivalence! Fully invest in it, pierce the earth in search of gold and the landmass on the other side – through the middle, and out the other side. Walk it in heavy mountain boots, drop elevators through the floor below ground – into the basement. Lie on the ground, sweet white sand between the toes. Plant powerful feet upon the earth and buy it with trinkets from aboriginals who measure by stars, tides, the eruptions of volcanoes. In straight lines place tape measures around the circumference of the purchase and declare ownership. If we are going to be unwillingly, terrifyingly captured here, well then we will turn the tables and make it ours, and in every way try to outwit the plans and devices of the Captor. Oh yes – and send that other one, the devil himself into the molten darkness, the sulphurous, into the very core, the incendiary navel of gravity.

And around the fiery umbilicus, shielded and

protected from annihilation by her rocky lap of flowery meadows, and river-waters, we drum and dance the rhythm of the earth's hold upon us. We are all in her gaze and in her grasp. Mama's gravity captures us all – and finally she receives our bones, our returned bones, into the hammocks and billows of her hips: and there, lovingly, intimately, absolutely, she digests her children, at the same time spitting out second by second sperm diving into ovum and from eggs we grow new bones, minute bendable twigs, a small architecture to support the tunnelling through and emergence – lifted out and then brought down, to lie down to the breast, to feed and become full. Each of us emerging infants, purposefully emerging and perpetually disappearing – each to make our own distinctive feelingful experience of landing, of capture, or the tease of jumping and then landing, flying – and coming back to earth.

Far away, untethered – or perhaps deeper in than we ever might know, and more achingly, profoundly tethered than any of us might ever expect – despite received wisdom, speculation and inquiry – maybe the Captor resides in Gravity itself, in the love of landing, and forming – and being brought to bear, to root, to signify. One of the most ravishing messages from the Holy One, the Wholly Other, resides in Trees. Their roots burrow downwards, sucking towards nourishment. At the same time, an elastic energy like a catapult is sucked upwards and responds to elements within the sky-vault. We observe a triumphant emerging upward of leafy reed, fruit, flowers. This organic outcrop is essentially tethered and yet also free to disperse seed and pollen. These elements fly and land. They burrow and wait and grow.

The One Being refracts itself and tethers itself so that we might know creation. An act of profound mystery and love. In the world and not of it. The foolishness of man – untethering the Principle from its Manifestation – sending it separated and untethered into the perceived heavens – into the blue of material distance – where it becomes an unassailable but defined form – for punishment, control and projected dependency, fear and love.

The spirit that lives within us is of and beyond gravity.

The Captor resides in the darkest fiery heart of the planet – where we manifest the minor deity Pluto and arch-enemy Satan, the most dense, the tightest material, the most destructive.

Outer space – bridge between material and non-material reality. Black holes sucking matter into themselves, to a point of intense vibration, releasing this intensity into the dark otherside of the cosmos as starmatter. Black umbilicus of whirling spiral nebulae.

Captor and Rapturer. Drumming, rooted to primal heartbeat, given a taste of the original heart, imprisoned in aliveness! And so we make an art of our captivity. Dancing and singing and howling as we are eaten.

Miriam is emptied of words. She is astonished at what she has written. She bends forward and rests her head on her arms. Her back aches slightly and she moves to a softer chair, tucking her legs beneath her. She remembers the evening when she clings to Jack in anxiety, escaping from space and darkness by holding onto the warmth of his hand. He brings her a piece of chocolate and she is grateful. In that moment she wants only the comfort of the mundane, the presence of a small detail of kindness. Now, she looks back across the room at her laptop, wondering when she will read what she has just written, wondering how it might sound to her. It is not to be shown to others, she knows. Not even to Jack. Something will leak. She attends to the varying corners of her being: loving Jack, hating and fearing him; longing only for the safety of his hand and the dark room, the bed, the bedclothes and their supporting feather-weight. She discovers also a self that seems to be making a bid for freedom, thrusting out of containment into an airy place, unknown and disconcerting.

22

Hannah is feverish. Since Marie leaves – that girl, ignorantly courting disaster – she has a new lease of life. Something can be done. Find out, quick. Maybe there is a child involved and then there is going to be trouble. She looks through her address book. Yes. That young man, the balletomane, who so doted on her. He must be in his forties now but always sends cards. He adores her. Said so. Funny name – Broderick. Bad enough to be a Roderick but with a B in front as well. Such nonsense. Anyway – all that is beside the point. And he has an interest in martial arts. Didn't ever do any. Should have, really. Flabby sort. He will be her investigator. She phones him.

'Darling Broderick ....' She pauses for his surprised tone and the consequent small silence. 'Do you know, darling, how you always said you would help me out if I needed? Well, a small thing. Probably unexpected. For reasons I can't tell you, I need you to find out about a young t'ai chi teacher – all I know is his name is Jack Goodman. And now, let me see, where does she go for her class? – oh yes, I remember – somewhere in King's Cross. A small hall near the station.' Broderick is carefully primed and told it's urgent. She needs the address of the school. 'Bless you darling. And are you still frequenting the ballet?' The conversation eases off and she replaces the receiver. It must happen soon. And now she is to plan how to find out if there is a wife and child. She knows that Marie is heading towards trouble. One of those quiet ones. They can be dangerous. She'll sit on a bench somewhere and that one will drive up on his motorbike and before you know where you are, trouble will be coming to her. She can't get Broderick to find out about the family address. That would arouse his suspicions. It's quite legitimate to find out the business address. Why shouldn't she? Quite old people do t'ai chi – and

Broderick doesn't know anything about Marie. She goes to the phone directory. Too many J. Goodmans all over London. Should she phone each one and ask about classes? That could be tedious. And not everyone has their number in the book. People use these portable phones now. She will have to get a private investigator. Now who was that man? Ah, remember that stalker. Many years ago. The investigator who tracked him down would be dead now or very old. But why not get another one? Flushed and buzzing with thoughts, Hannah picks up the business directory and her magnifying glass.

The third name she phones is the one she decides to hire. He is brisk and immediate. He will come and see her in two days' time. Yes, he can find out if the individual in question has a wife and child and what their address is. Yes, he understands it is a delicate personal situation. He has come across many things like this in his life. And yes, his fees are reasonable. This doesn't seem to be a complicated job. Depends on the time taken.

'There might be an additional requirement,' says Hannah in her most sophisticated voice, a firm autocratic voice which belies the sensation of shifting sands, of nausea which she is experiencing. She has not felt this way since the moment of the collision, the sound of the motorbike.

The scene plays itself through her mind. The motorbike swerves narrowly on the zebra crossing, the woman pulls backwards, the child not quite with her, clinging to the handle of the pram, a car impatiently starting, the driver presuming that the woman has already passed the middle of the road. The child and the car. Impact. A thud. Screams. People arriving from nowhere to assist. The little boy utterly still. Also still, but in a quite different way, in a paralysis of horror and disbelief, Hannah rigid on the bench. This is not what she means. A fright maybe, no – not even that. She doesn't mean accident. Yes, she might think of the woman suddenly removed, but not in front of her eyes. That terrible young man. How can he. She doesn't ask him, it is his idea. A mad compulsion arises. She will go straight to the woman screaming on the road and say it wasn't me, it was him. Hannah drags herself to stand, starts to walk towards the accident, shouts silently at herself to get away, don't talk to anyone, don't be crazy, no one knows it is you that makes this happen ... grips herself into a different direction, turns her back and walks away. Someone walking speedily past, tut tuts towards her 'Isn't that awful, isn't that tragic?' Hannah nods, her face reddening. Or is it going white? She might be going to faint. No, she must just walk. Slowly. And get away from here. She stops at the newsagents. When does the next local newspaper come out? Two days' time, ma'am. She returns after two days and buys the paper. Page four. A small photograph of a pretty woman, and a small boy. 'Child killed on zebra crossing. Wife of well-known international businessman Jeremy Faulks ....' Hannah never sees Jeremy again. She never hears from him.

23

For two days Miriam passes the laptop, sitting like an explosive device on the table. She wants to open it and read the fresh words that poured onto the screen through the agency of her rapid fingers and curved back. Instead, she makes tea, takes a sip, rearranges a few books on the shelf. She looks through the window, it is windy and raining. She sits down; she gets up and circles the table, looking at the small black machine, its logo etched in gold, the A of the word like an upside-down V. Almost absently she opens the laptop, types in her password. Creates a new file: Gravity 2. Stares at the screen, blank, but for the title. Her mind is scattered with thoughts, none of them clear. Don't think, don't think, she tells herself, remembering a creative injunction from previous theatre days. Hal Burlington, the last director she works with, has a unique way of stopping the whole rehearsal when he is not satisfied. 'Don't think!' he calls out, clutching his arms around his body. 'Wait! Sink down! Listen ....' Sometimes there is an agony of foolishness as everyone stops, self-consciously waiting, sinking and listening. And then there is a collective release, a breathing out, and something different happens ... or does not happen and there is a break. Miriam loves Hal though she is a little intimidated by him. He seems so sure of himself, of what he wants. Such a sense of entitlement.

A memory comes to mind. She is about nine. She is seated at the family dining table. She doesn't want the vegetables. Only the meat and potatoes. 'I am entitled not to want what I don't want,' she says suddenly, to her own surprise. There is a silence, and then laughter and a chorus of who do you think you are? Entitlement, huh? Where did you find that word, young lady? The response is not unkind, but she feels silly and shameful. She doesn't know where she finds the word, it sounds nice in her mouth as she says it. But the aftermath of the word feels dusty and unpleasant as if she's eaten something unwashed.

Hal has an oddly asymmetrical face. She once looks at a photograph of him, covers the left half of his face and then the right. She's done this to a photograph of Edgar Allen Poe. Two entirely different people look back at her. With Poe and with Hal. Two people living in the same face. One clear and looking outward, the other sunken and tight.

Miriam starts tapping the keyboard. An idea: the stage is empty and then people enter, carrying large stylised masks of their own faces. The masks are cut in two but initially held together. Turn one half around, and you have the two left sides together; turn the other and you have the two right. Each doubled side has its own energy and its own dance. Now – music? Miriam leaves the desk and ruffles through her CD collection. The Penguin Light Orchestra maybe ... the Rachmaninov piano trio Elegaic 1 is lying on top of the pile. That isn't the one but she wants to play it. The lyrical sound has her moving around the room. In front of a mirror, she covers the left half of her face and looks; and then the right. Yes, another difference. The sad side and the neutral side, she could say. Photographs. That would be good. Cut them in half. She finds her camera, steadies it and photographs herself. She looks straight into the camera's eye, no smile. She transfers the image onto her computer and plays with it, cutting her face in half and re-assembling it two ways. And then the dancers would change faces and look at their face held by another. And what's the point of this? Staunchly, she stays with her meandering ... who knows what the point might be?

Jack is picking Paul up from nursery today. She hasn't thought about supper. She'll make rice and stir fry, and one of those big salads Jack likes. Leaving everything where it is, she steps out to the supermarket, wandering through the High street as if ... yes ... as if she is entitled to. She's not been easy to live with this last while. The more lost she became the more she poked at Jack. And that serious-faced woman. She thinks of Simon. His two faces. Charming and zestful – and behind that, something hollow. A thin, dark-looking man, passing her, looks directly into her eyes. She looks directly back and moves on. That feels good. Here's looking at you. Here's looking at me. What face does she wear when she frets about that serious-faced t'ai chi woman? She induces the sensation, a slimy, grinding feeling in her guts. A signal of something not all right. A contracted face, narrow, seeking assurance.

Miriam moves through a thickness of bodies, women clutching children and shopping, young men with their arses barely clutching at their trousers, old people stepping hesitantly, utilising some remnant of capacity. Each paving stone a treacherous reminder of how unsafe the world is now. Miriam's heart flickers a little. How is it? She can be in the depths of paranoia and misery about Jack. And then she can be okay. What makes the change? Better not ask. Enjoy it while you can. Miriam flirts with the stallholder at the corner shop. He is handsome. And he arranges his fruit and vegetables on the tables outside with care and artistry. Too bad the car fumes pour all over them.

Gravity; masks; two faces; the dream. Miriam is preoccupied with something. It is giving her pleasure. Sometimes in her there seems to be a hole that only Jack can fill, and she doesn't mean sex, though there's that, too. And when that hole is there, through the front of her chest all the way out, as if hit by a bullet, there is no end to agitation. And all she can see is that he is filling someone else with something that's meant for her. Oh what the hell – enough of all this. In the supermarket she chooses carefully and with pleasure.

When Jack and Paul return, an olive-skinned, smiling goddess greets them at the door. Smells of lemon grass and coriander rise from the kitchen. Paul flings himself at his mother and shouts that he is hungry and what's for supper. Soon, soon says Miriam. But I want it now. Nearly ready, she says catching his hand, but now now now he shouts. Miriam meets Jack's eyes above Paul's head. He looks tired. Been a little shit, he mouths and then says that he's just going to do a couple of emails and he'll be in the kitchen as soon as she calls. He kisses Miriam, aiming for her mouth and just missing. As Jack hurries off and Paul scrabbles at his mother, the goddess feels a rising fury which displaces the light and pleasant feelings of before. She entreats herself to stay tranquil and maintain equanimity and why shouldn't her son be hungry and her husband tired but she first goes into the bedroom, takes off the new top she is wearing and puts on something old and familiar. With the exchange of garments, something shrugs within her, humorous and sad at the same time.

'One of my students is messing me around with fees,' says Jack, a forkful of rice and green vegetables hovering. He has a shred of spinach caught in the corner of his mouth. Miriam decides not to tell him about it. 'They don't realise this is my living. Some of them think if they don't come, they shouldn't have to pay.' This complaint is an old one and Miriam doesn't reply. They have been over it many times. Agree a contract. It's a school, there's a syllabus, you pay for the term. Finished. 'Yes, yes I know,' says Jack in a weary way. 'The contract and all that. He has one of those. Anyway – enough of that. Same old, same old.'

'Who's old?' asks Paul, loudly.

'Your dad,' says Jack, but with a smile

'But why are you the same old? Same as what? Will you be the same old tomorrow or different?'

'This child,' says Jack looking at Miriam with humour, 'is precocious beyond his years. What do they teach you at nursery school these days? Busy with existential philosophy, are you?'

'No,' says Paul laughing in an artificial way, 'we don't do eggs and posophy, we do games and squares and colours.' The child sits like a little king between his parents, his dark hair fluffed around his head and his eyes bright with the pleasure of attention and the sense that he has done or said something clever. He wants to keep saying eggs and posophy louder and louder and jump around the room but he bites his lip and looks at his mother. She might get cross.

Jack looks at this child and can feel only the weariness of an unsatisfactory day. The teaching is nothing special, and this arsehole Trevor can go to hell and find another school. Doesn't really concentrate or pick up the essentials anyway.

He wants Miriam's sympathy, wants her to find a way to dissolve this irritation, this sense of futility and repetition. And yet if she does or says anything sympathetic he would feel irritated. He knows that. She's changed her top. Had something nice on when he came through the door. A nice colour. What is it? Why doesn't she leave it on, he's sick of this thing she's wearing. Taken for granted. They all take him for granted. Before he can stop himself, Jack slides into a dark corner within himself. He knows it well. He doesn't want to be there, he knows it is approaching and he doesn't side-step. Don't practise what you preach do you, he reproaches himself. T'ai chi – side-stepping, not taking the brunt of an attack, turning the waist, letting it go in another direction. He gets a spoon for the last of the rice, sits down again and then asks Miriam if she wants one. She is busy with Paul, and shakes her head.

Sometimes the cloth of the day, the weaving of the events one into the other, assumes a quality of fine linen, or of lace. This evening around the kitchen table suggests everyday cloth, a little worn, small stains here and there despite faithful washing. The grit of a London evening gathers on the window, specks of dust, grime and damp. An ambulance siren calls faintly in the distance, someone walks past the window pulling luggage on wheels which bumps and rattles over uneven pavement stones. Miriam takes Paul in her arms and begins the bedtime ritual. Jack switches on the small radio, not listening, but liking the sound of voices blending into discussion. And Han? Not felt, not seen. Where is the joy from that day in the class when the Ancient One rides out on the chariot woven from Jack's exultant heart? Jack decides: shit day. Dig a hole and bury it.

24

Jack awakes, thrashing in bed, a creased portion of the sheet wound around his neck. Those two, the two men, his father and grandfather, appearing in a dream. Miriam turns around, grumbling in her sleep, exposing arm and shoulder. He replaces the bedclothes around her. He can't remember the dream, but feels irritated and imprisoned. Jack gets out of bed and walks noiselessly to the living-room. He sits in the big armchair, Miriam's favourite chair, the one she sits in with her legs tucked beneath her, the one made rich with embroidered cushions flung, haphazard, into its back. Jack closes his eyes. How frustrating the day, how limited his feelings. Where is Han? He looks for him everywhere. Bastard. Shows up, creates all that illumination and then buggers off. Immediately, Jack winces at his temper. He whispers to Han that he is sorry. He knows Han is not simply at his beck and call. If he were, the mind would be rubbed, would it not, at will, and the genie would appear. Han is miraculous, unpredictable, and as real as the breath in Jack's body. Han gives him essential and vital food, his heart's necessity ... Jack loops into himself, brooding sharply, forsaking again humility, lifting his head, greedy and loving, begging to see his Beloved again. Soon. Now.

When Jack's father dies, apologetic demeanour curtains the sick-bed. With scarcely any breath, he whispers, 'I am sorry ....' Jack's mother weeps loudly, taking three and four tissues at a time from the big bargain box, blowing heavily and tucking the tissues into her sleeve. Her sister-in-law, Hennie, sits by her and strokes her arm. There there, don't take on so ... Give me those ... and every now and then taking the swollen bundle of tissues from the sleeve and putting them in the waste-paper basket. Jack sits in a corner, furious, unhappy, unprepared. He is twenty, his father fifty-one. Liver cancer takes him quickly. Painfully. Jack is astonished at his mother's grief. How come after all those years of sarcasm and teasing she has all this other feeling in her? Too late. He feels, sitting in the corner, angry with her, disorientated. Why not weep when he is alive? For the sorrow of him and her unkindness. He regards his mother critically. She is quite unaware of his gaze but auntie Hen gives him a warning look. He hates the apparatus of sickness around his father, the stink of the hospital. Not dirt, but the controlling smell of hygiene and medicine. Outside, it is snowing. Big chunks of snow, clumsily falling and displacing the dreary colours of the ground. A large number of people come to the funeral. Your dad was such a sweet guy. Jack's mouth goes into its usual firm and not-smiling position. You'll be looking after your poor mam, then. He nods and nods, speechless. His mother loses her sharp spirit, loses weight … and dies two years after her husband. Jack now has two graves to visit in the cemetery at Enfield. Side by side.

Clearing the house after her death, he comes across his father's record collection. Disc after disc of piano sonatas, mostly Chopin. This part of his father never ceases to astonish Jack. An untutored man, son of a rough combative bully, doesn't read, go to films or have commentary on cultural matters, but in his spare time, takes himself off to the little room at the back, the junk room where the ironing board sits, and leftover packaging and old magazines, and his turntable. He listens to Chopin with the door closed.

Jack sits quietly in the big chair, comforted by its rich tapestry cushions, remembering. A flicker from the window tells him a short, fine, freak snow-shower is unexpectedly falling, a soft white delivery, measured and neat and brief, arriving at the wrong time of the year, soon to lift up its transparent skirt and disappear. Jack thinks of winter when the house might be wrapped up, all three stories, his family and the neighbours above blanketed in whiteness. But now, not enough for wrapping, only enough to surprise the eye. His irritation starts to subside. Jack senses a nearly-white emptiness around his head, and a feeling of density and substance dropping down his spine, taking itself also through the front of his body into his balls, legs and feet.

I stayed near to my young friend. I could feel his desperate longing for me, or for that which I represented for him. I was there. He would see me when he was able.

An event, I sensed, was about to emerge.

Ha! Yes! Into the shadows of the room, within an astral continuum, again became revealed the two ancestors, father and grandfather. A clumsy configuration of the three of them: the younger in flesh, the elders beyond the confines of material form. Although the grandfather had passed on earlier in measured time, his astral body retained more density than that of the father. The father was more faded in definition, and somehow, there was less unhappiness pressing onto his field. Musical, softly percussive sounds emerged with him as he took ephemeral shape. These sounds – clearly struck notes, one following the other in lyrical suspension – were also those that came from Dzukh's moment of recall as he sat in the curved chair. The musical memory opened up discomfort, followed by a releasing tremor within Dzukh's heart. From him to his father came a transmission of this tremor, and the father received it with delight. Such an exchange had not been a common transaction between them. Dzukh inherited the penetrating and assertive energy of his grandfather, although without the old man's coarse and bullying characteristics. I sensed a multitude of other forms gathering towards this configuration but gave not one of them attention, as it seemed to me that the three needed an economy of presence and application.

Receiving this unexpected gift from his son, the father's field flared into the colour of deep rose. The grandfather became restless and started to insinuate small darts of aggression towards his son. The roseate field, beautiful in hue, and equally of a steely enmeshed quality, caught the aggression before it could land and deliver. I could see once more that the grandfather remained stubbornly attached to the psychic lineaments of his last life, not willing to shed that identity during the post-mortem process, and therefore left (under scrutiny) to wander through the in-between state, neither here nor there, neither this nor that, but still caught and hungry. Part of the attraction to staying fixed to his last identity was that – even in this discarnate state – he could still re-play his son's subordination, and the fretting of his grandson. When he was in life, his manner of bullying estrangement gave him a sense of power and pain-seeking satisfaction. To release this fragment felt terrifying to him, meant the dissolution of himself. And the apparent fixity of his son's fear, even after death, kept the two of them locked.

In utmost quiet attention I observed this fixity begin to undo itself, to unravel and release, allowing the rosy energy around Dzukh's father to rise into wave-formations which now could gather into themselves the aggressive darts and return them, still clutching their sickly burden, to the grandfather. The stubborn remnant of the old man winced, when thus stung by his own arsenal. He drew from himself a larger thrust of hatefulness, sent it ... and this too was returned. Dzukh, the male of the third generation, was not aware of what was going on between his discarnate ancestors but he felt a shift within himself, a movement of change and dissolution. He felt an authority he had never experienced before coming from the memory of his father. The sound of strong chords continued from the little room where his father used to retreat. They hammered and struck brilliantly, creating an arch of rising rotation, an ivory staircase.

Father and son aligned over the bridge of sound and focussed, each on the other, via the transmission of heart. I couldn't do this before, signalled the father, without words. I let you down. Couldn't undo the fear I had. I am sorry.

And I am sorry, Dzukh responded to his father. The music subsided and left a luminous enclosure, within which father and son were held.

A powerful intelligence entered the enclosure, a magnitude of shining as of polished steel enclosed by velvet, the capacity of a sword honed to cut through dense and intractable material, the sword held in the hand of a time-warrior in service to the Lord of Karma. This Being was not fully visible, but in Intention clear and defined. We could say, this was an Intention taking form.

As the phenomenon settled, the ancestral field received its message. Are you ready to declare yourselves, asked the time-warrior. If it be so, Open your hearts, and let this moment be forever recorded. If you seek the cutting of the ties please be sure this is what you truly desire.

This is my son and I love him, the father communicated. I let him down by being weak. My heart now feels stout and true. In this time after death, I've been helped to see clearly into my life and the constriction I created between me and my son. Up till now I have not been ready for the release. I wish to continue, emptied of this particular story, into the unfolding of Death and Re-birth. The terrifying father no longer pulls at and weakens my heart-strings. I am finally free of his manipulation. I need no further meeting with this soul. I wish also to aid my son in the release of his unhappy time with me.

An interim moment arose, into which Dzukh poured out his heart and wept. I am sorry, he declared. I looked down on you, I hated you. This disrespect is over. Respect is restored. Thank you father for your courage, and for teaching me. He paused, and a youthful, longing expression came over his face. He questioned: Will we come together again in another life?

Response emerged from the presence of the time-warrior. That is not for you to ask, or know. The only question for Now is: Are you ready for the sword? This is a Severance without return, after which the father may continue upon his path of purification and eventual rebirth, and the son may face a ceremonial farewell of dutiful and sincere gratitude to his father. Think profoundly before agreeing to continue

The father, I could tell, was at peace and ready to depart. His Guardian Angel fleetingly appeared, and touched the man's forehead. Dzukh bent his head, tears flowing. He took his time. Many memories assailed him, and he murmured to himself. We around him were patient, as is appropriate. It was still possible that Dzukh might want to prolong association with his father's spirit, and the time-warrior would obediently vanish. There was no favour within the gathering of one decision above the other. Two paths arose from this time Now. Each chosen path would bring consequences.

Dzukh became still. Resolution settled. His heart-cave formed an arena of intense wonder. Within that space he beheld his father, felt the beauty of the man's revealed soul. His tears ceased, and within an odd, humorous momentum he smiled, and it felt as if father and son were slapping and patting each other on the back, wishing each other well, travellers parting at the crossroads, and waving.

Acceptance delivered from both father and son.

Bow your heads and Receive, requested the Mighty Being, after contemplating the acceptance for a short while. Thus did they, father and son. And a flash of brilliance split the air and a terrible cry came from the grandfather, whose astral body spiralled and recoiled and was whirled away back to his path of lonely wandering. Angelic sorrow followed his departure, signified through folded arms and closed eyes, and a waiting in the wings, the great folded wings. Father and son remained bent and chastened. The air quietened and the time-warrior blessed them and slowly withdrew, asking them to remain in the position of prayer until the air ceased entirely to move ...

I stayed, wrapped in a moment of quilted substance and joy, a weaving of completion. The father-remnant began to dissolve, and Dzukh breathed, and felt strength, strangeness and relief pour into his soul as his physical body re-entered present time and space.

Jack is motionless, his eyes closed. A set of memories moves in front of him like a pack of cards deftly fanned open: aunt Hennie, of the grizzled hair and bright squirrel eyes, who also suffers the sarcasm and bullying of her father and whose method of survival is to go glassy, to switch off and think of other things, to create a smooth exterior so that the onslaught rolls off. She can see that her brother is transparent, too open, the meat of his body flayed by their father's domination. Their mother cultivates solidity and truculence. Her husband doesn't lash at her as he does with his children; he ignores her. As a small boy, Jack finds Hennie unattractive. Sensing her presence now he remembers kindness and generosity of spirit. He apologises.

Jack sees Marcia, the girlfriend who takes him to the t'ai chi ballet that opens his life into the practice which is his heart's delight. He cuts off from her after that evening of wanting the whole experience to be his, unshared. She tries to re-connect, but he is gruff and indifferent. He remembers now the pained and resentful look on her face as he throws out another oblique, unexplained exclusion. Eventually she gives up. He requests forgiveness.

Jack remembers, age sixteen, sitting in his small bedroom,

trying to shut his ears to the regular life going on downstairs. The furniture around him looks as if it is for someone else; a small desk, blotted and scarred, a wooden chair with a round cushion on it, posters on the wall of Bruce Lee. What is he doing with all this? The next day, Jack takes down all pictures and posters and paints the walls blazing white. He ransacks his mother's cupboard for anything of one colour, preferably pale, and removes from his room patterns, floral and linear, curtains and a small rug and the cushion from his wooden chair.

Aged seventeen he leaves this bleached rabbit hole behind for a smaller rabbit hole at the university residence in Leicester. Lectures in psychology; the wirings of the human mind. But every possible moment Jack is training in various schools of the martial arts. He manages a minimal pass at the end, acquires a lukewarm degree, and avoids any possible job or further training in the subject. There are rows at his home, his father remaining silent and his mother showering contempt upon his intentions. How the hell will he earn a living? Why did they waste money on him if he was going to give it all up? Jack barely survives on a small amount of money he pulls in for teaching the earlier self-defence crafts he learns. It is only when he begins to teach t'ai chi that his classes settle down and become financially viable. He learns to live on very little money, eats cheap food, practises until he falls exhausted into bed. It is a lonely time, a hard time. He manages to put aside cash for his year in China at the t'ai chi school of his grandmaster, the year of blissful attrition, he calls it, his rite of passage into self-respect.

After the death of his mother, Jack inherits the small house in Tottenham, and adds some ballast to his bank account through letting. At first it is difficult to be a landlord, now he is easy with it. He takes care of all details of the property, mending, re-painting when necessary, coping with unreasonable tenants and learning how to make businesslike contracts and follow clear boundaries. It is surprisingly sad to clear the house of his parents. When he folds his mother's clothes into bags, Jack handles each garment with care. Who is this woman? She is a handsome woman, but the mockery with which she receives the world stitches a sneer around her mouth. When she dies, her mouth loosens its stitches and the sneer unravels. As death hovers, Jack watches the face of his mother change into what she might have been without the sharpness of her mind and tongue.

From the deep comfort of the big chair in his living-room, noticing the warmth and solidity of the chair and the street outside quiet in the early morning hour, Jack speaks to his mother: I am sorry I did not make more effort with you. I am sorry I took the sharpness to be the truth about you. Thank you. I loved you, yes I did. Yes I do. I thought you were beautiful actually. In that red dress especially, the one with the big skirt. Do you know what has just happened? I hope you know, I hope you are at peace.

Jack opens his eyes. They are wet and stinging. He feels around his body as if to assure himself he is still physically intact. He is shaking, cold and hot, sweating and shivering. The meeting, the sword, the Being, clearly do not emanate from the three-dimensional reality his body is returned to. Equally, he knows the event is not of the substance called dream. His sense of himself is shaken, reorganised, shocked, expanded. He thinks of his father. It is disconcerting and odd to connect without old feelings of shame and frustration. It is like coming round from a sudden, radical operation. Something has been surgically removed.

Jack looks wildly into the corner, and meets the illumined gaze of his ancient friend. Han is draped in a cloak of authority and power, as if the substance of the ritual now sits materially upon him. The cloak is emblazoned with images of silver and gold and pewter-grey shimmering within its folds, inaccessible to the grasping eye, but available as a sense of shape and archetype as soon as the glance shifts. Implacable, the old man holds Jack in a moment of love and terror. Of course. What else? Surely he has some participation in the atonement between father and son? Does it happen because of his presence? Surely he too feels the flash of the sword? Jack, cut through – is this what is meant by cut to the quick? – closes his eyes, weeping again, and whispering, 'Thank you Beloved Han. I am sorry for the lack of courtesy towards my family, towards some of the women I knew ... to Miriam, towards my students, to you earlier.' Answer comes there none. 'The sword, Han, the Being of steel and velvet, did you ... ?' Jack opens his eyes. The corner of the room is empty.

25

The detective – or fact-finder as Hannah prefers to call him – is swift and efficient in his work. He finds Jack and Miriam's address in Kentish Town. He is a small man, neatly dressed, with surreptitious eyes and a manner strangely both obsequious and sneering. On the surface, however, he deals with Hannah politely. He receives a cheque from the old woman whose haughty manner and elaborate curtains and burgundy surroundings don't fool him. She is disturbed. Her eyes are glittering and her body betrays panic. He knows the symptoms. Easy job. He departs, and more or less forgets her.

Hannah is now on the way to prevent a terrible thing happening. From a small aperture of awareness she is watching herself, aghast, and wants to stop herself, but the flood of horrified memory that is awoken crashes over her and a wall of water pushes her along and she is helpless. A rupture is happening on the floor of her buried memories and Marie's face is all she can see, and there is a child who is going to be hurt and it will be Hannah's fault again if she allows this to happen, and this time she won't walk away.

It is her duty. She is what she always really thought herself to be – beneath lifelong recrimination, self-hatred and blame – a noble woman caught up in someone else's evil. That dreadful man with the motorcycle. She draws herself up, elongates her spine, and catches a glimpse of herself in the mirror. The shrouded light offers a view of a graceful woman, a woman who knows the experience of loss and pain. If the child hadn't died, the man would properly be with Hannah. He grows naturally tired of the wife and leaves her the house and a sufficient income and he comes to his love, his angel, and they have a divine and public life together. There is nothing wrong in her going to sit on the common at Ealing.

She is finding out the truth, simply. She needs to see the woman, and, by seeing her, understand that this is a woman who can be left. How can this woman, with babies and nappies and shopping lists ever match up to the being who illuminates the stage night after night and who sets fire to this man's heart? Divine fire has to be tended; it is a duty.

Tomorrow is Jack's class. She will take a taxi to Kentish Town and plead with the wife to come with her to the class. And they can sort it out. She and the mother will sort it out. And the child will be safe.

Jack leaves and Miriam settles down with Paul. She lights a fire, gas-fired flames. She holds Paul and they look at a book.

Miriam is surprised at the knock on the door. 'Who is it?'
An elderly female voice replies. Miriam opens the door, on its chain. An old woman stands on the doorstep, a handkerchief to her cheek, elegant in dress but dishevelled in expression. She is dressed in a deep red velvet cloak. Miriam's instant response is that the woman looks disturbing, though beautifully groomed and well dressed, in an old-fashioned style. She could be on her way to the opera, behind her surely is the waiting arm of an elderly gentleman, a white kerchief pouring from his pocket.

'Mrs Goodman – we must go. I have a taxi. Your husband and your child are in danger. We must go and warn him, come with me.' Miriam looks beyond Hannah and sees a black cab waiting. Hannah has her back to the driver and he meets Miriam's eye and makes a small expressive gesture indicating possibly that he thinks the woman is somewhat unhinged.

Miriam releases the chain, remains standing in the doorway. 'Let us talk first.'

'No time! We have to go now! You must listen to me.' Safer outside than in, perhaps, thinks Miriam. She steps back into the room and unwillingly, fearfully, switches off the fire, wraps Paul in his coat and gets her own. She wonders what the hell she is doing – could the taxi driver be implicated, she wonders. How can Paul be in danger, he is safely here with her. She sees another taxi driving by, red light on, and, on impulse, flags it down.

'I will go in this one – follow you.' Hannah looks angry and distraught. She gathers herself.

'You absolutely must follow me, do you promise?'

'Yes, yes, anyway I know where to go ....' As the two taxis move off, Madeleine steps back from the window upstairs. She wishes she knew what that was all about. Perhaps a fancy dress party, but then Miriam would be in a fancy dress, wouldn't she? All very well for some, riding in taxis. She used to when her husband was alive. Just on their wedding anniversary they would get a taxi and go to the West End.

The bizarre caravan makes its way to King's Cross. Miriam holds Paul very tightly. No point phoning Jack, he will be in the middle of teaching. Paul is delighted. What a lovely diversion. Should she not have held her ground? Surely she could have prevailed if she had kept talking. This is ridiculous and unnerving. Miriam grips Paul too tightly and he wriggles away from her. She relaxes her hold. It feels as if she hasn't taken breath since the moment she opened the door.

The two taxis drop the women and child at the small church hall in King's Cross. Around the church and its hall, silent cranes squat on their building sites, within a sprawled tenancy of seedy, unkempt history, now subject to change and architectural invention. Just before they open the door, Miriam, having regained some control of her thoughts, grabs Hannah's arm.

'What is your name?'

'Hannah Bloom. If you knew anything about ballet, you would know me.' Hannah glares at Miriam. 'You will be grateful to me, my dear.' Miriam feels anxious and nauseous. Shouldn't she hail another taxi and take this woman away? Jack won't be at all pleased. Hannah shrugs Miriam's arm from her and reaches for the door.

'Wait,' says Miriam urgently, 'let's go and talk. This is all too fast. There's a café nearby. We'll go there ....' Her voice is rising, becoming shrill.

'Don't shout at me, you silly girl!' screams Hannah, her voice cracking in an unpleasant way. Paul starts to cry. Hannah opens the door. Miriam pulls at her arm. 'Let go of me, you are assaulting me!' Paul's crying rises to a pitch. Miriam, bereft of normal sense, follows the maddened old woman as she strides into Jack's class. The stillness of the class magnifies the panic and agitation that come pouring through the door. Jack is at the front, and about fifteen students, including Marie, who is standing near the back, are absorbed in a slow, complex movement. The entire class freezes. Hannah shouts at Jack. 'Do you see her?' – pointing to Marie – 'She is plotting to make trouble.' Hannah turns wildly to Miriam. 'Can't you see? – she will sit and watch you and hate you and ....'

Marie, white and shocked, stares at the crazed face of her employer. She wants to step forward calmly, coldly, and say stop this, this is ridiculous, but can only think of getting away. No, she must stay and engage. No, impossible, what would happen, only more ugly words and screaming. This can't be true. What the hell is going on? She cannot look at Jack – or Miriam, or the child. Adrenalin pushes her to flight, not fight. Painfully, swiftly, she gathers her belongings and leaves through a hushed line, each individual adjusting position as the devastated figure passes by. Marie is covered in a cloud of shame and cannot – will not – speak. Battling within the cloud, too fast for anyone to get a hold of her, Marie moves to the door and disappears. Jack – after a moment of paralysis – grabs Hannah's arm. 'Come with me – who are you? You have disrupted my class.' He steers her to a small room on the side, and asks the class to continue its practice. Miriam and Paul enter the room behind Jack and the door closes. The class struggles to remain composed and to continue with the instruction, but discipline breaks up and Jack's students whisper amongst themselves, worried, excited, curious, titillated. One or two are longing to put their ears to the closed door of the little room but restrain themselves.

The small room houses a rudimentary kitchen, with white cups and plates, an elderly urn, a small fridge, two chairs. It is shabby, but clean.

'Sit down, please,' says Jack to Hannah, pointing to a chair. 'And you darling and Paul, you sit here.' Jack strokes Miriam's arm, and stands near her. After the shock, he feels stony and calm. Hannah sits, trying to retain an imperial and confident look but, in truth, her eyes show bewilderment. She knows why she is here. Why does it no longer feel quite right? – she can't altogether remember what she is supposed to say. Or has she said it – that dreadful girl ran out, didn't she? Isn't that enough? Does that not mean she has been successful? Does she want to sit? Who is this man, ordering her around? He is nothing special in his silly trousers and she doesn't like the functional discomfort of the chair. In a faint resurrection of something familiar she says in disdainful manner, looking mostly at Jack, 'Do you not know who I am?' Jack thinks suddenly of his class behind the closed door, and comes to a decision.

'No, I don't, but you will have to wait for me to find out – I have something more important to do at the moment.' He steps out of the small room and tells the class he will have to end the session, that he doesn't know the old woman but she is clearly disturbed and will have to be taken care of. He will make up for lost time the next week. Yes, he replies to a question, everything is all right. And yes, he will check with Marie.

Jack moves back into the kitchen, closes the door and looks at Miriam. 'Do you know this woman, Miriam?'

'No, she came to the door and said you and Paul were in danger. So I thought I'd better not take a chance.' Jack goes to stand next to Miriam once more. They both look at Hannah who seems now to be shrinking, a thin figure in a voluminous and inappropriate cape, any sense of personal clarity dispersed, a face of confusion and struggle.

'Is that your boy?' asks Hannah.

'Yes,' says Jack, 'and I don't like him being disturbed.' The odd figure seems momentarily to recover her original sense of indignation.

'That girl, that one who ran away – she was going to disturb him ....'

'What do you mean?'

'You visit her, don't you – you bring her flowers and make promises ... silk and grapes and mirrors ....' Miriam gives a gasp and looks wildly at Jack. Jack grasps Miriam firmly, looks at her.

'Miriam, I don't know what she is talking about. I never visit Marie. She is my student. That is it.' Something subtle and powerful passes between man and wife. Miriam calms down. Covers Jack's hand with her own.

'She told me she is in love with you!' screams Hannah. 'And you are another liar and cheat and you will stay with your wife and forget the woman who has given you everything, all her life ....' Hannah stands up, Miriam cradles Paul and covers his ears, seems to will her body to provide a protective pouch for him. Unexpectedly, Jack laughs. A hard laugh.

'I have known Marie several years. She hardly talks to anyone, not to me. She is probably the most private person I know. Would she possibly confide in you? Ah ...' Jack breathes. 'You are the ballet dancer, ex-ballet dancer she ....'

'What do you mean ex? I was on stage with the greats and he would watch me week after week ....'

Jack turns to Miriam. 'At least now I know who she is – Hannah Bloom – I know that Marie works for her, helping her write a book.'

'Hannah Bloom, Hannah Bloom!' screams the old woman. 'Who cares?' She crumples, snorting dry sobs into her handkerchief, at the same time trying desperately to stop crying and regain dignity. It is a performance of painful schism.

'Miriam – I will take her home. Can't leave her like this. And I will come straight back afterwards. Take Paul out of here. Let me get you a cab first, see you safely in.' Nodding obediently, Miriam stands up, avoiding the old lady, wanting to be gone from her, aware of the anger of her husband, aware of his shielding arm. She can't quite believe that she is not finding her husband guilty, guilty – after all, here it all is, the woman she had suspected, running out of the room ... she should be hissing at him, side by side with Hannah Bloom, hissing with this avenging goose-woman, she should thank Hannah for revealing the awful truth, a truth she has long suspected. So why does everything in her breath, in her marrow, tell her that the woman is deranged, and that she, too, Miriam, has been deranged in constructing a fantasy of betrayal? The woman is like a hideous phantom from her own imaginings, a paranoia made flesh. She doesn't know how she knows this, she doesn't altogether trust it but she is going to be obedient to it, and allows her husband to lead her from the room, find a cab in the dark whispering street outside, hearing him instruct the driver in urgent tone of the address and to look after his family and drive carefully. Jack pays the driver and kisses Miriam and Paul through the open window. They drive off into the night, the cabbie, a man with a peculiar, nasal voice, chatting without awareness to the dark shape of the woman and child behind him.

The last student is leaving as Jack re-enters the hall. 'Are you all right, Jack?' she asks, her voice lilting with interrogation.

'Yes. One of those things. See you next week.' She goes out, reluctantly, slowly, as if Jack might suddenly call her and involve her in the drama, but Jack is back in the kitchen. Hannah hasn't moved. The young man looks at the old woman. Out of long habit, now that there are no women around, Hannah looks shyly up at the man, surely he will pay court as they all do ... all did ... on their knees, stammering and helpless in front of her beauty, the neatly shaped, turned-out feet, the slender back and the light definition of shoulder blade and clavicle. Ah, but all this is hidden within the cape. Hannah allows the cape to fall open. But Jack is oblivious to the charms within – he stares at her, not without compassion, and addresses her:

'What is troubling you?' Hannah teeters, trembles ... where will she go? Two roads open. The fastening of her cape comes adrift and a silken material reveals itself. Shot-silk peach. An old blouse, but still perfect. Hannah's hand reaches and automatically checks that the top button is done up. Her skin isn't quite flawless any more. Better a little discreet cover. More becoming. An unknown youngish masculine face is looking at her. He wants to know about her. See, there is always someone who wants to know about her.

'What is it you want to know?' Hannah asks in a kindly voice. Encouraging. The unbecoming kitchen vanishes, she is only aware of the gentleman looking at her. Her chin arches, her neck straightens.

Jack sighs.

'Why did you frighten my wife?'

'Darling – ' Her hand reaches towards him, touches his sleeve. 'It's all over now … don't worry.' Jack looks into Hannah's eyes, sees a flat surface. There is no exchange of glances. She has withdrawn, the curtain has come down. A hollow female shape nests in front of him within silk and velvet. A lost soul, waiting for her wedding, surrounded by finery and cobwebs. Jack, exhausted, sighs again.

'Let's get you home. Is there anyone there – at home?'

'The world, darling, it's all a stage and the world is there.' She extends her hand to him with unbearable aplomb and wraps the cape once more around her. Jack, with difficulty, finds out her address from her; she is in turn arch and defensive and then capitulates. Jack takes another woman to the front of the small church hall and, under the shadow of the squatting crane, hails another cab.

26

Marie holds herself together through an act of will, keeps herself steady. No-one goes after her, though there are some who would like to. She gives no backward glance to what she has left, but if she did, would see only negative space etched around Jack and Miriam, empty mirage within which their bodies shimmer; Hannah momentarily obliterated, a ghastly remnant like a fraying piece of old cloth, drifting beneath hazy, deceitful currents of air.

Marie travels on the underground, holds onto the rail as the carriage sways. The cool support is almost pleasurable, and she feels an odd gratitude to her fellow passengers, as they know nothing about what happened. They are innocent and she can borrow some of that quality from them. She gets off at Hackney Central and tries to maintain connection with the crowd pouring down the side entrance, but then, suddenly differentiated, feels distress as she gets to the bottom of the stairs, rapidly losing this unexpected comfort as she follows the familiar route home, opening her front door automatically, closing it and collapsing against it in tears.

The door offers solidity, safety, shelter from any prying eyes. She can barely move from it, her bag still hangs from her shoulder. Anger rises through the distress. 'How dare she!' she shouts. 'How dare she!' and the She – an amalgamation of Hannah the traitor and Miriam the gullible accomplice – the roaring She – taunts her with the rotten smell of failed sisterhood. She sees her own sister's face, the dangerous lovable Louise. And then the thin dark face of Hannah Bloom shows itself again and Marie almost chokes, shouting feelings of hatred and shame. 'I could kill you, you bitch, you stupid old woman you – contaminating my privacy!' No time here for the backward step away from distress and rage, to examine and contemplate disturbance. She is catapulted right into devastation. No escape. Marie drops her bag, steps out of her coat and leaves it on the floor. She lurches towards her bed, and falls on it so that the soft cover, the neatly folded cream cover, can act as bandage to pain. For unmeasured time she lies, weeping into the cloth into the relief of darkness, privacy, and the familiar shape of her bed.

Unseen by her, near her bed, is Han.

Tears slowly cease, bringing a troubled and exhausted peace. Marie lights a candle, takes off her clothes and gets into bed. Her swollen eyes slowly scan the room. She looks at her altar, gives a tired laugh. Not tonight. Of all nights. But can't. Too tired. Too washed out. 'What the hell Mims – fuck them all.' Louise's voice is so loud that Marie momentarily sits up. This is the common battle cry of her robust, reckless sister. Marie lies back down again, the warm furrow carved by her body receiving her in damp solicitude. Louise.

Marie recalls the sensation of trotting behind her sister through their tangled childhood garden in Greenwich, south London, the asymmetrical shape of the family home almost lurching at them. The tiles always look as though they are sliding off the roof, the doors seem to be swinging on inadequate hinges, no floor-line is straight, windows don't fit. The garden fights for space from the elderly but tenacious building, ivy covers the main wall at the rear of the house and has regularly to be hacked from the kitchen windows.

Louise switches from sweetness to cruelty without warning. It isn't so much malicious, Marie thinks. More like relentless curiosity about this small live object – her sister – and how it works. What makes it laugh so that it can't walk, and what makes it cry. Yes, all of that. However. What about the betrayal. Never talked about. Staring into the steady candle flame, Marie remembers.

Older than Marie by five years, Louise has her first serious boyfriend, Tom, when she is fifteen. The wild garden serves her beautifully during this period as no one can be seen through the mass cascades of green – ivy covering Virginia creeper, honeysuckle battling with roses, wisteria running amok around a derelict pergola. Louise sheds her knickers and her virginity without delay and handsome dark-haired Tom pushes his fresh testosterone ardour into Louise and they tumble into the hollows and the brambles and the nettles and the mulch. Marie – skinny, shy and ten years old, thinks Tom the most wonderful creature the world could possibly provide. She loves the way his rough jacket hangs on his lanky figure, she loves his almost blue-black hair, thick and wavy and very often pushed back in its profusion – pushed back with a weary and beautiful gesture only to flop forward again. Louise catches her once looking at Tom with her mouth open. 'Oh you dopey pet,' she says and then whispers into her little sister's ear (without unkindness), 'I think you fancy him ... you're not a baby any more, are you?' Marie shuts her mouth so abruptly she bites her tongue, the sudden pain underlining for her the danger of the moment. Fortunately, something else distracts Louise at that moment and she turns away from her sister.

Marie becomes obsessed with Tom. Since early childhood she has learned to track Louise so she continues to do this, against her better judgement and always in a state of delicious fear and excitement. Over the years she becomes a silent follower, skilled in moving quietly and blending her shape against tree and undergrowth should it be necessary. Maybe that is why she loves t'ai chi so much – the softness of the movements, stealth, the precision of alignment, the skill of invisibility.

One warm summer day, amusing herself on her own, a small, thin figure in a pink dress, Marie notices Louise and Tom. He is wearing jeans and a vest and she sees the hair under his arms and this makes her feel almost sick. They are so absorbed in each other they don't see her. They are kissing. Marie feels a different kind of sick watching this. A hurting sick in her throat. She has to keep watching even though it is so awful. To see. Their bodies pack together, pushing their tummies together and moving strangely. The four-legged monster moves away into a dark and overgrown corner of the garden behind a shed. Marie doesn't want to follow, but she can't not follow. Quietly, she finds a place where she can just about see. Louise is lying down, Tom lying on her, fussing with his pants, his zip, they are kissing and moving up and down, Louise's dress is up around her waist. Where are her knickers? They are on the grass near Tom. Marie can see Tom's bum and it is moving up and down and he is making funny grunting sounds and grabbing Louise's hair. Louise is making noises too. Marie suddenly wants not to be there any more. Stealthily, she moves from her hiding place but a twig cracks and – for one unforgettable, dreadful moment – Louise and her sister stare at each other over the humping back of the beautiful Tom. Snivelling in terror, Marie hastens back to the house. Her mother, busy, fretful, irritable, brushes Marie's hair from her face. 'Where've you been I've been calling you and I want Louise to do something.' 'Don't know where she is, she's out I think I saw her go out ....' 'What's the matter with you?' 'Dunno – a bit sick – berries ... I'm going upstairs.' And she bolts.

That evening, around the noisy family dinner table, Tom, now a fixture, sits next to Louise. They sit very close to each other, giving each other sidelong looks. Marie can see their legs pressing together. She crouches over her soup in terror. 'What's the matter with you?' her mother says again, more in irritation than concern. 'You look peculiar.' 'I'll tell you why,' says Louise loudly. 'I'll tell you why,' she repeats, until everyone looks at her. 'She's in love with Tom.' A silence falls and everyone looks at Marie. Her mother in irritation, her father in abstraction, Louise with hateful intent – and Tom with discomfort and some degree of kindness. 'Lay off babe,' he says to Louise mildly. 'I'll lay off if she lays off,' says Louise with a meaningful look at her sister. 'She knows what I mean.' 'Oh you two,' – their mother's mouth wrapping itself around the phrase with the tiredness of repetition without success. 'You're always...' 'Oh enough of all this nonsense.' Paterfamilias speaking. 'I want some more gravy please. This chicken is too dry.' A confused babble arises in Marie's head. She wants to deny the accusation and shout at Louise and she wants to say I saw them in the grass and they were doing something. But she keeps still. 'Hurry up with your soup, dear,' says her mother. 'Your father's on his second piece of chicken.' 'Well,' says Marie's father, Henry Deverell, solicitor, 'if you'd have given me a decent size in the first place ...' 'These chickens are smaller,' says Judy Deverell vaguely. 'Now what exactly do you mean,' asks her husband, suddenly animated. 'When you say "these" what are you referring to? All the chickens in London? Or in the dreadful supermarket where you shop?' 'Oh dad, leave her alone.' Louise's voice, sharply. 'How would you like to do the shopping? No, no,' she adds hastily as she sees her father take in a long breath. 'Don't answer that.' Tom bends over his meal and Marie wonders in agony how he can bear it and why doesn't he leave them never to come back? To her surprise, his mouth seems to be folding itself together as if he is stifling a laugh. She sees that he is squeezing Louise's hand. She catches Louise's eye – and wishes instantly that she hasn't. Louise gives her a look charged with a thousand meanings, all malevolent. After a fraction of time, Marie drops her head.

Marie looks back at this drooping child. A will to redeem arises within her. Undoing time, she cradles, with two strong hands, back and front, the child's head, raising it from its heavy posture. The space across the child's narrow chest widens, her head settles. Breath moves freely within her.

Aha! A resilient act, echoing from present time into past time! She couldn't do this for herself as a child. These conscious acts of alignment most of us cannot do as children. As a child she was bullied by the older one. Not seriously, but then she was a sensitive being and felt more than another who might have been able to push against the aggressive glance, or devise acts of reprisal.

Now I witnessed the awakening of an ancient soul and understood that she carried the imprint of many lives of training and discipline in the art of self-alignment. She sat up, raised her head, breathed steadily, filled her belly and her chest. Filled her body with calm intention – in the middle of the storm. She now let it rage around her but not within her core. She stepped away from the distortion, saw that it was not of her making.

I could feel her responding to the fruits of inner practice. Her spine gently straightened and lengthened, a small area of neutrality and calm entered her core. As I witnessed her, I felt tenderness bite me. I wanted to stroke her hair. I did not move ...

Marie rests in softly in her body. She feels relief. Pain is still there, frustration and betrayal. But it no longer chokes her, it no longer has possession of her. The simplicity of her act of redemption touches her. The holding of the child's head is followed by a movement from the base of her spine, through the spine and emerging, as it were, through the top of her head as a silken thread, pulling her out of the roaring waters and onto the shore. Odd memories, without form, touch in and out of her awareness. Eyes closed, she decides she will later phone Louise. They have not spoken for many months; theirs is not a highly communicative relationship. She will phone her and ask if she can come to Wales and stay with her for a while.

27

'Miriam ....' Jack stands before his white-faced wife. He is back at home. He tries not to think of the shocked and prurient faces of his students, of Marie's exit.

'Miriam. I know you are frightened and angry. You might even believe what that grotesque woman said.' He stares at her. Again, she knows this is not the look of a guilty man. She feels light-headed with shock, almost wanting to laugh and say did you see how her lipstick was running off the side of her mouth, the face of a mad clown ... 'Listen to me ... we've been wronged - you, me and Marie.' Miriam moves away from Jack. He grasps her arm. 'Please stay. We're in this together. I want us to recover from this nonsense.'

'Must you keep saying her name?'

'Whose?'

'Not ... that ... I mean Marie.'

'Yes, I will say her name. She is a decent woman who has not done anything divisive towards me or you. She is my student. And that's that. All the jealous thought has come from your mind – this disturbed woman is almost born out of your mistrust.' Miriam flinches as she realises this very same thought has come to her mind.

'It's weird.' Jack continues. 'I realise how I've been nervous about your jealousy and that's made me almost feel that I've done something wrong. It takes something like this to blow the shit out, doesn't it? Look at me ....' Miriam twists weakly to come out of his grasp but once more she is compelled by his manner and tone to stay where she is. 'I have to do something right now – and that is go and see Marie and clear this thing and put a line under it. I want her back in the class.'

'Why can't you phone?'

'No. I am asking you to accept this, Miriam. You are my

wife. I love you and want to be with you. Things have been scratchy between us for a while. Yes, I know that. Sometimes it has felt like the end. Sometimes I have wondered what you have been up to – there have been days when you looked different. I even wondered whether you'd been fucking someone else.' Miriam drops her eyes. 'Have you?' he demands – suddenly red-faced. 'That would be a fine thing,' he laughs without joy. It is a bitter sound and his cheeks look flayed.

'No. I have not cheated on you,' she says. Jack stares at her.

'I wonder if you would, if you could,' he murmurs more to himself than to her. Miriam thinks of Simon. Was that a cheating interlude? They didn't have sex, but they toyed with each other. No, she decides, I didn't cheat.

'I have not cheated on you,' she says more firmly, raising her head. Jack pins his eyes into hers. He sighs deeply and kisses her. Who would she cheat with? He conjures up a saturnine bastard with black eyes – someone she knows from the old days? Or maybe it's a blonde bastard with long wavy hair. Astonished that his libidinal self should arise at just this moment, Jack notices a corner where he might relish the thought of Miriam being with a saturnine or blond bastard – or the two together. He feels heat in his belly and a secretive joy. No, not for real he wouldn't like it, but in his mind, safely tucked into the confidential folder, he enjoys a moment of grandiose generosity to two men who are attracted to his wife and who give back to him a woman more desirable. Are women like this? he wonders. Don't ask.

Miriam looks dispassionately at the sharp lines around his mouth. Has she noticed them before? Are they always such a precise groove? She stares at her husband, as if trying to work something out.

'I am going now,' he says, 'and you are not going to make

a fuss. You will wait here for me without creating stories and alarm in your mind. And when I am back we will ... I don't know ... we will draw together. Wake up, Miriam. This whole thing is a wake-up call.' He moves from her, then comes back, clasps her under her thick mass of hair, gripping her by the neck and pulling her face to him. He rests it on his shoulder momentarily and then leaves. Miriam stands without moving. Her mind is scrambled and she looks for distress. This is completely distressing, isn't it? All she can find is a strange, unknown kernel of quiet within her. She is not who she thinks she is. She doesn't know who she is. Her body feels cold. She puts on a coat, and a scarf, and sits in the kitchen with her eyes closed.

Jack checks Marie's address in his work diary, calculates the journey and heads towards the station. He has no idea what he is going to say. He knows he must go; something needs to be done and he doesn't know what it is but it is of vital importance. Around his moving body, he experiences a compact fluidity. It seems to carry him along without effort.

I have been attentive all the while to the unfolding of event. I am moving with him even as I keep vigil with her. She is exhausted from weeping, but strongly held into her alignment. She waits and he moves with speed. A dedicated moment positions itself.

Jack knocks on the door. Waits a while. A soft and stifled voice calls out – 'Who is there?'

'It is me. Jack.' Marie opens the door. He is aware of her swollen eyes and drawn face, and of the patterns on the dressing gown she is wearing. Abstract flowers, he thinks. Poor girl, he thinks.

'Oh, for goodness sake ... what is ... well, please come in.'

Marie holds the door open and a small flicker of glamour lights itself in her ... in a place she knew before Hannah's devastation. Her dream; here he is. He is here, in her home. She is opening the door and he is coming in. The flicker vanishes. She feels shame and confusion. All that is over now, her secret love. It is rudely displayed, wrenched and embellished in an untrue way, its delicacy smashed and contaminated. That hateful woman, that .... Breath nudges at her, a graceful reminder. She straightens her head and the angry thought collapses.

'I would like to talk to you,' says Jack. 'may I sit down?'

'Please.' She indicates a chair.

'Will you sit down too?' Obediently, she sits.

'I am sorry,' she says.

'What for?'

'What she did.'

'Not your fault.' She is silent. 'A time like this,' Jack continues, 'needs honesty. It's odd, I feel something important is happening. Never mind that witch. Who cares. Look, Marie ....' He takes her hand in a neutral, friendly way. She allows her hand to be held, stiffly. 'I know there is feeling between us.' She tries to withdraw her hand, he holds on to it. 'No, not romantic ... I don't think. Hard to define. A kind of love, I think ... teacher and student maybe ... yes and no. It's as if ....' Jack pauses. The fluid state that envelops him as he travels seems still to be present. It has movement and yet also stability. It surrounds him as if he is wearing a gown of antiquity, a gown of deepest green billowing cloth, shot with gold. A glimpse of Marie from the corner of his eye shows her to be clad in the same material, clad in gold shot with green, the proportions of her colours inverse to his. The invisible – yet visible – fabric coils and uncoils around them, Marie's face changes; behind her he receives a glimpse of the outline of

Han's face. He seems to be hovering behind Marie, and she has the face of an oriental woman, small, with round cheeks, her eyes, looking downwards, eyelids, like elongated half-circles, resting their weight, their feathers, upon those cheeks. It is a face of familiarity. His heart is full. He knows his own face is different. This woman is very important to him – but he is compelled, forced, to leave her. Sorrow drenches his full heart with moisture. It is too heavy to carry. Something has to happen; the heart has to shed its load, the cloud has to break.

I formed again the third point of a Triangle. This time he and she held the two horizontal points and I was the rising point. This third position pulled their awareness to a different vibration. Holding the point strongly for them, I accessed the Records, and they and I received the images and experience of the last moments of their life together in the direction east from here, in that land, the land of my last human life, where the Palace was built and the Wall, and he one of the Emperor's guards and she his wife. Their eyelids were quiet and I knew they had achieved adequate reception. He remembered pain and annihilating blackness as the knife came down, and his desperate thoughts of her; she remembered the impact into her body of the knowledge of his death. They remembered, and I could feel a shift of resonance into their hearts and I aligned my heart to theirs. The two wounded figures from the past reached out to each other and were encircled by grace and a sense of relief. She held him and compassion poured into the horror and the loss. There was no altering of the destiny which called forth this tragic event. But through the thickness of time, we three extracted ancient memory, and they two made peace with it. He murmured; she sighed – and the sounds pulled them into the present.

Marie and Jack look at each other. It is a look of knowledge without words, of dissolving completion, as events fade rapidly, in the manner of the sea withdrawing pattern from the sand, leaving clear surface, time after time.

'I ... I ... don't know what to say,' Marie says quietly. 'Something feels better. I don't know what has happened. Something has happened. I think I knew you, and then lost you. And now I know that, it rests more easy. I feel a sense of gratitude and relief.' She sighs deeply. Jack gently releases her hand.

'I don't know what has happened. Yes, I also feel we knew each other. Very deeply. And had to part. This is extraordinary. Isn't life strange, Marie? If not for the old woman's crazy intrusion, we would not have come to this place. It's a kind of settling isn't it? And ....'

He is about to tell her about Han but decides not to. This reticence feels valuable and correct. Jack leans back. He notices, for the first time, the objects in the room. He wonders, without desire, whether men visit her here. He continues: 'Marie – please come back to the class. I value your contribution. We will find a way to ease you back again. We can think about something to say to the group. Or nothing. We'll see. The woman Hannah. Let it just vanish ... one way or another.'

'Okay, Jack.' Marie rubs her hands over her cheeks, she breathes deeply and stifles an odd yawning sensation. 'Yes – let me be truthful now. I have felt as if I were secretly in love with you. Didn't want to break up your marriage – anyway couldn't. I think you and Miriam are strong, if I may say so.' She yawns fully now, smiling a little, covering her mouth with her hand. She finds herself talking again. 'It feels kind of different now. As if I was in some kind of enchantment. As if it wasn't even really you. Well, yes and no. I like you very much – I love the way you teach. And I love t'ai chi. It gives me such a lot – but in a way the obsession was' – unexpectedly she giggles. Jack smiles. 'Yes, it was a nuisance. Got in the way. I felt like a foolish teenager.' She stops smiling, looks grave. 'No – that's to belittle something I don't understand and yet I feel very deeply. There was a way I saw you that was of the past – or inappropriate. Oh, I don't know. I can see you more clearly. And myself, in a way.'

'Yes,' says Jack, 'and maybe it kept you from opening to someone else. Well … None of my business.' She doesn't contradict this thought – looks at Jack carefully.

'What a day. What a night. You better get back home. I need to sleep anyway. And Jack, I probably will go away for a short while.'

'Yes,' Jack stands up. 'Whatever you need to do. Thank you, Marie. Thank you.' She smiles, her eyes are dark and there are deep shadows beneath them. She longs for her bed. She can feel sleep approaching, she wants to lay her head on a dozen pillows filled with goose-down. She wants to be lying still, in warmth and softness, white sheets and bedcovers around her. She wants the windows darkened and the room utterly quiet. She sees Jack to the door and he goes without ceremony. 'Sleep well. Thank you.'

I stayed with her. The sense of completion was fitting, yet, mysteriously, there was, I knew, an unknown strand in the field, not yet woven in. The sweet incarnate being I was watching folded herself into sleep instantly and I knew the blessing of karma appeased which was coming to her. I was aware too of the safe passage back home of

Dzukh; he moved swiftly and strongly.

A lamp is on in the bedroom. Miriam is asleep. Jack takes off his clothes. He looks at her face. It is smooth and young-looking, He sees the lineaments of Rebecca at the well; Ruth in the field. How could he ever imagine knowing or understanding this woman. She is his unknowable wife. Desirable, exasperating, mortal. Faithful – perhaps. How extraordinary that she is not sitting up in bed with a look on her face like a knife. The knife that cuts him and makes him stubborn and cautious. Moving under the sheets, he seeks out the curve of her hip, lays his hand there gently. His eyes flick to the corner of the room, suddenly dark as he extinguishes the lamp.

28

May I beg your attention for a short while, Dearest Brothers and Sisters. There was a contemplative mood fallen upon me after the witnessing of the Thread between Dzukh and Ma'li, and I paused to dwell upon meandering thoughts.

I was contemplating Hunger. I saw and felt the Hunger all around me.

We leave the great Sea of Becoming and take root (after seed and egg have fused) within human form. After a period of sheltered growing, the delicate physical form leaves its mother-cradle and is un-tethered into fragile earthly beginnings. The hungry mouth searches.

And we grow, and love and fight and fear, and leave home. And the hunger continues, seeking ever more elaborate versions of satisfaction available in the human realm, ever more wonderful promises of taste, distraction, reward, satisfaction. Bright eyes, comely bodies, brilliant minds, mischief, love and outrage and wickedness beckon and call.

There are those who complain, fight, howl – or make song – as they seek for the feeding ground in the body and soul of another. There are those who are more secretive in their search and snuffle around quietly, nudging their way towards possible connection. Some swear by starvation. I do not need; do not offer, do not give.

What can we expect of others, our fellow human creatures landed here upon the Green Planet? Promises broken, not maliciously, just sometimes too tired to love, to respond, to give the full quota of nourishment as came from that mother-sac. Babies cry, dwelling-places require care, survival demands work and food and shelter, creativity demands expression, attack and terror shatter peace. At times we arrive at the door of another who awaits us, and we are emptied and separate. Forgive me – I am not the Abundance that you need me to be.

In my long-ago time upon Earth, there was one who rooted into me and I into her and we called each other wife and husband. And yes, when she had to leave, I did suffer the loss of this kind of nourishment. And wept. And I was hungry and the rocks for a while were hard and unyielding when I tried to write on them. It puzzled some then that I seemed to forsake creature comfort for the discomfort of aloneness and exposure to weather, but that was what I did.

There have been men visiting the heart and body of the quiet one, Ma'li. Men who have come, and gone. With each had come promises, and the lilt of her flesh and heart believed that for now, maybe, there could be nestling and feeding and someone who would understand the bouncing heart in its cave and feel its pulse and its violence, this naked beating thing. And then, an unanswered question, an arrangement forgotten, an eye straying and not returning ... and one day, the heart registering again human separation. Or one day that hand of the other making savage with heart-strings, tearing and wrenching ...

After the visit from Dzukh, she intuited, without rancour, that she could not look to another to hold her heart. She began to understand the necessary death of hope and transference to another. She began to understand that we stand closely side by side with lovers and friends, giving and receiving, holding them in our hearts and being held, but not giving to another for safe-keeping this treasure within. The encounter with Dzukh helped her towards the initiation of this necessary, seemingly bereaved self-containment.

Then I rested my mind upon a beguiling aspect of dear Dzukh. His voice. Friends, have you noticed the delight you feel when you are accompanied by a human creature whose voice has a musical quality? Dzukh's voice was light but carried with it a darker timbre, an additional series of chords and notation to accompany the lighter sound. He would have been astonished to hear of this quality to his voice, that it soothed, that the after-resonance lingered and fell into raw ears, and deeper, injured listening places. For someone like Ma'li – allow me to use her name in my way – whose mother's voice had been critical, sharp, monotonous, and whose father's had a fussy, contentious tone, this restful quality entered her being like honey, coating abrasion and settling her restlessness, like a child who has been told she is to put on her night-clothes and go to bed, and her father is coming to tell her a story as soon as she has done this. And this is a father who will be there, who won't fail her. Quite like magic, he can decode the soft impressions of his child's feet as they pad into her room, and be there just as she settles under the bed-clothes.

So now, Friends, I wander and digress into an area of exploration about Father. The quality of father-nourishment in Dzukh's voice is not the experience I had in my incarnate life upon Cold Mountain, and yet upon my soul is a different and effective impression of a faithful father. I was taught by a father of few words, a sombre mien, and sense of discipline and attention to duty. He was not harsh; he was reserved. His care was demonstrated in consistency and effort. And when my attention moved from that Long-ago into this Time and Place, I felt, emanating from the young men who prowled the streets, empty and angry, a nervous wave of hunger for father, for the Yang that teaches a younger one his place in the unfolding. These boy-men, restless and lacking of focus, displayed movements jerky and fast, and hid in apparel pulled over their heads and covering their faces. I witnessed through the Records, a period, a short while back, of uncontained breaking and burning, where they ravaged parts of the city and caused fear, and at first the discipline of elders and the policing machinery of the state could not prevail. The broken, ashen fields of destruction caused loss of home and work to many ... and the city for some days held an atmosphere of disbelief and terror. The hunger for Place, for Purpose, for the dignity of a man moving his energy into the world, for arenas of legitimate battle between men testing their muscle, battle encoded into rituals and ceremonies within community, was palpable to me. Lost children, unused to discipline, containment and patience, and, above all, not trusting that the world they inhabited wanted them to succeed or provided support and opportunity for this to happen. A starving, maddened, grabbing and taking, and burning of the playthings on display.

In my previous sojourn upon the Earth, it was brutal indeed to be a young man. To survive and to have food on a plate one day and the next day, meant effort and work and struggle. And of course there was devilry and thieving and envy and killing. And friendship and loyalty and the passing on of rites of passage.

I felt sadness as the records showed me looting and burning as the young ones ran through the streets, watched in horror and anger by ineffectual elders; and then one arose, and, over the dead body of his youngest son, counselled peace. This elder, of noble countenance and powerful intelligence, shone like a star over the battlefield.

I was unmoved by the abstract speaking of those supposedly in high and moral and teaching positions. It is not from learned scrolls or dogma but in each and every action of our lives that we learn of the Mystery. Not decipher it, you understand, but learn of its presence. The practice of intelligence, awareness, silence and compassion, as some have understood, takes us towards the subtle hidden quality of the Mystery which hides in each one of us. The further we come away from this practice, the more our bodies and minds become restless and lost, the more hunger turns into torment and appetite is misunderstood and misdirected. The nearer we come, the more contented we are ... and this ultimately paradoxical nearness becomes implicated with not seeking, not finding, not having, for we know the Mystery we are seeking is, in truth, not to be found. Any Holy Fool will tell you this joke!

Ah, but I will cease now, Words are failing to convey, they are turning into snares and homilies. Forgive me, Dear Brothers And Sisters.

In my previous time upon Earth, when I was a young man carving poetry upon stones, the angry ones came at me with cudgels for what they thought I was doing or saying. I knew the effects of blind violence. I was at times the aggressor in previous lives. I knew what it was to see red and to raise a fist.

Angels we are, and demons, living our heaven and hell upon the Mother's soothing, miraculous and violent lap.

Allow me this little stream of language, Dear Friends, but if it tires you or offends the nature which seeks stillness, let the language flow past without settling or consequence.

29

When the sun begins to lower itself behind the hill, dark shadows come up quickly over the fields. Marie, accustomed to the way London dusk is compromised and mitigated by artificial light, finds in this rapid arrival of shapes an oddly frightening quality – long dark eels coming to wind themselves around her and drag her into muddy, brackish oblivion. These twisting shapes bridge the reality between her inner state, and the present visible world around her. She arrives in Wales to be with her sister, managing travel and packing, the organisation of money and leaving her flat in some sort of order, but she knows she is still deeply disconcerted. She is on the other side of something within herself. And she hasn't been to stay with her sister in maybe five or six years. City sister and country sister.

In the farmhouse near Abergavenny, Lou is careful with her, brisk and allowing. Anyway she has endless things to do involving her daughter, dogs, the house, the vegetables, and her friend Mart, labouring at the next farm. Marie is left to herself, to watch hills and shadows, as she adapts to different surroundings.

The sisters talk. It is evening, Becky in bed, the supper dishes washed up.

'Who is this bitch anyway?'

'I've mentioned her before – I've been ghost-writing her memoirs. Ballet dancer.'

'Oh yes. I can just see her, feet pointed sideways on one end and a scraggy neck on the other – she's off her fucking head, isn't she?' Marie bursts into nervous laughter at the juxtaposition of neck and head ... seeing a scraggy neck without a fucking head ... and ... but Lou has a way of saying these things with serious fury, and then Marie gets the picture and laughs. Lou doesn't know what's funny. 'What's funny?' she asks. 'One minute you're suicide miserable and the next ... are you okay?' She looks at her sister with sharp care. Marie lays her head in her hands.

'No, I'm not. I've had a horrible time.' She tells the story, the invasion of the t'ai chi class by Hannah, with a white-faced Miriam behind her, reluctant and disbelieving, and yet compelled to follow the shrieking woman. She doesn't reveal to Lou the extent of the complexity between Jack and herself, but does admit that she 'likes him very much' when Lou presses her. She doesn't reveal at all the strange, indescribably precious change that occurs between her and Jack. She allows Lou to follow a more mundane reality. She enjoys this level of exchange with her sister, if truth be told.

'How much?' asks Lou, sniffing like a bloodhound after a rabbit.

'There was nothing between Jack and me. He's married with a kid. I saw him at class and that's that. I know I am a good student – I always turn up and I practise hard – and teachers like students like that.' Marie gives Lou a keen look. 'Are you insinuating that I ...?'

'No,' says Lou firmly. 'The woman's clearly a nut-case. Why though does she pick on you? You worked for her, did you confide in her that you liked the guy?'

'Well,' Marie pulls a face. 'I did once say I really liked him but that he had a wife and child – just like I've said to you – and so that's it. End of story. It was while we were talking about her love affairs. Dahling.'

'But why,' says Lou slowly, 'does she pick on you? Was it pay-back time for something? Did you say something that made her mad? Was she jealous of you?' Marie gets up and starts drying and stacking some of the plates left near the sink. 'Leave them love,' says Lou. 'I never dry. Only cutlery, funnily enough. Doesn't make sense. Why not leave them to dry too? Is it something in our childhood do you think? What did mum do with cutlery?'

'Haven't a bloody clue. I tell you what though. After I said this about Jack having wife and kid, her face went really peculiar. It seemed to go peaky and sour – as if she had a lemon jammed up her nose ....'

'Juice running down her scraggy neck ....'

'Yes!' Marie laughs. 'No really, Lou, it was like a really bad smell ... as if everything inside had turned to garbage. Cancel the lemon. Just that garbage smell coming out. After that I left – half an hour early. And I think I heard something saying go now, go now ....'

'Was that the last time you saw her, before the denunciation?'

'Yes.'

'And from what you've said, the class didn't round on you but felt for you – this lunatic coming to mess up your patch.'

'Yes, more or less ... Yes. But still, you know – I keep myself to myself there and even decent people get excited about a bit of scandal and there it was.'

'Indeed.' Lou gets up, absently takes the dish-cloth and begins drying cutlery, taking particular care with forks, cleaning between the prongs. Marie watches her, different expressions criss-crossing her face. 'You're a picture, Mims. What are you thinking now?'

'Why do you clean the forks so carefully?'

'Dunno. I'm a disturbed child. Mum used to clean forks when she breast-fed me?'

'No, you saw the parents having sex and you thought fuck meant fork.' Lou makes an indecent display with the plain, decent fork she is drying, puts it away and sits down with the cloth in her hands.

'So what will you do for a job now?'

'Least of my worries – I have some money – been living like a nun in London. Oh and I can pay you for being here.'

'Don't be silly – I mean yes, of course – shopping will be nice. Adding to the food store – we'll talk about that. It's fine for you to be here. Never thought you wanted to come. Just thought you wanted to have your meditation and your t'ai chi and London stuff. Well, I don't know about all that. It's quiet enough here – well, different quiet. Quiet is quite noisy in the country, come to think of it. Anyway there's the spare room so just stay.' Lou adds thoughtfully: 'It's nice for me. You could keep Becky company when I'm not here sometimes.' Marie looks at Lou with narrowed eyes. Does she still feel like little sister? Yes and no. In this moment she feels older. Louise is pretty. These days she leaves her prettiness alone rather than enhance it as she did in younger times. She has a small nose, broad cheeks, a full lower lip and bright eyes. In the make-up days her mouth would be generously painted and the full lower lip would glisten and call attention to itself in a tantalising, combative way. Louise, looking at Marie, notices the refinement and delicacy in her sister's face. It is beautiful – the kind of beauty which takes time to reveal itself. A rising sense of light, washing itself through her skin. Most people, rapid rather than slow, miss this subtlety.

'Not here?'

'Well, I stay with Mart now and then.'

'What do you usually do?'

'Becky stays with friends. Not often. Mart comes here, too.' Louise's mouth, the plump bottom lip, makes a suggestive shape.

'It's come to that?'

'To what?'

'With Mart?'

'What do you mean "that"?'

'Forks.' They both laugh, and a potentially sensitive moment of how much to say, or see, is – just for now – averted. Marie flickers through her memory – how much has Lou told her about Mart? She remembers phrases from infrequent emails and phone discussions ... a friend ... nice man ... amusing ... helps around the place ....

Marie is suddenly as tired and flaccid as if someone has punched her in the middle. Her whole substance is doubled over, unable to hold itself up. She needs sleep, privacy, time. She needs to cry. By herself. 'I think I'll go to bed. Thanks, Lou ...' They pat each other as Marie passes her sister and walks heavily upstairs. The stairs seem particularly steep. Isn't that always so in farm-houses? Steep and malicious somehow, as if loose pieces of wood are out to trip her, and each step further away from the next as she climbs higher. She suddenly feels uncomfortable in this farmhouse, and then offers herself the possibility that a person, her sister, is sheltering her and offering kindness.

30

Marie settles into the Welsh cottage, the containing landscape of rolling hills, sheep, the routine of time and daily requirement, and the weave of her sister's life. The little room she has at the top of the stairs takes on the character of her flat in Hackney: clarity of space and object, the placement of a few things she brought with her, a white silk cloth over the bed, and her dressing gown hanging from the door. The stairs are no longer hostile. She finds a flat piece of ground behind the house where, daily, in the early morning, she practises t'ai chi. The horror of Hannah's invasion of Jack's class has not disappeared, but it has receded. A small ache in the heart reminds her; missing the class reminds her. Jack's arrival at her flat, their conjoined experience of unspoken and yet known revelation and the words he afterwards offers her remain as an astonishing palliative spread over the shock.

In the fenced-off field behind the house, a nearby farmer grazes six young Welsh black bullocks. They have strong glistening bodies and chew, sleep and stand around the field all day. At about five in the afternoon, daily, they push and butt at each other. Marie has come to watch for their position on the field as she steadies herself for practice. Their blackness against the intense green of frequently rained-upon meadow delights her.

As the days pass by, Marie draws closer to her sister and enjoys her active, pragmatic qualities. Lou presents a lack of self-consciousness, an immediacy of thought and reaction. When the two sisters grow up, Lou takes on the role of tough pioneer, and Marie of hidden poet. As is the way of families, the differences become stamped on them through family nicknames – rebel, and dreamer – and they occupy two ends of the same line, exhorted, each of them, to be a little more like the other. Lou, can't you be a bit more thoughtful ... Marie, can't you be a bit more confident ...

The sisters are shelling peas and grating carrots for the evening meal. Mart is coming, as he often does, and is bringing a friend from London.

'Has Mart always been a farmer?'

'Oh no,' says Lou briskly, throwing carrot tops and scraped skin into the kitchen compost bucket. 'He's older than he looks, you know. Mart is in his late fifties.' Marie looks up in surprise. 'Thought you'd be surprised – he's always been an outdoor man – very clever, started as an academic and couldn't stand it – has to be working with his hands, preferably outside.'

'He doesn't talk much.'

'You've noticed.'

'But for you, Lou – you're such a conversationalist – you love words and ideas – how does that work?' Lou pauses, resting her hands on her lap. Marie looks at her sister's bright face – broader than hers, the pronounced cheeks and lip – would anyone know they were sisters? Perhaps from gestures and expressions rather than from features and colouring. And who would have imagined, after Lou's spectacular sexual escapades as she escaped the family home in Greenwich, that the aggressive and rebellious young woman would end up on a farm in Wales, living within a small, minimally organised community, bringing up a child on her own.

'Well,' Lou gets up from the chair and reaches for a large saucepan from a rack near the cooker. She fills it about halfway with water, puts it on a gas ring on the big old cooker and lights the fire. Marie watches the flickering flame beneath the metal with pleasure, pleasure based on nothing but the sound and sight of fire against metal. 'He's a quiet man. It's good for me, and sometimes I could kick him. He's a big stone

I can lean against and he's a big stone I want to kick ....' Lou grins and Marie sees a younger face.

'And you and men, Mims?' Lou is moving around the kitchen, bringing potatoes for Marie to peel, and onions and garlic to slice.

'This might sound weird – I feel a little haunted. As if there is someone I can't see but he's there. I thought it was Jack, you know, my t'ai chi teacher, but it's not him. He came straightaway to see me after the nightmare and we experienced something strange but it felt right.' Marie sighs. 'Am I rambling?' But Lou is now distracted by the requirements of cooking, and says so. Marie continues her task silently, reprieved by Lou's loss of attention from having to tell Lou about Jack's words to her. She doesn't want to tell, but within the sisterly intimacy she could feel herself tempted into confidences she might later regret. She focuses on the uneven floor of the kitchen, her sister's hands, busy, the light fading outside, the absence of city phenomena. She likes the reduction of thought and pressure within her own mind but she won't stay here too long, with Lou. Weeks? Certainly not months. She will want to go back. And she will go back to the class and look for another job.

What to do about Hannah? She owes her a month's salary, Marie has substantial written material on her computer, not yet passed on to Hannah. Her mind gives an irritable shrug, she loses the peace of a moment ago. And she is missing Hannah's narrative. Although the experience in the shrouded flat is sometimes claustrophobic, this is an interesting story and a rather remarkable woman. Marie has pride in her work and enjoys shaping words. She has become involved in the task, and the unfinished story tugs at her. What next? She wants to know.

'Do you know the one thing I miss about not having telly

here?'

'I cannot guess.' Marie looks at Lou in surprise.

'It's watching running. Really good athletes giving their all. Always makes me cry. Not just athletes – anytime I see anyone really being applauded because they're busting a gut – giving it their all, you know ....' Marie notices a photograph of Becky, now aged nine. The photograph was probably taken when she was about six. It is a school sports day and the little girl is flying towards the finishing tape, her mouth wide open and her eyes squeezed shut. 'Yes,' says Lou, 'I love that picture. I hugged her nearly to death after she'd won that race. I loved her so much it was unbearable.' She begins to combine flavours for a sauce. Cooked apples, nutmeg ... she looks for the grater; it is lying in the sink, shreds of carrot still attached to some of the holes.

'It's the parents, you know – our good parents. Decent folks, yes. But no praise, never. Don't spoil the children. It was more like very nice darling but you could always do better ....' Marie remembers the sense of disappointment that always accompanies these small, measured doses of praise. A permanent insufficiency, hardly acknowledged, because, after all, weren't they lucky and no one should get above themselves.

'Oh exactly,' says Lou as her daughter walks in, draped in necklaces and brightly coloured scarves.

'Good evening, darlings,' says the child in a grand tone. 'I am Madame Fifi and when I come in you have to curtsey.' Lou and Marie meekly bow to the gleaming child who then adopts a different tone and says that she is hungry, extremely hungry, and wants to eat right now.

'Ready soon – Martin is coming with a friend of his, Terence.'

'Terence! Yuk! What a silly name.' Remembering the

constant, limpid stream of mild reproof they were fed on, Marie waits for Lou to remonstrate with her offspring, and caution her not to offend the guest. This does not happen. Becky is given a piece of bread to eat and chews it in front of a small mirror, exaggerating her jaw movements and opening her mouth wide to examine the sticky, masticated mess within. Beyond the kitchen, seen through the window and a filter of steam escaping the pot, the day loses its light and dusk begins to play its tricks. The hills, accompanied by their shadows, resemble vaporous figures, moving slowly towards the house, visible only to Marie, who is suddenly melancholy from the remembered lack of whole-heartedness from her family of origin. She wants to open her arms to Becky and tell her she's wonderful and what funny faces she's making, but Becky is seemingly quite happy without her commentary or approval.

The door opens and two men walk in. Martin first, his cheeks red and his eyes bright. He is a fit, wiry man and he brings an atmosphere of energy and competence with him. Behind him comes a man with grey hair, thick and wind-blown. 'We had a race up the hill,' says Martin happily. 'This is Terence and he nearly won.'

'Terence Faulks,' says the man shaking hands with Lou and Marie and then turning towards Becky but clearly not sure whether to shake her hand or not.

'Don't risk it!' calls Martin playfully. He moves up to Becky and gives her hand a vigorous slap. She slaps back. 'See what I mean?' says Martin. 'This is a tiger. The only remaining tiger in Wales. Very rare beast.' Terence moves back, holding his hands up in mock surrender.

'Okay, I have been warned.' He looks around. 'What a lovely kitchen.'

Becky moves up to Terence and looks at him candidly.

'Do your friends call you Terence?'

'Mostly. Why?' Marie holds her breath.

'Can I call you Terence? I don't know anyone called that.'

'Sure.'

'Do you have children?

'No.'

'Can I show you my toys?'   Lou taps her daughter on the shoulder. 'Excuse me, my dear, we need your services here ... table set yet?' With a lack of quarrel which surprises the two visitors, the child rummages for cutlery and begins to place knife, fork and spoon at each place. She measures distances carefully: knife, fork, spoon at the top.

Martin removes a bottle of red wine from his jacket pocket and finds the corkscrew. He knows his way around here, thinks Marie, feeling a flush of envy. What would it be like to have a man in her small place, someone who knows his way around? Normally, Jack's face would arise at this point. He would be the figure she is longing for, taking up place in her home, her bed, picking up the corkscrew with confidence and knowing where the wine glasses are. It is an odd thing, but true, that this fantasy simply dies after Jack's visit to her on that dreadful day. He becomes a brother, a protector, his hand grasping hers without sexual interest or romantic intent. And after that neutral but loving gesture, she has no need to make an effort, no need to force herself to see Jack differently. When he touches her hand in that way, a particular view of him, loaded with emotion, discharges itself.

Marie looks at Mart, at Terence, in naked scrutiny, a woman looking at two men without the containing shell of connection to another man not present. Her mind, her body, make blatant inventories. She hasn't felt a capacity for this kind of looking in a long while. There is a smart sea-taste in her mouth. Fresh salt, something alive. And at the same time, still, lightly, that haunting feeling of someone ... not Jack. Someone else. Marie shivers, and then becomes distractedly involved in the business of eating and drinking with new friends.

'What work do you do in London?' Terence asks her. He is a large and serious man and his shock of grey hair is now settled after battle with the wind and the running race up the hill.

'Well,' says Marie carefully. 'That is why I am here. I am not sure if I still have work. But my last job was with a ballerina – an aged ballerina – ' Lou sniffs loudly and starts to speak but then changes her mind and helps herself to more wine.

'My father's mad about ballet,' says Terence.

'Your old fellow?' asks Martin. 'He's still with us?'

'Jeremy? Almost. In a home now ... one of those fairly decent places where people talk to each other and there are discussion groups and music evenings and so on ... so he is being looked after in that way.' An uncomfortable look passes over Terence's face. Marie wonders whether he feels guilty that his father is in a home, but decides that this is none of her business and anyway, it is a cliché to think that way.

'You didn't really have much time with him?' asks Martin, sitting with his arm around Lou's chair, his wiry frame benevolent and inclusive not only of Lou but of all around the table. Becky slides off her chair and comes to sit on Lou's lap. She has eaten earlier and is now chewing on an apple.

'No,' says Terence. 'Well, my parents split up – there was an accident. They didn't separate right away, I had perhaps ten years with them as an only child. So to speak. You could say they had split up even though they were together.' Terence looks uncomfortable, as though he wishes he had never spoken ....'

'A bad accident?' asks Becky, looking intrigued and upset

at the same time, forgetting her next bite.

'Do you know what?' Lou announces. 'This is way past your bedtime. What an unthinking mother I am. Let's go up, young lady.'

'But I want to hear about what happened ....' Becky's lower lip begins to tremble.

'I am going to tell you a story,' says Lou swiftly. 'In fact a continuation of the one we started last night. Say goodnight to all.' She picks Becky up, and the child drapes her long skinny legs around her mother, half-eaten apple still in one hand, and pushes her head against Lou's neck. Marie feels a prickle of tears against her eyelids. She notices her sister's skill with the girl and knows that she wants to be the mother of this sweet girl; she wants to be the daughter of this intelligent mother. She gets up and kisses them both.

'See you in the morning, ducky.'

'Will you tell me about the accident in the morning?' asks Becky.

'Say goodnight to Mart and Terence and Marie,' says Lou, moving off swiftly.

Martin opens the door to the hall and the stairway to the bedrooms, closes the door after them and gathers the bottle of wine as he returns to his seat.

The meal continues as a kindly and amiable event. Marie's inventory has done its work and left her neutral and unattached to any outcome with either Martin or Terence. Martin because he is with Lou and Terence because he is not her type. There is no chord between them whatsoever. And actually Martin is not her type either. Once more, this is the moment when the Jack-anguish would kick in; bleeding her and filling her at the same time. It doesn't happen. She feels around her psyche gingerly. It is odd. A hole, an absence, and also a relief.

'Tomorrow, my esteemed sister, we are going for a drive to Llanberis and I am taking you up Snowdon in a steam train. It's not far; Becky will stay with her beloved Martin who, despite his appearance, can be twisted around her finger. Right?'

'And what man does not want to be twisted around the finger of a sweet woman?' Martin smiles at Lou and she gives him a steady look. Terence and Marie build a temporary, flimsy bridge between each other and talk about London and working freelance. Terence is an accountant, gave up a job in a large company and now works for himself with just a few, long-term clients. He asks Marie what she might do if the job with the ballerina comes to an end.

'Do you know – I haven't given any thought to what next ... I suppose the job hasn't officially come to an end though it's hard to see how I can go back after what happened. In fact, I didn't tell you,' – Marie looks brightly up at Louise and then briefly at Martin and Terence – 'the small independent publishers I told you about have offered me part-time work editing and I might pick up on it.' Louise smiles. Terence's face remains politely interested but he doesn't question further. He has a mute quality around him, a sense of privacy. Marie imagines him to be a reassuring presence to his customers. Perhaps she should have a conversation with him about her finances. That is something she never thinks about. Money comes in; it goes out. There is enough. She has always been like this. What need to talk about it to anyone else? She might emerge looking foolish. She doesn't feel foolish. The system has always worked. Lou seems to have a similar attitude. Neither of them has pensions or investments. Their father had a rigorous portfolio. He was an old-fashioned investor, looking for rock-solid companies, substantial. He would have hated cyber banking and dot.com investments.

'I'm just thinking about dad and money,' Marie engages Lou who is pouring cream over portions of gooseberry crumble.

'What are you remembering?' Lou licks her fingers, with candid enjoyment.

'Well,' says Marie, looking this time at Terence. 'I think each time he drove past his bank he would imagine that in a vaulted corner, under lock and key, his money would be sitting in neat piles.'

'Dusted each day by a uniformed bank attendant.' Lou's mouth is lightly touched with cream and crumbs. She reaches for a paper napkin.

'That's advanced!' Martin joins in. 'I think my dad had his under the mattress.' Marie anticipates that Terence might accelerate the narrative but he doesn't. He has a reserved and thoughtful look on his face and Marie wonders whether the arrival of money as a theme sends him immediately into dutiful attention. A defence against havoc? A shock of remembered havoc enters Marie's awareness; the door opening, Hannah's gargoyle face, followed by Miriam, strained and white and holding a sleepy little boy. She sees Martin, Terence, Lou and herself sitting in a warm kitchen in a solid stone farm-cottage in Wales, the child upstairs, safely tucked into bed, four adults eating around a sturdy oak table. Who's to say a long-sleeping Welsh dragon won't awaken and shake its blood-red stifled wings and grind its teeth against rocky platelets and heave itself above ground, hurling fire and sulphur over forests and grazing lands? What unimaginable hazards lie buttoned under Wales's green carpet? What vengeful dragon might be picking its way through the casings of Terence's heart? Through any of their hearts?

Marie is first to leave the table. She goes carefully up the steep steps, placing one foot in front of the other heel to toe, mindful of the boiling empty space beneath her, whirling with meteors, dragons' eggs and stars newly forming and dying in a whirl of gas and fire. In an excited state, she ascends to her room in the attic.

31

After the spoiling conjured by the crone-woman, Ma'li, upon whom this contamination fell, gathered together a few belongings and left her dwelling-place. She went to a large gathering point under a high roof and of a particular sound of metallic purring. From this building issued parallel metal lines and upon these moved elongated carriages, one yoked to another, and with a powerful leader-chariot at the front. It was a marvel to feel the surge of energy as the leader moved from its stationary position. There was a constant coming and going and many people climbed onto the carriages to leave and be taken away, and many emerged from the opening doors when another carriage and its faithful leader arrived and brought them back.

Days and nights passed after this departure, and, within the witnessing of all that was unfolding, I waited to receive awareness of where Ma'li had concluded her journey. As I concentrated and descended into silence, I began to see green fields, upon which were sheep grazing and rivers flowing; nearby the mysterious and varied shapes of mountains. This delighted my soul and tears came to my eyes for the memory of my beloved Cold Mountain, far away, found by following a yellow ribbon which winds around the Emerald Planet and brings us to the East.

A quite particular contentment entered me as I felt the being of the young woman held by the mountains' detached benevolence. I felt also the movement of inner landscape, the lines and contours of fate and destiny which arise from cosmic patterning and weave us into our lives. I particularly saw the man she had met at the farmhouse near her sister's home. He carried an element within his story which tied him – though he knew it not – to the old woman, initiator of the spoiling. It could be that fate was drawing him to Ma'li so that she could bring him to the old lady and a circle drawn around the terrible story of the death of his brother ... and yet, and yet ...

Long have I studied the workings of the Great Lord of Karma and I have learned that under his Eye, events do not always take such an obvious turn. Although Advanced Souls may be granted moments of insight, there is no prediction possible from the restricted perception of everyday mind. We humans, within our fledgling fragment of consciousness, often call out 'Not Fair!', not being able to see that This Great Being holds an Intelligence so terrifying, so beyond our comprehension that to tug at Its Garment is to bring a shower of mist and tarnish before our eyes. We are only able to agree, and surrender to that which we cannot control, and cannot grasp. Stories unfold, and unfold in their own Time, and in their own Way.

Ah! I momentarily saw a beautiful journey into mountain peaks, some of them already dusted with snow, which Ma'li took with her sister. They were drawn up the mountain by a steaming machine, beautifully polished and painted of black and red colour, and pulling two carriages within which sat men, women and children. Upon their return, they walked down, and a winding path took them through vistas and valleys, rocks and grasses and trees tolerating a cold wind, coming eventually to a lower incline, upon which were sheep, looking at them and chewing. They had stopped at a hostelry at the very peak of the mountain and there they drank warm liquid and ate food. Then the sisters walked quietly and strongly together on the peak, and I had access when they looked down upon the valley from a high point.

Consequent upon communion towards the quiet one in the mountains and the Awareness that followed, I found myself attracted to the ribbon leading eastward. Thus did I send messengers, a cohort from my very Being, to the corner of the Green Mother where I had my last incarnation and thus, remaining anchored to the Ancient Isle, did I roar and tumble and slide past cold climes and tundra and gatherings of northern animals upon snowy ground, through myriad qualities of light and apparition until I descended in consciousness to the very place of the birth of my last embodied self, and Cold Mountain felt my presence and the poetry from countless Whiles before rose up and whispered, he is here, Han Shan is with us ... and Thou, Spirit of my Beloved Mountain – unchanged – but of course your Holy Body affected by human curiosity, requirement, greed. The movement of humans upon place and time had wrought pressure and change upon the land and landscape. Habitation pressed down upon green shoots and many a tree had given its life in man's service. I manifested continuous contact, retaining my connection with Cold Mountain, and absorbing as well territories Further North, and prevailing also toward the Great City where Emperors once dwelt in the Palace. Here, now, tall dwellings and working places and working compounds pushed towards the heavens, these constructions no different in style and structure from those I saw on the Ancient Isle where Dzukh has his life, and indeed saw I the same on my journey thitherwards, dotted here and there upon the Earth's face, upon all different landmasses. Tall buildings, straight, like trees, with many shining windows. And though the people speak in varied tongues, the small device for speaking and listening appears everywhere in their hands and speedy words fly from one corner of the Mother to the other incessantly, day and night, and this Eastern corner signals to the West and back comes a signal, within the shortest While.

The faces of people from different landmasses continued to express a variety of colour and shape. The particular dress from My Time, full trousers and flowing shirts, with delight and recognition I saw, and, interwoven into this contour of expression, hither and thither I also saw people, clad as their Brothers and Sisters in the West, displaying cloth of the same cut and colour, of a style and quality that is now common in many places. Whether this is good or bad is not the point. Neither is it good nor bad. It is what is happening. The Ten Thousand Things continue to spill out from The One, forever changing, forever the same.

Hovering over the entire Land of my Previous Incarnation, observing both the detail of the end of one street corner and the turning into the next, observation of the bricks and stone of the walls, to observation of the undulation of fields and valleys, rivers and mountains, I felt an uneasy movement within my awareness, as if blood were altering its course and turning around upon itself. Then beheld I the great river, of a colour not green or blue, of a colour not brown but more of a yellow and brown, and I heard the pain of this Being for She had been obstructed in her course and forced to cluster her waters in a great container, and the direction of her Essential Nature had been altered and the body of the land around her, shocked and disrupted, sought to recover itself. Dwelling places were fallen into disrepair and human community dismantled and despatched. Then did I weep and my tears entered her Body.

Multiple impressions did I receive, and I knew that the diligence and stoicism of this tribe of my body-memory was still intact. The postures of people bent in the field, cultivating crops, working with beasts, replicated images from my history, demonstrating obedience to labour and requirement. Different, however, the constant rapid calligraphy streaming through the ethers, these ethers previously of relatively pristine and clear quality: what you, Dear Friends, may be calling Air but is more than – and less than – air. Ethers: the sensitive non-material upon which is written the resonance and echo of daily life.

Layers of experience shuddered through the ethers, Friends. Remnants of war, of industry, of family joy and sorrow, of sickness and death, of killing and love, of song and dance, decoration and the cultivation of animals and plants, and all within the particular calibre of this Place and its People. The Great City in this particular Now I observed to be inhabited by many of different races, but the central plains knew mostly their own people, barely an Elsewhere inhabitant in these parts. Bodies born from this corner of the Earth and returning, born and returning ...

Scanning the Central Plane, the mighty Henan Province, did I let my awareness rest, gently and with pleasure, on the burial ground of a great t'ai chi family. From a visit to these Masters did Dzukh learn his craft and hone his skill. I saw the stone memorial tablets of each vanished Master. Terrible times visited this place, when the tyrant who initiated himself as benevolent began to turn one family member against another and who wrote in a Red Book of the iniquity of this Art, distorting its beauty with descriptions of betrayal and encouragement of wrong-thinking. He attempted a strange insistence, requiring, as it were, that all sheaves of corn grow in the same way and bend to the wind and receive the rain in the same way, that there should be a uniformity in each growth and that difference be trained out through the binding of each plant to a rigid metal pole. As it were.

I saw in the village around the burial ground a school of excellence where young men and women gathered to absorb the art. A very small child in bright blue silken robe kicked the dust and projected his body from the ground, to return with ease and grace, his form elastic and compact. As I took delight in this child, I required no material listening and talking device to communicate my joy. On a sweet impulse did I send a message to Dzukh. I co-ordinated my Being with his, and did impart a picture of this place for which he feels great reverence. Halfway through a movement in his class – the movement which I have previously described, Wave Hands like Clouds, requiring a turning of the waist as a millstone and the hands to circulate, mirroring each other, the feet stepping lightly one after the other – he received my message, and delight infused his body and this transmitted to those around him.

Young Dzukh. Ah! I think on his mouth. The cast of facial and body feature, you see Dear Friends, always tells a story. This element of Dzukh's face tells of strength and determination. His mouth does not open and shape words when this is not necessary. He waits, he feels no obligation to amuse or impress. This gives him additional inner strength. Words are exquisite instruments when used with finesse and care. Without care, they tumble and fall and thus create noise and confusion. Some human creatures of agitated nature need to talk all the time; this shows an unquiet quality of heart, for heart and tongue are linked in the body alliances. Thus was it discovered by the Great Taoist Sages who showed also kidneys and ears, lungs and nose, liver and eyes to be in special mutuality. The body is a system in communication with itself. When we disregard this, we create alienation and damage for ourselves.

Dzukh the Warrior, in this life on the Ancient Isle, is sent to repair damage along the masculine continuum of his ancestral family. He will be turned to examine his irritation and selfishness. He will also hone the skills hard-won during other lifetimes, skills in the practice of t'ai chi, and this will bring benefit in an unexpected way. Ha – but I am leaning into the Future, and the Future, as I mentioned previously, does not exist, so I am playing with insubstantiality. I bring my attention to neither past nor future and see the child in the blue silk suit playing with a cat. The creature is lying in the shade of a tree, away from the hot dust in front of the school building, and the child is teasing it with a small twig from the tree. I am of course not embodied as I observe the scene. The child is too young to attune himself to a Disembodied Poet unless I were deliberately to engage him. This is not for me to do.

When the Being of Abiding Wisdom did request my agreement to sojourn upon the Green Planet, she breathed no intimation of the detail of what I was required to do. To apply the trajectory of language to the task required of me is to misrepresent. Dearest Friends, you who are attending upon the telling of my visit, let me rather tell you that the life I had as Han Shan was a life of distinction, creativity and obedience, a life of crystallised knowledge and perfection, even though on the human plane there was hardship, loss and suffering. Of course. The life as Han Shan was a diamond-point of obedient and loving devotion, and after that While upon the Green Planet, in this Eastern corner of Her Body, it was decreed that I was to journey the non-material realms for rest, replenishment and learning. This is how my faculties of awareness and understanding developed. I have travelled to many worlds that carry life in all its differing forms, but of course the Mother Earth, whom I most love and recognise, is my primary home.

Dearest Friends, it is love that has brought me back. I returned to dwell alongside Channels and Gates of Excellence and Compassion within the Field of Being. Those of you with a response of love towards this Field did receive from me Radiance beyond your imaginings.

It is written in many Great Traditions that amongst you always walk Beings of Another Order. Mostly unseen and unknown. In one Wisdom School it is written that there are always Thirty-Six Just men amidst humanity.

Let me now discuss with you a little of the Knowledge we call Science, that is, deciphering the laws and principles of Creation, learning how to harness discovery and knowledge. Of course some turn this knowledge to harmful use. Our Mother being the planet of Duality, free will is present either for fusion or for fission. Joining and blending opposites, or encouraging opposites to such a point of division that only hatred and destruction can prevail, are two possibilities always available. Other souls attend the Schools of Learning called Art (meaning dance, music, painting and sculpture – anything which is expressive of the beauty, mystery and originality of life here upon Earth). We may also understand the nature of humankind politically and psychologically, philosophically, medically (the Ashram of Healing).

There are seven great Ashrams of Learning, and these are represented here upon Earth by beings incarnate and discarnate. I have been a student in the Ashram of Art, diligent, patient and then flowering into the life of Han Shan, poet. At the same time, because I had many incarnations previous to that of Han, and these incarnations always in the East, I am steeped in the martial arts. Yes, I have been a warrior of some renown, trained by Taoist monks whose dwelling place was in high and remote mountains, and who experienced lives of arduous hardship and extraordinary physical and energetic capacity. There are Masters today who come from this lineage. Dzukh is not yet a Master, but in many lives, he achieved brilliance and in the last life in the East, came near to Mastery. The brilliance became clouded over in recent incarnations in the West but in this current life he is breathing fire and ice and coming through clouds of forgetfulness and speedily regaining strength. And I found my way immediately to him.

32

'Jack ....' Miriam meets the candid gaze of her husband. She sees a preoccupied light in his eyes, his body strung like a bow, back slightly curved, shoulders and arms tensile. He looks as if he is going to explode – carefully. Release a charge. A planned detonation. She knows something of what is going on and is curious. He is wholly taken up by current events in his life and yet he is not absent from her. She flinches slightly as she wonders how she might have been experiencing this taut husband, had she not been similarly brought to attention by her own pursuits. Two loaded creatures, each packed full in their own way.

'Yes?' He pulls at her wrist and brings her to sit at the chair next to him. The kitchen table is covered in books and diagrams. 'Do you want a kiss?'

'No. Yes.' Paul comes through the door, in his pyjamas, frowning, his mouth soft with the disrupted onset of sleep.

'Why should I be in bed when you're having fun?'

'What fun are we having?' Jack picks up his son and puts him on his lap. 'We're working.'

'Kissing fun!' says Paul and then in oddly adult mode, clicks his teeth together in a tsk tsk sound. 'You were going to kiss mummy.'

'Why shouldn't I kiss mummy?' Paul stares at his father, his mouth working. He struggles for words. 'You are always having fun and not me.'

'Come on.' Miriam takes Paul from his father's lap. 'I'm going to take you back to bed and give you a cuddle and a kiss.' Paul lies tightly against his mother's shoulder, his arms wound around her neck. He shoots his father a superior look as he is taken from the room.

'Little bastard,' says Jack as Miriam returns, half an hour later. 'I never have any fun ... he's always stealing you from me!' Miriam kisses Jack, putting her hand into his hair. Jack's eyes moisten and he puts a hand on his wife's belly.

'No,' says Miriam, pulling away. 'I wanted to ask you something – no, discuss something.'

'Fire away.'

'The old woman. The retired ballerina. I've got all sorts of thoughts about her – one is that Marie should come back and help her finish the book. First of all,' she hurries on as she imagines Jack thinking she might want to tell Marie what to do, 'it's an interesting job and there's pay and Marie I am sure is doing it well; secondly the old girl was clearly in some sort of madness or pain when she came roaring around ... she needs help, not condemnation.'

'Thirdly,' says Jack, 'it will help you in some way with your project?' Miriam purses her lips.

'Yes, yes – but that's not the only reason. I just have a feeling it will be a good thing. All round.'

'What do you want me to do?' Jack looks at his wife.

'Well, nothing, actually ... I would like to call Marie, if you'll give me her mobile number – and I'll put this idea to her. And of course I won't say "should". I don't mean should – oh, I don't have to explain this. So – just telling you – after all, she is, or was – a student of yours.' Jack looks at Miriam narrowly.

'Am I justified in feeling a little nervous, Miriam? This is the woman you couldn't stand for a while. The one I was supposed to ....' He falls silent, aware that perhaps this is still dangerous territory.

'Jack – it's faded, that thing I was in. Well, I mean, my preoccupation is more to do with Hannah, the harridan. And yes, I am planning something with her to do with the project – as you know. And I think Marie could be part of that. So yes

... ?'

'Is fine with me.' Jack's eyes turn back to his books. 'I am sure you will be graceful about it all. I will leave the number on the table.' Miriam's exit from him at that moment is scarcely graceful. A scratch of the pain that the name Marie could evoke not so long ago disturbs her; the name barely able to be said ... the strike at her heart upon seeing at times that neat, still figure, patiently and whole-heartedly following the slow movements of the form.

So fragile, to Miriam, the alignment between Jack and herself. He is a whole world she knows very little about and surely her world is as unavailable to him. And yet they try to keep two worlds in some sort of rapprochement and degree of transparency. Daily acts of alignment, consciously and unconsciously carried out. For the sake of maintenance. Meet some of my needs, and I'll meet some of yours.

A fierce feeling of separateness arises in Miriam as she fills the kettle. Not separation against Jack, but separation because of him. Acts of agreement, acts of respect, acts of compromise. And all this goes sour and lop-sided if there isn't an own territory, inner and outer. An own unknown. This is surely sexy to the other; attractive at least. Miriam breathes deeply and feels herself angry and also happy as she moves around the small kitchen, making tea and reaching for Marie's phone number, hastily scribbled on an old envelope by Jack, gone now to the bookshelf in the bedroom and rummaging for something he wants.

A noise outside brings her to a stop. Since the riots she has been an anxious citizen, nothing quite as it used to be. Youth taking to the streets. Feels like a cliché. For centuries people have been taking to the streets. It's not going into the streets – it's taking to ... what difference does that phrase make? It makes a difference. She feels hurt and helpless, protective of her property and belongings, and also wanting to be one of the league of youngsters, searching for an encampment of fellows, a place to feel unstoppable and connected, ripping out of restraint and normal behaviour. The Arab spring; the London summer. Miriam shakes her head as if loosening irreconcilable thoughts. She goes into the living room, heedless of its pleasant ochre colours, the touches of ivory and blue as a complementary theme. Miriam phones Marie.

Marie is alone this evening with Becky. She likes this situation. Becky is devoted to Lou and when her mother is around, everyone else is at the back of the queue. Becky is in bed, reading and drawing, Marie is downstairs, looking out of the window at nothing, autumn is deepening. It is dark; Welsh dark, not the London variety, debilitated by street lights, buildings forever illuminated, car lights momentarily catching the unseen and then throwing it away, like rags left on the road. Marie wonders whether it is time to go back to London though Lou makes no sign that she is no longer welcome. She is getting to know the few neighbours dotted around the hill. Martin is a frequent visitor, though it is clear that he too wants Lou for himself. An uncomfortable identity as a vagrant upon the earth forces itself upon Marie. She has no established home or family, no vocation. Her parents are still alive but narrowed down, fussy, preoccupied by the routine of small habits, hardly leaving their new home in the Lake District. She visits and keeps in touch. In truth, she feels she is relating to two shadows, remnants of the hardy parent-folk she once knew. Her way of life has always been a mystery to them. She used to try to explain, no longer wants to. She can't permanently hook onto her sister; doesn't want to. This is not the life that feels right for her. So what does feel right? T'ai chi. Each time she settles into the posture she feels she has a place. Permanent life as a student? In a t'ai chi school? No. A dry sadness begins to settle into her throat. She lifts her head – is Becky calling? No, this is a wish for distraction. She wants to run upstairs and pile into the little girl's bed. She envies the safety and identity the child has: home, mother, Martin, school. Auntie. A routine. She wants Becky to call her and say please come and stay next to me.

Breathing softly, Marie sees herself, anchored temporarily in a field in Wales. She could let herself sink into terror, and call out as Becky does sometimes when she has a bad dream. Who would come? Becky? Running in fright to her aunt, her small arms fluttering at her sides. That would be quite out of order. Marie wraps her arms around herself and this gesture is strangely comforting.

The phone rings, and Marie is jolted out of temporary cradling. She answers and it is Miriam.

By the time Lou comes home, a little drunk and with Martin heaving her intimately through the door, Marie is ready with a decision. It is not the time to tell Lou now. They sit at the table and talk briefly, Marie aware of being outside of the sexual ambience embracing her sister and this likeable man. Thus was it ever. Somehow, when Marie finds her own various pairs of masculine arms to steer her through the front door and then hurriedly on to bed, Lou is never present. This thought accompanies Marie as she climbs to the top of the house, to her asymmetrical chamber beneath the eaves. Lou must think she's a sexless woman. No, that's not so – they have conferred long and hard about men, hers and Lou's. It's the visceral witnessing that is lop-sided. Her sister hasn't seen her in a state of sexual arousal and about to get laid.

She should have cultivated the worthy fellow Terence, Martin's friend, now back in London. He clearly had an eye for her. A not very hot or juicy eye, she reflects ... and no reflecting lurch of juices within her. It either has to be very juicy or not at all. And this desirous state is also to do with crucial details, such as the way he – whoever he is – takes a loaded fork of food to his mouth or deals with traffic jams. Or teaches t'ai chi, she thinks ruefully but without excitement. Yes, well and truly over, whatever it was with Jack. And an interesting new beginning initiated by Hannah yelping and barking into the group. She keeps turning it over, tasting the strangeness of his being in her flat, holding her hand without drama or romance, her speaking to him with words she has kept concealed for so long. From anyone. And now Miriam phones. And of course there has been a time when the very existence of Miriam carries a charge. Times when she thinks Miriam should not be the wife, it is her place. And then feels guilty and tries to expunge the thought from her mind. A strange, almost hallucinatory period; living in a fantasy, an uncomfortable day-dream that persistently tries to tell her its nature is truth. What a relief to be out of it, though an odd emptiness not to have the companionship of fantasy. And now Miriam phones with an interesting suggestion.

Marie settles into an almost thoughtless reverie. She closes her eyes. Lou's smothered giggles are barely noticeable. There is no accompanying question: shall I go back to London and pick up again with Hannah? For Marie, at times of decision, the process of question and answer yields very little fruit. She sits quietly, upright, hands loosely in her lap, breathes quietly, her alignment within becoming deeper and freeing her from connections and attachments to the external world. This steady breath plunges her into a watery space, a vast confinement in which her heart drums its beat, thud-a-thud, echoing through shoals of unexpected fish-creatures without form, but with a movement that disturbs the water and creates patterns, sensation, ripples. Feelings arise, inchoate, without description. Marie drops into a priceless seam of richness, noticing, noticing, noticing ... no words, no grammar, no language.

At breakfast, Marie tells Lou she will return to London in three days' time. She embraces her sister.

'Is it because Martin and I were too noisy last night?'

'No –'

'Well, I hope you're going back to something better than the crap that happened before you left ....'

'Who knows?'

Lou surveys Marie with a look her sister knows well. Part love, part irritation, part loss of interest in favour of anything else that might be happening more obviously around her.

'You're so fucking obtuse ... is that the word I mean? I don't think I really know what it means. Anyway little sis, you know best.' Momentarily Lou looks searchingly into Marie's eyes. 'I know we are different – chalk and cheese as they say and please can I be the cheese. Chalk! Urgghh! But you are something lovely. We like having you around. Peaceful and also surprising.' She kisses Marie, holding her very close, and then gets Becky ready for school. It's a chore this morning, Becky wants none of it, preferring to stay in bed with her favoured notebooks and pens. Her screams echo from the garden as Lou propels her towards the car.

33

Miriam phones Tilly, examining her own reflection in the mirror as she waits for connection. She has taken care to look elegant, subdued rather than colourful. She has an appointment to see Hannah. Kentish Town to Oxford Circus. Oxford Circus to Warwick Avenue. She finds a charming photograph of Warwick Avenue Station exit on Google. She can imagine herself emerging from it. From there, not far to Hannah's flat in a house beside the canal.

'Miriam?'

'Wish me luck. I am going to see the old lady.'

'That witch? What for?' Miriam grimaces at her reflection. The mirror has a dusty corner and she wonders if she could wipe it while talking. The cord isn't long enough. She leaves it.

'I have something in mind.'

'Well, watch your back, masochist ... by the way, that Simon was asking after you.'

'He wears nice jackets.'

'You are such a fool – no, you weren't, I am glad you didn't.'

'Me too. Well, wish me luck.'

'You already said that. How much do you need, babe? Call me when you're back. If she gets nasty beat her up.' Miriam replaces the receiver. She needs the dose of straight-forward confidence Tilly delivers to her friends. Her own mind has started weaving unsteadily. Why am I doing this? The woman's mad. Perhaps there'll be a scene – and how will I get out? Her thoughts turn momentarily to Simon. What a good thing that didn't happen. What a disaster that would have been. Tilly didn't receive the full story, but enough to bring her sharp little face frowning into Miriam's. 'He's a tosser, didn't you notice?'

Miriam remembers Jack's head on her shoulder from the

night before. Who cares if he doesn't have such impeccable taste in jackets? Who cares if he likes Chinese jackets with interlocking frogging all the way down the front? Who cares if he's a stubborn arsehole at times? Miriam locks the door and heads off to Kentish Town station.

The exit at Warwick Avenue is exactly as the photograph suggests and Miriam experiences déjà vu stepping out: she is now the blood and bone version; before, in front of the computer, she imagines herself coming up the stairs and into the light. She is a fractal facsimile, one way and the other, reduced in size now expanding. She imagines taking Paul to see the boats on the canal, and enjoys the sprawl of pot-plants on one particular boat which can hardly be seen for its leafy and left-over-from-summer flowery cover, the occasional cat prowling on the side, and signs of life from the boats: smoke from a crooked chimney, disassociated words floating from portholes, deriving from conversation or radio, She arrives on the dot and knocks on Hannah's door. Time elapses, mostly in her chest, nerve-wracked, before the door slowly opens.

Miriam sees a beautiful old woman, dressed in elaborate and plentiful black velvet and overlaid stuff of an old-fashioned starched quality, swathes of material around her slight frame. Her eyes are veiled, with secrecy and suspicion, and yet behind the veil there is a perceptible glitter, as of two lights at the small end of a dark tunnel. Her mouth is carefully rouged, and visible at its corners sits the collision of many words said, and unsaid. This dusty but fragrant relic beckons Miriam into a shadowy interior. The door clicks shut and excludes daylight. Miriam follows the fading figure, which then instructs.

'You must be the journalist. Follow me my dear and please stop at the kitchen and make tea, you will find everything laid out. I will be waiting for you next door in the lounge.' In an old-fashioned and cluttered kitchen, a kitchen in which there is no sign or feeling of cooking, more a place of storage of kitchen-associated objects, Miriam notices a tray covered in an embroidered cloth, slightly yellowed at the edges but clean and ironed. There is a canister of tea-bags on the tray, two cups and saucers, a teapot and a small jug of milk and a plate of shortbread biscuits, oddly arranged as the spokes of a wheel.

Miriam wants to giggle, but nothing is funny. She can't breathe very well. The air is stuffy – as if remnants of thread and powder stick to motes of regular dust. The kettle sighs and makes effort, and Miriam pours boiling water into the teapot. How many bags? She puts in three, hesitates. Then decides on three. It is not a large pot, is of elaborate design – a house with a small thatched roof as the lid. Like something out of Beatrix Potter. Miriam picks up the tray and walks carefully into the living-room. Hannah is seated on a large sofa, the room shrouded by profuse dark red curtains; two lamps burn softly, a large mirror dominates the wall to the left of the invisible windows; photographs cover the opposite wall. Hannah's body is still as if suddenly sprayed with an immobilising fluid. Miriam realises she is posing, has arranged herself in an archetypal position, neck elongated face tilted. It is effective in the darkened room, but also grotesque – a congealed beauty, trapped in a thought, in a pot-pourri of narcissism that is now a permanent habit.

'Thank you so much, darling,' says the figure, moving slightly. 'Do put it down and pour. I will have very little milk. Just a touch. And no biscuit. Now then, which magazine do you write for? And is a photographer coming?'

'I am not a journalist.' Miriam pours tea. Her hand is steady. She is sitting on a small chair next to the round table Hannah beckons towards as she enters with the tray. 'I used to work in the theatre and I am creating something about gravity ... you know, the experience of it, the mystery of it, the physics of it, and I thought that's what ballet dancers have to deal with ... '

'I don't teach any more dear.' Hannah smoothes her cheek and looks wistful.

'No, it's not about teaching.' The words in Miriam's mouth feel difficult, inappropriate.

'But I could come and watch, and make some suggestions.' Hannah's face brightens. Miriam takes her time stirring a teacup empty of sugar.

'Miss Bloom, I am in the early stages of developing an idea – and I wanted to meet someone who has spent a lot of time in the ballet – '

'Oh, I see,' but it is clear that Hannah does not see. And how would anyone see in this gloom, thinks Miriam, claustrophobic and as if the darkened patina were laying a shroud upon her and wrapping her too in antique swathes and swatches.

'What I'd like to know – can I ask you? – how on earth does a human body make that consistent effort of lightness and lifting and leaving the ground?'

'Because you want to; because you have to,' says the retired ballerina with some retrieved sense of pomp and importance. The dying Miriam grabs at life. She puts the cup down and moves towards the wall of photographs.

'May I look?'

'Of course.' Miriam feels Hannah's eyes upon her as she moves from image to image but loses her sense of unease as – with just enough illumination – she discovers the previous arch, imperious, oval young face of the aged woman behind her. Curved eyebrows, curved mouth, a look of innocence; innocence just on the cusp of experience. So beautiful, the curve of the neck, the elongation of slim young arms, the delineation of muscle in the leg.

'You were ... you are ... beautiful,' says Miriam quite sincerely. She feels a wrench in her heart for Hannah.

'Come and sit here,' says Hannah. Her voice has changed. When Miriam returns the old woman is looking at her in a different way.

'I remember now who you are. The woman with the baby. We went in a taxi ....' Hannah stops. Her face darkens.

'Yes,' says Miriam, picking up her cup of tea and taking a sip as if to indicate something normal. Just two women having tea, that's all. 'I know something was bothering you. You were very worried for me, weren't you?' Hannah looks at the younger woman. There is something about her that ...

'Are you Jewish?'

'Half. My father.'

'Well then, you are not. However, you remind me of my mother. No, not my mother, my aunt, my mother's sister. She was artistic. My mother was ... well, you could say ordinary.' A little corner of Hannah's face looks ragged; her eyes are no longer sharp. 'Why are you here really?' her voice is fearful. 'What do you know? What do you want to find out? You don't know anything about me and it is all long ago.'

'I don't know anything about you but that you were a well-known and beautiful ballerina – and that the other day something bothered you that seemed to be to do with another woman ... in my husband's class ... do you remember?'

Hannah knows a young woman is sitting next to her, who wants to ask her about dance, and she looks like auntie Greta. She is kind. And she is leaning towards her, holding a tea cup. Her hair is like Greta's. In the same style. Thick like Greta's was. Or so she was told. No photos, such a pity. Poor woman, wiped out. At last, she can tell someone. But she mustn't tell everything. Not the bad things. An odd disjunction of images and thoughts irritate the back of her mind, memories of a plain rather shabby small kitchen and a row of people and Marie ... Faint, but clear, comes the knowledge that she misses Marie. And the book at a standstill. How can that have happened? Perhaps this woman will ...

'I was in love once, you know.'

Miriam sits still and receives the synopsis of a love affair, hears of loving someone who could never be with you, someone so extraordinarily attentive and yet – not there. There are photographs from that time. Not of him. How poignant. Just her, and the only clue about him is that the young dancer's eyes suggest that some enchantment is giving them lustre and enlargement. Two large, shining black eyes evident in image after image – matching the ballerina's exultant pose, feet turned out, neck extended. Miriam feels the clutch of Hannah's hand as it grabs hers and holds it, using the other to point to details, to embellish stories. There doesn't seem to be a clear and specific ending to this story. Love and attention are pouring in and then suddenly a gap, a hole somewhere in the narrative and Hannah is on her own. Miriam experiences a strange vertigo, as though she has been thrown over the hole, dank and full of strange murmuring, or perhaps she heaves herself over it, and is landed heavily and summarily on the other side, without knowledge or understanding, wretched and damned.

'I feel for you.' Miriam is still holding the small, dry hand.

'Yes, dear. I think you do.'

'Do you remember Marie?' There is a silence, and Hannah's mouth forms a sour and sad shape.

'That one who left? She was helping with my autobiography. It is all high and dry now.' Hannah draws in a quick breath, lets it out with an odd, sibilant sound. Miriam wants to laugh, wildly and rudely.

'How about I ask if she will come back? Then you can continue – and I can be filming you or interviewing you for my project – you know, the exploration of gravity. Could be interesting,' says Miriam.

'It might help me,' says Hannah in a moment of businesslike lucidity. 'I have a chapter looking at the mechanics of dance.'

'You must have a whole store of film – of yourself. We could think about using some footage. All with your permission, of course – and whatever I produce at the end will only be with your permission.' Miriam is frowning with excitement. 'Do you still dance? I know that's a cheeky question – but I mean, do you do any sort of practice?'

Hannah rises disdainfully to her feet and moves to a corner of the room. Miriam notices a rail, perhaps chest height, along this part of the wall. Hannah places her hand on the rail. 'One and two and three ...' The complicated outfit rustles and shimmers, and an old elegant leg is raised. It moves slowly, extending itself as Hannah looks straight ahead, unsmiling. The leg is raised not quite parallel to the ground, but almost, and then is slowly brought back down. Miriam is enchanted – the large skirt rises like a tent, under the pole of an ancient, almost fleshless leg, but one still willing and able to follow an imperative.

Miriam claps. The sound disappears into the carpet and the furnishing of the room. 'There you see my dear, gravity defied, even as it attacks skin, bone and the enduring leftover of the once lyrical ....' The small movement animates Hannah into a startling, different version of herself. 'There. See. You think I'm a thundering old dame, but I still have poetry in me. I am not a stupid old thing, but it is damnable, this thing ...

losing and losing. And getting up in the morning is an act of defiance against the cold dark soil that's calling me ... No!' Hannah gestures towards Miriam who is moving towards her, tears in her eyes.

'Hannah – please – I am sorry.'

'No! Do not insult me. Do not be sorry. I am an artiste. We have pride. It is in our blood. I am vain, I suffer the loss of my youth and beauty. But the book will re-vitalise the whole story. Well ....' Hannah pauses, stares at Miriam, surprising herself with the unexpected arising of coherent language in support of truthfulness. Miriam, she suspects, did not anticipate this quality of expression either; was busy writing her off as fossilised and a bit mad and that perhaps with some careful digging, a few nuggets could be found ... but this monologue just rendered makes the sound of an archaic bell, aging bronze, still authoritative, through the dust and the flakes of elderly skin and the fallen crumbs from tea biscuits. 'Well, young woman, you'd written me off, hadn't you? Amusing old relic? Yes.'

'Yes. No. Hannah, Miss Bloom, I think you're brilliant. Yes, you did surprise me, I didn't know you would speak in this way – you didn't let on, you kind of give the impression ....' Miriam stops; Hannah is making her way back to the tea-table. She walks in stiff, stately fashion, pauses, looks at Miriam.

'Do you know what? I will be honest with you, young woman. Miriam, I had forgotten I could speak in this way. I have been sunken into a gloom. Even when doing the book, I was in a restriction. Sad, everything sad. Everything over. Not a book, a tombstone. This project of yours is interesting though I confess I don't altogether understand what you're talking about. I don't care about that. That's your problem.' Hannah looks spiteful and mischievous, colour comes to her cheeks, amplifying the artifice of make-up already present, and rapidly disappears, leaving her strangely discoloured.

'You can talk to me and take away what you are looking for – though I will have to check it ... and perhaps I can continue my book. Please bring back the other young woman, I made a mistake about her,' Hannah dabs at the air with her hand. 'I went into a horrible remembering and everything looked peculiar. And I became peculiar. I am not easy, I know, and I don't care. I never set out to be easy. But that wasn't right. It was a terrible time and that other time was beyond terrible.' Hannah subsides onto the couch and seems to lose all substance. Miriam believes for a moment that Hannah's body might dissolve from the shock of partial revelation.

'Can I get you anything? You look very pale.'

'Make some more tea. And bring me that bottle of lavender. I need some drops on my wrist.' Miriam, suddenly exhausted, is reminded of the time. She must go and collect Paul.

'I will make you tea but I need to go and collect my son.'

'I remember the child. In the taxi.'

'Yes.' The two women survey each other. Each is surprised, in her own way, at the emergence of event between them. 'I will speak to Marie and bring her back to see you if I can.'

Hannah insists on taking Miriam to the door. The rush of light and sound from the outside is a shock and a relief to Miriam, though Hannah hastily shuts herself back into her cave, frowning as light hits her face.

Miriam moves swiftly into the arched entrance to Warwick Avenue station. She feels pleasure and triumph. And a finger of grief at the same time prods at her innards, jabs her heart in a tender place.

34

Awake, and reluctant as yet to arise, Jack turns over and seeks again the sleep that wants to throw him out of its embrace. A bit like his mother. Big enfolding arms, the beat of her heart, the odd selection of smells that live on her skin: salty, perfumed, as if a signature is written into her pores. And then – get off you; you're heavy. Not unkind, but definite. That is it. Enough. For her. But often, a premature removal for him. And this is what he looks for now. More.

Miriam is up and out. She and Paul gone to the park. Jack runs his hand over his chest, down his legs and back up again, scratching, stroking. Sweet to be on his own, tasting his own texture, his own embrace. His breath can reach the wall; no one to stop its passage. More of himself, this is what he wants. No interruption. To lie, and taste and soak up whatever he wants, for as long as he wants. No requirement of another to throw him out of touch with himself.

Attuning to this man today, to this Being under my Guardianship, I follow an oblique line into his reverie: he is remembering his mother, and thinking of his wife, but actually he is wanting the company of men. He wants stimulation and challenge of a particular quality, the quality of men in easy fellowship together. Since the Severing by Sword of the painful restrictions passed to him through direct ancestry, he has been naked and yearning, The gift of noble and intelligent male entitlement was not delivered to him during his growing time. And yes, Beloved Beings, those of you in attention to this unfolding tale, these gifts, of intact masculine or feminine entitlement, are rare for all of us. Is it not so, however, that lack and loss can wake us up, and then do

> our sinews strain and we wrestle and weep and our
> encircling arms bring to us, through our own endeavour,
> the shapes that articulate our souls ... ?

The embrace that you want; and then it becomes suffocation. So that you can't think. Jack scratches his chest. Since marriage and fatherhood, has he lost the sharp, airy quality that unencumbered men bring to each other? With this thought, Jack hastily genuflects towards his wife and child. He wouldn't want them not to be there – strange double-negative kind of sentence. Re-phrase. He is glad they are there. He sits up in bed and looks around the room. Miriam is artistic, no doubt, and creates a tasteful place to sleep in. Not a lot of clutter – unlike some women. His mother on the other hand ... boisterous piles of stuff. On every surface the artefacts of a vigorous life of domesticity. A way for her to show her domination over space and any tendency towards emptiness and the unknown.

Suppose it can't be helped, Jack reflects, getting up slowly, shovelling his feet automatically into the soft trousers left on the floor. Friendship changes. As far as they have socialised at all in recent years, he and Miriam have tended towards other men-women with children. For which club Maliphant, for instance, is ineligible. That name. So perfect for him. No one can really remember his birth name, or how he acquires the appellation that so fits. His car door is never locked or unlocked properly, so that there are always procedures, complicated to everyone but the man himself, for getting in and out of the vehicle. His flat (rented to him – not quite legally – by a friend) has three rooms, and he is always relocating into the smallest one so that any passing others can stay in the two bigger. Beds and mattresses are moved around and then placated for their disruption by having heavy, embroidered Indian cloths draped over them. Maliphant is fastidious about food, and the small, crowded, ill-fitted kitchen is often the scene of steaming, sieving, chopping. The last time Jack sees him, Maliphant is host to a thin, small Croatian woman who is so anxious about London she hardly ever gets out of bed, occasionally moving from bed to bathroom in a large, ghostly-white dressing gown. As a diversion from bed, she lies in the bath until the water is cold, the door left open so that anyone passing sees this pale, cold form, seemingly imprisoned in watery aspic. The open door is never an invitation to carnality. It is more of an unnerving glimpse into inertia and despair. Maliphant never closes the door on her. One of the wonderful things about him is that he seems to be able to let people be. At the same time he is not a pushover. If there is something out of order, he protests – fast and furious. But the way people play out their habits, their odd, quirky states orbiting like slightly lost planets within his hospitality, none of that disturbs his equilibrium. He proceeds within his own ellipse, incorporating all that flows through his life with curiosity and gusts of amusement. Occasionally, Maliphant drinks a lot and goes into an extended period of creating mayhem wherever he goes. Mad events are started and then abandoned, such as the idea of buying an ice-cream van and selling ice-cream koans to seekers after the truth. And then Maliphant disappears – and ends up in Eastern Europe or in Greece. Or in a village in Essex. Maliphant has some kind of job with young delinquents, and, by the sound of it, inspires devotion in those who find themselves under his care. In terms of work obligations, his disappearances are covered – just – by friends at work. Jack holds his breath sometimes as he witnesses Maliphant declaring it is time for a walk-about or a drive-about or a fly-about. He has a gleam in his eye – and then he is gone. There is a time when Jack serves as shoulder for crying women who fall deeply in love with Maliphant, loving his long curly hair and the wild, unreachable places he goes to in himself, loving his utter disdain for regularity and domesticity – and commitment – and longing to be the one for whom this will all be laid down. And yet of course if this anarchy ceases, there will no longer be Maliphant. And they will turn away and seek for another disturbing male to stir up their juices and wrench from them cries of abandonment and frustration which make the object of this pain all the more desirable.

Jack wanders into his practice corner, smiling at the thought of his friend. Maliphant likes to tease him about t'ai chi. No time for this slow stuff, sorry mate. And yet there are conversations into the early hours and one of them is Maliphant's challenge of Jack's unquestioning acceptance of his teacher's method of imparting the practice. Just because it's old, doesn't necessarily mean it's good! Maliphant dances around the room, making feinting movements, standing on chairs, jumping off, poking his face into Jack's, running his fingers through his tangled hair. Wake up matey! Yes, of course I understand there are movements and principles, and you have to learn them, and then there's a critical point where you have to let go of your dependency ... and see what's there when you rely on your own experience. There's the humility and effort of learning from a good guy and then you have to kill him. When you meet the Buddha, kill him. This is what I tell my kids. They think I am saying when you meet the bugger, kill him. And this is what puts them back on the road. You get stale, man. You don't live in anyone else's pocket.

This fluent, powerful Maliphant also has an edge of brokenness and despair, visible only to a few. Jack's heart swells with memories and thoughts of his friend. He will ring him today. He wants to see him. There is a conversation he

wants to have.

Something is connecting for Dzukh. Ah! Just as I did not know, all the long while back when I was in human form, that the outpourings of love that I inscribed upon the willing pages of nature – rocks, bamboo, stone – would remain alive until these very days, that men and women from different landmasses would find them and attribute to them lasting value ... yes, just as I did not know, so does the young one not know that from this moment, from the seed of his meandering thought, something valuable is going to be born which will thrust itself, lively and joyous, into life ... Yes, Beloved Beings, I have told you that I am granted sometimes the Sight that can look into that which we call Future as well as that Sight which can see into that which we call the Past. Neither of which of course are in a specific place of backwards or forwards; being, rather, understood and known as part of the constantly generating Present.

In this moment my earthly brother was tasting the willingness to forgo received wisdom, and step into his own unknowing, his own blunt forest and adventure-ground. The shape of his entitlement was being writ and carved by his masculine hand. Thus, all that While before, did a potent mystery enter my soul when words seized hold of me and refused to be pinned to a formal page and flew out into the ethers and landed like whirling seeds to penetrate the ground and from there, to grow.

Jack settles his body, and breathes out slowly, As he breathes, his shoulder-blades discover themselves to be of a quality of plasticity, of spreading delicacy; and between a vortex of intense deep movement which originates in his

balls and his heart, and these delicately spreading shoulder-blades, a spiral continuum, generating itself, increases in substance and texture with each breath. Maliphant's crazy sweet smile is there somehow and Han is there, not sitting in the corner, but, Yes! Standing! A nimbus, radiant ochre and brilliant turquoise, circles his ancient form. Jack knows that somehow a shell of limitation he's been living in is cracking. And opening. And now, being created, is More. It is not his mother, or Miriam. It is not Maliphant, though each affects him in a certain way. The yolk of his substance, his original stuff, is irradiated, struck and sung by adventure. Add venture. Something More – and a moving toward. He can't go back.

35

'Maliphant?'

'You still alive? Thought you'd perished under the yoke of domesticity.' The voice is just the same, a familiar rising lilt and tilt into friendly skirmish and contradiction. As is always his way, Maliphant does not paddle in the shallows but leaps into the wave, without disrespect cutting through any possible opening preamble. No recrimination about time passing, no immediate curiosity about why the call now, They arrange to meet the next evening. The conversation is only about this: hello, and when and where. Jump in, swim.

Jack knows very clearly he wants to see Maliphant, he thinks about him before meeting and is waiting at the stipulated time though he knows Maliphant probably won't be. Indeed. Maliphant arrives late. He is thinner, somewhat drawn in the face, his hair touched with flecks of grey. Some kind of strain floats around him, as do almost invisible spores float in the wind.

Maliphant embraces Jack, they look at each other like two dogs suddenly, happily, met in the park.

'She let you out? How long you got, mate?'

'Once she knew it was you, she gave me the shortest parole imaginable.'

'And how is that lovely woman of yours?' Maliphant, in the early days of Jack discovering Miriam, freely confesses to Jack that he finds Miriam delectable and tells her that she is wasted on Jack and should rather be travelling the world with him.

The Hare and Dog, a Camden pub, is known not for its beauty but for its faithful clientele and the prodigious memory of the woman behind the bar – a large blonde with a sharp gaze and a ready laugh. She remembers nearly everyone, and their drinking preferences. Jack and Maliphant find a small table, littered with empty and half empty glasses, squeezed next to another small table where two young women are seated: blackened eyes and silver studs and rings decorating lips, ears, noses and eyebrows, architectural hair forced into geometric brilliance around patterns of shaved, revealed scalp. The women fix them with momentary steely scrutiny, in this way letting Jack and Maliphant know that they have failed a test they didn't even know they were taking.

'How long has it been?'

'Last saw you a couple of years back, I reckon,' says Jack. He looks at Maliphant's tired face. 'How many women crying for you these days?'

'Oh – ' Maliphant takes a deep pull from his glass. 'Hard to say – I am circling two or three at the moment. One in Germany, one in London – another ... she travels, don't know where she is now. Keep 'em guessing – you know me. Suddenly I am there and they are pleased – and when the little requests start to come in like do you like babies or shall we go to Sainsburys, Maliphant is off, you know, And then back ... And if they can't take it, well, that's it. Women. So lovely. Bless 'em all'

The two neighbouring women are talking intently. An air of drama and exclusion surrounds them, their words are incomprehensible to Jack. He wonders how it might be to approach them, to make sexual overture. It would be like taking his trousers off in an iron-monger's.

'There was a conversation we had way back,' he says, 'and I am remembering it for some reason. And remembering it made me want to pick it up again.'

'And which one of our many ravishing dialogues was that?'

'All about killing the teacher.'

'Ah yes, that's one of my favourite conversations. But first you will please bend an ear to my woeful plight. You know of course, being a Londoner, that our streets have been hit with disorder and anarchy, looting and burning, and that some of the individuals involved have been under fourteen years of age.' Jack nods. Some of the destructive events happen very near to his patch of earth, and he knows fear and a determination to see off anyone who threatens his home and his family. 'Well, some of these kids are mine. Not paternally of course, but, well you know, this is my job. What the hell am I going to do, Jack? Some of them behaved like thugs – but some are lost and malleable. Do you know what it is?' Jack puts own monologue on hold.

'Tell me.'

'Get me another beer first. And for you ....' Maliphant makes way for the full glass, moving the empty into the row of other empties. For a moment he gets lost in this movement, placing the glasses in a line and then a circle. And back to the original line. Jack watches. Light from a nearby lamp illuminates the discarded liquid in some of the glasses, and shows up sad lines of foam in those that are empty. The glasses become players in an as yet untold tale. 'Okay, see the ones with liquid still in them; some kids are like that. Still something there. Others are like the empty glasses – it's gone. Yes, sure, it can be re-filled, but that's a tough job. Being an empty glass with a few smudges in it – it's shit. You become shit.' Maliphant looks at Jack. His eyes are sad. 'I'm interested in the not-empty ones. I can still do something with them.' He leans back. 'Do you know, when I was in Spain recently – in the south – someone told me about the rituals men get involved in – where a bull is let loose in a village and the men deliberately put themselves in its way. In present time, there is a heralded bull, Rattan I think it's called – and its owner is immensely proud – the bull is a celebrity. If there is such a thing as *Ola!* magazine he's appearing in it wearing an Armani suit. And why? He has killed three men. Tosses them in the air. And do you know – when I heard this story, I felt a rush of testosterone – I wanted to do it. I wanted to get into Rattan's path, to dice with death – to feel that incredible rush of adrenalin, to feel my manhood. And test it. And I am not a young one with overdosing hormones flooding me ... and I wanted to do it.'

Jack thinks about Paul. One of these days his voice will be breaking, he will be part of a gang of friends who keep secrets and create their own laws. Maliphant continues. 'Our young ones, half empty, have nothing to test themselves against but the structure they live in – police, government, parents. The establishment. The establishment which also is seen as withholding, indifferent. Not even a decent enemy with respectful levels of fear so it's an honourable battle. The enemy is withholding and indifferent – and it teases. It teases by advertising its culture – some of which emerges from youth, and then is thrown back packaged. You can have this, and then you'll be ....'

One of the goth girls shrieks at something her friend has said. The sound hits the glasses, half empty and emptied, it is a salvo fired from the other side. Jack feels that at any moment, war could break out. Maliphant rests his hand on Jack's shoulder. His touch is dry and sinewy. 'You know that thing you do – what's it called, Pushing Hands? That t'ai chi stuff where you pit yourself against the other, but in a more subtle way.'

'Your kids would never do that, would they? It's a slow, quiet practice. Takes time and patience.'

'Yes – maybe ....' Jack smiles.

'There is something else chewing my mind,' Maliphant continues, 'it's called neural pathways. You with me?'

'Ever agile, the mind of the Maliphant,' says Jack. 'No – I am not walking neural pathways yet, first you listen to me.'

'Okay. Do I have enough beer?' Jack's eye passes over Maliphant's glass, two thirds full. He ignores the question.

'The conversation we had back in the mists of time – about killing the teacher. I had an experience the other day – and it was as if I knew something for myself that I hadn't been taught. Words are useless here, mate. I just know I can't go back to where I was before. It's as if that reality has sort of vanished. I haven't forgotten what I know – it's not amnesia. I know it differently. Does that makes sense?'

'No. Yes.'

Jack laughs. 'Doesn't to me either. And does.'

'So there we are then ... You have to stay with does and doesn't and see what happens.' Maliphant looks at Jack with a bright gaze, the tiredness gone from his eyes, and Jack feels there is nothing more he wants to say at the moment. How odd, he thought he had a lot to say. An evening-full of words, questions, demands.

'Well,' Maliphant continues, 'shall I go on?' There is a sudden altercation at the door. Three young men are looking for someone, their manner is hostile, their movements aggressive. They look into the interior, scanning faces, then turn around and leave, bumping into each other, their language explosive, random showers of words, crackling and burning. After they leave, a vapour is left in the doorway, smoky and inchoate. 'See what I mean?' says Maliphant with a crooked grin. 'Now let me tell you about some interesting findings in the world of neuro-science. It concerns the limbic brain. This is the place where we are able to feel into another's reality, experience empathy. If we are not met adequately in this way when we are babies, we might not be so easily able to feel in that way towards others later. Witness the arrival at the door a moment ago of several crocodiles. If you're in reptilian brain, you have no empathy whatsoever for any passing mammals.' Jack leans forward. He asks Maliphant to start again, slowly, so that he can pick him to pieces, get into decent argument and debate. He wants cut and thrust. And he has a worthy partner.

By the end of the evening, Maliphant despatches three more beers to Jack's single pint, and is weaving into their dialogue other conversations around him and then returning to Jack, without altering the flow (the two girls have long gone and their table is now a resting place for a very drunk and weary man with a long face).

Jack leaves first, knowing that Maliphant will most likely create flurries of excitement here and there before finding his way to the door. He waves to the blonde barmaid who smiles at him, and decides to walk home, even though it's quite a distance, enjoying the swing of his arms and the steadiness of his feet.

36

The streets are unusually empty as Jack walks, buildings shuttered as if in recoil from recent riots, additional clumsy extra protection hastily added to windows and doors. Jack feels as if he is in a newsreel from a bombarded country somewhere else. He is not nervous, but feels hyper-alert. It is this sharpened sense which picks up, after about ten minutes of solitary walking, the sounds of other footsteps, and breathing. He keeps his pace measured, the sounds increase and then he is walking within a quartet of young men; they are either side of him and it is not friendly. From the corner of his eye he notices trainers, hoods, two black men, two white. A menacing dance starts to move around him, a soft-shoe shuffle and then a voice.

'Hand over your wallet and no trouble.' Jack stops, and turns to face the nearest figure. He looks into the eyes of a young man, the rest of whose face is covered by a scarf. Two other men move nearer, exclaiming in sharp tones that the dude does not know what aggravation is coming his way. Jack feels fear, but more intensely, he feels anger. He drops his awareness down to the soles of his feet, and into his belly, and could be in his classroom in front of some of his more eagerly aggressive students. The nearest man brings his hand to push Jack's chest – Jack breathes in, receives the weight and intention of the other – and twenty years of diligent practice and the bright mysterious resolve of the last few days bring forth their reward, immediately and wonderfully wrapped in energy of an unknown, luminous, elastic quality he has never felt before. This man's weight is received and turned around. Shot back. With a hiss of joy, Jack, through the intelligent catapult of his body, and an explosion of breath, returns the oncoming aggression and the man stumbles back, falls over the pavement edge and lands painfully on his shoulder. He remains supine, a baffled look in his eyes. A second man moves in rapidly but he is clumsy and Jack, poised and burning, receives him in the same way and sends him spinning in a different direction, an eerie guttural sound in spontaneous accompaniment. The man staggers backwards, shouting with rage. He collides with a parked car and the sound of flesh on metal is satisfying to Jack, who turns rapidly to receive the other two, advancing on him. This time, he releases two punches, each carefully aimed at the solar plexus. Just before his fists connect his body pulls back in a taut parabola, a finely tuned bow releasing an arrow. The men stumble clumsily, grunting. Jack removes himself fast, turning into a wider street, and then walking more swiftly, not running. Adrenalin is humming in his ears, he is panting. His body feels exalted and powerful, surprised.

He hears again the sound of footsteps. Running. Fear touches him. He turns. Two of the men, one white and one black are advancing on him again. Jack breathes deeply, centring himself. This is not what he wants. Second time might be more difficult. He notes a metallic taste in his mouth, his heart is racing.

'Hey dude, peace man. We want no trouble, We want ....' Jack is not convinced. He waits, looking for the glint of a knife. The bigger of the two speaks. 'What shit you laying down there? You some kind of ....' Jack starts walking again.

'You want to talk to me, you walk with me,' he says.

'Okay, okay. So what style you use? Is it some kind of boxing? I ain't seen nothing like that.' They are passing a mini-cab office. There are signs of life in the office, and two drivers are smoking on the pavement. Jack stops.

'What do you want to know?' he asks. His tone of his voice is neither friendly nor unfriendly.

'I want to learn this stuff,' says the shorter man. He wears a black shiny anorak and black and white trousers.

'It takes time and discipline.' Jack looks at him. The man meets his eyes.

'I don't care man. I want some of that stuff, it's cool.'

Jack gives him a dispassionate look. 'I teach this stuff,' he says, 'but this is an old school and you have to fit with the rules. It's very strict that way. And it doesn't fit you to be aggressive and thieving, it fits you to be cool with yourself.'

The second man speaks. 'Yeah – I don't mind rules if they don't mess with me. Give us the name of the place.'

'No,' says Jack. 'No. You give me your numbers and I call you.' The men look suspiciously at each other, and a tremor of aggression starts to emerge.

'We not messing around man. What's the problem? Just give us the address and we turn up.'

'I have to think something through,' says Jack. 'And then I will call you. Tomorrow. And you have my word.' Irritably, they give Jack their numbers. He shakes their hands, giving time to exchange a glance with each. They leave, loping, unevenly bouncing on their cushioned shoes, down the road, and disappearing round the corner.

'Trouble?' asks one of the cabbies.

'No,' says Jack, 'but I could do with a ride home.'

When Jack gets home, he opens the door quietly. All lights are off except for a small one in the entrance hall. He sits in the living room, in the dark. His body feels vivid, his mind suffused with a quiet brilliance. He looks into the corner, expecting to see Han. There is no sign of him. He whispers, 'My friend ... it's you isn't it? It's you doing this. How can it be me? I am good enough, I know, but tonight took a lot of nerve. And skill. And power. Where did it come from?' No answer. No sound. No image arising between the two blinks of an eye. Jack sighs. He closes his eyes and sighs again, deeply, dropping his awareness into his belly. He smiles. It feels as if he has a granite obelisk planted in the middle of him. Heavy, but also airy. What an odd experience.

Soon he will lie with his wife. Now he sits with himself, knowing that there is a current, an unfolding, and he is being carried by it. A slow boat to China he thinks, and grins. In the quietness of the night, in his living room, Jack suddenly punches the air as if he has just scored the mother of all goals in the World Cup – and he is running around the pitch and everyone in the stand has arisen and is roaring and he is running, leaping and running, and his smile is to be recorded on the front page of every daily newspaper worth reading.

37

Jack is on the net, and on the phone. He needs a good room, not as big as the one where he runs his school. He doesn't want to open up his school for this. And not in the same area. Something solid, clean, near transport. Eventually he finds one between Angel and King's Cross, a loft used by a Thai boxing school – free for hire on Tuesday evenings. He books it for the following Tuesday, from 7 to 8.30 in the evening. He speaks to the owner, pays a deposit and receives instructions about picking up a key. Easy. There – step one. Step two – he sends a text to the two young men whose numbers he has taken. Be there at 7. You will have a lesson for an hour and a half. The charge will be £5.

My beloved friend has surrendered to the current. It came his way, and he leaned in, gave up his weight and shape, and leaned in, let it take him, allowed the unknown movements to take him, to hold him. These tremendous, shy invitations come unbidden to us – sometimes only once. They hold and manifest another Way, or a direction deeper into the Way, shall we say. Many of us sit at the edge and let it pass, many of us are not even aware of what it is that is inviting us. And it goes; passes on, humming softly. You see, Beloved Beings, (to describe the experience through a different sequence of language-image), these openings are not presented as golden and bejewelled palace gates; they are more like small wooden doorsills, sometimes hidden in bramble and weed. We need to be very quiet, open and deeply attuned to the currents within us. Then, when the visitor comes, the delicate invitation, we are already prepared, so to speak. Ah, alas, this language is not an easy way for me to give you the gifts that are here for you. These words are a humble, clumsy gate into a glowing terrain. And, of course, this movement can also induce terror, as that other dimension lifts us out of apparent safety and proximity to the known.

I am bereft of speech now. May I sit among you and breathe a cloud of stillness and unknowing around each of you. Each of you.

Jack arrives early, bringing with him a portrait of the grandmaster of his lineage, and a framed depiction of the yin/yang symbol. He is wearing his black cotton teaching suit and soft black shoes. He lights a small candle and a stick of incense, and waits, sitting on a rather worn-out wooden chair. The boys arrive on time, and bring with them three others. Jack can't be sure if two of those three were part of the original four he encountered in the shadows. The five stand in a little knot, looking sceptical and uneasy.

'Please stand in front of me,' says Jack, rising and standing in the front of the room. He indicates five positions, with space in-between. The boys shuffle into place. 'My name is Jack,' he says, 'but you call me Sifu, which means teacher. This isn't personal, it's a tradition of respect for the teaching.' The boys look at each other; there is a rising frisson of impatience.

'When you going to show us that stuff?' says the biggest and therefore probably the boldest. Jack nods at him but does not refer to the question.

'I will learn your names out of respect too, respect for students of this art. But first I want to tell you something. To learn the art of defence within the t'ai chi tradition, there are many hours of practice and effort first to get the basics. So any of you who want to go straight to the defence may as well leave now and not waste your time or money. It's fine by me.' Jack pauses, looks at each of the five, patiently, courteously. Two of the boys turn and hover and look at their neighbours, one looks at the door – but none leave. 'Okay,' Jack continues. 'What I require is that you now stay for the entire session. This builds up a field for the rest of us. I will explain more about that later. At the end of today, anyone who wants to quit – that's fine. And those who want to continue – we meet once a week. It is a feature of this discipline that each of us affects the other. If we all focus and concentrate, everyone gets the benefit. Enough for now ... Can you tell me your names.'

Nemo – the smallest. A sharp face, vigorous alert body, brown skin and a halo of curly hair. Steve – possibly the oldest. Shaven head, wooden studs in each ear, a vicious scar trailing a ragged red line above his pale eyebrows. An aquiline nose and thin lips which give him a sneering expression. His eyes though tell a different story. When Jack looks into Steve's eyes, he feels hurt and his heart lurches. Hardcore – handsome, confident, spells his name to Jack and then smiles without humour. He has cultivated an abundant shower of beaded plaits, caught up in a piece of blue cloth. Jackson – slight, evasive, avoiding eye contact, swallows his name as he says it, has the refined features of someone who might be of Sudanese origin. Reminds Jack of one of his neighbours, the son of a family who live across the road. Finally – Terry. Jack thinks of him immediately as the artful dodger. He might have been a cloth-cap kid on the streets two centuries before. An engaging grin, easily offered. Nemo and Hardcore are the two who followed Jack around the corner.

'Thank you. Now we start.' Jack holds up his left hand. 'This is our salute,' he says. 'See my left hand – this is us. Brothers.'

He twists his hand around so that the fingers are hidden and the thumb sticks up. 'Not this,' he says. 'No number one.' He raises the fingers once more and tucks his thumb onto his palm. 'Brothers,' he repeats. 'No number one.' Jack raises his right hand. He makes a loose, clenched fist, thumb holding back second and third fingers. 'This is the martial art,' he explains. 'Used with care; only in self-defence.' He brings his hands together, so that the four fingers of the left hand fold horizontally over the right fist. He rotates his fists so that he is looking at the back of the left hand, extends his forearms so that the enjoined hands move towards the group. Jack bows his head. 'This is our salute,' he says. 'Now you to me.' The five salute him. 'Okay, now we begin.' Something in the air has changed; feet are no longer pointing towards the door.

Jack introduces the group to the basic standing position. He demonstrates the quality of rooting into the ground – and the lack of it. He can dislodge each one from their position; none can dislodge him, though Jack is clearly not the most muscular in the group. Time after time he patiently demonstrates dropping the centre, maintaining equilibrium, emptying the upper body. The five begin to engage. There is a degree of play, as well as seriousness. And the evidence of Jack's skill is that which holds the attention of all five. Each time he engages one to one, a connection starts to develop from the feet, through the legs, through the lower abdomen up the spine, through the arms and into the hands, into the eyes. Even Jackson manages eye contact, though his momentary gaze is fleeting and mistrustful. When Jack takes the group through the practice of standing for a length of time, knees bent, shoulders relaxed, arms raised in a loose half circle in line with the navel, after a short period some are sweating and slightly shaking. All complain of aching in the legs. Jack has brought water for them and they have a break at this point.

Fifteen minutes before the end of the session, Jack brings the physical practice to an end and asks each to sit on the floor, cross-legged if possible. He asks them to breathe deeply and into the abdomen, and to keep their eyes closed. 'The biggest battle we have,' says Jack, 'is the battle with ourselves. We allow anything to rise up and control us, even sometimes if we'd rather not. This practice now is inner qi gong – or working with energy in an inner way. Using the mind, not the body. Chi – energy – follows the mind, as you probably know.' There is a silence. Jack instructs the group to follow the breath and simply notice feelings, sensations, thoughts. 'Don't make anything of what you see. Allow everything. Even uncomfortable thoughts or feelings. Just let them pass by, like clouds in the sky.

'This is possibly our greatest strength,' Jack says quietly and thoughtfully. 'Being able to watch ourselves and choose our reactions ....' After a few minutes' silence, Jack asks the boys to arise, and to salute again. 'Please practise,' he says. 'Just five minutes a day done with real concentration, will really help you get this strength. Thank you for your effort. Please pay me before you leave, and I will see you next week.'

Hardcore and Terry don't have the required fee. Jack asks them to bring it next time. Each protests a little. 'No pay, no lesson,' says Jack. 'Simple as that. Next time we do the payment first.'

'Hey ... er ... whatsit, Sifu – is this the training Bruce Lee had?'

'Don't know,' replies Jack. Nemo has asked the question. 'Something similar, anyway. And years and years of practice.'

'Jeez,' says Nemo as he follows the others out of the door. Jack sits on the nearest chair after they have gone. He remembers his year in China at the training school. They would have laughed at this introduction. There it had been in at the deep end. Standing for so long that the legs buckled and tears came to the hardiest practitioner. The teachers gave no visible encouragement. Simply looked and walked away. It had been the hardest time of Jack's life. And the most satisfying.

There's a knock at the door. Odd, it's open. The five are back, huddled together on the threshold. Jack immediately thinks they have had a brief conversation outside and have decided, after all, this is not for them. He says nothing, looks at each one in turn.

'We talked,' says Hardcore. 'And decided....' He looks at the others and continues: 'We not going to get nowhere just a day a week. We want two days.'

'Grab a chair,' says Jack, following an intuition which tells him to run with this. 'We'll work an extra day into the schedule, I don't think this place is used very much. Anyway, I'll check that... and my own time-table, and let you know tomorrow.'

'Pay?' Nemo's voice rises.

'Well,' Jack is surprised to hear himself say, 'I said five for one class. Should be ten for two. If ten works for you, that's what you pay. If it doesn't, minimum for two sessions is six pounds. So you each decide what to pay from six to ten ....' No one says anything to this plan. Almost in unison, they turn, nod and disappear.

Dear Friends, I watched the movement of the men towards Dzukh and knew that, in parallel to this quickening, I needed to negotiate my own expansion of Chronos time. Remembering my early encounter with the language of sacred arithmetic while still in the

Heavenly Realms, I invoked again the number three, which then acted upon the seven to produce twenty-one. The twenty-one added itself gracefully to forty-nine to produce the number seventy, and I knew that this was now be the measure of my time upon earth. The unfolding tale of Dzukh required seventy. This was quite clear, and satisfactorily agreed.

38

Dear Friends, in these days of close accompaniment to Dzukh, I have been gratefully aware of my two Beloved Friends, Master Yang and Madame Li, who showered me with delight and education in the Heavenly House of Learning and Apprenticeship. Our most common mutual joy was the Transmission of the Tao in all its forms: written, told as story and myth, practised as moving prayer and also as martial art.

I of course was steeped in the Tao during my time upon the Earth. This was misunderstood by people who later began to put IST to the end of words of beauty like Tao and Buddha and who tried to enIIST me into their human tribe. You know what I mean by tribe. I observed they still existed – and dangerously - in your reality: if you're this kind of IST, you're not that kind of IST. Such a boxing in of human consciousness! 'Leave me alone!' I would cry as I scurried from their kitchens and palaces. 'Take away your paper and bound books! Take away your definitions ... the Tao that can be described is not the Tao ...' (Thank you, Lao-Tzu. And by the way, I am not going to be pulled into a discussion as to whether Lao-Tzu was human or legend. Leave that lyrical being in peace to disseminate its artistic and playful wisdom.)

Yes, I was steeped in the Tao. I lived in Cold Mountain, in its embrace, and the only way I knew to express my joy, vulnerability and astonishment was to decorate trees, bamboo, rocks and walls with love letters to the Way Things Are. Later, in the Discarnate Realm, communion with Master Yang and others like him, and verily memories of my training in the martial arts, provided the hint of a sensation of how the microcosmic body of a human experiences the macrocosmic body of the cosmos. Yes, a grand statement, but why not? As above, so below. The Tao cannot be told or measured or compared, but it can be experienced.

Madame Li, a swirl of elegant consciousness touched with the lightest violet and deep blue shimmer, had been a swordswoman in Eastern China of the Earth even before Master Yang's time, disguised as a man until she was given a nunnery through the complex and myriad weavings of the forces of Destiny. With delight did she commune to us that the chaste poring over of sacred texts and the cultivation of innocent vegetables were but a front to conceal training in the martial arts. The women who chose, or were chosen, to enter the whitewashed high walls showed love and devotion to the practice of energy-cultivation and artful self-defence. Devout figures were seen bending over rows of seedlings and plants; their lowered gaze never met the eyes of local people as they went about their business of tending to the poor and healing the sick. However, deep within the Sacred Portals, these beings rose early and faced the East and learned to move from the tan t'ien, softening the waist, making light the upper body, and making cool and obedient the mind. They worked with the sword and the staff, and Madame Li made delicate alterations to traditional forms where appropriate. I understood from Madame Li's communion that the radical position she took concerning the practice of qi gong (the basis of t'ai chi, hsing-hi and bagua martial arts forms) was to teach that the self-knowledge embedded in the practice led to a profound understanding of one's own nature and how to work with one's angels and demons.

I recall a time when the three of us were drawing upon memory and telling tales of previous incarnations. Master Yang amused us by telling of Master Wu, a fierce teacher he had had when very young and mischievous. Master Wu had already reached older age when the young student had been brought into his school. Master Yang told us that Master Wu's hair was long and thin, like cobweb about his head. The students used to joke that he had a spider living in his ear and that spinning happened while he was asleep, so that his hair in the morning was shining and intricately woven but came into disarray and tangle towards night. The other students, sensing the strong spirit of the new arrival, told him that an initiation practice for such as he was to creep up on Master Wu while he was asleep, carefully remove the spider from his ear, and bring it back to be witnessed by all the students. Master Yang related that he had felt unsure, but found that he could not refuse to carry out this act of daring, as he did not want to appear cowardly to the other students. He also thought it was possible that they were not jesting, and that indeed, this was a genuine task. Late at night he crept to the Master's room, noticing its rocky walls and lack of any object but a mat upon the floor, and swords against the wall. The Master slept quietly and Yang, anxious and nervous, crept forward as softly as he could. He watched the Master's eyes. They were deeply shut. He stretched out his right hand, and, suddenly, it was held in an iron grip.

'Foolish young man,' said Master Wu, wide awake and terrifying in his sinewy strength. 'Go back to bed and listen only to your own counsel, and to mine.'

Madame Li listened to this tale with a sweet smile

upon her face.

'Did you notice that night, that Master Wu had a scar upon his forehead?'

'Yes,' Master Yang replied eagerly. 'Extraordinary. In the shape of a bird.'

Madame Li said nothing, but concentrated with quiet intent into her translucent form so that we might begin to see some suggestion of a previous incarnated body within her. A shadowy shape slowly emerged. Whether it was masculine or feminine was not quite evident. A wave of hair spread from the forehead. Madame Li moved it from her face. Master Yang and I beheld a scar, in the shape of a small bird, a little egret, in perfect detail, and no more than a fingernail in length.

We three. Companions through life after life.

There have been times, during my guardianship of Dzukh, that I have called upon Master Yang and Madame Li and they have directed additional brilliance and power into the whole circumstance. I bowed my head, and received the golden colours of sunlit grass, and the amethyst hue of distant stars. And Dzukh, Beloved Initiate, absorbed into the marrow of his bones these delicate splendours, these unsolicited gifts, from me.

39

The trees in Little Venice are shedding their leaves, yellow and brown remnants lie in clumsy piles on the surface of the oily water and on the pavements. A mellow autumn sun, further away and seeming to journey elsewhere, casts reduced warmth. Marie kicks at the leaves in her path. Back in London two weeks now, seeing anew the effects of the riots. An English agitation. In Hackney she sees scars; not here in Little Venice. Walking quietly along this select waterside path, she carries a bunch of four sunflowers, looking into their black hearts, enjoying the irregular thick crisp cluster of yellow petals and green leaves. She will give them to Hannah. Why not. As she walks, a handsome man, possibly of Middle Eastern origin, walks in the opposite direction. He strides firmly, his coat looks expensive, he carries a bouquet of sunflowers. Marie smiles, and wants him to notice the two bunches of sunflowers being carried in different directions. There is something distinct about this moment – does it matter if he doesn't notice? Yes and no. If he had noticed, and exchanged a smile, not altering his stride or making any other contact, something mutual and mirroring would have sealed the distinction. Now it is simply her experience. Unmirrored. Second handsome man of the day. In the morning a ring on the bell and a parcel for the neighbour who is not at home. Marie signs under the gaze of a beautiful man with long rasta plaits and a smile of easy connection. She swirls her name onto a plastic notepad, smiling as he smiles, and there's a joke about her getting pulled out of bed for a parcel that isn't even hers and there is nothing risqué or suggestive about the remark, it is sweet. She likes this man a lot; she feels liked by him. Then he jumps into the white van and speeds off, waving. Maybe it is the warmth of that connection that attracts her later to the sunflowers.

Marie is meeting Miriam at the café on the edge of the canal before they go to Hannah. She is early and dawdles at the railings, staring into the water. The image of being an obedient traveller upon the lap of Mother Earth as she gyrates around the sun comes again to Marie and she shivers in the mild autumn sun, feeling in the presence of something magnificent and delirious. She thinks of Leonard, the eccentric who picks her up – three, four years ago? – at an arts festival. A short and odd time together. He asks her to make bread with him, naked. Both of them. In a mood of peaceful obedience and curiosity she agrees and the two of them make dough and knead it, adding to it several different grains. He looks to her neither sexual nor comical, rather like something out of a fairy story. Two children who are in a spell and have to make bread for days and days. Never stopping. They work conscientiously and without speaking. While the bread bakes and rises, they lie quietly in his bed. She wonders if they will make love but this doesn't happen. They are quiet and sleep a little. The bread is lifted out and breathes and cools. They eat a slice with butter and cheese.

'Marie – I am almost sorry to call your name. You look so peaceful and thoughtful.' Miriam stands at the railings, a vivid and intense presence. Marie notices her thick hair, twisted into a knot low in her neck. She looks exotic, foreign. Full lips, bright, swinging earrings, a skirt of varying colours, cut on the cross, an uneven hem, tight black sweater, swagger coat.

'Miriam – ' Marie stands quietly in her dark cotton trousers, delicate even in strongly laced boots and a thick cotton jacket with a round collar. Her face is pale and there is a suggestion of brown rivers and mountains in the peat colour of her eyes, a landscape which Miriam enters respectfully, carefully, moving slowly. The two women walk towards the café without speaking, as the dark, viscous canal water shuffles along its leisurely dark course under the bridge to the left of them.

'Gravity! Yes of course – you will know from Jack that it is a big part of t'ai chi.' Marie speaks with enthusiasm and knows immediately that the name Jack floods the space between them and, for a long and impenetrable second, dangerous waters threaten to rise up and engulf and erase any structure and connection slowly building. Miriam forces herself not to mind Marie displaying the name so soon, this display emerging from the intimacy her husband and this quiet woman experience as teacher and student; she holds her hand hard not to slap and her mouth not to utter Mine. Marie blushes deep within her soul, her face remaining pale: has she offended? The dark waters lap and tease, and then recede. Each woman stirs unnecessarily at her cup of coffee. Neither has taken sugar but there is a nervous stirring of the froth and the coffee. Miriam speaks.

'Yes – and coming now to Hannah. Hannah to her face doesn't feel quite right. She needs some kind of appellation – Dame or Madame, you know.' Marie nods slowly.

'I think I called her Miss Bloom. She was never married – but I gather there were many suitors.'

'Marie – she was so beautiful. Still is in a strange ancient way. And there was someone special. But of that she seems very secretive.'

'Did you tell her I was coming?'

'Yes, but I said nothing about whether you would continue – just that you were coming to see her. What's your feeling?'

'Well, I have to see her to know what I feel. She was vile. Crazy.' Marie looks steadily at Miriam. 'Is there anything left over for you about this – in terms of what she said, Miriam?' In the space between, where before flood waters threatened, now there is the holding of breath.

'Marie – well ... somehow the way Jack was, and the way he went to speak to you seemed to put it right. I felt she came with madness of her own, and you two got caught in it. Players in her fantasy.' Miriam is quite sure she does not want to open her earlier paranoia to Marie. For heaven's sake, she doesn't really know her. She feels a twitch, an unwelcome leftover nervousness at the quietness and depth of the woman, seeing her with Jack's eyes. Stirring her coffee once more Miriam dares herself to conjure up a picture of Jack and Marie together sexually. The image does not coalesce. Enough of this. New phase. It's over. 'And what about you?'

'I am anxious about seeing her. And I am enjoying meeting you. Your project interests me a lot.'

When they get to Hannah's and Miriam knocks on the door, Marie stands slightly behind her, as if receiving protection from the taller woman. Hannah opens the door and smiles, a hesitant drawing away of the mouth from the teeth, a mouth outlined and filled in with scarlet red lipstick. A large red artificial rose is pinned to her dark red chiffon blouse, the sleeves are full. She wears a long, black velvet skirt.

'Oh girls,' she says, 'I have the tea-tray all ready for you.'

Marie knows she is willing to let Miriam lead the conversation. This has not been agreed between them, but it feels right. If Miriam falters, she can step in. Marie is aware of Miriam's qualities of fire and air. It is not just the red lips and the vivid eyes and the way she walks. It is a sensation she transmits, of speed and immediacy. Like those cartoon characters that have dots and a spiral drawn behind them to denote rapidity of movement. If Miriam is a hare, she, Marie, is a tortoise. If Miriam is fire and air, she, Marie is earth and water. Words do not come easily or swiftly to her, her interior reality is more affixed to feeling and sensation than thought and language. When she expresses herself, it is with economy, and, for those who stop to listen, what she says is often sensitive and finely crafted. Now, with the explosive fiery force of email and text msgs and colliding flying endless words denuded of vowels and spelling, Marie's tortoise-shell calligraphy, the scrupulous, patient scratching of patterns of expression, is left behind in the dust. Out of the blue comes an image from a family holiday in North Devon. It is wintertime, and mother, father, Louise and Marie are walking on an alternately stony and muddy coastal path near Clovelly. Louise and her mother are talking fast and furious about three girls at the hotel, and their mother, and the ins and outs of their faces and their idiotic views and conversation. Marie is walking behind – father is way in front, striding, even through the mud, his boots furiously lifting and spraying damp red crumbs onto his trouser leg. From far away she notices a white gash in the brown rocky cliff below them. Now as they approach the gash, she sees that it is water pouring in full stream, down a fissure in the cliff into the sea. Marie sees a wedding dress exploding out of the rock. The stuff of the dress, the whiteness and the brilliance, is the downward rush of the water; the wind catches it and teases it out, into a billowing marriage-skirt. It is wild and magnificent and somewhere spliced into the rock is the bride, forever trying to run free in her dress, and Marie pauses, and fills her eyes and her heart with the sight. She is about to call to her family to look ... and then decides not to.

'... isn't that so, Marie?' Miriam is regarding her with inquiry. Marie shakes her head and smiles. 'So sorry, I was miles away ... what was it you said?' Leaving the fresh sky and wind of the

Devon coastline, she is back in Hannah's fusty drawing room and the old lady is looking like she used to when Marie would come to work with her, and there is no hint of the monster who appeared at Jack's class. Well, hardly a hint. Marie can't quite see her in the same way. These quietly glittering eyes could suddenly start rolling savagely again, the crabby finger could point at her. But no – Miriam is here and something else is happening.

'Well, Miss Bloom – is this the manner in which you would like us to address you?' Marie notices that Miriam does not pause for answer to this question but continues smoothly. Hannah does not seem to notice that she has a choice of title, and even seems to have forgotten that a tea-making ritual is to be named and announced. 'I know Marie is doing excellent work for you on your autobiography and of course something rather unfortunate happened at her class where we do believe you mistook her for someone else and thought something bad was going to happen ....' This time Miriam pauses and looks gravely at the powdered and straight-backed elderly ballerina. 'I imagine you would like to say a few words to Marie to make good a most difficult experience for you both.' Hannah seems to be mesmerised and for once not outraged that she is not the queen of the moment, directing the movement of her courtiers and adoring ones and slaves. This other unexpected queen is visiting and while she is asking her to eat humble pie – is she? – she is also quite clearly impressed by the dancer's pedigree and Hannah is pleased about this and will play the game because it feels as if something interesting is going to happen for her and god knows the days can be long and tedious and she has missed the wretched girl who is helping with the book – or anyway, she has missed talking about herself and knowing that this meticulous person is taking notes and the book is developing.

Actually, she acknowledges to herself, perhaps the queen Miriam is correct and she needs to put things right. Perhaps she made a mistake, can't exactly remember what happened but does remember a rush of appalling fear that a dreadful deed is about to happen ... is that it? And she must step in. Goodness gracious, what a terrible responsibility. Hannah removes a lacy handkerchief from her sleeve and dabs faintly at her forehead.

'My dear,' she says in a suffering voice, and leans forward and nearly lays her hand upon Marie's. Festooned in a fingerless glove of black net, the long bony fingers hover ... and to Marie's relief, do not land upon her. 'My dear, I was badly mistaken. I was doing my duty, heaven knows some of us have to ....' Hannah's mouth is pursed, to indicate that a story of great suffering could be told, but not now. 'If any grief has been caused to you by the actions of another, it is required that you receive deep apology.' Marie looks away, anywhere not to catch Miriam's eye. What an adroit side-step of an apology. She will be equally adroit. One step two step from the ballerina; a skilled dropping of the centre from the t'ai chi practitioner, and a turning of the waist, so that the evasion can spin off into the far dusty corner, and not land on her.

'Miss Bloom, if anyone has received injury and has suffered as a consequence, it is surely possible that the true sorrow of the heart will lead to forgiveness.' Hannah, spinning a little in the re-enactment of her grand jeté, is summarily stopped ... and looks sharply at the innocent face of her amanuensis. Miriam looks intensely at the photographs on the far wall, recording with delight the exquisite play she has just witnessed. She feels respect for Marie. These quiet ones, often very powerful. She wonders if she will tell Jack of this moment. She'll see.

'Shall I make the tea?' asks Marie quietly and firmly, beginning to rise before the haughty nod can be delivered from the old one who knows somehow she has been properly – but politely – put in her place. And that this is right, even though she doesn't like it. Spitefully, she remembers that the biscuits are nothing special. Glad she didn't ask her weekly shopper to spend too much on the contents of the packet that would now be fanned out on the plate next to the teapot.

The visitors drink tea, and leave the biscuits. Miriam picks up her original thread. 'This is my suggestion – my request, Miss Bloom. You continue the work with Marie, and I come along too. Unpaid,' she confirms hastily as she sees a shocked eyebrow beginning to rise into the powdered forehead. 'And of course I don't interrupt your autobiographical flow, but I ask questions here and there for my own purposes, the purposes of my exploration of gravity ... and the possible expansion of that into some sort of work ... I don't know yet what that might be – film, collage, radio play. I have no idea – I just want to follow the impulse. Improvisation!' says Miriam strongly and leans forward as if she has suddenly found common territory with the ballerina. Stepping together.

'Improvisation? This is not something we did. We followed the choreography, my dear. Step by step. Woe betide improvisation.'

'Hmm, yes, of course, absolutely right,' Miriam agrees with rapid sincerity. This time it is Marie who disciplines the howl of laughter that wants to arise and distracts herself by intent observation of the photographs. 'Of course – that's not what I meant. Perish the thought, what was I thinking? No, we follow step by step the learning process of the ballerina and how she develops through constant and rigorous practice, the art of leaping high and pirouetting seemingly without effort ....'

'Don't you believe without effort,' Hannah sips her tea carefully. 'None of this can happen without effort.'

'That is exactly what fascinates me.' Miriam looks carefully at Hannah. 'How on earth you extraordinary beings managed to make this supreme effort so that we in the audience could imagine that you were floating.'

'All sorts of people come to the ballet.' Hannah replaces her cup as if it were made of the thinnest and most valuable china. 'Not many understand what they are seeing.' Okay, okay, you old trout, game set and match if you want it, thinks Miriam. This is going to be quite a struggle.

'Oh yes, I am sure you are right.' Miriam too replaces her cup on the small table, her voice soft and amenable. Arrangements are made for the return of Marie to her previous employment and that Miriam – discreet and unpaid – will come too. 'Tell you what,' Miriam pauses at the door, as Hannah prepares to let them out into the cold and windy day outside. 'Let me know your favourite cakes or biscuits, and I will provide next time. It is not fair that it is always you.' Hannah thinks deeply, a little strange smile playing on her lips.

'Well now, you know those cakes with the poppy-seed in them, can't remember the name, I haven't been able to find them anywhere. For years.'

'Done!' Miriam assures her. 'I know the ones you mean and where to get them.'

Marie and Miriam hold their breath and say not a word until they have descended the few steps from the front door, turned to the right and hurried along past several houses. In synchrony they look back as if to make sure there is no trace of red chiffon and black velvet, and only then, in unison, do they release puffs and gales of laughter, as if the years have rolled back and they are teenage and nothing in the world is as funny as what they have just seen and they don't care how loud they are being, and their eyes are watering and their sides heaving and they get stitches and have to put their hands on their hips and hold onto the garden wall of a grand mansion. And after the explosion has quietened down, they look at each other once more and it starts all over again.

40

'Guess who wants to contact you ....' Tilly looks mischievous. She walks briskly through the cold air, sniffing with glee as the trees in Victoria Park receive gusts of cold wind around their fading red skirts.

'The Dalai Lama.' Miriam has Paul's tricycle in one hand and Paul hanging from the other. 'Paul, you are dragging on me ... come on, little fellow, walk for yourself or ride your bike.' Paul shakes off her hand and makes a vigorous rush into a dirty flock of pigeons. He applauds as they rise and scatter.

'Warm.' Tilly dodges as Paul roars back from the pigeons and launches himself at his mother's knees. 'Have mercy on your mother!'

'I give up.' Miriam lifts Paul and Tilly automatically takes the red tricycle.

'Oh, all right then – Simon.'

'Really? What for?' Miriam sends a sharp look at her friend even though the name no longer disturbs her. Simon has long been taken down the river of time, swathed in his floppy jacket, recumbent in a flat boat, floating away out of her life.

'No seriously, honey, the guy remembers you talking of an interesting idea and wonders how far you've got. He has some kind of amateur dance group looking for a project.'

'Let's go to the caff.' Miriam shifts Paul from hip to hip. 'Tilly, do you think it's worth checking out?' Tilly puts a free arm around Miriam's shoulder.

'I think he's okay around work if he's interested. It's seduction I would stay away from.'

'As I did,' retorts Miriam, feeling the weight of her son and the ache in her arms. 'Paul, sweetie, how about riding for a bit, then we'll get to the caff quick-quick and have some tea.' Paul, in a moment of unexpected obedience, descends from his mother's hip and receives the tricycle from Tilly. He shoots away from them, paddling his feet on the ground rather than pushing pedals. 'Don't laugh, Tilly!' Miriam smothers her own laughter. The child is comical, puffing and flapping his feet like a determined goose landing on abrupt ground.

'What's the project, Miriam?' The women drink tea, Paul carefully licks a vanilla ice-cream.

'Paul, let me lick the melty bits so your hands don't get covered.' Miriam leans towards the ice-cream and Paul digs his mouth possessively into the centre of the cone. Miriam manages to scoop displaced ice-cream with her finger. Paul starts to howl that the streak on Miriam's finger is also his and he should have it. She holds her finger at his mouth, he holds on to the cone, and licks Miriam's finger intently. Squinting up at Tilly from her awkward position, Miriam takes her mind to the series of notes and drawings currently sitting on her desk. 'Gravity, which is what I am fighting now so that the you-know-what doesn't descend to the gravel.'

How does she do it, Tilly wonders. The constant interruptions to conversation, the mess, the endless negotiation, the ice-cream stain on her jeans. Tilly tucks herself neatly into the short black dress under her autumn coat, enjoying the long, elaborate sleeves, the bell skirt. Her mind wanders to her schedule later that day. She surveys a mental checklist, tucking reminders into corners. Tilly enjoys the working of her mind. She regards it as a complex, strategic operation requiring overview and care, oiling and dusting. Out of this comes the optimistic, straightforward support she presents to friends. Within it sits a deeply secret refuge she provides for herself in times of depression or sorrow. A small chamber in her mind without words, without tactics and mechanism. In here she sits when she has to.

Blank, holding her breath. Until the engine of life demands comment and her mind picks her up and hurls her into complexity and process. She is a linear, rather than lateral thinker and supposes that if she had a child, the whole child-care thing would similarly have to be a straight-line procedure and that a lot of energy would have to be spent drawing the child back onto that line. For instance, the ice-cream episode. How would she have managed that? Well, not a cone. Asking for trouble. If it had to be an ice-cream, rather something in a tub, with a spoon. Better containment. She inches her bell skirt further away from Paul's explosive licking. Miriam watches her with a smile. 'You've got one of those thank God I am childless looks on your face.'

'Dead right. I was busy inventing a flawless, mess-free form of child-rearing.'

'Involving a cage? A straitjacket?'

'Not there yet. Meantime, protecting my haute couture from milky debris.'

'I'm not a milky debris!' shouts Paul. 'I am having a treat!'

'Yes you are, you delicious person!' Tilly throws caution to the winds and plants a kiss on Paul's dripping cheek, elongating head and neck so that her body is as far away as possible. Miriam giggles.

'So – gravity. Didn't I sent you a copy of what I have written? It's all very rough so far.' Tilly shakes her head. 'Well, I was taken by the notion that we are tethered to the earth. We can fly off, jump, elevate ourselves by living on the upper stories ... but we always have to land back again, glued. Stuck if you like. Or safely anchored? Which? So I am fascinated with ballet – points, leaps – defying gravity. Hopeless defiance, isn't it? We always return – but there's rebellion just in that moment.' Tilly stares intently at Miriam, her geometric hair swinging into its points.

'Yes, I can see where you are going ... are you talking physical or existential? '

'Both. And poetic, and surreal – and mystical ... all a mixture at the moment. No clarity yet – just playing. Birds, of course. Well, except for pigeons and vultures. Sorry to discriminate. But they're ugly. And I won't have that.'

'I want to play!' shouts Paul.

'He listens to everything.' Miriam stands, picks her son up and swings him round. 'Not too much – you just had ice-cream. That's enough.' She wipes his face. He shrieks and darts off towards a small, ragged-looking bunch of pigeons, their scruffy grey heads pecking back and forth. 'Yes, I am thinking about film – I'm talking to the old lady who disrupted Jack's class – she was a prima ballerina and still carries a degree of straight back, turned-out feet and general hauteur.'

'Well ... Keep me posted. And do you know, in all seriousness,' – Tilly stands up and unnecessarily dusts off the back of her coat – 'I think Simon might be quite a good resource for this kind of thing. If it grabs his interest, as I said.'

Miriam and Tilly part company at the ornate gate, Miriam to load her tired charge onto a bus, and Tilly striding, a little precarious, on her high-heeled boots in the opposite direction. A late afternoon wind blows rubbish from the pavement, paper and cans lodge against the park railings. On her lap, on the worn-out material of the bus seat, Paul falls asleep, the red tricycle parked in the luggage bay. Miriam is weary, her shoulders ache. Paul is inert, breathing deeply, a sweet burden on her body. She lets her attention move from him to remembered images from a recent television programme about Japanese cranes. Her heart seems to beat deeply within her body. She checks again: seemingly dislodged is the restrictive pain from the days of fear about Jack, his life, his creativity, his interest in Marie. The thought of

Simon no more gives rise to fantasy and the shrill, hurting pleasure of tit for tat. She had let herself run dry, become empty, deficient. An echo of the times when her father turns away from her poetry and gives attention to the sculptured Annette, his wife. Same feeling. Scorched earth, no rain. Dry everywhere. She must get out, must leave, it is unsafe. Out into the desert. And hatred then, for those who have turned their backs on her.

The bus jolts over a hole in the road, a heater beneath the seat scorches passengers' ankles. Paul grumbles in his sleep. Miriam notices rows of houses, and parked cars, people walking. Nothing of distinction catches her attention. She is dwelling within; noticing uneasy scratches of remembered pain within her heart, now better understood and soothed, the sharp markings softened.

Cranes fly in to dance in pairs, to hurl themselves upward, springing off the earth so that their mate is attracted, wings outspread, muscles quivering, dainty stick-feet together. Tortoises move their flippers, diagonal, one by one, inching forward, earth-bound. Tortoise: gravity, stone and flesh; crane: lightness and extension. Jack talks about Crane Form and Tortoise Qi Gong, perhaps t'ai chi and qi gong could be part of the exploration. Martial artists working with dancers? If Simon knows a dance troupe, they could work with Hannah. Miriam smiles. And she'd have to be a crane, not a tortoise. An ancient crane – dressed in rusty bird-feathers, bowing to the young ones who will never know the experiences she has had. Hannah, unforgiving of the movement of time, still pulling herself erect even as dust calls to her. A puzzle remains. Why did she think Marie was doing something harmful? Why did she come storming into Jack's class, must have taken a lot of effort to find out where it was and then get there? Miriam shrugs the question out of her mind and decides to wake Paul before the bus gets to their stop, looks in her bag for some small edible thing she can push into his mouth before he starts to protest.

Later, an email goes out to Simon. 'Tilly tells me you have contact with a dance group looking for a project. Mine might suit. Let's talk about it.' By the next day he replies. Yes.

41

Marie catches Louise with her eye as she steps down from the Newport train at Paddington station. She is wonderfully not yet seen by her sister. Martin follows Louise, holding a bag. Marie studies her sister's face, its lively immediacy, the look of rushing into things, helter skelter, no brakes, trusting the ride. The time in Wales shows her that this impression is not of the whole truth. Louise acquires additionally, surely from time as a parent, and living in Wales, a quality of cautious travelling, sobriety and tough scrutiny of the route and its hazards.

Martin, comfortable in his sinewy body, wears jeans, t-shirt and jacket, and his regulation unassuming expression. Louise is in a frilled skirt, brightly striped knee-high socks and – visible as she comes nearer, smiling as she catches sight of her sister – strappy red, retro-heeled shoes. A jacket bounces on her shoulder. Marie opens her arms and hugs her sister with warmth and delight. 'You look gorgeous! Happy birthday!'

'Mm – second teenage. It's shameful. Good thing I'm travelling with a proper grownup.' Martin embraces Marie.

'Going to take two of us to hold her down – you wouldn't think she's a London girl by birth.'

'Okay – what I want right now is to go to town and mooch about and have lunch in Chinatown. That place with the rude waiters – as long as I don't get too many green peppers in big chunks – '

'The bag?' Marie gestures to Martin. 'Do you want to leave it here? Is it heavy?'

'I am not wandering round London with this.' Martin eases the bag from his shoulder. 'We are going to Bayswater first – dropping it at Terence's flat. He's left keys for us.'

'Oh and by the way – he's invited you for dinner.' Louise looks at Marie. 'We think he took a shine to you.' Marie wants to declare that she is not shining in response, but doesn't, and the day opens out into eating and walking and talking. Louise asks how the old bird is these days since the reconciliation and Marie tells her briefly of the project. It is easy to be with Louise and Martin as a couple. They are relatively free of the intimate self-referencing litany some couples almost unconsciously perform: the exclusive repetition of the We as it moves through shared history, the drone of irritation at the emergence of well-known habits; secret looks, words, gestures. Insulated forever by the sex-in-the-Greenwich-garden episode, Marie has well-trained antennae for the invisible electrocuted fences around her sister's privacy. She seems not to have to be on her guard this easy day in London, but does not take apparent safety for granted.

In the noisy restaurant, brusquely treated by busy waiters, she, Louise and Martin follow disparate lines of observation and reflection. Martin remembers his mother's first visit to London and how she tentatively enters Soho and Covent Garden with a shopping bag of home-made sandwiches and a flask of tea. While he and his father eat pasta and drink wine in a small Italian restaurant, his mother remains in Soho Square, within sight of the restaurant, and there she consumes her lunch, feeling safe and independent, and free of any worry about foreign food getting the better of her hitherto invincible Welsh-reared good health. Martin relates this tale with delight and Marie warms to him, sensing a loving, if limited, relationship between mother and son and wondering in the back of her mind whether men who have good relationships with their mothers prove to be better husbands.

Louise is intent on shopping and after lunch drags Martin and Marie to a shoe shop in Covent Garden, renowned for footwear sprouting flowers and bows and miniature fruit made of painted clay, buttons and polka dots, velvet and lace. These seductive works of art wink from the shelves, in comparison with which even the halfway decent footwear of customers appears clumsy and functional. Marie is tempted, but decides to return another day, on her own. She leaves her sybaritic sister to an elfin salesgirl, a decorative creature as delicious as the merchandise, who should be sitting on a mushroom, sipping nectar. Martin has a half imbecilic look upon his face – as Bottom probably looks just as he enters the idyll with Titania. Marie idles her way home slowly. Dinner at Terence's Bayswater flat is timed for 8 o'clock. At first she is sad that Lou and Martin decide not to come and stay with her but, in truth, it's a relief. Place is too small.

Terence greets her at the door. There is no sign of Louise and Martin. 'Are they still out?' asks Marie.

'Well, they're in – but not yet out. Of their room I mean, or the bathroom. One of those, I think.' Terence smiles in a nervous way. To placate whatever makes him nervous, Marie, without waiting until her coat is hung and she is invited into a chair, gives him a box of ginger coated in dark chocolate, and a selection of fruit: mangoes, apricots, cherries. She doesn't want to placate him, actually, she doesn't want to do this soothing thing with anyone, so why does she start off in this way? Perhaps to save herself from his painful smile.

Dark wood, plain carpets, very little ornamentation, A sense of impersonal but good-quality masculinity. A comfortable, neutral space to come home to.

'You've taken the biggest towel!' comes Louise's voice from the bathroom, followed by a slap and a shriek of laughter.

'Oh dear, just a minute.' Terence disappears down a corridor, Marie hears him opening a cupboard and then tapping carefully on – presumably – the bathroom door. 'I have another towel – also a bath sheet. Do you want it?'

'On no, darling Terence, we're fine – just teasing him.'

'Marie's here.'

'Okay, we won't be long.' The sound of the cupboard door opening and closing again. Terence returns.

'Oh what a bad host I am – let me take your coat – what will you have to drink?' Terence takes his time opening a bottle of wine. Martin and Louise emerge, tousled and damp and hastily dressed. Louise's face is scrubbed clean of make-up. She looks young.

'Well – did you get any shoes?' Marie looks at her sister's bare feet.

'Oh you wouldn't believe how long we were there – and then I didn't get any. They are pricey and didn't quite fit – but what fun, hey?'

Terence apologises and says he has ordered a take-away Chinese selection. Home too late to cook, do they mind? The order is varied so everyone should have something and it's mostly vegetarian. Some fish. The dumplings are always good.

The easy-going atmosphere of the afternoon vanishes. Instead there is worthy and earnest questioning of routes followed, shops entered and goods observed. Martin clearly likes Terence – they have a long-standing friendship. It is easy to imagine Terence being reliable and loyal and Martin gives detail of the day in good faith, but his main attention is on Louise and the movement of her smile and the sparkle of her language. The delivery arrives and Terence finds bowls and plates so that the take-away containers can be discarded. The food is tasty.

Terence is trying to eat. He has had nothing to eat all day.

Truth be told, he is not back late from work. He's been at home all afternoon.

He can't eat, shuffles food around his plate, hiding prawns under rice and then scattering the rice. His mind is on a small leather suitcase in his room, old but in good condition., JKF, Jeremy Kingsley Faulks. It is one of the objects he brings back to his flat when his father goes to the nursing home. A terrible time. Only him to deal with it, of course. His mother is so cut off from everything. And gone away far from London. In her small flat, photographs of Rufus, the son who died. On the wall, and on the mantelpiece. There he is, a handsome little boy, looking into the camera in an inquiring way. It is not permitted, however, to mention him. He is present, and never spoken about. Terence spends a lot of time selling furniture and giving away expensive suits and ties, and the leather case is stowed away on top of his cupboard after a desultory look within. He notices old programmes and articles about ballet – his father's fascination – and closes the case without interest. Only last night does he open it again. He is looking for hangers to give to Martin and Louise. Doesn't usually have guests, and so is concerned that the spare room be comfortable and properly equipped. People always want to hang up their clothes, surely. Dusty, beneath the hangers, he finds leather under his fingers, brings the case down. Unlocking it once more, he finds theatre programmes, photographs, newspaper articles, and a pair of shoes. Ballet shoes. Small, ivory white, slightly discoloured in places, the ribbons worn, the toes stiff and rounded.

Most of the night, and through some of the afternoon after a hasty arrival at work in the morning and then a masquerade of illness – headache and stomach ache – which brings him speedily home again, Terence is confronted by the archive of his father's obsession with ballet. And in particular with one dancer, though there are photographs of a few different women. The one who dominates is called Hannah Bloom. There are newspaper cuttings, reviews of her performances. Not top class, but pretty high up. And by heavens she is pretty. Some of the photographs are formal studies, but most of the others, dated, seem to have been taken in someone's flat. Her flat? According to the dates, this affair (yes? what else to call it?) goes on for about a year and a half. And he is born during that time. And then the accident, his brother Rufus dead and the whole family messed up. His father vanishes, comes back into his life much later when Terence is independent and away from his mother. They form an uncertain, hand-shaking formal relationship, eating out together, occasionally spending time at Jeremy's home. After years of Terence being solely in the care of his mother, he then experiences an absence of mother. She cannot deal with the absence of a second son and cuts off from him, becoming vague and distant when he calls.

Terence is aware of a shining face looking at him in a puzzled way.

'You all right?' asks Louise.

'Yes, oh yes.' Terence looks at the remains of green vegetables, prawns, rice, dumplings .... He can't eat. His eyes fall on Marie. This woman has a calm face. He notices this in Wales. Puts it out of his mind, just doesn't know what to do when he fancies a woman. Well no, not fancies. Likes. Desperately he wishes she could rise from the table, ask Martin and Louise to go to their room, take him by the hand and ask him to tell her what is troubling him. This is all crazy.

'Lychees,' says Terence. 'That is what we will have. And the other fruit Marie kindly brought. Excuse me a moment, I will bring them from the kitchen.' No one offers to help him. Not from lack of courtesy but because his rising and leaving happens within an agonising plume of steam. Terence is hot and wet with some kind of anxiety. He clearly needs to bolt for a moment's respite. Privately, Louise and Marie imagine he is quite unaccustomed to entertaining and that all this is throwing him into distress. Martin thinks the poor bloke must have problems at work, and resolves to talk to him on his own after Marie leaves. Or maybe it's because Marie is there. In all the years, Martin has never been able to help Terence ease up with women. Terence never discusses the strange paroxysms he goes into when skirt is around; Martin never asks.

In the kitchen, Terence forces himself to concentrate. Lychees. Two cans. Open them and bring spoons and dessert plates. Oh and a bowl for the fruit from Marie. He must wash it first. Slowly, steady now. Those damn photographs. In her flat. Must have been her flat. She is staring into the camera with her tongue just visible between her full lips. She is bent towards it, her tiny hard breasts poking at the lens. Worst of all, in another photograph, her leg is raised, parallel to the ground – how do they do that? – and she has no underwear, just that idiotic ballet stick-out skirt. Where did he get these printed? Oh yes, didn't he have small developing room where the downstairs toilet used to be? ... with a lock and key. Private. No entry. Did them himself, didn't he? Did some landscapes which were dotted around the walls, framed. Black and white, like the pictures in the suitcase. Curling now, some damaged. Pouring the lychees into a bowl, Terence is appalled, looking at them. They look like fishy eyeballs, denuded of qualities of sight, washed clean of everything but eye-jelly. He turns his face away. And unwillingly remembers those shots in the mirror. distorted but you can see the two of them, fondling. Disgusting stuff. Terence puts the cherries under the tap, he wants to crush them between his fingers.

He wants them to bleed, to hurt them. He can't do this, go back into the dining room with these people.

Martin comes into the kitchen. Stops short when he sees Terence's face. 'Terry – what's up, man? You look terrible.'

'It's not the Chinese food. Not feeling very well – look old chap, I will leave you to it ... terrible host, what will they ....' Martin interrupts him, takes his arm, steers him out of the kitchen.

'You get in there, and then to bed. We'll have the dessert and clear up, you don't worry.' With a grateful, tight-lipped look at Martin, Terence disappears towards his bedroom. Martin carries the fruit in to Marie and Louise. The night drops a heavy curtain and not much dessert is eaten. Marie soon leaves and closes the front door with care.

Later, hardly moving, wrapped around each other, naked in the spare bed, Martin and Louise whisper that they must be very quiet making love. When they go to bed, Martin taps on their host's bedroom door, gets a muffled goodnight and no more. 'See you in the morning,' says Martin, knowing that Terence prefers life simply to go on. No fuss.

Marie is relieved to be walking down Bayswater Road towards the station. It will be a while before she is home. Poor man. Louise and Martin go back to Wales in the afternoon. How sweet to spend time with her sister. Sad about the evening. As she concentrates on her journey, distracted by the sights and sounds around her, Marie stops thinking about Terence. She knows he would like to see her again. She knows this is not going to happen.

42

'I need to place you in position.' Jack's eyes move around the floor. It's the sixth meeting of the want-some-of-that class, as he privately calls it. Thursday. Twenty young men face him. He is surprised and yet not surprised. The original five have been doing well and attending faithfully and new people come each week. He anticipates the class will continue and equally that at any minute it could close. This razor-edge of uncertainty excites him and also he likes the men. He likes their vivid language and the way they are tough and ebullient. He likes the way their collective stance towards him suggests that if he fails them, he is going to feel very sorry. These men have a hard quality, Jack can't be sure about their spoken and unspoken rules of conduct and is not sure he wants to know. They have no reason to like him or trust him. He is only as good as his last class. Well, he won't bullshit them; and he will not tolerate bullshit from them. If it's t'ai chi they want, that's what they'll get, And yes, he will style the class toward the particular cut and flourish of who they are. He is their teacher, and he could be a brother, though a brother from a different tribe. Other side of the fence brother, truth be told.

'And I also want to let you know,' he moves a tall newcomer to the back and places him after the two already standing behind Nemo. 'Yes, we will have to close this class now. Can't take any more in the room, and also, after this date it would be too complicated to have new people coming in and catching up.' Jack notices an expression on Nemo's face. As he is placed in the front, leading a row, his sharp face softens, his upper lip almost perceptibly swells. A look of pride. Steve leads the second row of four, then Hardcore, handsome in black silk trousers, a red-and-white checked cloth pulling his braids from his face. Jackson next. He lingers at the end of each class, never quite speaking to Jack and yet there is a sense of something wanting to be said. Jack wonders whether Jackson is being bullied. The evasive air he has ... is he dodging a blow, or is Jack imagining things? Jack Son, son of Jack. This is a murmured tease, once half-mentioned as the group grabs jackets and bags and leaves. Finally, Terry, the artful dodger. He stands with too-stiff attention (Jack makes a note to soften this posture) at the head of the fifth row.

Jack faces the group, synchronised now with the five pioneers in front and the others, standing in second, third or fourth rows according to how long they've been attending. His heart stings with pleasure looking at the faithful and dogged quality of the original five. With the newcomers, he is watchful, alert. He takes his time with this placing, looking at each before he speaks. 'Those who have been here before know what I am going to say. I say it again for the newcomers. It is also probable I will keep saying these things to you even when you have been here a long time.' He talks of commitment, discipline, practice. He talks of the salute, and the meaning of courtesy and discretion. He is brief and to the point. He goes through a warm-up, the qi gong standing position - knees slightly bent, weight equally distributed left and right, alert and yet relaxed – and then into the form, giving instructions that are methodical, and also visually descriptive, metaphors which provide the essence of the experience. 'Imagine the air around you is thick – almost like water – it is buoyant. As if you don't need muscles to lift the arm – it rests on a cushion of air, and the waist turning, the centre, the tan ti'en turning, move the arms .... Look ....' and he demonstrates.

Jack decides to start the 'pushing hands' practice with this group, unusually early on in the teaching. He wants them to work with each other, and to learn how to feel qualities of weight and intention from another. There is always a chance, as he moves between the pairs, demonstrating, for someone to try to uproot him, often someone taller or bigger than he is. Jack's rootedness, elasticity, experience and a developing sense of profound mischief and authority allow him each time to bounce the advancing fellow backwards. He is economical with this particular demonstration. Doesn't want to set himself up. Just enough, a little drop of spice here and there.

Jack is directed by a rudder of interest and passion as he explores depths of himself and draws to the surface new levels of understanding and intelligence. In some ways the thinking and practice is no different from that utilised with his regular class, but his body tells him he is accessing treasures from hitherto uncharted layers. He cannot make assumptions, he is not altogether comfortable, does not feel altogether safe. He is listening to the hairs on the back of his neck as he dives. He is not alone, and he has resources he never dreamed of. An unknown is unfolding. The impetus, the initiation, he is sure, emerge from the small, illuminated form of Han, now dwelling within his life, he knows not how or why. Jack does not speak of Han to Miriam, or to anyone else. Nor will he speak of the development of urgent and passionate prayer he is starting to deliver to this Aged One, matters of the heart which are almost inarticulate, a manner of speaking which is, as it were, beyond language, and how could he ever pass on the most immediate and unselfconscious manner in which he addresses the Luminous One as Beloved Friend? Is he mad? Deluded? If he is, time will tell, and the whole thing will fall apart. Egg on face, big time.

Jack ends the class with a sitting meditation. He suggests a posture of alert relaxation, he describes the possibility of moment to moment connection with body, emotions and thoughts. 'This is my body; I live in it, I am responsible for it, my awareness is the director of my actions, feelings and thoughts. If I am afraid of someone and let that feeling run away with me, if I hate someone, if I envy someone and let those feelings run away with me, I am giving away what I am, I am giving away my strength, my dignity. We feel what we feel; we can't help that. But we don't lose our balance.' He thinks of his father, of his grandfather. He feels heat up his spine, tingling in his hands. What he is saying is true for his own rapidly developing, private and unexpected sense of autonomy. If it works for others, they will use it. If it doesn't make sense they will forget it or not come back. He is talking to himself. This is what he needs to hear. This is what the bullied need to hear; and, indeed the bullies. Three have left since the class began. One of these has since returned.

The class is over; some shoot rapidly out of the door, others, who like to hang back and talk or repeat moves, exit more slowly. Jackson is once more the last one to go. Jack replaces the chairs. Is Beloved Friend present? He never sees him when he looks, never hears him when he listens. In a pale flash of something dull gold and red, unexpected and within a movement of time unaffiliated to clock or watch, there he is. Or not.

Walking to the station, Jack reflects that he knows nothing about the lives of these students. He is offered more biography from the members of the other class. These guys melt away at the end of the session. He has phone numbers but no addresses, home or email. Is this professionally acceptable? Perhaps he ought to start a register. Something to think about.

'Hey!' a voice coming at him from the shadows. Jack frowns, then makes out the shape.

'Jackson?'

'Can I walk with you?'

'Well, I am going to the station. Sure, if that's the way you're walking.' They walk in silence.

'Sifu ....'

'Yes.'

'It sounds a bit stupid saying that name outside the class.'

'Mm.'

'Do you ever get scared?' A group of girls goes by. Despite the cold air, they are wearing short skirts and skinny tops, their faces are lit up with colour; lipstick, blusher, blue metallic paint on their eyelids; they are shrieking at each other, waving and gesticulating strong bare arms and laughing. Jack and Jackson make way. The entourage, driven by alcohol and hormones, flick at the two men eyes dangerous as pieces of sharp stone. 'These sisters they can fuckin' kill you man.' Jackson's voice is a whisper. 'Sometimes I think they more worse than the brothers ....'

'You asked me if I ever get scared?' Jack stops walking. He faces the young man. 'Yes, sure I do. Scared of people, things ... things in my imagination that make me fear even if there's no reason.' He stops talking and remains standing, looking at the younger man. 'What about you?'

'Yeah, this and that. Anyway, got to go. See you next week.' Jackson moves away lightly, rapidly, Jack watches him dart between groups of people, his eyes low, his head down. At the corner he turns, looks back, notices Jack in the same place where they parted company, and, with a crooked little smile, brings his hands together in a small, discreet version of the salute. Jack does the same, with equal discretion, and moves on, his heart touched – and heavy at the same time with the sense of an unshed story, a story that might never be told. In a sudden movement of sorrow, he hits his right fist into his left palm. Disappointment, Jack tells himself. Take care, there is always disappointment. Not as a negative, not as a glass half-empty, but as a discernible, ever-present, inevitable, neutral event related to hope or expectation. He could start now to imagine some kind of epiphany with this class, with Jackson. Dangerous. It is as it is. Has its own life. Could go to epiphany, could stop, go sour. He could get waylaid and beaten up by a posse of brothers who don't like what's going on. Moment to moment, responding truthfully to whatever is presented to him, this is the only real possibility. Jack smiles, swerving down into the underground, breathing the gusts of impaired air pouring from unseen vents. As he observes, without malice or correction, the meandering of his hopeful mind, this very act of noticing, the directness and simplicity of noticing, gives him joy.

Jack boards the carriage and removes a ragged newspaper from his seat before sitting down. The Old One, the Beloved, occupies the seat opposite! Travelling without a ticket on the Northern line? He is smiling. His cheeks round up like apples, his skin resembles the beaten quality of old iron, his eyebrows rise and flow, arc around the curving line of his oriental eyelids. Smiling, and then gone. Fleet, sharp, powerful and mischievous. Thus accompanied, Jack sits, quietly fizzing, amidst the cast-off newspapers and sweet wrappers.

43

Thursday evening again. A week since the brief talk with Jackson, and Jack walks through the side-streets of Islington and Angel, avoiding rotting piles of fruit scattered around locked-up market stalls. He's a little early for the class and his mind automatically runs through the familiar opening ritual: the salute and the bow. The original five are starting to bow with a flourish of entitlement and pride, in contrast to new members who give a brief inclination of the head, barely concealing their disbelief and cynicism.

The practice room is a little stuffy and Jack opens windows as students arrive. Before long, a group of men, known and unknown, stands before him. Jack works through the warm-up. The practice is not flowing as usual, it is jarred by increasing tension between two of the new students. Tall, serious Raj and the cocky fellow who gives his name as Skipper. They are following the instructions, but Jack senses that a quarrel is wordlessly developing between them. He decides to let it be. He ends the routine with a meditation, bows and salutes. The class responds and leaves, clattering down the stairs, taking the sour, oppressive cloud of Raj and Skipper with them.

Jack, gathering his belongings and making sure the room is left in good order, becomes aware of shouting and swearing from the street below. He looks out of the window. Raj and Skipper grip each other, staring and mouthing unintelligible aggression. Several men from the class add excitable voices. Jack stares as a glint of metal pokes an ugly element into the scuffle. Visible, and then gone. Without hesitation, he drops his jacket, runs down the stairs, arrives into the midst of glowering, feral radiation between Raj and Skipper. Jack's thoughts clamour, as if he thinks them all at once, a collision of questions, none of them answered: What is he doing? What about the fucking knife? This is outside of the classroom, not his responsibility. Does he also want a fight? Or is this part of the whole new thing?

Well, too late for speculation. He is here, in between two powerful and angry men. If there is a knife, it has disappeared. He can smell sweat, and a pungent and disturbing odour of men's after-shave. Synthetic lime. Raj is trembling and an unattractive line of saliva trickles down the side of his mouth. Skipper grabs Jack's arm. With a practised shrug, Jack shakes him off. Jackson and Hardcore are nearest to their teacher, open-mouthed and breathing hard with excitement. Will this be another demonstration of what they originally saw? Will Jack throw these two onto the sides of cars, into the gutter?

Hardcore suddenly recalls the knife. Hisses at Jack in fear, trying not to be heard by others. 'Sifu ... there's a weapon.'

A realisation, sharp and clear, whistles into Jack's mind, cuts out Hardcore's whisper. This whole thing is not just about the classroom. This is Han imparting deeper initiation into the Warrior's art. The warrior doesn't stay upstairs straightening chairs while downstairs explode the effects of the y chromosome men inherit from their ancestors who hunted with spears and who savaged their enemies' limbs from their bodies.

Jack also knows he could end up bloodied and foolish.

Too late. He's involved. River of no return.

Raj tries to push him out of the way. He lunges towards Jack, his eyeballs twitching side to side like bruised small fish, smashed onto the quayside but not yet dead. Skipper once more tries to grab Jack's arm. Jack feels a power rising within him, from the ground to his feet through his balls, tan ti'en, through his arms. He clips back his fourth and fifth fingers beneath his thumbs, and with the pincers now created by second and third fingers and with the motion of an arrow leaving a bow, with the fast movement of a cobra towards its prey, he jabs left-right his sword-fingers first into Skipper and then into Raj, into vulnerable points in the solar plexus. Not too much – he doesn't want to injure them. Just enough to stop them in their tracks. Startled, winded, the men's bodies buckle. Raj lets out a high yelp as he staggers back. Hardcore and Jackson take hold of him. Skipper doubles up, he groans. Neither man has the capacity at that moment to retaliate. Jack puts his hand onto Skipper's arm, and then looks at Raj, still supported by Hardcore and Jackson. He notices strangers, hovering on the outskirts of the throng, fearful and righteous, some taking out their phones. One he observes in particular, a man with a high-pitched voice who keeps saying, 'Someone must stop this – I won't have it – ' Skipper hoarsely tries to shout but his voice won't come through.

'Let's get out of here!' Jack says quietly to the two men. 'Keep away from the public. Upstairs.' Jack keeps Skipper by the arm, Skipper wrenches him off. 'Get up there or you are out of my class,' says Jack in a low and tight voice. Glaring at him, Skipper follows the group now heading back up. His feet want to walk away, all of him wants to walk away, shouting and swearing revenge. So why the hell is he letting himself go upstairs? 'And you, please,' Jack looks at Raj. The tall man's eyes flicker hatred but, drawn by critical mass and persistent curiosity, he too returns to the training room.

Once inside, Jack fetches an empty metal box that usually lies on the window sill. 'Your weapons in here. Now. You'll get them back.' No one moves. 'One by one – put them in.' He swiftly counts heads. Twelve of the usual twenty are in the room. 'And then take your places in rows as usual.' He stands. He waits. Three men, including Skipper, approach the box. When they have returned to their positions, Jack covers the box with his coat.

'I want you all to breathe – right down into your feet. Several breaths, you know how.' The room fills with heavy silence, disturbed suddenly by the sound of a police siren. A car stops. Doors open and close. Rapid voices rise and fall. Jack can hear the high-pitched tones of the earlier spectator. Footsteps clatter up the stairs and the door is opened. Two policemen. They look irritated. Their bodies are solid, packed tightly into regulation dark uniform. The heavier and slightly taller man has very large, red hands, his fingers play oddly around the clasp of his belt. The second man stands quietly; it is his eyes which have movement, scanning the room and the faces with sharp gaze, his lips tightly pursed.

'What's going on here?' asks the heavier man. His thumbs hook into his belt, and his large fingers now rest motionless against dark trousers.

'This is my t'ai chi class.' Jack speaks courteously.

'What's that when it's at home?' asks the second uniformed man. His eyes stare at Jack. 'We were called because of a fight.'

'These are my students and I am dealing with it.' The second man continues looking at Jack, with an expression of disdain.

'So let's have a demonstration if you're a class,' says the first, with mock weariness. Something has shifted in his demeanour. He moves his large left hand and glances surreptitiously at his watch.

'Certainly.' Jack gestures towards the chairs and offers the audience of two the possibility of being seated, but the larger policeman waves his hands in a fussy gesture, and the men remain standing. Every member of his class is watching Jack without a flicker of distraction. Silence reassembles in the room. Jack – as he would under normal circumstances – instructs the class to settle into the posture, and then begin the form. Obediently, breathing deeply, the class moves into the first posture, slow and deliberate, all together.

'Okay okay,' says the taller, bulky man. 'Enough. I see it in the park.' And then with icy protocol and politeness: 'Excuse us for entering your class, sir, but this is our patch and we are here to maintain law and order.' He turns to his partner. 'Let's go.' The two men make a belligerent exit. Car doors slam, an engine starts up. Jack waits in case the high-pitched onlooker is still present to insist that more action should be taken, but there is no further dialogue from the street.

'Raj and Skipper – please come to the front.' Jack places the two combatants facing each other, and instructs them to bow. The rest of the class remains watchful. 'You may be angry.' Jack addresses the two before him. 'There may be good reason for being angry. But right now I want discipline and courtesy. In this bow, I want agreement that in spite of difference and dislike, you will be respectful of the other. If you bow, it doesn't mean the other guy has won. No winners, no losers.' Sullen, but willing, the men incline their heads. 'Now – pushing hands,' says Jack. 'No force, no muscle, just following the energy of the other. The rest of you, please observe.

'Raj and Skipper please stand like me. Right leg forward, left leg behind, feet shoulder-width apart, left foot angled 45 degrees. Body facing squarely forward.' Raj takes position, still glowering, shooting quick glances of reproach at Jack; Skipper's face is impassive as his body settles.

'Now – watch me. Shift your weight backwards and forwards so that we get the sense of right leg full, left leg empty. Additionally, allow a sense of pushing from the floor, as if a coiled spring of energy rises from the floor into your right foot up the leg, through the tan ti'en – and then as you shift weight, the energy, the spring, moves into the other leg. Now the left leg is full.'

Jack is in the courteous detached mode he adopts when teaching, fully absorbed. 'Okay – now from the left to the right.' The three men move slowly and with increasing gravity backwards and forwards.

Satisfied, Jack calls a halt. 'That's the first principle. The shifting of weight. The second principle is the receiving of the weight and force of the other – and the third is to use the weight and aggression of the other to your advantage by the dropping into the tan ti'en and turning the waist. With the turning of the waist comes the circulation of the hand – hence the term Pushing Hands.' Jack stands opposite Skipper. 'Let me demonstrate.'

The large, angry man stands opposite Jack. Now a sickly smile hangs on his lips, his body is peppered with the resentment and unease. He is bigger than Jack, stronger, broader. He looks at Jack with disbelief. He has heard about the capacity of this pale man but he is new to the class and hasn't seen it. As far as he's concerned, rumours are always exaggerated. Nonetheless guys he respects have been coming to learn. Every week. He wants to know what's going on.

'Okay, Skipper,' says Jack. 'Raise your right hand about chest height.' Each man is in the designated stance, facing one another. Jack edges closer so that they are touching, back of the hand to back of the hand. 'Now,' Jack instructs, 'turn your hand, and push against my arm as hard as you can.'

The smile turns into a willing grimace as Skipper puts all his aggression and tension into pushing the irritating man in front of him. Jack receives the push. After years of practise he knows – don't brace the arms, the upper body. Keep it all soft, fluid. Take the push down, receive it, into the tan ti'en, move it through as the weight shifts from forward leg to back leg, and then let the back leg and the central column of the torso drill themselves into the floor, earthed, powered by the energy they have received. With a vivid, corkscrew turn of the waist and his right hand flipping to show the palm outward and guide Skipper's body away from him, Jack releases charged-up energy and feels a rush as Skipper's heavy weight spins past his right side. Skipper is moving as if blasted by a powerful wave, juddering and bouncing. Jack's hand completes a half-circle and then snaps onto Skipper's wrist, steadying him. Panting, startled, Skipper rights himself and stares at Jack. Jack looks at him and then bows to him. 'Thank you.' Everyone watches, breath held, to see whether Skipper will respond in kind. An endless second passes. Then – a very small bow – a mumbled thank you.

Skipper is confused. This weirdo has had two occasions where he could have hurt him. There's a place in his solar plexus that is still tender from the jab of Jack's fingers. But he knows – it could have been worse. The guy obviously held back. And now, with a strange sense of spiralling elasticity crackling through his body, in spite of himself Skipper feels quite excited. He won't show it. Oh no. Puts on his best poker face and makes way for Raj.

Raj is not sure whether it's better or worse to go second. He's watched very carefully – what can he do that's smart? He and Jack take their positions, They place their hands back to back. Raj decides: as soon as Jack turns to the right and tries to take him in that direction, he'll yank him to the left. He's bigger than him. he won't be expecting it. He pushes – forcefully. Jack takes it in as far as he can, and notices in the push, something that wants to go both directions. As he sinks down and roots himself, he allows himself to receive this energetic intelligence. He twists his waist to the right and then suddenly turns it to the left and Raj, his mouth agape with astonishment, bounces past Jack's left side and heads towards the back wall. Three students rush to catch him before he collides with it.

'Jeez!' shouts Raj. 'Shit! – got to say that's something.' Everyone laughs, the laughter grows and rolls. Skipper, after a while, joins in. Jack watches everyone around him. He claps his hands.

'Years and years of practice,' he says. 'So, Raj and Skipper, want to work together on this? While we do it, you others pair up and have a go.'

As Raj and Skipper begin, back of hand to back of hand, Jack issues careful instruction. Initially there is a tendency to push too hard but slowly the practice softens and becomes more elastic. After twenty minutes, Jack requests the men step back into the initiating stance, to make eye contact, and to bow, signifying completion.

'Thank you everyone,' says Jack. 'I appreciate you staying and coming back to support us going through this extra bit of teaching. We are all like Raj and Skipper. We get mad. Things get hot. Suddenly something's happening that's like wildfire.' He looks around carefully, 'There is another way.' Jack pauses. 'Take your weapons from the box,' he says, 'and I never want to see them in my class again.'

As the group disbands for the second time, curious glances find their way to Jack who begins to pack up once more. Voices and feet clatter, once more descending the stairwell. His glance pulled into the darkest corner, Jack senses heat, a burning unseen package of will, wisdom and love. He murmurs 'Beloved ...' and then realises Jackson is still in the room.

'Sifu,' – Jackson's eyes are wide – 'that was awesome man, and' – his eyes flicker – 'what is that in the corner? I can't see nothing but I know something is there ....'

'Jackson,' Jack puts his coat on. 'Some things just can't be explained.' Jackson hops around him as they leave the room.

'There's more wanting to join – what are we going to do?' asks Jackson, forgetting that he usually shoots oblique glances rather than give full-faced attention. His eyes are wide, looking at Jack, with a mixture of love, envy, fear.

'I have an idea,' Jack walks quickly. He is hungry; wants to get home. 'Tell you next week.'

'Awesome man, Sifu man.' Jackson darts off into the shadows.

'Beloved,' whispers Jack as he walks to the station. A prayer without coherence rises from him, in which he communicates joy, gratitude, accomplishment, in which he communicates the sense of courtesy he feels towards the policemen, courtesy he invites into the classroom as knives lie under his jacket. He could get into deep shit for this. Is he colluding with violence? If he thinks back to the moments of action as he runs down the stairs, disrupts the two men physically and orders the class back into the room, he feels only calm decision. If his adrenalin had been up he would have felt more excited, a key player in a drama. Now, all is quiet. Time will tell, he murmurs to himself. And receives an inner injunction: take nothing for granted, be aware, be watchful, outward and inward.

Jack looks towards the corner of the street – it's always possible, the Ancient One could alight at any moment into the most mundane fleeting habitation. He sees nothing, but feels the presence of weight in his belly; a dark rock. His body is shaking a little, he can't quite feel its periphery, his skin. The core, the molten core – and wide space. Endless. He shoves his hands into his pockets and onto his lower abdomen, and enjoys the rhythm of walking. On the edge of his eye caught, flickering, a trembling of light, a vivid shape of moving illumination, softening the irregular paving stones for the flash of a second.

44

Maliphant sends a text to Jack: wot u up 2? ivry 1 talk of it. we eat fri eve? 7? Contadino. kntsh tn rd. Jack replies: u pay we eat. Maliphant: u pay. u rich and gonna get richer wn I tell you wots up.

The home-made tomato soup is the best. Huge plates, creamy red thick liquid lapping generously at the edges, decorated with spirals of cream, parsley chopped into the middle, rough black pepper discharged onto the surface from an absurdly large pepper grinder Afterwards, spaghetti with tomato, mushroom, chorizo, lavish parmesan. Olives. Thick pieces of crusty white bread. Beer. Perfect. Neither friend says much until at least half the heaped portion of pasta is demolished. Jack and Maliphant have been here before. The bill is always reasonable. The owner tucks a sleeveless cardigan into his trouser belt, managing still to look elegant. Today he wears a mixture of cream and green. He is affable, courteous and easy with his customers – most of them faithful returners. His son, swarthy and plump, mops his brow and dashes and dives between tables. They don't look like father and son.

'Right.' Maliphant chases a thick pool of tomato and mushroom gravy with crusty bread, then holds the bread steadily in the gravy, watching its spongy texture absorb liquid. 'That hole in my stomach is now partly filled. Another beer to go with the gravy and I'll tell you what's on my mind.' Jack, face almost dug into his bowl, grunts agreement. Maliphant crams the sodden crust into his mouth and manages at the same time to order two more beers. Italian. Not the best, they acknowledge, but goes with the food. Taking a break, finally, his eyelids heavy with satisfaction, Maliphant turns towards Jack.

'Your school – your new school, I know all about it.'

'You would.'

'Yeah – course I would. Some of them are mine. Not mine possessive, you understand, but responsibility-wise. In my patch, you know. No names no pack drill. Don't need to tell you, and this isn't tales after school, okay?'

'So?' Jack's mouth is full, he chews and swallows slowly, eyes down, one hand round the neck of his beer bottle.

'First of all, it takes some guts. You could trespass on very carefully drawn lines of allegiance. Quick encounter in the dark, and you're done for, or very hurt if you trespass.'

'So?'

'Do you know, my friend, you are losing your rhetorical skills. But – seriously now – you appear to be doing something that really works. And all sorts of ears are listening.' Jack pours half the beer from the newly arrived bottle into his glass, sits back. 'Word has come to me through the wires that the prison service is interested in you.'

'Maliphant you bastard, you're turning me in.'

'Won't be a moment too soon – you are a menace.' Maliphant, for Jack, is a fresh pleasure after the discipline of work. He wonders what his friend would make of the Ancient One. Wouldn't make anything of him as he wouldn't be able to see him. Is the seeing because of an ability to see? This question seems to radiate from a different language, the flavour of the Beloved. At the same time, Jack, redolent with good food, feeling the satisfaction of eye, tongue and belly, tastes also the satisfaction of friendship, of men, of sitting square on the seat, within the comfort and strength and capacity of his body.

'I'm on a roll – could stop or go pear-shaped at any time.'

'Two prisons, one in London and one in Birmingham, want you to teach prisoners t'ai chi.' Jack picks up the glass in front of him and studies it thoughtfully. He puts it back on the table and remains a silent for a further moment before replying.

'Tell you what, Maliphant – I can't do that. Takes too long, too time-consuming. But I could teach others to teach. Better use of my time. Tell you something ....' Clear and without reservation, Jack continues, his hand remaining around the glass of beer, ignoring two people noisily leaving, evidently familiar customers. They embrace the owner, promise allegiance and attendance the following week, praise the food, arms around the owner's solid body in its green sleeveless tucked-in knitted jersey. The son looks on without expression. 'This is a plan stewing right now. I am planning to train my five musketeers, the originals who tried to hammer me.' Jack's face has a quality his friend has not seen before. Curiously, if he were to name it, he would call it happiness. Further, it is usually he, Maliphant, who is the initiator, though never would Jack be thought of as passive. Usually Maliphant would drive the conversation, holding the conversational aggression, as it were. Now he can feel Jack full, primed and ready to shoot. Leaning back into his chair, sipping thoughtfully, his mouth loaded with taste, Maliphant listens. 'If you are ready to learn, you can be one step ahead and teach well enough. You have to be awake and aware of what you are doing and teach exactly what you are told. And then – adding to that – have you heard about *El Sistema* – Venezuela – started over three decades ago by an economist and politician called José Antonio Abreu? One of his most famous pupils – Gustavo Dudamel – is a well-known conductor now. Street kids were pulled into garages, any vacant space big enough for a makeshift school room, given musical instruments and – this is the special quality – started playing together at once as an orchestra, rather than going through years of individual painstaking tuition through scales and graduated exercises. Learning, right from the word go, from nothing, to play together. We went to one of the early concerts by the first orchestra that developed from it, at the Albert Hall, and they played *West Side Story* – you know, Leonard Bernstein.' A dark shape materialises at their table. The owner's son asks if they want to see the menu.

'Ten minutes – ' Maliphant keeps his eyes on Jack. Doesn't want the flow interrupted. The boy moves away, wiping emptied tables.

'I wish you'd been there.' Jack regards his friend with a smile. 'These kids were rising from their chairs with the energy of playing. And the sound, the impact – sensational!' Jack takes a long pull of beer, wipes his mouth of froth, breathes out audibly. 'Well – what I am doing and what was done in Venezuela is not the same – but there is a small element that connects me. What Abreu saw, I think, was exclusion. Kids excluded because they were never going to get training as classical musicians. Too expensive – too loaded with formality and time considerations, shortage of teachers. No entry into one of the marvels of our life. So he devised a way of collaborative teaching. Disciplined, focussed – but also chaotic. And of course – out of chaos, creativity.' Jack reaches over the table and touches Maliphant on the shoulder. 'So ... I could say a lot more about this, but what I am doing is kind of collaborative, though I stay strictly with the principles of t'ai chi. Tried and trusted. People are talking a lot these days about mindfulness. We are not mindful about our bodies – kids adorn their bodies in tribal dress, and gestures and language develop and spread ... but there is very little awareness of inner feelings relating to the body. Of inner awareness. Of the skill and strength of self-awareness and discipline. Not discipline from an outer system of moral exhortation – but from one's own understanding and experience. Self-respect and autonomy and autonomous choice is what I am talking about.' Jack leans back and closes his eyes. Maliphant checks himself. Is his friend turning into a fundamentalist, has he been listening to a messianic monologue? He'd be off – in a flash – if this was so. No, the guy is genuinely alight with something. He is not imposing it – well, not yet.

'No shit,' he says, released now from acute concentration. 'Dessert? Coffee?'

'Coffee.' Jack gestures to the son, who takes his time arriving. 'I'm nearly done – I think – okay, let's get down to the plan. The system. Yes, this class is going well. It's astonishing. I am strict, I respect them, I teach the basics, no messing. I demand punctuality, payment and attention. And so many want to come, I could open new classes for every day of the week. Not on. I don't want to. So what I am planning is to give teacher training to the five. And you might be able to help here. We need rooms. Got a spare garage?' He turns a sarcastic, interrogative eyebrow to Maliphant. 'Well, I reckon one guy takes on five – anyway, haven't the total picture yet – this is as far as I've got. And I check those classes regularly. Lay out strictly what and how they teach. And then – every now and then – maybe once every two months, we all get together – big hall – for fine tuning, questions and all.' Jack pauses. He laughs. 'I think that's it. Never known you so silent mate. I've run you over, hey? About time.'

Maliphant slaps Jack lightly on his back. 'Just this once … don't get used to it. So, over to me. News travels fast. Something also about a fight. Don't tell me, I don't want to know. Well, the prisons offer, as you know, all kinds of stuff. Someone at Birmingham – Bleesdale Prison – you've heard of it. Relatively new, some radical views being tried out there. A little like what you said about exclusion. Well, their boss –

indirectly – and through his secretary – heard that I know you, asked me to get in touch. Here's his number. They want to discuss el English System with you. Right – over to you. No shit if you don't, I've done my bit.'

No one would know, not even the astute owner and his watchful son, but there were three of us at a corner table. Yes! Three! I had visitors and it was an unexpected joy. Strange was it not that no one approached this table. The son did not adjust plates and eating implements. And yet, not strange. The table remained wrapped in a benevolent indescribable substance, a sacred space declared, though no-one heard the declaration. One or two guests looked our way, puzzled, and then returned to conversation. Dzukh had his back to us, but that which his companion called 'Happiness', seeing it writ upon his features, was also that We Three smiled and encompassed him within our Threefold Heart. He knew not that we were there; he knew without knowing that we three were there. Yes indeed, Dear Friends, you who accompany my telling of this beautiful tale, it was indeed Master Yang and Madame Li who sat with me. That is, for the esteemed Madame, the arrival of a violet intensity, and within and roundabout, Threads of transluscent ivory: Master Yang sent an emissary of himself which expressed itself as deep red, a flash of fire from unearthly realms, the fire of experience, deep knowledge, and the collected wisdom of those who have gone before along the same martial arts path. In contrast to the delightful babble between folk dining together, we three exchanged no words, but adjusted our Accord, and Communed. Deeply and lovingly. Humorously too – for Master Yang signalled that he might request a sojourn upon the Green Planet were he able to obtain a large white plate and the red soup steaming within and remember the visceral delight of tongue upon liquid, and liquid edging downwards to warm the belly, and the eye feasting upon colour and the nose feasting upon aroma!

Signalled by their visitation was that my time upon Earth was coming to an end. Seventy days, and Han would return to the Heavenly Realms. For so it was agreed. Healing and cleansing had begun within the direct family realm of my dear bother Dzukh – and also, on a wider scale – healing had begun for our young brothers of this great city, and would continue to pour towards brothers and sisters further afield. Indeed, Master Yang and Madame Li had latterly cast their Influence upon the entire journey, the influence of their particular practice. How fortunate that Madame Li's unique distillation would continue to be received. Dzukh would absorb the powerful transmission that she formulated behind the walls of the nunnery. Dzukh, being of strength and sensitivity appropriate, was being elected next in line incarnate .... The vessel needs to be strong and of clean materials, otherwise the transmission burns, and the vessel cracks. Those whose foundations were less strong would not have been able to hold the fire. Dzukh is an old soul – a strong old pot! Weathered through the ages, devoted and one-pointed and deeply loving of the martial art. The work that we had done together in that immediate while had cleared his pot of some of the cobwebs that previously lined its form.

A barely discernible tremor signalled that my Beloved Friends were about to depart. A question from me hovered lightly in the field of our Communion. It was not phrased – it suggested itself as a raised eyebrow upon a human face suggests a question. The ivory and the violet wrapped itself into intentional velocity, and left; the red similarly vibrated itself into a spiral forcefield ... and left. And I remained with my question: There is something else that is manifesting here upon Earth for Han. And as yet I know it not. The question settled into agreeable equanimity, and, delighted and humoured by the brief visitation of Friendship from the two Great Beings, I twined myself into rapturous Silence, and sat without requirement, deeply folded into Trust and Agreement.

Jack turns around, notices an empty table for three, and sees, for the flash of a second, sitting cross-legged on one chair, clad in a robe of soft, unadorned material, his Beloved, eyes closed, a peaceful smile upon his face. Jack's heart leaps, moisture rushes to his eyes, and he grabs a napkin and puts it to his face. Maliphant observes him curiously. Jack stays still, briefly, acknowledging with gratitude beyond expression the mystery and accompaniment that is granted to his life. Something is happening which changes him forever.

The two men embrace, affectionately, outside the restaurant. It is less cold than usual, a brief tease from spring, sending out a messenger, not ready to arrive herself, but around the corner, under the ground, waiting until ready, knowing she has first to wait the duration of winter. Jack and Maliphant stride off, in different directions.

'Jack!' Maliphant has swung around on his heels. Jack pauses. 'One question, mate!' They walk towards each other. 'Just a thought ... you're not setting up a youth army, like Putin? He rounds up scores of the disaffected young ones, teaches them martial arts and anti-Western propaganda and sets them loose every time there's dissidence and a gathering in a square ....'

'Well now, your deductions are immaculate. Today Kings Cross, tomorrow Trafalgar Square!' Maliphant pokes a mock right fist into his friend's chest. Jack brushes him away and kisses him smack on the cheek. They embrace and set off again on their separate routes.

45

'Miriam ....' Miriam removes her glasses, reminding Jack of the habit she has of taking aids to sight from her face when she needs to listen. A query in her eyes, she gazes at her husband.

'You've got a look of heavy intention. What do you want from me? I'm suspicious.'

'Well might you be. I want a favour. A boon, fair maiden ... I know I said I'd look after the little fellow this morning but I desperately need time.' Miriam looks at him in a less friendly way. 'I'll be as quick as I can. Going up to Soho with a student from the new group. Getting some kit ....'

'I need time too – have a meeting on Friday.'

'I know – can we swop? I'll do a few hours before Friday?' They bargain, and Miriam agrees, but as the door closes she feels irritated. She can't quite hold her corner and match Jack's urgency with enough of her own. She feels a flare of aggravation and resentment from the soles of her feet to the top of her head, and wonders at the disproportion of this reaction to the minor importance of the event that triggers it. Must be the 'I want' factor ... something she sees clearly in Paul, but then he is not yet three years old. She is a fully grown rational woman who loves her husband. So why can't she let it be?

Guiltily putting Paul in front of children's TV she sits in the kitchen, cradles a cup of coffee and lets herself sink into a strange place of sorrow and resentment, a sensation of being at odds with herself, at odds with the energy and well-being she has been basking in of late. She wonders at the inevitable interference with sweetness. Jack is robust and bursting with his new project, she is moving ahead with hers. She will meet Simon and the dancers on Friday. She has a lightly sketched proposition, and this is the way she wants it now. Nothing fixed yet. Space for new input. Tears, surprising her, run down her cheeks. It is all so fragile, she murmurs aloud. What is it that is so fragile? We, the human we. Subject to many strange tides and rumours. She lies in bed with this husband and they hold each other and say words of love, and their life is benevolent. The fragility? The sense that good fortune and sweet times cannot run forever? These days, running one into the other, she and Jack float in a mutual erotic stream. So different from the paranoia and anxiety of recent times. The Marie fear-time, as she privately calls it. How different now. Marie is becoming a friend. Delicately, slowly, but real enough. Jack's reasonable request this morning should not jolt her into this unhappy state – though yes, it jolts her.

That's it – in the swim of things as they are now, a kind of confluent murmuring between them, the moment of change and negotiation with him feels like an intrusion. She arranges in her mind that he will go off with Paul, or at least keep him occupied at home, and this arrangement is suddenly disrupted. That's it. Her mind is living a continuum which creates itself out of the 'I want', and when this continuum is disrupted she feels fury. The plan, the desire, is fixed, inflexible.

Her tears are drying now. I will not let the narrower end of my mind dictate my reality, Miriam thinks – and then laughs. The mind deciding to disempower the mind? No, this decision to unseat the narrow thought isn't a mental one – it's a wish, from her bones, from her heart.

Miriam studies herself in the mirror. She looks tired, and as though she has been through a small, private war. Gathering the wounded, soothing the ground, moving slowly behind a ragged soldier playing a solitary tune, she goes to rescue her son from another onslaught of small moon-faced creatures presently cavorting on the screen.

'No, no, no! I need to watch!' Paul is desolate. Miriam determinedly scoops up the resistant child, now fighting his own war by struggling in his mother's arms. They make peace in the kitchen by agreeing that they will make gingerbread men.

Jackson is in seventh heaven. He is with strange white Sifu in the heart of Chinatown. He walks with his distinctive hip-enhancing lilt next to Jack, glancing surreptitiously at him every now and then, noticing his movements, mannerisms, the way he speaks. Jack weaves his way with familiarity through streets vehicle-free and overflowing with Chinese vegetables, groceries and bric a brac. The Martial Arts shop is small, bursting with shelves, shelves laden with neatly packed boxes, further shelves and walls stuffed with photographs, weaponry. Jackson is spellbound before the swords, decorated with calligraphy and dragons. Jack calls him away.

'Come here, please Jackson, I need your advice. You, and the other four. We have to guess the sizes. Small, medium or large. I am getting you each one of these black t'ai chi suits.'

'Sure, sure Sifu.' It takes time to choose and decide. The Chinese assistant is simultaneously patient and taciturn, Jackson ransacking his brains with answers to questions he can't ask. Why are you doing this? Are you paying for them? Will we have to pay you back? What's going to happen? He struggles to keep his face expressionless and consequently it is unusually rigid. His usual look – a combination of cynicism, excitement and pride – is ironed out with a determination to maintain a mask of mature indifference. He also has a worry he wants to talk to Jack about. How to do it? When to do it? Finally, the purchase is neatly packed into a parcel. Jack pulls out his credit card. While he is busy tapping in his pin number, Jackson wanders to the weaponry corner. 'Sifu man, do you use these?' Jackson points to the swords.

'Not sure what you mean by use. I have learned two sword forms. One broadsword – the curved one – and one straight.'

'Will you show us?'

'Not for a while. That's how it is, you need to train a while first. It extends the form as we do it – instead of ending at your fingertips, you end at the sword tip. So first get to know your own hands, see?'

'Cool.' They are walking rapidly now to the tube.

'Jackson – can you get in touch with the other four? I want to meet you all an hour before class tomorrow. No extra cost. You have my number, will you let me know how many can come?'

'Sure.' Jackson puts on an impassive look, attempting once more to disguise his reaction. This time it is pleasure at being entrusted with the message. Jack would like to engage with him further, but he wants to get back to Miriam. He and Jackson smile at each other like conspirators as they are about to part company but all at once there is a worried look in Jackson's eyes that is more pronounced than usual.

'Jackson? Everything all right?'

'Yes. No. Can we just stop?' The two men pause. Jackson looks furtively left and right, then turns around and looks in front and behind.

'Jackson, are you in trouble?'

'No, Sifu Jack – Maybe you ....'

'I'm in trouble?' Jack's voice rises a little and Jackson hushes him. They are standing next to a functional-looking tearoom in Charing Cross Road. 'Let's go in here – we get some tea.'

Jackson, hunched over a thick white mug of tea, looks carefully at Jack. 'There might be grief coming – some guys don't like what you're doing.'

'Anyone speak to you specifically or make threats?'

'No, for sure no, but I hear things.'

'So what you think we should do?'

'Learn weapons?' Jack smiles. He looks at the face before him, noticing how Jackson has squeezed his features into an earnest and worried expression.

'Is that why you were interested in the swords?'

'No, man, that would be a joke ... but I saw some other fighting gear there.'

'Jackson,' – Jack looks carefully at his student – 'we can't prevent things coming our way. We don't look for trouble but if it is on its way we just have to handle it. And our best weapon is to keep practising and to keep the mind intentional and strong.' Jack reaches out and touches Jackson's shoulder. 'You and the other four are doing really well. I am proud of you. We will take care of our school best we can.'

'Yeah. I guess.' The younger man's expression is unreadable. Jack pays for the tea, and they part company once more.

Jack feels a flicker of fear as he walks. Who are the ones who are upset about him? What conflict might be coming his way? Day at a time. That's the way. Deal with everything as it comes. Han will help. Jack shrugs. No. That's not the way to see it.

Parallel to this felt sense of equanimity and acceptance, Jack imaginatively accepts into his right hand a sword of lethal sharpness, and runs through a horde of enemies with it, slicing so close at their heads that they find their precious beards trimmed. And if they don't have beards, he carves the logos neatly and squarely out of their t-shirts, leaving their chests bare. The last image is of an unimaginable number of men, their faces shaved and their upper bodies exposed, running in a pack away from him. Jack allows himself a postscript. The next day they all come and sign up for a class.

Miriam presses herself hard against him when he returns before the agreed time. She looks flushed, has she been crying? Nothing to worry about, it seems. She gives him a radiant smile as he and Paul decide which part of the gingerbread man to eat first. The child wriggles on his father's lap, punching him lightly and making him squeal.

A dark night is settling in as Miriam looks unseeingly at her notes on the laptop screen. She feels a kind of vertigo, as though she has pulled herself back from falling into a hole. What she wants to do now, rather than work, is secrete herself into the kitchen and – invisible – watch her husband and son, devour them with her eyes and place the received images under her skin, storing them where they might be safe. A little moment of protection.

Miriam closes her eyes, breathing softly and deeply, and slowly it is as if she rests around an elongated, palpable column of air. Anxiety takes a backseat, waiting for another day. Her imagination, released, brings her towards the outlines of a film set ... Hannah is enthroned in a beautiful, dusty room. Not quite Miss Haversham; not so many cobwebs. There is something regal and piteous about her. A group of dancers, clad in black, lie around her. Music – Handel – the aria from Queen Anne's birthday ode ... the one transposed an octave higher, where voice and trumpet alternate and tenderly support each other. The main feature of this moment is that the figures are transfixed. The more airy the music, the heavier they become. With a requirement of intense empathy for Hannah, each young figure follows her movement as she slowly lifts a hand ... and lets it drop, circles her head, letting her chin move towards her chest and then – very slowly – rise again. Yes – you'd expect heavy music, a doleful plunging of notes towards the lower octaves ... but no, the sound is ethereal, rising. And then? Doesn't matter. Miriam is allowing inconsequent patchwork into this dreaming. A square of colour and pattern arises and she notices it ... but what it will join to and how the completed cloth will look, she has no idea.

Is this an illustration of gravity? Gravity as a force pulling between two objects ... so it was thought, in Newton's time. No, turn to Einstein, and the theory about mass bending space, and space pushing ... Hannah is on a trampoline, falling into its net, distorting the square shape, and the dancers in orbit around this, streaming on the fermions, the chunked ripples in a field, the one-dimensional oscillating lines within each atom. Everything altered and affected by everything else ...

It is the time that Hannah usually goes to bed. She prides herself that she needs very little care – how she despises that word. She has her cleaning lady, and a part-time carer (isn't there another word for this?) comes in three times a week to check on her health and capability. She has a hideous neck object which she never wears. It has on it a red button which, if pressed, brings emergency services to her side. They are given a spare key to the front door. She also has a bracelet with the same red button. These two aids for emergency lie on her big table. Certainly, she needs to tread a bit more carefully these days, but at the same time the excitement rising from the new thing that has come into her life brings strength and energy. Advising young dancers, isn't it? Taking part in a film about ballet? No, it's more about how she does it

– these difficult movements, the stretches, the elevation, the extension. That is what they want her to tell them about.

Hannah walks carefully towards the tape-recorder. Damn woman hasn't dusted it. She sweeps at its surface impatiently, then looks among the tapes in the box next to it. No one uses tapes any more. It's CDs, isn't it? Or is that the new word for films? Doesn't matter. She searches, not able to read so well any more but seeing the illustrations. Yes – there it is. *Coppélia*. She hasn't listened to music in a long while. Clicking the fast-forward button several times, she comes to the mazurka. The drum roll, the exultant strings fill her heart. She raises herself onto her toes. Not quite but nearly. Hannah loses her balance a little then settles. She raises her arms, she is first on in the corps de ballet, in that gorgeous red skirt with white petticoats abounding beneath. There is a photograph on the wall somewhere. She doesn't want to look, she wants to dance, for there he is, in the shadows, in the front row, middle seat. The first time their eyes meet. He stares at her face and at the little red bodice and white puffed sleeves and at the glorious shapely legs twirling the frothy skirt. She is the most radiant and expressive of all the girls. They say so. That's why she is chosen as understudy for Swanhilde, and does the solo those few nights. Oh, what a time. And now she will be in a film and he will see it and come back. And for a short few years they will re-live the love that was meant to happen, and flower and flourish.

Hannah turns, and her thin brittle legs remember, faintly, what to do, and she gasps as the music gathers and she lifts herself, yes! She can still do it, but now she stumbles, and there, in the way, is the sharp end of the table and she comes down from the desperate, raised posture and she falls against this sharpness and the carved edge stabs her in the hip, and she staggers and a chair is in the way and she hits her head against its unforgiving wooden corner, the upholstered seat not available to cushion her. And the table and the chair have cruelly stabbed her and she is on the floor, dizzy and confused. Hannah tries to get up but something is quite wrong in her hip, a stinging pain keeps her to the ground. Something out of its socket, in an odd angle? Damn, a doctor will have to look. Thick liquid wet and warm touches the corner of her mouth. She has gashed her head. It is bleeding, and blindingly painful. Quite a lot of blood it seems. She touches the viscous stuff with her fingers and stares at it. Dark red it appears in the sombre gloom of her room. She hates blood. Remembers how pleased she was when, for a while, being at her thinnest, she stopped menstruating. Well, she must simply get back and press that confounded alarm. But she needs help to get up and the cleaner – she has been today, so she is not coming back tomorrow. And the carer (horrible word) – when is she coming? And the Hebrew girl, well, half-Hebrew and the typist – when are they coming? Clarity of thought is obscured by waves of dizziness, nausea and pain. Through the shrouded curtains, Hannah hears the sound of a motorbike and then she realises – ah yes – she always knew he would return. The one on the motorbike. And he has raced his motorbike and she has fallen. That's what is happening. And she stops struggling, and cries, desolate and lost. Longing for her overweight peasant mother and her clumsy inarticulate father; longing for Jeremy. She stretches an arm up towards the table. She can't reach the button. She can't even reach the table-top. She tries to grasp the cruel chair and heave herself up. She can't do it. Once more, she stops struggling. The waves of darkness turn into the darkness of the auditorium. There he is. Looking at her. With love and desire and ruthless self-interest. She pirouettes, she is divine, he is captivated, she holds her arms aloft, and turns,

and turns, and turns ...

Blessings upon you, dear soul. May you walk with your angel through this dark night. The man you long for, the old one now sitting in the home for old ones, is back to his child mind. He will see the obituary in the newspaper, a photograph of you at your most wonderful and beautiful. His heart will shriek, and he will be utterly distressed and not be sure why. The nurses will take care of him ... Blessings too upon him and may the karmic lord cast his neutral, compassionate and just eye upon the struggle, the love, the desperation that emanated between the two of you.

46

I was located in the particularity and circumstance of Dzukh and the field around him, including of course the elder now passing into the locus of in-between, that which is neither of life nor death, and at the same time, of course, I could be anywhere and everywhere.

I altered my focus from the Dzukh field and guided myself to a highly charged point in this great city. I looked at the statue of a winged young male with a bow and arrow. It was situated on a high column. Around and about, diverse moving metallic forms were surging and darting, and lights and images and words radiated from the sides of the buildings. A congregation of mostly young people collected at the foot of the statue, some sitting on the rising rings of steps, at lower and higher levels. All this immersed in persistent, immense clamour of noise and electrical energy. Conversations happened between people physically present and also with disembodied voices heard through the small instruments held to the ear. Again I was struck by rapidity of thought and expression, and by a distinct lack of focus. Bodies made theatrical and elaborate gestures, eyes darted hither and thither. It was rare to witness steady and receptive contact between people. Astral debris – thoughts, fantasies, discarnate references, intentions – writhed and spread through the gathering, an immense library of moving information. Every now and then I noticed a thought of great beauty, of luminosity – but more often than not I noticed those hateful, mean, fearful or banal. At one point I picked up on a murderous whisper, and then realised that it was from past time, from a time when horses trotted the street, and the mechanical vehicles now available had not yet been envisaged. Someone was going to be pushed under moving hooves, and with a knife in his back to ensure quick despatch.

Not at any time upon Earth did I feel requirement to take a physical body. My alignment of will, love and wisdom was force enough to move me as a coherent whole to wherever I wanted to be. I took myself to the winged boy – and settled, and then did I let a preparatory sound move as far as it wished. It always touched me in this kind of communing to notice who has the hearing. It is a hearing of the heart or of the subtle being. The sound is not obvious to the physical ear. Most of the human creatures immediately gathered around me had not yet developed antennae for receiving such as this, but, here and there, I knew, Earth beings did light up in joy to hear harmonic tuning of the deeper world – sometimes called the higher world, the inner world, the invisible world, or world without end. No matter. This nomenclature is irrelevant. Sufficient be it that I talk about Attunement, and the way our innermost landscape receives Original Sound, and how this provides clearing, a dissolving of dense and distorted thought patterns and feelings. Some incarnate beings, particularly those from spiritual orders, know of this procedure, and use sound – chanting – as a daily act of refinement.

I maintained resonance and the note circled, beyond the winged creature and beyond this dense area of the city, the area of commerce and entertainment and artistic display; beyond the further streets and their merchandise from my land of origin, food and materials and musical instruments and martial arts swords, it travelled, the golden unheard sound from the golden unseen bowl. Thus did I stir the citysoul and thus did I call, and answer came riding through the ethers, souls tuning into the vibration. And within those gathering strands did I detect a cry of anguish and I followed it and – without moving my centre from the statue and the steps –at its source did I find the presence of a man, grieving and praying deeply. Respectfully, waiting, did I request permission to join. This permission I received.

'What ails you beloved?' The weeping continued. I did abide. Swirls of colour flared from his heart, a distraught kaleidoscope of sorrow and helplessness. And within that, at the same time, a relief that his prayer had been heard. Wordlessly, the contents of his heart spoke. He had witnessed, on the moving picture box that many people have in their homes, scenes of acute cruelty to animals in the large continent where live people of a different colour and where the landscape and the animals are wild and powerful. Many travel there from other lands to steal animals and make of them spectacles of curiosity. He saw an ape, called of the sort gorilla. And it had been snatched from its nursing mother and put in a box in a market, dressed in ragged human clothes, and its eyes, brown and innocent, were filled with terror. This particular sight had driven a spear of anguish into the man. 'How will we humans ever change?' and in his despair did he lose faith in the essential beauty of the universe and could feel only fear. And from that an anger towards the Creator. 'It is too difficult, life on Earth. Dangerous. Human nature hasn't changed since we wore animal skins and carried clubs. We have just become more sophisticated. We are hurtling to oblivion in this dark blackness. And children are being born who are going to be cruelly hurt and terrified as things get worse. And this is why I will not have children. And this hurts my wife who would like to be a mother.' I stayed close to him, wordlessly in agreement, for who am I to contradict the state of a man's heart? And with that exploded a tumult within him. And violence of thought and anger and a kicking against helplessness. Yes, I said to him wordlessly, yes it is like this. Yes it is.

And I saw all of us on this perambulating planet, all of us screaming children, grabbing each other in the dark. And then seizing on the distraction of our extraordinary toys, different in this space and time from the ones I had when I previously lived in a body on this Green Mother.

What a leap of courage and unknowing to leave childhood and its dreams and embellished objects, and embrace the still, cool vision of maturity. How difficult a thing for us when we know not what we put childish things aside for, when we fear that this quiet emptiness contains annihilation.

Momentarily, the tantrum and violence subsided, and the tender-hearted man rocked softly back and forth in the embrace of my abiding. From his capacity to lean into my embrace, he found a governing tenderness within himself in response to the howl that had come from him, and in that manner, that moment, his prayer, to him, felt answered.

Now I came to amplify my own distinct note, cultivated over the Many Whiles upon Earth and within the Heavenly Realms. Think of the lines of written music in the Western fashion: six lines; five spaces. The encounters, incarnate and discarnate, within the circle around the young Dzukh, and the momentary encounter with the man I have just described could be seen as small markings within one line. Microcosmic notation, but nonetheless significant, as everything is significant. Or completely insignificant, if you would rather see it that way.

If I break out of the form, resonate beyond the lines and the spaces, if I focus my range and sound through further distinction and elaboration of notes and scales, chords and melodies, themes and variation ... I create a vibration, a ringing and a stirring which touches all sentient beings whether they know it or not.

When the Being of Abiding Wisdom invited me to return to the Green Planet, she charged me with understanding the dissonance and discord which has taken hold; parasitic sounds which lie upon radiant notes and suck the resonance from them. Through the activity of free will - unconditionally granted for its own mysterious purpose to humankind - dissonance started to emerge through thought, feeling and action ... and the divine Om became encrusted with babble. One can only speculate that the presence of this profound lack of courtesy and understanding is part of the birth and learning of humanity, arising after the emergence from the Holy Unknown; an emergence possibly required by the Unknown wishing to release Itself and then Call Itself to Return.

But I will trespass no further with fruitless musing. As a tribute to courtesy and understanding I can make an offering of Attunement. This act requires sublime contemplation and concentration and afterwards I am to rest, emptied and silent.

I brought my being into Accord, and waited within my vibratory alignment until I found the One Note. I poured a quantity of love and commitment and whole-heartedness into this note and then breathed it out. Precision and clarity spread from me, moving through density, ugliness, fear, power, illusion, greed, love, hope, terror, longing, desperation, humility, forgiveness, moving through all the manifestation of human life within this city within this great island, and then beyond the sea, touching upon other land masses. Those who might have been meditating at this moment would receive a cleansing and an awakening that they had never experienced before; those consciously contaminating the Om would experience an inner detonation, causing anguish and confusion, and also a possibility of swift awakening. Many who were simply going about their business in harmless enough sleep might experience a moment of inexplicable, acute well-being. There were varieties of possible consequences through the myriad receptors all humans carry. Creatures, too, would resonate. I had released a quickening wave which would circle the entire planet. My total Beingness was offered up, given and spent in this action. I knew no more beautiful thing to do for the Beloved I Am; For That which We Are, Have Been, and Will Be.

After completion, I did what was necessary and compressed my entirety into a pinhead, into a dense and minute black dot of existence. The recuperative powers of Yin, the Great Feminine, surrounded me; a velvety black net, not of light and action but of darkness and density, restoration and silence.

47

In her abode in north London, Madeleine, tired after the long walk up three flights of stairs, rests for a moment in a sagging soft chair. She closes her eyes and smiles. Suddenly, for no apparent reason, life is sweet. She remembers her confirmation ceremony at a church near her family home in Suffolk. The priest had touched her head in a kind way and smiled at her. How strange. It is as if he is in the room. If she opened her eyes this benevolent and good man would be standing there, giving blessing once more to a neglected child.

48

Two days later, Miriam, light at heart, recent anxiety quiescent, prepares for an outing with Paul. He is going to play with a friend from nursery, and Miriam will stay with him as she rather likes Carol, the friend's mother. The foursome works well. Carol and Miriam seem to know intuitively that one mother comes forward to pull the children apart when they fight, leaving the other to rest and draw strength for the next explosion. Hostilities usually erupt over toys. Neither child wants to know what it means to share. Desirable objects are just that, and there is only swiftness of eye and hand, and then loudness of screaming and degree of injury and pathos when one child seems to have more. Miriam brings a few toys with her so that the onus to share isn't heaped solely upon the host.

Jack delays his practice so that he can have breakfast with them and wave goodbye. The silence when he closes the door is welcome. Paul is currently in a particularly loquacious frame of mind and insists on replies to his endless questions. 'You need to answer me,' he says solemnly, with a fixed look at the parent who is required to respond. This fixed look carries with it such a compelling mixture of entitlement and reproach that it is hard to evade or dispute. This morning, not quite awake, Jack needs to explain why fire makes things hot.

Jack is grateful for a morning to himself. He wants to think. Or rather, not to think, but to let events and experiences jostle and shift in his mind. Jackson, the eager messenger, managed to round up the other four and they were all present the evening before, for the meeting an hour before the class. The 'trouble' Jackson referred to over the thick white cup of tea near Chinatown is pushed to the back of Jack's mind. He knows it won't stay there.

Jack goes back to bed, putting all four pillows behind his head, feeling the support with pleasure. He moves his awareness from head to toe, noticing areas of relaxation and areas of tension. He stretches his arms, his legs, breathing softly and deeply. He particularly feels his abdomen rising and falling with breath. He anchors himself into this place, feeling weight, gravitas, stability. Jack senses additionally the point on his forehead between his eyebrows, and the centre of his heart. Locating these Three Treasures calms his mind, and settles his chest. A pleasing wave of energy rolls down from head to toe, carrying with it an experience of integration and wholeness. He is aware, too, of the sharp and stubborn qualities of his nature. He likes this edginess. Sometimes he scratches at Miriam and she at him. There is an excitement, an aliveness to these tussles within himself and with others, a thrusting through the arriving creative layers of his life, unusual power running through his body. Responsibility. He tastes again the meeting with The Five. They listen carefully as he tells them of his offer.

Each week – for nothing – he will teach them to be teachers. And after six weeks of this, each of them can set up a weekly class. No more than five in each group. And he will tell them exactly what and how to teach. And each month, all the classes will come together – he will find a big place – and he will give a lesson. There is to be no pushing hands in the Apprentice Classes, as he calls them. This will only be taught under his supervision in the big class. Occasionally he will call in on the Apprentice Classes – they might not know when. Not to check up on them, but to give them support and, if truth be told, to keep the whole thing usefully unsettled. They will charge for the class – a nominal fee – enough to pay for the venue, and some extra cash for themselves. They will run everything – seeing that the venue is cared for and left in good order, seeing that everyone pays, arrives on time, and follows the requirement of commitment and respect.

This is an experiment,' says Jack, 'and an honour. I am placing trust in you, and others will too. Anyone takes the piss – they're asked to leave.' He scans their faces. 'Any questions?'

'No one will want to come to us – they want to come to the horse's mouth isn't it?' Terry lifts his cheeky face up the Jack, meets his gaze.

'Well, fact is, this horse can only take a certain number in the class, and I don't like taking on beginners week after week. Up to a point yes, then it slows things down. Oh, also to say that, for extra training and experience, and to help me, I will be asking you in my class to help the beginners we have already taken on. All of this is great practice for you guys. Yes – some people won't want to come. That's all right. Let's see what happens.'

Hardcore looks at Jack, his handsome face expressionless, his voice flat. 'I'm up for it.'

'Any one of you not up for it?' Jack asks. 'This isn't a have-to. It's choice.' Jackson is quiet. The conversation in the tearoom is not mentioned. Jack looks at him carefully. The squeezed look is absent, but his face is a little subdued. Jack looks around at the plain, functional room. It is ready for the class. Clean enough, the chairs stacked at the side, the external glass of the windows carrying irregular grey sheen, product of the daily deposit of London grime. Jack brings his eyes back to the Five. Nemo, Steve, Hardcore, Jackson, Terry. Each of them has attended every class, they are good students, they have aptitude. What a strange bond exists between him and them. Again, he feels the precarious and somewhat unreal nature of it all. Any minute and he can imagine the sneer on Steve's face deepening and a jet of saliva expertly spat out of his mouth in aggression and contempt. Jack visits this disturbing place in an almost superstitious necessity to placate the masters of fate. Take anything for granted, and you're done for. And yet Jack also knows that this sour thought is a creation of some devil whispering into his ear. They reality of it is that skill is being transmitted, and they know it. Not of its extraordinary source through Han, but of its emergence through his own accelerated capacity. Trouble? Well, there's always trouble. Somewhere, somehow.

'Did I tell you about *El Sistema*?' They all shake their heads. Jack elaborates. 'It's not the same as what we're doing – but it's not that different ....' Jack is finding that the Han-infusion also develops in him a power of speech previously not accessible. He has weight and authority in a way that is new. Choice to do the right thing. For himself. That's about all he knows. He wouldn't want to be doing anything else, in any other way.

Lying back on the cushions, the taste in his mouth sweet, Jack knows that every part of him is being used – mind, body and heart. He remembers his faltering early days, the sense of hopefulness as he stood in front of a small group of students. He remembers the days of tension with Miriam, the night-times of uneasy dreaming, where he is always looking for a place. Surrounded by others who seem busy and confident, he is trying to look similarly assured, and he isn't.

The pleasant quality relating to his mouth seems to extend now to his nostrils. As he breathes in, the sweetness that sits on the edge of his breath, the perfume, is not like the incense or oil Miriam often burns. He closes his eyes and opens them anew, noticing the wall-hanging to the left of the bed. It is of a spray of plum blossom, just beginning to open even though snow still lies on the ground, and filaments of frost hang in the air. The artist has delineated each form with precision. The branch doesn't just hang diagonally in space, it hangs into cool wintry space. And it seems as if it is this flower that is delivering perfume to Jack. From the painting on the wall to him, a line of affect arrives: crisp, clear, cold air, carrying fragrance; and as the fragrance moves up his nose, it becomes more intense and seems to penetrate the cavity of his head, an icy radiance that seems to scour the nasal cavity, the eye sockets, the internal volume between his ears, the Jade Cushion – that area where the skull meets the neck vertebrae. The sensation continues to sink downwards and Jack, eyes now closed, experiences a shocking, bright awareness inching its way to the base of his spine. He might as well be in Lapland, sliding down a bank of vivid snow, he might as well be tumbling through the aurora borealis, and its roaring colours painting him beneath his skin, tattooing him from the inside. The fragrance is everywhere, inside and out. Jack opens his eyes.

Han is standing in the corner. Arms outstretched and palms facing outward. 'It's you, it's you ....' Jack whispers. 'I knew it was you.' The little man changes size, becomes enormous, and then small again. He is wearing a brightly coloured cloak. He has a gnarled stick in his hand. 'Oh no!' Jack's heart beats desperately. 'You're going – does this mean I lose my capacity – you know – is it dependent on your being here?' Jack's eyes fill with tears – 'Never mind that, I will miss you. I love you, I love you in my life, I love you with my life.'

It touched me so to see dear Dzukh in his alignment. Noble Being – he does not know, does not trust yet, that what he has, strength, wisdom, is now his. Capacity – as he called it – resides neither in him nor in me. It simply resides, and those who are able to align themselves into this continuum, find themselves fully imbued.

Influenced by the intense narrowing of this moment now, when indeed I am to depart and shortly return to the Heavenly Realms, my exquisite friend Mei Hua – plum blossom – extended himself to find purchase in Dzukh's soul and Dzukh too is now associated with this glorious creature. He has passed through another portal of teaching, and his quiet and subtle endeavour will continue to stretch into surprising quarters and bring forth companions: perfume, the friendship of nature, power that will enhance as long as it remains embedded in humility. This will cause challenge within himself as his human facilities collide with the imperative that now lodges in his soul. But our Dzukh is a warrior, and will advance towards this inner battle with energy and relish, even when it is difficult.

Seventy days. One more night and one more day, and completion will claim me and I will surrender, and Return. During my time upon Earth, I anchored myself here in the land of Avalon, the land of fairies and ley lines, and ancient bards and magicians. My time of anchorage brought me to know and respect and feel for the sense of history, struggles within present time and a prevalent film of tiredness around me, longing for rejuvenation. This land has known many changes and is now a land where humans of many colours abide. Literature and artistry have flourished here and particularly has this been an island of justice. Many unfair and ugly events have I seen here, but so it is everywhere, and here there is a mature understanding about civil matters. Yes, and now even the soil is tired. Bless this land. May nutrients and minerals and energy generate again to provide for the human souls gripping this particular surface of Earth's body.

Oh, our Beloved Mother, how I weep for you. Such wondrous things do you provide – and such terror too from your killing floods and wild cyclones. Let us never undermine your strength. To you, Beloved Mother, we humans when we are unsettled can be an irritant, fleas upon the surface, causing you scratches, rashes and aches and pains. But your life sustenance comes from a source beyond human. You could give one gigantic sneeze and blow us away! Bless you, Mother, Bless you!

Feeling acutely the moment of departure from Earth, and a tremor of softness as I contemplated farewell to Dzukh, I determined, within this last while, to touch down momentarily in further realms of habitation . And thus it was that I travelled in the wink of an eyelid, to the great country across the sea, where a man with brown skin did ascend into power. And he is a beautiful being, and yet it is a cobweb of influence and tension he has stepped into. I breathed into his ear and watched him smile. This was once – and still is – a country of tremendous influence and wealth and yet now, the corner which was my habitation is arising out of coercion and manipulation by the one who put thoughts into a little red book; is arising into influence and substance. I brought myself there, to a new city of shining towers where did live twenty million souls. I passed the country where Buddha walked, and sat under the Bhodi tree. This country took my heart, yes it did, for the way that crazy holy men and women can walk the street, side by side with holy cows, in the middle of noise and smell and the same rapidly moving vehicles as I found here. And amid smoke and mischief and beggars and Maharajahs, I saw tall buildings and all the contemporary trappings that now spread from one side of the Emerald Planet to the other. How might it have been to have the identity as Han Shan poet, of the wild hair and tattered coat, and wander the streets singing and inscribing poetry, without being pelted by stone and garbage? I saw emaciated bearded ones, almost naked, lying on a rack of nails and smiling. And no one jeered at them.

And then, Beloved Friends, did I touch into the great continent where the first in human form, born rising from the dusty red ground, had its habitation. A continent of beauty and richness of wild creatures and vegetation. And such sorrow of conflict and murderous activity. There did I pause for a short While, praying over sickly children and their mothers walking across hot sand, no water, no food. And elsewhere north, east and west, did tables groan for the weight of food, and excess food thrown away. Thus has it always been, Beloved Friends. When we take human shape, we take an imprint of savagery, each of us, a will to survive and have what we want; and we are given too the possibility of selflessness and compassion. We choose, and we continue to exercise choice. It is not easy. There are many material and psychic temptations. But we are helped. Not in the way that you imagine, but in a way you can only know once there is Awakening. And this Awakening is an act of Grace – delicate, unexpected, sideways. We need a certain kind of strength for it.

Dzukh, dearly Beloved, I turn to you now and I know you are with me in the thoughts that will commence and which I direct towards you.

We are aligned and communing. Dzukh, I will never leave you. Where could I go? Dzukh, many whiles before, we had human life in the same eastern corner of the Mother's body. We had a strong apprenticeship there. Not at the same time, but of the same Lineage. We are steeped in love of the same Great School. And thus aligned, do we also love each other. Dzukh, flowering has come for you. And it will not always be easy, for you have been given – and have accepted – great responsibility. If you become exhausted, rest and step away into solace. Have care of yourself. Stay simple and empty. Stay grounded. Find safety in the void, in the No-thing. Taste and love the Ten Thousand Things, but do not become beguiled by them, or by your thoughts and feelings. Be always courteous to your thoughts and feelings, understand their nature. Do not become seduced by the power that has entered you, it is here to serve the greater good. Do not be afraid of envy or aggression. Stay in quietude and all will be well. Bless you, Dearest Brother.

Jack, weeping, and loosened of the usual workings of his mind, moves from his comfortable bed and lays his body on the floor at the Beloved's feet. He remembers brief lines from Rumi's poetry and knows that the wrenching sense of hovering bereavement that he is feeling is that which Rumi poured out through the burning of his own breaking heart. He closes his eyes and still can see Han, smiling at him, his eyes brilliant with love and humour and a quality of wisdom that is almost unbearable to witness. Air dances around him, it touches his face, it is cold and warm, light and heavy, it is dusting him with radiance and fragrance. Mei Hua is dancing too.

Shedding one more layer of resistance to what is clearly unfolding, Jack surrenders, His heart rips open and into that gaping hole, Han extends a mighty out-breath, a ribbon of wide, wild gallantry, an act of extraordinary courtesy and grace, allowing Jack's breaking heart to be lined with silk and fragrance, plum blossom and orchid, chrysanthemum and lotus.

'Thank you,' breathes Jack, barely moving his lips. 'Thank you.'

Into the quiet he speaks, for now it is quiet and in the room is only himself. Han is neither visible nor present. Jack lies for a long period, a ragged man bleeding to death, a blessed man, his heart blooming and ravished. After a long while he stretches his arms, gathering sweet blossoms, pulling them to him, covering himself. Hours later, it seems, he slowly stands up. The room is empty, Han departed, flowers disappeared. Jack looks at his watch. It cannot be. It cannot be that Miriam and Paul left just five minutes before. Jack washes his face, comes back to the corner, the corner where the Ancient One ....

He takes his stance, feet shoulder-width apart, relaxes his shoulders, breathes into the deep illumination lodged within his aching and bruised, intelligent heart, breathes into his abdomen and begins the precision and poetry of his practice.

49

A shortest While remained for my presence upon the Earth planet (that which you would describe as 'one day'), and then would I be piloted into the agreed return to the Heavenly House of Discourse and Apprenticeship. If I declared, at this point of departure, that my work was done, this did not imply completion. It implied that I had, moment by moment, focussed on what I was required to do within the allotted While. There is neither beginning nor end.

I aligned myself with the vibration of the Being of Abiding Wisdom, the one of feminine essence who initiated me into this project of Returning to Earth. I wanted to know whether there was ceremony needed before departure.

Truth be told, more compelling than that question concerning ceremony, I was still being touched, and deeply so, by the delicate sense of something yet to unfold, something of which I knew not.

I awaited in unknowingness until I felt her field interlacing with mine.

'Beloved Han.'

'Beloved Being.'

Within a shimmering wave of communion my question presented itself. And then did her answer prevail, soft and clear. 'There is only the task of looking into your heart, for there you shall see what it is that is calling you, what music is yet for you to hear this Last While of your sojourn upon the Green Planet.' In the silence that arose between us, I thanked her without words, felt her graceful withdrawal and remained for a goodly While meditating upon the State of my Heart.

I was hastened back through tunnels of collapsing time, through memory and acquired history, and arrived at the sensation of my last incarnation upon Earth – more than a thousand years ago as Han Shan, crazy poet. I knew again the experience of carving language into tree bark, and onto the skin of stones. I recalled both the effort and exultation of the work. I was an incarnated human, and, with awareness of the Imprint of the Holy One stamped upon me, refusing to be corralled into two- and three-dimensional time ... Yet, equally, I was finite as a body and a temporary identity, and there was heartache and exhaustion and struggle. And the joys of respite when beauty arose and laughter and the joining of human to human, through flesh, heart and soul.

Her face rose into view, as if veil by veil the mystery removed to reveal clearer lineaments, the wife with whom I joined, the ivory princess whom I loved. Revelation of her brown oval eyes, differently folded into a lid of Eastern persuasion, a small skin-curve that held them, her features composed by a slender stroke of a brush, the soft swift movements of her slight body as she came and went. She loved me, yes she did. She loved the poet. But the crazy poet was difficult for her. As indeed it was difficult for me – but I could not stop myself bursting the fetters, avoiding court and library and dignitaries, and running up the mountain to carve upon nature and there to leave words and songs and declarations of love. There was no other way I could do it, I was encoded this way and to ignore the primal calligraphy of my destiny meant suffering and withering of essential life-force.

Scorn and torment were heaped upon me, and indeed upon her. And this was unfitting and unfair but was the way of the folk around. And I had the burning to run and to write and to exult and to know myself free but she did not have the wild, running quality. This was not her story. Her story was of stillness and the love of the everyday in the small house, planting, cooking. Beautiful was this for me to receive. Balm at the end of the day, the outbreath after the passionate inbreath. The yang receiving the yin.

Painful was it for me that I could not prevent this ugliness falling onto her and into our home, I could not protect her from the feelings of unhappiness that the sour words provoked in her. For a time we moved high into the mountains and lived far away from other people, but this was difficult too, the soil hard to dig and cultivate – an obstinate patch instead of the flowing garden she had produced further down behind the valley house. We had to make journeys for food and the re-entry into the community was signal for a more intense ribaldry and shouting. I watched her beautiful face become anxious, and unhappiness interfering with her posture, creasing her upright spine. We moved back to the valley.

The other sorrow for her – and for me, but less so – was that no child took seed to bless our union. This was a garden she could not cultivate although our bodies flourished when joined .... She often felt sure that the movements we generated thus created a furrow, a sweet dent in the ground of her body and there would a baby grow. But not.

Over time, my empress withdrew. One evening I returned – and she had gone. She left me a poem, and that she had carved it onto wood touched me as much as the words themselves.

Beloved I will never leave you
I love you beyond this life
The wind circles without visible form
And so do I circle about you

I left our home, walked higher and higher into Cold Mountain, and lay for days in a clearing, without food, poetry or solace. The wind – she – touched my face and I wept, dark soil and rotting leaves mingling with salt water and coating my cheeks. The loss of my wife gouged a hole in my heart and then-after my poetry carved itself deeper. I did not try to follow her or find out where she had gone. My life could not be any different. I had to be the solitary poet.

I sang and wept and carved, writing of the unknown and mysterious cycles of happening, of which we fragile ciphers in human form know very little, but experience and feel every day through the Ten Thousand Things, the myriad spilling phenomena within us and around us. And the more we learn and know and penetrate with science and with poetry, the less we know, and the more vast that which we do not know.

Over time, the wound in my heart healed, though I never forgot her, and the wind always carried her to me. Sometimes I wondered whether she had met another and maybe created a home, a child …. It pleased me to think she might be happy, It was painful too, to contemplate her cleaving to another. I would put this thought from my mind, this image – and invoke a different one which suggested that she had joined a group of contemplative women and that they were looking after her! I was amused at my preference for her future.

No one in the village ever spoke to me of her. And the teasing eventually died down. Indeed, some people, I noticed, secretly walked up the mountain and read what I had written. Some contrived to be in my company when I was in town, hardly speaking, but communicating with me through eyes and heart. I developed the capacity to tune in to whatever was happening for them, and to register an unspoken response which was somehow healing. Sometimes the message I received for them would manifest – in lightly disguised form – in a poem carving. Oddly, I knew that the person to whom the poem referred would somehow find it. The quality of solace which was developing between myself and others through the carving craft left me with peace and gratification. I began to know that the epiphany for my soul, the most beautiful way for me to be here on Earth, was to know of the fear and trembling of others, and to commune with them in love and quietness, and to gather the language of rock and air and tree and water and to let this language speak its consolation.

Two, particularly, stayed near to me, Not too near, for I wouldn't tolerate that. Big Stick and Pick-up appointed themselves guardians. I would find small items of food and water. Sometimes useless and ineffectual messages to return to the world and have shelter as it was felt proper. They loved me and I them but it was a silent procedure between us.

I barely noticed how old I was becoming, how emaciated! How ragged my patchwork cloak, the colours fading. My wooden clogs became as thin as splinters … criss-crossed with markings from the many pathways I had travelled.

As the weathering and aging gathered force, my two guardians and other people became more attentive to me. I had to escape their ministrations and creep my way up the mountain to my favourite sanctuary. I managed a sleight of eye whereby the last two witnesses of my presence, Big Stick and Pick-up, thought I disappeared into a crack in the rock. They stopped following and began instead the telling of tales and stories about me as if I had already died, and I was free to escape to the place where I had wept the loss of my beloved.

And a time came when, as I lay quietly, I felt that the force remaining in the leaves around me was more vibrant than the force presently in my body. My body felt almost transparent, a strange unease took hold of me, a sensation of disengagement, confusion and unfamiliarity. I began to weep, and to call out (To whom? For what?). My body contorted in pain and terror. For a moment I felt her with me, the breeze came, my ivory empress; she laid her hand to my head. Then came a rushing, as though the back of my head had opened up and my entire pained, delicate substance become a wave birthing itself out of me with tender and firm intention. Except the wave was also not me, I was being drawn – and then came the light ... and I was no more and I was more than I had ever known I could be.

How sweet and tender the memories from my heart. Was this what the Great Being had pointed me towards? The cessation of that last life upon Earth? I closed my eyes again and waited. Something was calling me. A sound, its weave and texture creating a path – I walked along it, turning and rising and falling. The injunction, the call, brought me to the house of Ma'li. She was asleep. The trial she had been through had lost its pinch upon her features and her face was less drawn, more tranquil. I took my place and waited. I felt greatly at peace in her small home, its altar and Taoist treasures were familiar to me. The aroma of something equally familiar came to my senses. Dumplings!. She had been steaming dumplings!. Just like .... Is this? I gazed upon her face, my heart turning, as her face shifted and dissolved and became many faces, old and young. And then, the dissolving ceased. Before my eyes lay the ivory princess, my wife of long ago. She, in her Now and from her Long-ago While, opened her eyes and we gazed upon each other and absorbed each other. Everything stood still, held its breath; every atom of breath in the room gathered around us, the breath of plants, of steaming water, breaths gathered and released during all of our lives ... these drew around us to hold and cherish that which was revealing itself.

I am dreaming. I am Marie and I am other. I am one and many. I am in a small house and I am cooking. Steam pours from a pot over the fire. He comes home, my husband. I spring towards him and take his colourful cloak and kneel before him and help him out of his clogs. His feet are cold and scratched. My love for him swells my heart and I bring him to sit and without speaking we eat together. We wash each other in warm water I have poured into the wooden bowl. Each one washing and then being washed. We go to bed and his tender hands seek me out. I feel again the furrow in my womb, waiting and wondering. We wind and curl around each other, tasting and touching. My eyes are closed and suddenly – touched by imperative – I open them. It is I Marie and I also other ... and he ... he is in the corner. Without speaking, without blinking I let my eyes fall into his. This is a moment in my life unlike any other. This is he and this is I and nothing else matters and all time dances and then stands still and disappears, and all space collapses in on itself and is no more.

He talks to me, but there is no sound and no words.

'We are together again, beloved wife. My ivory princess. Last time you left me. And that was how it had to be. And I never knew what happened to you but I never forgot you. The air, the wind, brought you to me night after night.

'This time it is I who must leave but before this imminent moment, we are permitted joining and meeting. It is so beautiful. And I will never leave you. The air, the wind will carry my love and care to you each day and night as you did for me.

'And we will meet again. And again. And again.'

'My beloved. My heart is at peace.' Her beloved – yes, it is Han, she knows him, it is Han Returned to Earth .... Marie closes her eyes but can still see her husband. A swirl of light, of inevitable invitation, full of colour and yet of no colour, surrounds him, and the sound of intricate harmonies pervades the light. The cohorts of light and sound wrap themselves around Han and take him up, and the roof opens, and the night sky hollows itself into a whirling vortex, and Marie's heart is wrenched violently; and singing. She rolls from her bed and falls to the floor in gratitude and wonder and sorrow ... and there, her eyes open, her fingers move towards, and find – a small square of material. A fragment from the corner of his colourful cloak. On it, an ancient twig, on which rests Plum Blossom. Mei Hua. Two blossoms. Pink and fragrant.